· bread alone ·

bread alone

JUDITH RYAN HENDRICKS

WILLIAM MORROW 75 YEARS OF PUBLISHING
An Imprint of HarperCollins*Publishers*

HENDRICKS
HENDRICKS, JUDITH
BREAD ALONE

*Excerpt from "I Only Have Eyes for You" by Al Dubin and
Harry Warren © 1934 (renewed) Warner Bros., Inc.
All rights reserved. Used by permission.
Warner Bros. Publications U.S. Inc., Miami, Florida 33014.*

Excerpt from The Tassajara Bread Book *by Edward Espe Brown © 1970 by Chief Priest,
Zen Center, San Francisco. Reprinted by special arrangement with
Shambhala Publications, Inc., Boston, www.shambhala.com.*

Excerpt from Becoming Bread *by Gunilla Norris © 1993 by Gunilla Brodde Norris.
Reprinted by permission of Bell Tower, a division of Random House, Inc.*

HarperCollins books may be purchased for educational, business, or sales promotional use.
For information please write: Special Markets Department, HarperCollins Publishers Inc.,
10 East 53rd Street, New York, NY 10022.

FIRST EDITION

Designed by Claire Naylon Vaccaro

Printed on acid-free paper

Library of Congress Cataloging-in-Publication Data
Hendricks, Judith Ryan.
   Bread alone : a novel / Judith Ryan Hendricks.—1st ed.
      p. cm.
   ISBN 0-06-018895-2
   1. Divorced women—Fiction. 2. Bakers and bakeries—Fiction. 3. Baking—Fiction.
I. Title.
PS3608.E53 B7 2001
813'.6—dc21
                                                                00-069560

01 02 03 04 05 QW 10 9 8 7 6 5 4 3 2 1

To Geoff, for believing

Upside down I may take shape.

I may become resilient.

Kneaded, turned on end

I will become less

And somehow more myself.

from BECOMING BREAD *by Gunilla Norris*

· bread alone ·

One

LOS ANGELES, 1988

The beeping smoke detector wakes me. No, wait. The smoke detector buzzes. When I sit up, the room is wavy, an image in a funhouse mirror. The alarm clock? I turn my head too quickly. It's the old Apache torture. Strips of wet rawhide, tied tight, left to dry.

I swing my legs over the edge of the bed, blink my swollen eyes. My mouth feels like the lint trap in the clothes dryer. I'm wearing a half-slip and the ivory silk blouse I had on last night. My watch has slid up, cutting a deep groove into my arm: 6:45 A.M. An empty bottle of Puligny-Montrachet on the night table. I thought only cheap wine gave you a headache. What did I do with the glass?

I stand up, unsteady. Walk downstairs. Carefully. Holding the railing. Into the kitchen. The bread machine. How can such a small machine make such a big noise? The beeps are synchronized to the throbbing in my temples. I hit the button. The beeping stops and the lid swings open, releasing a cloud of scent. I wheel around and vomit into the sink. I turn on the water, rinse out my mouth, stand panting, gripping the cold edge of the slate countertop. Then I remember. David.

I lift out the still warm loaf, set it on the maple butcher block, a perfect brown cube of bread.

The employment agency is a busy office in a glass and steel building near LAX. The windows offer breathtaking views of Interstate 405, still bumper-to-bumper at ten-thirty. Applicants crowd the waiting area— mostly women who appear to be ten years younger than me, probably all named Heather or Fawn or Tiffany. The place has a sense of purpose worthy of the war rooms you see in World War II movies. All that's missing is Winston Churchill. No one lingers by the water fountain to chat. Everyone's on the phone or tapping a keyboard or striding res- olutely down the hall, eyes averted to avoid distractions. Like me.

The only exception is the young woman at the front desk. When she finishes filing that stubborn broken nail, she looks up with a smile. "Can I help you?"

I try for amused detachment from the whole process. "I have an appointment with Lauren at eleven o'clock. I know I'm early, but..."

"That's okay." She hands me a clipboard with several forms attached to it. "If you'll just fill these out, we can go ahead and get started with your tests." She gives me a pencil and points to some chrome and leather chairs against one wall.

Tests? Oh shit. I sink down onto a chair, my head still twanging in spite of two aspirins and a double espresso. One thing at a time. Name: "Justine Wynter Franklin." Maybe I shouldn't use my married name. I try to erase "Franklin" but the eraser is old and brittle and just makes smudges as it crumbles. I scratch a line through it, print "Morri- son." Now it looks like I'm not sure.

Address. Telephone. I nail those two. Date of birth. Social Security number. Type of work desired. "Don't know" probably wouldn't look good. I put down "Office." Too vague? Skills. I stare at the blank space and it seems to grow larger, defying me to fill it.

Well, I can still recite François Villon's "Ballade des pendus." Or discuss the effects of the Industrial Revolution on the English novel. Let's see... I can make perfect rice with no water left in the bottom of the pot and every grain separate and distinct. I know how to perk up peppercorns and juniper berries that are beyond their shelf life, repair curdled crème anglaise. And if you want to tenderize meat using wine corks or get candle wax out of a tablecloth, I'm your woman. I can tell a genuine Hermès scarf from a Korean knockoff at fifty paces. I have a strong crosscourt backhand. A long time ago, I knew how to type, but even then my speed was nothing to brag about. Someone told me once that I had a nice telephone voice. "Give good phone?"

"Justine Franklin?"

Startled, I look up.

"Hi, I'm Lauren Randall." The woman standing in front of me showing me her perfect teeth is obviously very much at home in this world. Fortyish, handsome rather than pretty, wearing a beige raw-silk dress. Her blonde hair is pulled back from her face so tightly that it raises her eyebrows into an expression of surprise.

When I get up to shake her outstretched hand, the clipboard clatters to the floor. Face burning, I scoop it up, ignoring the stares, and follow her down the hall while she does her standard line of chat. "It's so nice to see someone wearing a suit. You wouldn't believe some of the outfits I see. These young girls come in here looking like they're going to the beach instead of to work."

Now that we've eliminated me from that "young girl" category... She takes the clipboard from me and leads me into her office, a cubbyhole with two chairs and a tiny desk covered with file folders. "Let's see what we've got. What kind of work are you looking for?"

"General office. Filing, answering the phone..."

There's a fifties movie that my mother loves, where Doris Day, as the bright young thing who sets out to conquer the big city, gets a job in the steno pool—now there's a term to date you. And on her first day of work at a big, important ad agency, she—demure in a pink shirtwaist with a white Peter Pan collar—spills coffee all over this handsome young guy who works in the mail room. Coincidentally, his father owns the company. She's mortified, but he's so charmed by her sweet shyness that he falls in love with her instantly. After a lot of stupid plot complications, they end up getting married and she retires to become a lady of leisure, sort of like the position I'm just vacating. I want to ask Lauren if they have any openings like that. Receptionist with career path to kept woman.

"Have you worked as a receptionist?"

"Well—"

"How many lines have you handled? Have you used a Rolm system? Or Honeywell?" She ignores my silence. "I'm sorry. I guess I came roaring out before you had a chance to finish the application. I'll just make some notes and we can give you the typing test when we're all through."

"There's no point in giving me a typing test. I haven't typed anything in five years."

"That's okay." She waves a hand breezily. "It's like riding a bicycle. It comes back to you with a little practice." She looks at the blank spaces under the "Experience" heading. "Are you currently employed?" I've read plenty of articles that insist that experience as a homemaker and volunteer is just as valid as any other job experience. I'd be willing to bet Lauren hasn't read those.

"Justine—"

"Wynter. I go by my middle name."

"Sorry. Wynter, why don't you just tell me what your experience is?"

Deep breath. "Three years teaching high school," I say. "One year real estate sales..." She's looking at me expectantly, waiting for me to get to the meat and potatoes. "And I've worked on committees. Cedars-Sinai, the Philharmonic..." I'm ransacking my short-term memory for something more impressive.

"Why on earth do you want to do general office? You'd make more money if you just renewed your teaching certificate or went back to selling real estate."

"I can't sell real estate because I was horrible at it. I never sold anything."

"What about teaching? It's not difficult to renew—"

"I hated teaching." I grip the arms of the chair with damp fingers.

She sits back slowly, folds her arms, sizes me up. I can see it in her eyes: Another Hancock Park honey whose meal ticket got canceled.

Inside, she's probably laughing her butt off. She crosses one slender leg over the other and lets the strap of her slingback pump slip off her heel. Then she says, quietly, "I don't mean to startle you, Wynter, but I hate this job. Sometimes we have to do things we hate."

I'm on my feet, not knowing how I got there. "Thanks for the advice." I walk out of her cubbyhole, past the receptionist, out of the office. If I hurry, I'll look like I'm going to an interview.

I sit in the parking lot in the red Mazda RX-7 that was my birthday present three years ago. *Bitch. What the hell do you know about anything?*

Why am I even worrying about a job? David and I will sit down tonight and work this whole thing out. He's tired, stressed to the max. He'll probably walk in the door with roses or something, say he's sorry... We should go away for a few days. To Mexico. Drink margaritas, make love, sleep. It'll be okay. I turn the key in the ignition.

I don't need a job. Especially not one of their piddly indentured servant office jobs.

My car smells good. Whatever the detailers use on the leather seats perpetuates that new-car smell. It was a typical David gift. He wanted me in a Mercedes, but I always found them too stolid, too frumpy. I wanted something I could have fun with, something that had stick. Like a Porsche. Knowing my proclivity for speed, he nixed the Porsche. We stopped discussing it. Then, the morning of my birthday, when I came downstairs, there was a small package sitting next to my orange juice. I thought it was jewelry. Nestled in folds of white satin was a black key. My RX-7 was sitting in the driveway, top down even though the sky was threatening rain. We got a couple of miles up into the hills before it opened up and poured.

It's past noon and I haven't eaten anything. I pull into the first In-n-Out Burger I come to, order something at the drive-through window, barely seeing what it is. Back on the freeway, north on the 405, west on the 10, then PCH up the coast. For the first time I notice what a gorgeous day it is. On my left the blue Pacific, dotted with whitecaps, replicates the blue sky's scattered, wispy clouds. The whole scene could be turned upside down and you wouldn't know, like those pictures in children's books. On my right the earth-toned bluffs of Malibu still blaze with color—scarlet bougainvillea, orange and yellow nasturtiums, purple lantana scrambling over yucca and dry scrub. Everything looks exactly the same as always unless you know where to look along the road for the piles of rock that are always breaking off and sliding down the face.

As I drive and stuff French fries in my mouth, I keep sneaking looks at other drivers. Why do they all look like they know where they're going and what to do when they get there?

Memories of blissfully empty summer days urge me into the turn lane for Zuma Beach. As I pull into the nearly empty lot, I see a black Mercedes and my breath catches. David? Wrong model, wrong license plate. What would he be doing here anyway? The sedan drives slowly past me, a red-haired woman at the wheel.

I stare at the glassy curls of the breakers while The Supremes wonder "Where Did Our Love Go?" and I wonder when. Okay. Lately, there haven't been a lot of those television-commercial moments of tenderness or laughter or even shared objectives. But does that mean it's over? The first bite of cheeseburger hits my stomach like a rock in an empty swimming pool. I stuff the rest of it into the bag with the cold fries.

Out of the car, slip off my pumps, slither out of my panty hose. Walk across the sun-warmed asphalt into the cold, wet sand, hugging my jacket around me. Empty lifeguard stations huddled together forlornly are the surest sign of fall in southern California. Sometimes the only sign. Down the beach, a yellow Lab dances in the froth while his well-trained owner throws sticks. Scattered surfers in black wetsuits bob on their boards, waiting for a good ride. A gray-haired man and woman in matching warm-ups walk by, holding hands. Other than that, it's just me. An icy wavelet slaps my feet and I stand still, sinking up to my ankles. If I don't start walking, I'll lose my balance.

The salty wind whips my hair across my face, makes my eyes water.

I walk north, stepping over strands of seaweed, broken shells, half of a crab swarming with flies. I've read that when you become aware of your own impending death, your first reaction is likely to be, *I can't die. I have tickets to the opera next week.* Why is that? When we're face-to-face with the unthinkable, why do we try to defend ourselves with trivia? When my mother came to get me out of class to tell me my father had died, my very first thought, before I got hysterical, was, *So we can't go to Tahoe this summer?*

Now as my toes curl and cramp, try to get traction in the sand, all I can think of is how disappointed my mother will be. She's always adored David.

In her version of the story, he was the Handsome Prince who rescued me—not from a dragon, but from something even worse—from a boring existence as a high school teacher who rarely dated, and who spent vacations going on trips with other single women. He installed me in a house in Hancock Park, gave me a red sports car, beautiful clothes, expensive jewelry. All I had do was to look good, give clever parties, make the right friends, be available sexually when he wanted me, and not embarrass him. It wasn't a lot to ask.

Okay, it's true that I hated teaching. It's difficult to illuminate the glories of literature to kids whose reading skills hover around the fifth-grade level. Most of them were only doing time in my classes while they waited for the surf to be up or their period to start or the 3:10 bell to ring so they could cruise Bob's Big Boy.

It's also true that my social life revolved mostly around my women friends—CM and Sandy and Liz. Wine tastings, ethnic restaurants, French films, art exhibits, all the standard diversions of single women. This is not to say that I didn't date. My mother certainly doesn't know everything.

In my reasonably extensive experience, a man's good qualities—like warmth, honesty, generosity—are inversely proportional to his physical attractiveness. This leads me to the conclusion that great-looking guys are the biggest jerks of all, since they've been spoiled by every female they've interacted with, beginning with their mothers.

In spite of this fact, or maybe because of it, I am drawn to tall, blond, good-looking men like the proverbial moth to the flame. This, as my best friend CM is quick to point out, may be due to the fact that my father, whom I adored and who died when I was seventeen, was the tallest, blondest, fairest of them all. But he was also the last of the good guys.

It's been almost fifteen years since he died, but I can still walk into the den at my mother's house and expect to see him sitting in his leather chair, the paper open on his lap, a Manhattan in a sweating glass on the side table. He liked them dry with a twist of lemon. My mother had a fit when he taught me how to make them.

He taught me everything. To love books. To ride a horse English when all my friends rode western. He bought me a car with a stick shift when all my friends had automatic. He taught me to watch the Tahoe skies on still August nights, to look for the shooting stars to make wishes. How to tie a square knot, how to hit a backhand volley. How to strike a match one-handed. How to breathe when I swim. He taught me not to be afraid to open my eyes underwater. Or above it.

Most men I've known simply don't measure up. Oh, there were a few I was probably not smart about. Like Mark, someone's cousin from Del Mar, met at a wedding. Andy, the airline pilot with a wife in Dallas. A photographer with the unlikely name of Rocky Rivers. I always thought he was more interested in CM, anyway. None of them rocked my world.

Not until the night of my friend Paula's twenty-third birthday party. I remember her grabbing me the minute I walked in.

"There's someone you've *got* to meet."

I threw my jacket on the hat rack next to the hall closet. "Why?"

"He's tall. Taller than you."

"So was Frankenstein." I started down the hall toward the bathroom, but she spun me back around.

"This one's not Frankenstein. Come on. You can thank me later."

She physically dragged me over to the makeshift bar set up on a card table in the living room where the ne plus ultra of tall, blond, and good looking was opening a beer.

"Wyn, Dave. Dave, Wyn. 'Bye." She disappeared into the kitchen. I wanted to crawl under the rug, but Dave smiled and shook my hand, apologized for his hand being cold. His eyes were wide-open blue, the color of the ocean in July.

Then he said, "It's David, not Dave, by the way. And you're Lynn?"

"Wyn. Like Wynter."

In those days, most guys would invariably say something like, "Wynter? I hope that doesn't mean you're cold." And then they'd laugh like idiots.

But David smiled and said, "What a beautiful name. I bet your father picked it."

That rocked me back on my heels a little.

I poured myself a glass of chardonnay and asked him where he worked. Even I had heard of Jamison, Markham & Petroff, a very hip ad agency in Beverly Hills.

"Oh, so you're the guy who convinces people with bad credit to buy useless garbage they don't need and can't afford."

He looked down modestly at his Italian loafers. "Not exactly. I just sell our services to other companies." He paused. "But in my own small way, I help make it possible for the creative types to sell more useless garbage to sheeplike consumers with bad credit. What do you do?"

"I teach literature to kids who can't read."

"Sounds like a thankless job."

"It has its benefits. Summers off and all the burnt coffee you can drink."

"You must be pretty dedicated."

"I'm dedicated to eating regularly."

He looked thoughtful. "Well, you could always—"

"Wynter! Oh my God, I don't believe this!" Mary Beth Cole, whom I hadn't seen since graduation—and with good reason—was pushing her way through a knot of people in the hall. She fell on me as if we were twins separated at birth, then, without missing a beat, tossed her faux red hair back and held out her hand to David. Bracelets rattled up and down her arm. "Mary Cole," she said, smiling.

I noticed him noticing the plunging front of her black halter top while she gave me a look of horror. "I heard you were teaching high school. Please tell me it's a lie. I can't picture you— I'm working as a location scout for a teensy little production company called Feldspar. Pay's for shit, but I *adore* it."

I didn't have the energy to defend myself, knowing she didn't give a rat's ass anyway, and then another voice from the past screeched, "Wyn! Mary Beth! I can't believe this! It's like old-home week." Susan Carmody, blonde, tan, another fugitive from UCLA. "Is CM here?" Her blue eyes swept the room.

"She's in Baja," I said.

Her smile revealed so many gleaming white teeth, I felt like I was in an appliance showroom in front of a row of refrigerators. She described her burgeoning career as a freelance food stylist, which seemed to be the first stop on the career path for upwardly mobile domestic arts majors. The three of them started swapping business cards; somebody hit the volume on the stereo and Boz Scaggs was belting out "Lido Shuffle."

It seemed like a good time to disappear.

I've always hated the way women will trot through their paces like contestants in the Westminster dog show just to impress a man.

That night, like so many others, I ended up in the kitchen, drinking wine and gossiping with three or four friends at Paula's pink Formica table. After a while the birthday girl appeared, shaking her head.

"What the hell are you doing in here? Why aren't you out there lining up the rest of your life? Don't you think he's terrific?"

"He seems very nice." I grabbed a handful of cheese popcorn from the bowl she was carrying.

She was still shaking her head at me. "You don't find them like Dave on every corner, you know."

I took a sip of chardonnay. "It's David, not Dave, you know."

She expelled a loud, exasperated breath, picked up a new bottle of wine, and went back to the party.

By ten-thirty, I could no longer stifle the successive yawns. I fished my purse out from under the table and went to say good night to Paula. In the hall, I collided with David.

"You keep running away before I can get your last name. Wyn..."

"Morrison," I said. I couldn't believe he remembered my first name.

He told me again that his name was David (not Dave) Franklin.

"It was nice meeting you, David not Dave Franklin. But I really do need to leave." I grabbed my jacket from the rack.

He made a point of looking at his Omega. "Do you turn into a pumpkin on the stroke of eleven?"

"Eleven-fifteen. I always like to be back in the patch by then."

"Do you need a ride home?"

"I live upstairs."

The heart-stopping smile. "Why don't I walk you home?"

I looked at him, suddenly annoyed. "It's a Y-chromosome thing, right?"

"What is?"

"The way men are only interested when you're ignoring them."

"I didn't realize you were ignoring me."

I pulled on my jacket. "Well, now you know."

"So. Does that mean you won't have dinner with me?"

"I have a standing rule. I don't date men who are prettier than I am." I turned and let myself out the door.

I was halfway up the stairs before the first twinge of regret nipped at me. For a brief interval, I stood in front of my own door and considered the difficulty of going back to the party. What excuse could I use? I forgot my sunglasses. Well, fine, it was pitch-dark out. I could just apologize for being so snippy. But, no. You don't want to start off with a man by apologizing. That sets a dangerous precedent.

In the end, I gave a mental shrug, unlocked my door, and crawled into bed with my little TV.

The next day, Sunday, was one of those Raymond Chandler–esque days that L.A. gets in the fall. Dry and crackly, with a strong Santa Ana wind

driving the dust through the tiny cracks around the windows, and making firefighters nervous. The window unit in my apartment was on its
last legs and it wheezed from the effort of cooling my three tiny rooms.

CM was somewhere in Baja with her latest flame; I thought about
going to a movie by myself, but it didn't seem worth the effort. I was
hungry but I didn't feel like cooking, the weather made me tired but I
didn't feel like sleeping, and I sure as hell didn't feel like grading the
thirty-seven vocabulary tests that were languishing in my briefcase.

I decided to make bread. It always makes me feel better—or at least
more grounded.

I popped the plastic lid off the container that held the *chef,* the
starter, and inhaled the familiar, pleasantly musty smell of a living yeast
culture. This *chef* had started as a small piece of dough that I'd brought
back from the bakery in Toulouse where I'd done a work/study program the summer after my sophomore year at UCLA. By this time, the
original French yeasts had intermarried with the L.A. locals to the point
that the dynasty was seriously compromised, but I still liked to think
there was a little bit of France in every loaf.

"Souvenir"—a noun in English—the word sounds like postcards,
T-shirts, cheap metal keychains with the finish flaking off. In French,
souvenir is a verb. It means "to remember." Whenever I catch the scent
of good sour starter, *je souviens,* I remember that summer in Toulouse. I
remember Jean-Marc, the dark-eyed *maître boulanger,* the hot blast of
the ovens, the rhythms of kneading and shaping dough. The way my
breath would catch whenever Jean-Marc called me "Weentaire" in his
wonderful French voice.

I scooped a cup of the *chef* into a bowl, stirred in a cup of water and a
cup of flour, and left it to its orgy of feeding and reproducing. By
tonight, it would be *levain,* the leaven. I had just put the flour canister
back in the pantry when the doorbell rang. I figured it was Paula, drop-

ping by for a post-party analysis. I went into the living room and opened the door.

Richard Nixon stood on the landing, holding a brown pizza box that reeked divinely of garlic. Or someone wearing a Richard Nixon mask. A pinprick of fear tickled the back of my neck. "Pizza Shack Psycho Killer Claims Second Victim in Westwood." Then I noticed the Italian loafers.

"I think this takes care of the pretty problem, but I can't eat with it on," he said.

Against my will, I laughed.

"Garlic. No anchovies. I hope you're hungry."

How did he know that flowers wouldn't work? When I stepped back to let him in, I could have sworn I saw my life spinning away from me like the out-of-control space capsule in *2001.*

We sat on the couch and he set the pizza box on the coffee table, pulled off the mask. He couldn't resist running one hand through his hair to make sure it was adorably tousled, but even as he did it, he gave me a sheepish grin. Before I could decide whether to be bitchy or conciliatory, he said, "I think we got off on the wrong foot last night."

A fairly generous assessment of my rudeness.

"I wanted to apologize if I offended you somehow."

Unreal. All I could think of was how I was going to describe this scene to CM. I didn't know what else to say, so I asked him if he wanted a beer.

"What kind?"

"I think all I have is Molson."

He considered, then said, "Do you have any wine?"

After browsing my collection of four bottles, he opened a Ravenswood zinfandel. I got two plates and showed him where my mismatched crystal was hidden. He sniffed the air in the kitchen.

"What's that smell?"

"Starter. For bread." There are certain people to whom I avoid trying to explain the concepts of *chef* and *levain.*

"It smells great. Yeasty."

"That's probably because it is." It must have come out sharper than I intended.

"Would you rather I just go away?"

My own gracelessness made me blush. "It's not that. I just don't know what's going on here, and when I'm uncomfortable, I get a bit... edgy."

By that time, he'd located my dish towel and was polishing the water spots off two wineglasses. I wondered fleetingly if he was gay.

"Do I make you uncomfortable?"

"Well... yes."

Back on the couch, I cut the pizza and served it, stringing cheese everywhere. He seemed to want to clean it up, but he managed not to. "Why are you uncomfortable? I mean—" He took a bite of pizza and chewed as if he were tasting *Caille au Citron avec Beurre Blanc.* "We were having this really interesting conversation last night, and I turned around and you were gone."

"I was in the kitchen. It wouldn't have been too hard to find me."

He ignored the jibe. "And then when I finally found you again, you walked out and shut the door in my face. Did I do something totally disgusting?"

"No, it's not that. It's just—" Sitting in the friendly light of my south-facing window, munching on a really good pizza and drinking the soft, round wine, my apprehension was difficult to explain. I looked at him sideways. "Why are you here?"

"Because I liked you."

"Why? You don't know the first thing about me."

"I know you're very... attractive."

I shot him a warning look.

"Well, maybe not in the conventional sense, but you do have a certain... I don't know. You remind me of a camp counselor."

"A camp counselor?"

"Yes. You know, sort of outdoorsy. Clean."

I continued to stare at him.

"I'm not doing this very well, am I?"

I shook my head.

"You make me laugh. And you have an attitude."

"Let me see if I have this right. I remind you of a funny camp counselor with an attitude. And this appeals to you?"

He nodded, as if this were quite the usual thing to say to a woman. "You just seem so different from most of the women I know."

"You mean most of those beautiful, polished, wildly successful and sophisticated women you know."

He almost blushed, but not quite.

I arranged myself sideways on the sofa so I could look at him without turning my head. His face was perfect. Not pretty, but composed of only essentials, nothing extra, nothing wasted. Blake's fearful symmetry.

"You're not giving me a lot of encouragement," he said. "Are you seeing someone?"

"Not at the moment. Are you?"

"No," he said.

"Why not?" It was totally not my style to conduct an interrogation, but I couldn't stop myself.

"I've been busy."

"Busy?"

"I work a lot. What about you?"

"I'm picky."

His laugh was spontaneous, infectious. "I noticed that right out of the gate."

"So now all of a sudden you're not busy and you want to spend time with me?"

"If I meet your exacting specifications, yes. Is that so outrageous?"

"It's not that . . ."

He leaned forward slightly, resting his elbows on his knees. "You keep saying it's not that. So what is it?"

"I don't know what it is."

He aimed his most potent smile directly at me. "Neither do I. Don't you think we should find out?"

Two

※

We did find out.

We found out that we both liked classical music. Even opera. That we both liked scary movies and we both shut our eyes at the bloody parts. We both loved French food and good wine, particularly when cooked, served, and cleaned up by someone else.

I learned that David was the statistical one man out of every seven million who actually enjoyed shopping. He didn't seem to mind when I beat him at tennis and he liked it that I wasn't always fixing my makeup.

Like me, he was an only child, but there the similarities ended. His parents, Martin and Estelle, had retired to Monterey, and he talked about them in a remote way, telling me more about their careers—Martin had been a political science professor and Estelle an education consultant—than about them. When he talked about them, it sounded as if he were reading a curriculum vitae. He listened to my rose-colored stories about my father with a combination of skepticism and envy.

One evening at a bistro in Santa Monica, I got his take on other matters domestic as well—and, more surprisingly, my own. David had just finished besting the waiter in his favorite game of wine-upmanship when a young couple with a toddler and a very new baby came in and were seated at the table next to us.

David's glance fell on them briefly, but they hardly seemed to register in his consciousness. He looked back at me and we resumed our conversation about a new exhibit of black-and-white photography at LACMA. By the time the waiter reappeared with our wine, the woman had handed off the squirming toddler to her husband, and was shaking drops of milk from a plastic baby bottle onto her wrist. Suddenly David stood up, picked up my jacket, and indicated a table on the other side of the room.

"Lactose intolerant?" I asked as we made our way between the tables, waiter in tow.

"I just know what's going to happen," he said when we were settled.

We touched our glasses together and, as if on cue, the newbie across the room started to wail. David stuck his nose over the rim of the glass, inhaled, then took a sip and held it in his mouth for the requisite five seconds before swallowing.

"I've tried imagining myself as a father," he said. "Somehow I can't see it. Maybe later. After I've done everything I really want to do."

That moment was a modest epiphany for me. I realized that I had never tried imagining myself as a mother. I wasn't sure why. Maybe it stemmed from teaching school. There were times between classes when I'd find myself standing in the doorway of my room or in the faculty lounge or in the cafeteria when I had lunch duty, watching the barely controlled chaos before me, those children whose brains had yet to catch up with their bodies and some of whose brains never would. As I watched, I tried to pinpoint the stages of development in that awful metamorphosis from downy-haired cherubs to sullen, swaggering boys and noodle-brained, giggling girls.

It was no good reminding myself that CM and I had once been among those noodle brains, and had turned out reasonably well. The whole motherhood scenario just wasn't something that sounded even remotely interesting.

I set down my glass. The unasked question hung in the air. I shrugged lightly.

"Quite honestly, I've never given it a lot of thought."

His expression most closely resembled one of relief.

But I think the thing that clinched the deal as far as I was concerned was his attitude toward sex. I never felt as if I was being maneuvered or rushed. Ever since I'd finally managed to lose my virginity with Sylvie's cousin Gilles just days before coming home from France, I'd found sex to be a hit-and-miss proposition—mostly miss. I always enjoyed the preliminaries a lot more than the culmination, and I'd about decided that was probably just the way it was, although I'd heard some of my friends go on like it was something special.

I'd also found out how completely it could ruin a relationship, because once you'd slept with a guy, he expected that every date would end in bed. If that wasn't your destination of choice, you spent the whole evening trying to think of a way to decline gracefully. There were the inevitable discussions about whether to do it or not, accompanied by all the reasons. Sometimes you'd try being "just friends" but that never worked once the magic line had been crossed, and you ended up not seeing him again, never mind that you might enjoy his company.

I was reluctant to even start down that road, and David seemed to sense that. Maybe even to understand it. I allowed myself to think that he might be different.

Still, I couldn't imagine that this was serious. It was an odd, though not unpleasant, sensation for me, going places with a man who turned every woman's head. Sometimes when I'd look up into his smile, I'd have an impulse to turn around, as if the real object of that smile were standing behind me. Assuming that it would end, if not next week, then the week after that, I tried not to care too much and, failing that, at least not to show it. That became more and more difficult as fall turned to winter.

David continued to be thoughtful, attentive, and a perfect gentleman. The relationship hummed along, but didn't seem to be humming along toward anything specific. I came full circle and began to worry about why he wasn't trying to sleep with me. He was a great kisser, but it never went beyond that. Then one night he took me to dinner at Beau Rivage, a wildly romantic little restaurant clinging to the edge of a cliff in Malibu. We drank champagne and stared out at the black velvet ocean, dotted with occasional twinkles of light from passing boats and the lacy white froth of waves under the moon. The steady stream of conversation we'd kept up for the past six weeks seemed to have abruptly run dry.

Afterward, his black T-Bird cruised slowly down the dark Pacific Coast Highway; he turned off the radio and absentmindedly opened his window, even though it was early December and the wind was wet and cold. It was late and there were so few cars on the road that the breakers roared in the quiet. He drove silently, focused on the curves that loomed ahead, while I huddled into my jacket, certain beyond all doubt that this was the end. He'd just taken me to this wonderful place to soften the blow. Now he was going to tell me it was over.

We pulled up the suicidally precarious drive of his little house in the Hollywood Hills. When he pulled the key from the ignition, I turned my face to the window, making no move to get out of the car.

"Just tell me."

He said, "Let's go inside. It's cold out here."

"You're the one who had the damn window down. Just tell me."

"Tell you . . . ?"

"Don't be a wimp, just say it. Then you can take me home."

"What are you talking about?"

"That it's over, of course."

"Over?"

I turned abruptly. "Is this an echo chamber? Look, I'm not going to make a scene and get tears all over your squeaky-clean car. Just tell me you don't want to see me anymore, and you can take me home. I'll live."

His laugh broke the silence.

"Is that what you think?"

Without waiting for an answer, he got out, locked the door, came around and opened mine. I let him take my hand and tug me gently out of the seat.

"I don't know what's going on," I said. "And when—"

"I know. When you don't know what's going on, you get edgy. Come on. Let's be edgy inside, where it's warm."

I'd been to his house a few times, but always in daylight. It struck me as cold and sort of temporary looking in spite of the artsy black-and-white photographs on the walls and the caramel-colored leather sofa, more like a model home than a place where a real person lived. Nothing was ever out of place or dusty. There weren't any old newspapers or books turned upside down to mark the page. No glasses in the sink. No spare change on the dining room table. No mail stacked by the phone.

At night it looked completely different. Strategically placed lamps glowed, giving the rooms shape and depth. A fire was already laid in the fireplace, an Oscar Peterson tape cued up, more wine chilling in an ice bucket. All carefully planned. For me. He was seducing me. I was amused and touched and exquisitely flattered.

Near my grandparents' cabin on the Russian River, there was a swimming hole where the water was clear, cold, and deep. On hot summer afternoons, I'd haul myself out, wet and shivering, and lie down on my favorite boulder. It was warm from the sun and smooth from the river, and I loved the feel of its contours under my hands. His body was like that. If his lovemaking lacked spontaneity, he more than compensated with intensity. I'd never before had such attention given to every square inch of my body.

At some point, it began to rain. Gently at first, then increasing in speed and volume till I thought the hill would liquefy and send the whole house sledding down onto Sunset Boulevard, the two of us inside. Finally, toward dawn, the skies relented and we fell asleep, exhausted.

In the morning, I discovered that his ocean-blue eyes were gray. He saw me staring and smiled.

"Contacts," he said, pulling me over on top of him.

Ten days later, on my twenty-fourth birthday, he asked me to marry him. I was nearly as astonished and grateful as my mother was.

After we were married, I had one spectacular year of selling real estate—spectacularly bad. Eventually my company agreed not to make me pay for my training on the condition that I promise never to work in the industry again. I made a few half-assed attempts to find something else, because I liked having my own money, but then David pointed out to me that tax-wise, it was better if I didn't work. And I would have more time to do the things he wanted me to do. I didn't need much persuading.

What he wanted me to do was easy enough. I was to be the Executive Wife—the charming hostess, the source of contacts. He gave me books to read, subscriptions to the *Wall Street Journal,* the Sunday *New York Times, Los Angeles Magazine.* He made sure I read his copies of *Ad Age.* He told me in great detail what was happening at work, what they were doing for which clients, who he thought they might lose, who they were pitching.

We gave parties, went to parties, dinners, benefits, concerts, gallery openings, plays three or four nights a week. There were pro-am golf tournaments, political fund-raisers, walk-a-thons, wine auctions. I served on committees for the Philharmonic, Cedars Sinai Hospital, Sierra Club. I worked out religiously at LA Fitness, played tennis at the club where JMP paid for our membership. And in my spare time, I did lunch with my "friends," mostly women with strategically placed husbands that David might want to know.

I soon realized that when he told me he'd been too busy working to have a relationship, he wasn't kidding. He seemed to thrive on all the activity, but I was exhausted, and vaguely uneasy, like I was the great imposter and would be exposed sooner than later. I felt guilty about cultivating friends based on their potential to help us economically. But David explained that it was my job; I was his partner. As with any job, there would be facets of it that were less enjoyable, maybe even distasteful, but necessary nonetheless. In those too few, too brief times when we could relax by ourselves, he made it all seem okay.

And for a while, it was.

One morning when I woke up with a sore throat and a body that felt like the doormat for a herd of buffalo, I lay in bed, drifting between consciousness and un, like you do when you're sick, and I thought in strange little shards and crumbs about my life. I realized with a jolt that I'd been married for five years. That I hadn't seen my best friend in months and I couldn't remember when I'd last spoken to my mother. Or read a book just for the pleasure of it.

Or baked a loaf of bread. My *chef* that I'd carried home on the plane from France and nurtured and used for six years—or was it seven?—had long since expired because I'd forgotten to feed it. The thought of my faithful little yeasts starving to death and drowning in their own acid wastes had depressed me so that I'd cried for days. Scared the shit out of David. He was ready to bundle me off to a Beverly Hills shrink to get on the Prozac program, but I refused to go, having developed a deep distrust of the species after my father died.

Out of desperation, I think, he came home one night with a bread machine. From the start, he loved the thing, loved the whole concept of it. Loved the way you just dumped in all the ingredients, set the timer, and presto—fresh, hot bread overnight. Never even had to touch the stuff. Wouldn't mess up my manicure. I was appalled.

He listened patiently while I explained that bread is a process, not a product, but admitted that he didn't get it, and it just made both of us sad. I refused to use the machine, so he began to play with it. He got in the routine of making bread—if you could call it that—almost every night. But in the mornings, he was often so focused on work or in a hurry to go to some meeting that he'd rush off without waiting for it to be ready.

By then he was being mentioned as the next likely director of marketing—at twenty-nine, he'd be the youngest director in the company—and things began to change in earnest. There began to be even more meetings, weekend gatherings, sometimes including spouses. I wanted to be supportive, but these things were boring beyond all imag-

ining; I didn't handle them well. When I did attend, David was distant
and condescending. We'd fight about it while we were getting dressed,
driving in the car, or in our room if it was an overnight party. Then we'd
have to go in to cocktails and dinner and pretend everything was fine.

I'd watch him over the shoulder of someone who was describing to
me his hip-replacement surgery, and it was like watching a total
stranger, or someone famous whose picture you've seen so many times
that you recognize them instantly but there's no personal acquaintance.
His charm rarely failed him. One of the officers or the directors would
put an arm across his shoulders, and you just knew they were thinking
of him as the son they'd never had, or wondering why their son couldn't
have been like him instead of dropping out of school to be a surf bum.
David made every one of those men feel like his hero, his mentor, and I
think he sort of wished it, too. He never came on too strong, too challenging, too threatening.

And their wives—my God, the older ones wanted to take him home
for milk and cookies. Some of the younger ones just wanted to take him
home. I'd never considered myself a jealous woman, but there were a couple of times when I wanted to pour my drink down someone's cleavage.
If David hadn't been so absolutely circumspect, I might have done it.

Most ominous of all, however, was his new tendency to be annoyed
and embarrassed by my frankness and my disinclination toward social
jockeying—the very things he'd once said he loved about me. I tried to
do what I thought would please him, but I began to feel like I was walking on eggshells. Still, when the meetings were over and we were safe at
home, old comforts returned and we'd settle back into our life.

Nothing was really wrong. Things were going to get better. Just as
soon as this meeting or that project or the next pitch was over. After he
became director of marketing. We'd have more time. We'd go away for
more long weekends and long talks. We'd find it again.

In the movies, when it's time for The Bad Thing to happen, the music
changes. When the homesteaders have got all the crops in the barn and

they're having the harvest hoedown and everybody's dancing and having fun, then the menacing cello tremolo lets you know that the cattle baron's henchmen are about to show up and gun down a few innocent bystanders. I've always thought it extremely unfair that real life doesn't come with that sort of sound track. Not that it would change anything, but advance notice would be nice.

So I came home on a Friday afternoon from a meeting of the Hancock Park Green Spaces Association to find a gold Lexus parked in our driveway behind David's black Mercedes. I had to park my Mazda at the curb. Before I could even get to the porch, the front door opened and out stepped Kelley Hamlin, one of the account managers. Not just any old account manager, but the company MVP for the last two years. I'd talked to her briefly a couple of times at office social functions, but I'd heard from some of the other women on the management side that she was brilliant. Driven. She was also beautiful.

"Hello, Wyn." She smiled at me, flicked her blonde hair back over her shoulder. David stood behind her, a file folder in his hand. "Thanks for dropping this off, Kelley."

The faintest little *ping* sounded somewhere in my brain, so quiet that I almost missed it. I looked at him, and he looked right back at me, smiled into my eyes. But there was no exchange. It was like looking at someone who's wearing those mirrored sunglasses. All you see is your own reflection.

After a quiet and seemingly endless dinner, I was reading the new *Los Angeles Magazine* in the room I call the den but that David always refers to as the "library." He came in, sat down next to me on the black leather couch.

That in itself was a guaranteed attention grabber, because lately we'd been simply two people who found themselves asleep in the same bed every now and then. He sat on the edge of the seat, smiled almost shyly, as if he was going to start a conversation about something other than picking up the dry cleaning.

I remembered how it had been before. How it might be again. I smiled back. Détente.

Then he said, "Wyn, I can't do this anymore."

"Do what?" The wrong thing to say. It elicited his hurt/disappointed look.

"I can't keep pretending everything is fine."

"I know everything's not fine. You're working much too hard and the stress must be—"

"Yes, I *have* been busy, and there is a lot of stress. But it's not just that."

An image flared. David rolling over in our bed next to someone. Indistinct, no more than a shape under the covers. The scene evaporated instantly, but it left a white shadow, the way a match flame leaves a ghost of itself on your eye.

We looked at each other for a minute before I went for broke.

"Are you seeing someone?"

He frowned. "Seeing someone? You mean like a shrink?"

"No. I mean like a woman. Is there something you want to tell me?"

He took the magazine out of my hands and tossed it onto the aluminum-sculpture coffee table. "Of course not. I mean, yes, there's something I want to tell you, but it has nothing to do with a woman."

But he didn't look at me.

"I've just been really unhappy. I'm not even sure why, except I feel confined, like I can't move. Sometimes, during the day, I'm sitting there in my office and I feel like I can't breathe."

I started to touch his face, but he intercepted my hand and placed it in my lap. I said, "Maybe you should go see Dr. Geary and—"

"I just had a complete physical in January. There's nothing wrong with me."

"Then what is it?"

He blinked twice. "It's my whole goddamned life. The house, the job"—he paused, but only for a second before plunging on—"us. Everything. This guy I knew at the club dropped dead during a squash game last week. He was only forty-five, for Chrissake. It makes you question what the hell you're doing. What we're doing."

I felt a lurching sickness in my stomach. "Can't you tell me what's bothering you about...everything? I thought this was what you wanted. I mean—"

"So did I." His eyes had lost their clarity, become like flat, blue stone. "I don't know if JMP is where I belong. Whether I should try a bigger agency. Or even a completely different—Where do I want to end up ten or twenty years from now? Maybe there's something else, somewhere else I haven't even thought of yet."

While he cataloged possible causes of his malaise, my mind raced. I wanted to shout at him that he was too young for a midlife crisis. I had to stifle the impulse to reach over and trace the line of his dark eyebrows, his perfectly straight nose, the plane of his cheek. I remembered how his face felt next to mine, the crisp scent of his Polo cologne, the way his hair slipped between my fingers like corn silk.

"David, believe me, I understand. You're working too hard. The money's not that important to me, honestly. I want you to do whatever you want to. Whatever makes you happy. I don't need—"

"You're not listening to me." His voice took on a too familiar edge of impatience. "What I'm trying to tell you is that I need a complete break from the whole..." His hands opened, then closed into fists. "I need to have the psychological freedom to take risks, to fail. I can't feel like you're depending on me to take care of you."

"I don't want you to feel like I'm depending on you. I wouldn't mind if you depended on me a little more. I'm perfectly willing to go back to work, so you can—"

"Wyn." He cleared his throat. "You're missing the point here. What I need is to be completely independent. Of you."

A somewhat belated flash of insight. This wasn't about us, it was about him. What he wanted. What he didn't want.

He said, "I've wanted to tell you, but I didn't know exactly how to explain it. And the other problem is, you don't deal well with the unvarnished truth."

Sudden tears pooled in my eyes and overflowed, dripping into my lap. He handed me the pressed, white linen square he just happened to have in his pocket.

"David, the unvarnished truth is, I love you. Don't you——?"

"It's not that I don't love you." The words sliced cleanly through the mush of my sentiment. "I just think it was a mistake to get married. Like we did. So quickly. I don't think we really knew each other. And I need..." He picked up the handkerchief off the floor where I'd dropped it, handed it to me again. "I need to figure out what's important to me."

Sound concerned, but not hysterical. "If that's how you've been feeling, why didn't you say something before now?"

He looked pained. "I shouldn't have to tell you that we're miserable. Don't you even know when you're unhappy?"

"I know it hasn't been so wonderful lately, but we've had seven good years. Let's not throw it all away just because——"

"Wyn, listen to me." He eased closer, took both my hands. I hated that determined look on his face. "I'm being suffocated—not by you," he added quickly. "It's everything. I feel like all my options are closing off. Like I'm trapped in this——"

Outside, a car alarm began to shriek. One of ours? I remembered that rain was forecast for tonight and we should close the windows on the west side of the house. The housekeeper was coming tomorrow. Did I write her a check? Was I supposed to call Lisa Hathaway about the publicity committee meeting for the symphony fund-raiser?

My life was going down the toilet and my brain had picked this moment to go out on strike.

"I don't know." He took his hands from mine, carefully, as if he wasn't sure mine would stay put.

"So what are you saying? That you want a——"

"No." Too quickly. Then, "I don't know. Maybe we both just need some time alone, some space."

"David, I don't need any more time alone. That's about all I have right now."

He seemed not to hear me. "Maybe you should move out for a while. I saw a great condo the other day. Not too far away. We could still see each other." His voice rose just slightly. Like you do when you're trying to talk a child into taking her medicine: *Hmm? Wouldn't we like to do that? It would be so good for us.*

A tiny prickle of anger started at the back of my throat. He'd been looking at condos for me?

"If you're the one who needs some space, why do I have to move? Why don't you get a condo?"

He straightened, his gaze over my head someplace. "Because it's my house," he said.

I remembered this woman I knew who was hypnotized at a magic show and made to do all kinds of funny things. When the guy brought her out of it, and she noticed everyone in the audience laughing, she felt stupid without knowing why. Just now I had that same sense of having missed something important.

He slept in the guest room. We hadn't made love in months anyway, but sleeping by myself in the king-size bed without even the shape of his body nearby was cataclysmic. I couldn't have felt more alone if I'd been sleeping in a crater on the moon.

The weekend was interminable. He spent most of it at the office. Or at least that's what he said. On Sunday afternoon, I dialed his extension, listened to it ring six, seven times, till voice mail picked up. It didn't mean he wasn't there. He could have been in the men's room, the kitchen, a conference room, a screening room. He could have been on another line. I knew if I asked him, that's what he'd say. "I was talking to Hank." Or Tom. Or Grady.

I hesitated for a second, then called the main switchboard. When the automated receptionist started ticking off everyone's extension, I punched in Kelley Hamlin's number. It rang twice before I slammed down the receiver. I wasn't going to start checking up on him. I trusted him. If he said he was working, then he was working.

Obeying some ageless instinct, I took a long bubble bath. Too long. My fingers shriveled. I put on a classic black skirt and ivory silk blouse that he'd always liked. I stared at the naked face in the mirror, somewhat reassured that the woman reflected there still looked pretty good, hadn't changed all that much. *You're in your prime,* I told her. I reached for the makeup tray.

I had my mother to thank for the dark eyes and good skin. The straight nose and wide mouth came from my father. My hair was the problem. Why couldn't I have gotten my mother's hair, dark and shiny like an artist's brush? Or my father's—thick, blond, and straight as a Swedish sea captain's? Instead I got hair like my father's mother and sister—light reddish brown, thick and curly, completely unmanageable. I battled it now, smoothing the kinks out with a hot comb.

I chilled a bottle of his favorite Puligny-Montrachet. I put on the music he liked, the Brandenburg Concertos. And I waited.

I was sitting on the bed with a book and a glass of wine, doing more drinking than reading, when he appeared about eleven-thirty.

"Are you hungry? There's some soup."

He smiled politely. "No thanks. A couple of us were working on a pitch. We sent out for Chinese. You should hang up your skirt before it gets all wrinkled." He eyed the bottle on the night table disapprovingly. "Don't you think—"

Before he could finish, I refilled my glass with childish defiance, but he was already headed for the bathroom. I tossed aside the book, drank some more wine, riffled the pages of a magazine, listened to the water running in the bathroom. He came out, picked up his pillow. The sweet, clean smell of him wrung my heart.

"David . . ."

He turned, but not all the way around to face me. Like he was on his way to something important and I was detaining him. "Wyn, please. Don't make it any harder than it has to be."

"We could go to counseling." I rolled the hem of the sheet between my fingers. "Do you know how long it's been since we made love?"

He exhaled through his nose. "Things at the office are crazy. I've been working my ass off. I've got so much on my mind I can hardly sleep, and then I come home and you expect me to perform like a trained seal—"

"I don't expect anything." My voice cracked annoyingly. "I just miss how it used to be. I want you to hold me. It's not just the sex. You don't even touch me anymore." I swallowed audibly. "Do you realize that?"

"Haven't you thought about anything I said Friday?"

"I'm going to look for a job tomorrow."

A frosty smile of approval. "Good idea."

I closed the magazine in my lap. "But I'm not moving out of this house."

The smile vanished. He opened his mouth to say something, then closed it, setting his jaw. He turned and walked out of the room, pillow tucked under his arm, like a little boy running away from home.

When I drew my legs up under me, the magazine flopped open. "Hottest Careers for Women in the Coming Decade." I picked it up, scanned it hopefully. "Finance." *I can't balance my own checkbook.* "Teaching." *Been there, done that.* "Police Work." *I don't think so.* "Construction." *Are they serious?* "Child Care." *No way.*

I drank some more wine and pondered the realities of returning to the workforce, then I closed the magazine and heaved it across the room. When I stood up to take off my skirt, my knees wobbled under me. I sat down heavily, dissolving against the pillows.

Time to get ready for bed. I wanted to lay out the suit and shoes for my interview tomorrow. And the purse. Jewelry. But my head felt large. Unwieldy. I'd close my eyes.

Just for a minute.

Three

༺❀༻

My oma told me that the best friendships often start with a quarrel. She said there's a closeness that comes from a good, healthy fight that you can't get any other way, and I think it must be true. Look at CM and me. Our friendship started with a fistfight, and twenty-two years later it's still going strong. The friendship, I mean.

The fight was about a boy. It seems ridiculous now, but at the time we were the two tallest girls in the third grade, and Michael Garrity—while neither attractive nor pleasant—was the only boy taller than we were.

After the playground monitor had escorted us to the office, with CM holding wet paper towels on her bloody nose, and our mothers were sequestered with the principal, we were left by ourselves in the hall to await sentencing. We turned to each other as if on cue, and the instant our eyes met, we started to laugh. We got a two-day suspension from school. Our parents grounded us for a month. On our first day of freedom, we went behind her garage and gouged ourselves with her dad's rusty Boy Scout knife to become blood sisters.

She accepted a choreographer's fellowship position with a dance company in Seattle over a year ago, and we haven't seen each other since. But whenever we talk on the phone, it feels as if we're picking up right where we left off only a day or two ago. She's the one person I want to talk to now, but before I can call her, she calls me on Monday night. At the sound of her voice, my seething emotions attain critical mass and I start to bawl.

"Wyn?"

I blow my nose and keep blotting the tears that refuse to abate.

"What's going on down there?"

"I don't know. David is . . . We're—I think we're splitting up."

As I'm pouring my heart out, I suddenly realize she's laughing. Surprise stops my tears in their tracks.

"I'm sorry, Baby. I'm not laughing at you. It's just that I was calling to tell you Neal moved out." Now I'm laughing, too, albeit a bit hysterically. "I think we should fall back and regroup," she says. "Why don't you get your ass on a plane and come up here for a nice, long visit?"

The following Saturday, one of those blue-and-gold September afternoons, finds me on an Alaska Airlines flight heading for Seattle-Tacoma International Airport. My mother's reaction to my departure was predictable.

"Have you taken leave of your senses? This is exactly the wrong time for you to go away. You need to be there. Show him you love him. Cook dinner for him. Make your presence felt."

The fact that he's never home for dinner, doesn't want to feel my presence—in fact, acts slightly surprised and annoyed when we pass each other in the hall, as if I'm a long-term houseguest who's overstayed her welcome—none of this registers with my mother.

David's unabashed enthusiasm was depressing. "I think it's a really good idea, Wyn. I need to do some thinking. It'll be good for me to be alone."

The plane's docking ritual seems lifted from a religious service, as in "Thank God we made it." There's a final lurch, lights blink, chimes sound. The pilgrims rise en masse, pressing forward through the jet way, straining toward that first breath of fresh air. I scan the crowded terminal for CM. She's easy to spot, with her mass of auburn hair a good four inches above most other heads, but she's already seen me.

"Wyn!" She runs up and gives me a big hug. "You look way too good for someone who's just been dumped."

Actually, she's the one who looks great. But then she always does. CM—or Christine Mayle to the rest of the world—is the only woman I've ever known who even looks good the week before her period.

Analyze her features and she's not classically beautiful. But at just under six feet tall, with creamy skin, green eyes, and long auburn hair, she doesn't look like very many other women. Her taste in clothing is, frankly, weird—handmade this, ethnic that, strange color combinations. But somehow it all looks good when she puts it on, and she carries herself like the dancer that she is, striding rather than walking. I always expect her to break into a *tour jêté.*

Her apartment is on the fifth floor of an old brick building at the top of Queen Anne Hill, and it's very CM. Two bay windows frame sweeping views of the city and Mount Rainier and the ocean—"Elliott Bay," she corrects me. It has built-in cabinets and a fireplace, crown molding, green-and-black tile in the kitchen. No water pressure, but tons of ambience.

"I'm sorry I don't have a guest room." We settle ourselves on her couch. "This thing is a Hide-A-Bed. I think it's pretty comfortable."

I cringe, thinking of my back.

"We've had worse," I say, smiling. "Remember that place we rented in Laguna that summer?"

She laughs. "The closet with the adjoining sponge?"

I kick off my shoes and pull up my knees, resting my chin on them. "Tell me about Neal. I'm so embarrassed I just dumped all my toxic waste on you when you called. I didn't even ask about him."

"We made it to eighteen months, three weeks, three days. That's our new personal best." She shrugs philosophically. "But it was going downhill for a while before he left. I think it started when he lost out on a teaching job he was sure he had. He got in this downward spiral where he couldn't work. He got very clingy and insecure. Then he started dropping hints about how it was my fault—"

"Your fault?"

"Yeah, you know. Like I pressured him to move up here when he really should have stayed in L.A. and worked."

"You know he'll come back. He always does." It's about the best I can do in terms of comforting.

"I don't think so." She lets out a weary sigh. "We've never lived together before. It was . . ."

Instead of finishing the sentence, she goes to the kitchen, comes back with a bottle of champagne and two juice glasses. After a solemn toast to the Amazons—our high school nickname—she says, "What do you think's going on with David?"

I set down my glass and press my fingers into the ridge of bone above my eyes, where headaches are born. "I honestly don't know." The lump in my throat makes conversation difficult. "It hasn't been good for a long time. I guess I was trying to avoid it, just hold it together till things magically got better."

"Did he say why he's so unhappy?"

"He said he felt trapped—not by me, of course. It's marriage in general. Too confining. And he might want to change jobs. He doesn't want his options limited. I think for the first time in his life, he's looking for self-realization."

She looks at me. "Sounds more like he's looking to screw around."

"Thanks, Mayle."

"Sorry. That was a dumb thing to say. It's just that I never knew David to have a philosophical thought in his pretty head."

"He isn't stupid." My voice sounds stiff and hollow inside my head, the way it does when you have a bad cold.

"If he'd dump you, how bright can he be?" she says, indignant on my behalf.

I don't say anything.

"Come on, hate his guts. You'll feel better."

I take another sip of champagne and study her bare feet, curled over the edge of the couch. God. Even her feet are beautiful. Strong, slender. Maroon-painted toenails.

"You know any lawyers?"

My stomach turns over. "We're not talking about the big D. Yet. Maybe it won't come to that. Maybe if I just give him some space ..."

She lets it hang there for a minute, and then says, "Well, if it does come to that, be sure you check around. Ask some of your rich-bitch friends. Preferably a female lawyer. I think the men all subconsciously identify with the husband. If you can't find one you like, you should call my friend Jill Trimble. In Silver Lake. She divorced Roy a couple of years ago. Took his ass to the cleaners."

"Could we talk about something else?"

She leans over to hug me. "I'm sorry, Baby. It just makes me furious that he'd do this to you."

The sofa bed is like every other sofa bed in the world—lumpy and saggy. I dream strange, exhausting dreams about swimming or drowning, wake up, roll around, drift back to sleep, into another dream. Finally, at eight I get up, pull on my sweats, and sit in one of the bay windows, stare at the fog hovering over the water.

I left CM's phone number on three message pads—in the kitchen, in David's office, and in the bedroom. Just in case he gets an uncontrollable urge to hear my voice. I could call him right now. To let him know I got here okay. But Sunday's his one morning to sleep late. He'd probably be pissed off if I woke him up.

I picture him sitting on the flagstone patio with the *New York Times* and his coffee. That's what we do on Sundays when the weather's good. In the spring, there's the perfume of creamy white gardenias, wet from the sprinklers. On dry fall days, the pepper berries crunch underfoot, spike the air with their sharpness. He'd be all dressed, of course, but I'd be wearing his high school soccer jersey that I cut the sleeves out of, and my flip-flops. He used to tease me about sleeping in the jersey, said he felt like he was sleeping with some jock. I thought it looked kind of sexy. Maybe not.

CM wanders out, yawning. She looks at the rumpled bed. "You didn't sleep, did you?"

"I was a little restless."

"I heard you thrashing around once or twice. Is the couch awful?"

"It's not that bad. I'm just having weird dreams."

"Liar. You can sleep with me." She dismisses my protest. "I've got a queen-size bed. It'll be fine. Hey, in Laguna we did it in a double. Besides, since we're having such a bad time with men, maybe we should become born-again lesbians."

She insists on going out for breakfast. "There's a great little bakery just down the hill. We can have a brisk walk, get coffee and scones, and read the paper. I have to go to a meeting this afternoon at the studio, so you're on your own till dinner."

"You have meetings on Sunday?"

"Not usually. Right now we're working out an itinerary for a series of master classes at schools back east, so things are a little crazed."

It's nine by the time we leave the building, me bundled up in sweats, a windbreaker, Dodgers baseball cap, long scarf wrapped around my neck, velour gloves. CM, oblivious to the cold wind off the water, wears tights and a Seattle Mariners jersey.

I should have realized that her idea of a brisk walk just down the hill is my idea of a forced march, particularly when I haven't had my coffee. We weave through a maze of streets, commercial and residential. Small shops, cafés, a few bars. Victorian houses, craftsman bungalows, Spanish/Moroccan stucco, New England saltbox. Some old, some new, in varying states of renovation and decay. Sprawling magnolia trees, velvet-green pines, a few magnificent old hardwoods. Gardens spilling over with flowers, neatly manicured lawns. One shabby cottage has a wooden sign stuck in the weed-infested ground. It says "We like the natural look."

Half an hour later, we arrive at the block of squatty brick buildings that includes the Queen Street Bakery. By now, the sun has burned through the fog. I've removed the scarf and gloves, tied the windbreaker around my waist, and I'm still sweating like a prizefighter. The crowd of couples and families and kids and dogs spills out onto the sidewalk. One guy has a red-coated cat on a leash. I hear him tell someone it's an Abyssinian.

CM points at a vacant table near the open French doors. "Better grab that. I'll get the food."

I drop gratefully into a chair, disentangling my layers of clothing and looking around me. The place is laid out shotgun style; from the front you can see behind the counter to the serving station, past the backs of the big black ovens, straight through to the back door. The café part is full of mismatched tables and chairs, with bright cushions, artworks of wildly divergent styles and levels of expertise. There are plants everywhere—spider plant, wandering Jew, devil's ivy—obviously chosen by some unrepentant flower child. But it's the smell of the place that grabs me—not just the food, but the space itself—old brick and sun on freshly mowed grass.

When I was growing up, my family always vacationed at Lake Tahoe, in the High Sierra, right where Nevada's elbow pokes California in the ribs. We rented the same cabin every year, two weeks in the summer, a week at Christmas.

On Saturday mornings, my father and I would drive over to Truckee, a little town with a high concentration of Basque sheepherding families. There was a bakery there called Javier's, and we always tried to get there just as the huge round loaves of sheepherder's bread were coming out of the oven.

The owner of the place was named Jorge, and he and my father had a running joke about the nonexistent Javier and where he might be that morning. They would talk about the weather and the sheep and the fishing while I wandered around, eating cookies and watching the bakers in back. I could never get enough of the smell of that place—the bread, the strong coffee, the creaking, splintered wood floors—or the feel of the loaf, warm in my lap on the drive home.

The Queen Street Bakery has some of that same flavor about it.

CM sets down two mochas and an earthenware plate with two scones. "Don't thank me, just leave a big tip."

One bite of the scone makes me smile—golden brown and crisp on the outside, meltingly tender inside and not overly sweet, with just enough chewy nuggets of currant to provide counterpoint. Funny how the tiniest perfection can make you believe everything's going to be all right.

When CM parks herself in a chair and crosses one long leg over the other, every male in the place between thirteen and eighty is checking her out, some surreptitiously, some not so. It's always like that, no matter where we go. One look and their eyes keep drifting back to her like compass needles to magnetic north.

It's funny. Most women would kill to look like CM. They think if they were only beautiful, all their relationship woes would be over. They'd probably be surprised to find out that CM has just as much trouble with men as they do—sometimes I think she has more. Sure they stare at her, but a lot of them are too intimidated to do anything beyond that. Her looks scare off a lot of perfectly nice guys, and her in-your-face independence takes care of the others.

And then there's Neal. He keeps breaking up with her—or acting like an asshole till she breaks up with him—and coming back. Does that mean he really loves her? Or that he enjoys emotional upheaval? Or is he into the power trip of making a beautiful woman cry over him?

Oblivious to the testosterone wafting our way, she takes a long sip of her mocha and her eyes close in contentment. She sets down the cup and folds her arms.

"You know you'd be better off without him."

My head falls back. "Don't. I came up here to decompress."

"You came up here because you wanted me to talk some sense into you."

"No, I didn't. Between my mother pestering me to hang on for dear life and you nagging me to cut loose, I don't know what I'm doing. I just want to float for a while."

"If you ask me, that's what you've been doing for the last seven years."

"I didn't ask you."

"Wyn, can you honestly say you've been happy? I mean, there you are tooling around L.A. in your sports car and sitting through boring committee meetings and eating little artistic arrangements of sushi for lunch and giving dinners for people you loathe and spending shitloads of money on clothes that don't even look like you. Is this really what you want to do with your life?"

"What do you want me to do?" I say crossly. "Become a medical missionary in Zimbabwe?"

"I want you to do whatever makes you happy. Are you happy?"

"I love David and—"

"Why?"

I stare at her. "Why do I love him?"

"Yes. What is it about him that you love?"

"For Christsake, Maylo. I love him because I love him. It's a feeling. You can't break it down into components. I know you can't stand him, but—"

"Never mind how I feel about him. In fact, forget him for the moment. Is your life making you happy?"

"I knew when I married him how our life was going to be, and I accepted that."

"Answer the question."

"How many people are really happy?" I'm shredding my napkin.

She leans forward, grips the edge of the table. "Answer the fucking question. Are you happy?"

"How should I know? Stop badgering me."

She leans back in her chair. "I rest my case."

"Are *you* happy?"

"Yes."

"Even though Neal's gone."

"That makes me sad. I miss him. I like getting laid regularly. But for the vast majority of the time, I'm happy with my life."

Every morning on her way to the studio, CM drops me off at the bakery. I have coffee, read the paper, have more coffee, eavesdrop on the conversations floating around me, watch the women who work there. Most of them seem to be roughly my age, and it interests me how different their lives are and how hard they all work. Pretty soon, they know who I am, that I'm visiting CM, and I know most of their names and what they do.

There's Ellen, one of the owners, with eyes the color of espresso and short, dark hair. She wears long dresses with black Doc Martens and wire-rimmed glasses that keep sliding down her nose while she's waiting on people, and she must know every single person within a ten-block radius. She asks about their husbands, wives, kids, pets, always by name. She'll talk local politics with anybody who shows the slightest inclination, and she's a fount of neighborhood gossip—what shops are closing and why, who's moving in or out, who's pregnant or getting a divorce, whose cat or dog is lost or found.

A punked-out kid named Tyler is the espresso *barista*, the youngest of the lot. She's got blue hair and a nose ring, a tattoo of some Celtic knot design encircling her wrist. Lots of eye makeup and she dresses all in black. From her conversation with the other women, I gather that she just graduated from high school and is in career limbo. She works at the bakery in the mornings, dabbles in a few art classes late in the day, does the club scene at night. I wonder when she sleeps.

Diane is the resident cake baker and Ellen's partner. She's a Meg Ryan blonde, tall and skinny, with that coltish grace that's all elbows and collarbone. Ellen needles her about her tendency to oversleep; she usually rolls in around nine o'clock to start baking the cakes for tomorrow and decorating the ones for today. I love to watch her designs take shape. She does wedding cakes with real flowers. She does birthday cakes with buttercream roses and daisies and ivy, fruits, animals, or toys, and the dedication in nimble, flowing script. She probably could have been a sculptor, but when I tell her that, she just laughs and says she likes being a baker because she can eat her mistakes.

On Wednesday, after I have coffee, I catch a bus down to the bottom of Queen Anne Hill and stroll south along the waterfront. The breeze off the Sound blows fresh in my face, snaps the colored pennants on the light poles. I picture CM at the studio, giving class, writing grants, doing her own workout. Here we sit, both of us with a lapful of relationship disaster, and yet her life seems to have changed very little—at least superficially.

I wander out onto one of the wooden piers. Scents of creosote and diesel fuel merge in my nostrils with the iodine smell of seawater. Across the bay, the cranes and container ships of the working port look like an animated cartoon. I find a wooden bench that's relatively free of seagull shit and turn my face up to the sun.

Okay, she's not married, I am. She and Neal lived together less than two years; David and I for seven years. But that doesn't explain it away entirely. As long as I've known CM, she's seemed to have an inner compass that I lack. Even in grammar school, she knew she was a dancer.

While I was changing my major every year, she sailed through the UCLA dance curriculum and began getting work almost immediately, although not for much money. Sometimes I felt bad for her having to work two jobs, but she never seemed to find it any more than a minor inconvenience, a brief detour on the road to a destination that was never in doubt.

If I hadn't married David, I'd probably still be teaching bonehead English to a bunch of teenage delinquents and wondering if I should go to grad school and taking aptitude-assessment tests. I guess the truth is that she's driven and I'm drifting. But it's never made the slightest difference in our friendship.

The closest we ever came to having a second fight was when I got engaged to David. His charm never worked on her the way it did on the rest of the female population. She found him insipid, almost beneath contempt, and never minded telling me so. She called him Pretty Boy. He called her an intellectual snob and said she was jealous of me. He never understood why I found that hilarious, and he never understood our friendship. For years I nurtured the hope that they'd learn to like each other, but mutual tolerance was about as good as it got.

Of course, if the truth be told, I was never overly fond of Neal, either. He was our graduate instructor in psych 101 and CM was instantly smitten. He's attractive enough in that brainy/sexy way. Tall and lean, dark and brooding. He even wears a Van Dyck. He's been a Ph.D. candidate in clinical psychology for as long as I've known him. CM thinks he's brilliant. She says the reason he has so much trouble finishing his degree is that he keeps butting heads with the academic establishment. To me, he seems like the consummate bullshit artist.

Another reason I find him so irritating—aside from the fact that he's continually making CM unhappy—is that he always wants to talk about my relationship with my father. Like he's titillated by the possibility that there might have been something unnatural going on.

"Spare some change, lady?" A cigarette-raspy voice. A woman hovers at the end of the bench, shifting her weight from one foot to the other. She looks too young to be one of the hard-core homeless, but her skin has the leathery tan that comes from exposure and her eyes have that vacant hardness that eventually replaces hope. Spikes of dirty brown hair poke through holes in her red knit cap.

I hate looking at her filthy, ripped jeans and grimy parka, but I've never been able to just look away. David disapproves of giving money to panhandlers. "There are plenty of jobs around" is his standard line. He says I'm only encouraging them to remain dependent on handouts. I know there's a certain amount of truth to that, but I always have a hard time saying no when I'm standing there in my hundred-and-fifty-dollar Donna Karan T-shirt and my Calvin Klein jeans and my Bruno Magli sandals.

I dig in my pocket for a crumpled dollar bill, press it into her hand. "God bless," she says.

It reminds me of running to put pennies in the Salvation Army Christmas kettles when I was little because I liked to hear the bell ringer bless me. Right now I suppose I need all the blessings I can get.

Four

❧

On the way back to the apartment, I have a sudden urge to ward off the loneliness goblins by baking bread. I don't have a starter and it takes two or three days to get one really humming, but I still know a few tricks to give a plain loaf some character. Since CM's idea of using a stove is to set her purse on it while she laces up her Reeboks, I stop by the Thriftway for supplies and lug them up four flights of stairs because the building's creaky elevator is malingering today.

You don't really need a recipe to make bread. It's mostly about proportions—one package of yeast to six or seven cups of flour, two cups of water, and a tablespoon of salt—and Jean-Marc used to say that bread may not always turn out the way you intend it to, but it always turns out. Just the same, it's been so long since I've done this that I use the recipe on the back of the flour bag as a jumping-off point.

Plain Old Bread

1 tablespoon (1 packet) active-dry yeast　　*1 tablespoon salt*
2¼ cups warm water　　*6 to 7 cups unbleached white flour*
1 tablespoon sugar

Most recipes want you to use a whole envelope of yeast. This means the first rising will take only about an hour and the second maybe forty-five minutes to an hour—particularly if you put it in a warm place, which is what they usually suggest. Some go as far as telling you to put the dough in a gas oven warmed by the pilot light.

That works fine. If that's the kind of bread you want. Grocery-store bread. Wonder bread. Remember that? The stuff we ate when we were kids. It was white—a brilliantly unreal white—and it had the mouth feel of a damp sponge. When you took a bite, it left an imprint of your teeth suitable for postmortem identification.

Then in the seventies everyone jumped onboard the organic/whole earth bandwagon, and started throwing every grain they could find into the mix, but the recipes called for way too much yeast and lots of oil and eggs and milk, because we all still craved that soft and tender stuff we grew up on.

It wasn't until I went to France that I tasted bread that wasn't full of additives and air. It was like a religious conversion for me. In fact, it's kind of like sex—one of those things that everyone thinks they know all about and they tell you how great it is, but which is actually pretty uninspiring until you have it one time the way nature intended it to be.

So, the first thing I do is cut the yeast in half. You don't want the dough to set a new land-speed record. What you want is a long, slow rise to build the kind of texture and flavor that make people think you paid $5.95 for this loaf at the European Gourmet Bakery.

I combine the yeast with the water in a large crockery bowl, stir in the sugar, and let it sit for a few minutes while I measure the flour into another bowl. Then I stir in the flour with the only big spoon I can find in this pitifully underequipped kitchen. When it clumps together and pulls away from the sides of the bowl, I turn it out on the counter and knead it for ten minutes, adding just enough flour to keep it moving. Then I knead in the salt. Dead last. Because salt strengthens the gluten and makes the dough fight you.

When it's smooth and elastic enough to spring back when I poke it, I oil a big bowl, slosh the dough around in it, making sure the entire surface is oiled. Then I put a damp towel over it and set it as far from the stove as I can. Someplace like a wine cellar would be nice, but CM doesn't have one of those. I put it on her dining room table.

With half the yeast, it'll take twice as long to rise, so I pour myself a glass of sauvignon blanc and start scraping dough off the counter.

The scent of yeast hanging in the air reminds me of my *levain* and the day that David came to my apartment with the Nixon mask and a pizza. The sharpness of the longing I feel takes me somewhat by surprise. Maybe CM was right. Maybe I would be better off without him. But then why do I feel like howling right now? Why do I want to touch his face, smell him, feel his body against me?

I'd settle for talking to him. But I can't call him at work. In a small company like JMP, everybody knows everybody else's business as it is. We're probably already fodder for the gossip mill.

I'll call the house. He won't be home, but I can leave him a message on the machine. Just to let him know I'm thinking of him. Maybe he's lonely, too, and he's embarrassed to call me after all the things he said. This way, he'll have the excuse of returning my call to save his fragile male ego.

He'll call me back tonight. Probably late, because he'll be working late as usual. I'll sit in the living room in the dark, and I'll tell him about what I see—lights of the city, the ferries moving across the black water toward the shadowed islands. I'll tell him I made bread today. I'll tell him I miss him. We can start with that. Just "I miss you." We can build on that. It's not just him, after all; some of the blame belongs to me.

CM has one of those duck telephones that quacks instead of ringing. She calls him Dorian. I punch in our phone number on his belly. I'm expecting four rings followed by the recording, but after two rings there's a click. He's home.

"Hello." A woman's voice. I open my mouth but nothing comes out.

Unless I'm very much mistaken, it's Kelley Hamlin's voice. "Hello-o. This is the Franklin res—" There's a rustling noise and then a ringing crash as the phone hits the floor. Then David's voice.

"Hello."

Dorian and I exchange a meaningful glance.

"Hello? This is David Franklin." There's a distinct note of panic under the heartiness.

I gently replace the duck in his cradle.

Five minutes later, Dorian's quacking his brains out, but I let the machine pick up. "Wyn, it's me. Pick up if you're there." Pause. "For heaven's sake, Wyn, stop acting like a child. I know you're there." Pause. "Kelley and I are just working on some client files. Pick up the phone." Pause. "Shit."

The line goes dead.

I think I'm going to cry. Then I picture David's face if he could hear his call being announced by Dorian Duck, and I laugh first, then cry.

When CM comes through the door at about six-thirty, I'm working my way through a 1.5-liter bottle of Robert Mondavi cabernet. She throws her purse on the couch.

"And which occasion are we celebrating tonight?"

I hold my glass up to the chandelier and squint through the ruby light. "Chapter two. The phone call. In which our unsuspecting heroine calls the handsome prince at the castle, and the milkmaid answers the phone."

"I see." She purses her mouth. "And what did the milkmaid say?"

"Hello."

"That's all?"

I retrieve a glass from the cupboard and pour some wine for her, sloshing a little on the counter. "That was about all she had time for before the prince yanked the phone away and it crashed to the floor."

She drinks some wine before taking her coat off and draping it over the nearest chair. "And what did he say?"

A rather drunken giggle bubbles out of me. "I didn't talk to him.

But he told Dorian they were working on some files. Wouldn't you think an advertising prince could come up with a more original lie?"

She sighs. "Oh, Baby. I'm really sorry." I think it's the pity in her voice that undoes me.

Thursday morning my eyes are glued shut with dried tears. After I rip them open, I see that my tongue is still purple from the wine. Unfortunately, I remember most of the evening. Crying and laughing, drinking cabernet and something else when we ran out of that, walking to a diner because neither of us could drive, eating greasy hamburgers, arguing with some other drunk at the counter till the waitress told us to leave. Throwing up in the bushes on the way back. Poor CM had to get up and go to work today.

At least I had sense enough to put my dough in the fridge so it wouldn't overrise and fall flat. I take it out and set it on the stove to come to room temperature while I shower and dress and clean the apartment for therapy.

By noon it's workable, so, in David's honor, I shape it into two of the oval loaves the French call *bâtards*. I give them a two-hour rise, spritz them with water for a crackly crust, and pop them into a 425°F oven for thirty minutes.

I've read somewhere that the smell of baking bread is a proven antidote to depression. It's true. By the time my little bastards are cooling on the counter, I'm starting to revive. I feel good enough to take a walk. And I feel the need of something chocolate. I know the Queen Street Bakery closes at two so they can do wholesale baking, but I grab one of the warm loaves and put it in the bottom of a paper grocery bag to bribe my way in.

Instead of baking, Ellen and Diane are sitting at one of the tables, with coffee cups and stacks of paper. When I bang on the door, they look up and smile, but Ellen points at her watch. I unsheathe my secret weapon. I can tell they're wavering. I hold it up to my face and inhale deeply, close my eyes, smile. In a second, Ellen's unlocking the door.

"Where did that come from?" She sniffs appreciatively.

"CM's kitchen."

She touches it gently. "You made this? Ooh, it's still warm."

I pull it back. "Not so fast. This isn't a gift. It's a barter. I need chocolate."

Diane laughs, rocking back in her chair. "Have we got a deal for you."

In less time than it takes to load a bread machine, I'm sitting at the table with them. They've ignored my suggestion that they let the bread cool completely before tearing into it and slathering the chunks with sweet butter. I'm eating a piece of Patty's Cake, an innocent-sounding name for a lethal dose of moist, dense chocolate cake sitting on a pool of espresso-caramel sauce.

"Okay. Who is Patty and how does she make this?" I lick a smear of sauce off my fork.

"Patty was the woman who owned the bakery," Ellen says. "This was the only recipe of hers that we had to have."

Diane smiles. "And after we paid through the nose for it, we discovered that it's embarrassingly simple. You can mix it with a wooden spoon in a saucepan. You don't even need an electric beater."

"I won't ask for it then. Since you had to buy it."

She tears off another chunk of bread. "Good. Because we don't give it out."

"Is this sourdough?" Ellen's sniffing the interior of the loaf, examining it lovingly.

"Nope. It's just bread."

"It doesn't taste like our bread. It's more"—she gropes for a description—"complex or . . . developed or something. I don't know. What's the secret?"

I smile sweetly. "It's embarrassingly simple. But I had to pay for a trip to France to learn how to do it, so I don't give it out."

After they stop laughing, we agree to an exchange of information. Diane goes back to the work area where I can hear the unmistakable sounds of cleanup in progress—pans and metal bowls banging, water running, and women laughing. She returns with a sheet of lined note-book paper, hands it to me.

"Here's the cake recipe. You can run across the street to Dan's Market and make a copy."

God, I can't wait to make this for CM.

Patty's Cake
with Espresso-Caramel Sauce

7 (1-ounce) squares unsweetened cooking chocolate
¾ cup butter
1½ cups strong coffee
¼ cup bourbon
2 eggs
1 teaspoon vanilla
2 cups cake flour
1½ cups sugar
1 teaspoon baking soda
¼ teaspoon salt

Grease and flour two 8½ by 4½-inch loaf pans.

Put the chocolate, butter, and coffee in a heavy saucepan with a 4½-quart capacity. Place over low heat, stirring constantly, till chocolate is melted, then stir vigorously till mixture is smooth and thoroughly blended. Set aside to cool for at least 10 minutes. Beat in bourbon, eggs, and vanilla. Sift dry ingredients together and beat into the chocolate mixture till well blended. Divide batter between prepared pans and bake in a 275°F oven 45 to 55 minutes, or until a wooden skewer inserted in the center comes out clean. Cool in pans for 15 minutes, then turn out onto racks to cool completely. Serve with whipped cream, crème fraîche, or Espresso-Caramel Sauce.

E S P R E S S O - C A R A M E L   S A U C E

1 cup sugar
⅓ cup water
½ cup heavy (whipping) cream
3 tablespoons espresso

Whisk sugar into water and pour into heavy-bottomed saucepan—preferably one with a white or light-colored interior, so you can keep an eye on the color change of the caramel. Stir over medium heat until sugar is completely dissolved, about 1 minute. Increase heat to high and bring to a boil. Do not stir, but wash down sides of pan frequently with a clean brush dipped in water.

Meanwhile, heat cream to a simmer in another pan.

When sugar begins to caramelize and turn golden around edges of pan, lift pan very carefully and gently swirl mixture to ensure even caramelization. Boil until syrup is a beautiful, deep amber—3 to 4 minutes. Remove from heat and set pan in sink. Slowly pour in hot cream, whisking to combine. Mixture will bubble up and may splatter. You may want to wear glasses to protect your eyes. Stir in espresso and blend until smooth. If mixture starts to harden, return to low heat and whisk until dissolved. While sauce is still warm, strain through fine-mesh strainer. Makes about 1 cup.

Ellen clears her throat. "About the bread . . . ?"

"The secret to more interesting bread is to use half the yeast and let it rise twice as long," I tell them.

It's very quiet for a full five seconds while they look at each other.

"That's it?" Diane says. "Half the yeast and twice the rising time? That's all?"

I feel almost as if I've cheated them. "I told you it was simple."

"Shit." Her hand slaps down on the table. "Linda would never do that."

"Who's Linda?"

Ellen sighs. "Our bread baker. She's so set in her ways she's practically calcified."

"So get someone else."

She waves her hand as if she were shooing away mosquitoes. "It's not that easy. She came with the place and . . . I'm just a wimp, I guess. I don't have the stomach for firing people. It's not like she doesn't do the job. Besides, she's not that far from retirement. It's easier just to wait her out."

"But you learned this in France?" Diane's eyes are speculative. "Are you a baker?"

"Well, I did work in a bakery. Sort of. One summer when I was at UCLA, I did a work/study program at a *boulangerie* in Toulouse." Two sets of eyebrows go up.

"What an incredible experience," Ellen says.

"It wasn't like I was a regular baker. At first, I just washed the equipment. But eventually, Jean-Marc, the *boulanger*, started letting me shape loaves and rolls and croissants. Load and unload the oven. You know—stuff he figured I couldn't possibly screw up."

"Jean-Marc, huh?" Diane gives me a sly smile. "Was he gorgeous?"

"But of course. He was French."

Saturday morning, CM drags me out of bed at seven and down to Pike Place Market. By the time we get there, they've started the market day without us. At Starbucks we stand in line for extra-foam, nonfat lattes, then sip them as we stroll through the North Arcade past stalls of handmade jewelry and clothing, paintings and pottery, honey and olives and nuts, flowers and fresh vegetables from local growers.

We watch the countermen at Pike Place Fish toss their merchandise back and forth through the air, and listen while two guys dressed like lumberjacks in jeans, flannel shirts, and work boots debate the merits of cod versus halibut for fish and chips.

A woman whose rear end resembles a plaid double-wide trailer hoists herself onto the back of a bronze pig while her husband records the feat on the camcorder.

"That's Rachel," CM says.

"You know her?"

"The pig, not the tourist. Rachel, the Market piggy bank." She looks disgusted. "If I ever get to that stage, will you please shoot me and put me out of my misery?"

I lick my foamed-milk mustache. "I would, except I wouldn't want anybody to know that I knew you."

With a hand on my shoulder, she propels me outside to the street. Steam rises from the wet cobblestones to mingle with the smell of roasting coffee and truck exhaust, ocean breeze, the scent of flowers, garlic, cumin, frying fish. I inhale deeply, stealing a kind of comfort from the reassuringly earthy smells.

"Let's go over to the Corner Market and get some cheese for dinner."

My head swivels like Linda Blair's in *The Exorcist,* in a vain attempt to see and smell the offerings of every tiny ethnic shop—*hombow,* baklavas, tamales, spicy, red *cioppino,* chicken satay, wursts, crumpets.

"We have all this in L.A., you know."

"Of course." CM smiles sweetly. "The trick is, you'd be driving for three days to find it."

At one corner a familiar perfume reaches out like an invitation. Le Panier. A *boulangerie/pâtisserie* in the French style. This one's very high tech—lots of glass, blue-and-white tile, halogen lamps, and shiny stainless steel deck ovens. The windows are full of neatly stacked *palmiers* and *pain au chocolat* and napoleons and strawberry tarts.

"You want something for later?" CM says.

I shake my head, walk quickly past the open door wondering why that smell brings on a sudden melancholy.

At a natural-cosmetics shop, she stocks up on cucumber facial and green-apple shower gel. Just off a narrow passageway, we kill an hour laughing at filthy greeting cards and trying on gauzy cotton dresses from India. She tries to rush me past Sur la Table, but it doesn't work. I dart inside to check out the floor-to-ceiling *batterie de cuisine*—just like the little shops in Europe, they manage to cram an amazing amount of merchandise into minimal space.

By eleven-fifteen, we're casing lunch places. We end up at DuJour, a little self-serve café on First Street, where we carry our trays to a table by the window wall that looks out over the Market rooftops to Elliott Bay.

"Okay, I give up. Does every place in this town have a view?"

She takes a piece of sourdough bread and tears it, handing half to me. "You should think about moving up here."

I don't say anything.

"I mean if you and David..."

I shake my head. "I'm a California girl."

She flicks crumbs off her fingers impatiently. "Just because you were born there doesn't mean you have to die there."

"I'm just not the adventurous type."

She nails me with a look. "You used to be," she says.

Monday morning, I'm reducing a cappuccino-hazelnut scone to crumbs and working on my second latte when Ellen says, "Can I ask you a silly question? Are you by any chance looking for a job?"

"A job?"

She laughs. "Yeah. You know, a repetitive task for which someone gives you money. Here's the deal. Diane and I really loved that bread you made. Linda's getting ready to retire. Hopefully, next year. We were sort of thinking you could work with her and let her teach you the technical stuff—I mean the logistics of making bread in quantity are a little different from doing it in your kitchen, as you know—and then when she leaves... You have any interest?"

Her enthusiasm is almost contagious. "It sounds great," I say gently. "Except I don't live here."

"You could always move." Her voice goes up at the end, like a question.

I avoid her gaze by opening the "Lifestyle" section of the paper, folding it back, positioning it carefully on the table.

"I'm in marital limbo at the moment," I tell her without looking up. "I'm going back to L.A. tomorrow."

I left a message on the answering machine last night, giving David my flight number and arrival time. Not that I'm expecting him to meet me. But just in case, I give the gatehouse a quick scan. Feeling sad and self-indulgent, I throw my bag in the backseat of a green-and-white cab.

Traffic's heavy for midday, and the air is warm and brown. The driver, a thin-faced guy with yellow skin and dirty brown hair, subjects me to his Horatio Alger story about abusive parents and working his way through junior college. I suppose I should be more sympathetic, but I can't help suspecting I'm being hit up for a big tip.

My Mazda sits alone in the driveway like some neglected orphan. No client-file parties today. Having deduced from my lack of response that I'm not a nice, guilt-ridden rich lady, the driver doesn't bother turning around; he just holds out his hand, palm up, and says, "Twenty-six eighty."

I paw through the bill compartment in my wallet. "All I've got's a twenty. Wait here and I'll get the rest." I shoulder my bag and start up the walk, only marginally aware of something in the deep shade on the front porch. As I draw under the portico, I see my camera, a portable phone, one of the TVs. My God, I've stumbled on to a robbery in progress. Somebody's in the house bringing our stuff out to load it up. Then I notice the boxes of books and piles of clothes with shoes thrown on top. My jewelry box. My curling iron and makeup, a broken bottle of Bal à Versailles, saturating my slippers at two hundred dollars an ounce. My breath turns to ice in my throat.

"No." Then louder, to convince myself, "No way."

Pushing the boxes aside, I reach the door. My key fits into the lock but won't turn. This isn't happening. My shoes make scuff marks on the shiny black door; I pound on it until my hands are stinging hot—stupid, because he isn't here. I imagine windows opening up and down the street, all the neighbors watching my eviction. David wouldn't do this. It's against the law. You can't just throw someone out.

The taxi's horn reminds me that the guy's waiting to be paid. Now what? I set down my bag, thankful that I didn't put it in his trunk, and walk as nonchalantly as possible out to where he sits, drumming his fingers on the outside mirror.

I give him my most charming smile. "I seem to have grabbed the wrong key, so I can't get in my house right now. I don't suppose you take plastic?"

"No plastic." His dark eyes narrow.

"Well, I have twenty bucks. I can give you a check for the rest."

He sighs. "Jesus Christ, lady."

"I'm sorry. I can't get in. What do you want me to do?"

He bangs his fist on the steering wheel. "I could call the cops, you know. I can do that. I've done it before."

Hands on hips. "Go ahead, if you want to sit here and wait for them to show up. Maybe they'll kick in my front door for six dollars and eighty cents."

"Shit. Give me the fucking twenty." He snatches it out of my hand. Before I can pull out my checkbook, he throws the cab into gear and peels off, leaving part of his tires on the pavement. I walk back up to the porch, still trying to arrive at a different interpretation of the still life sitting there.

The lamp from the den—the only thing in the house I ever bought without consulting David, and naturally he hated it—sits precariously on one step. It's a ginger-jar lamp, yellow porcelain with painted flowers. When I saw it in the shop, I thought it would add some life or warmth or at least color to the den.

Or maybe it was just that I knew he'd hate it.

I pick it up. It looks fragile, but it's surprisingly heavy. The heft of it in my hand merges with the sight of my belongings strewn around the porch like trash, and ignites a sudden fury in my brain. I give a roundhouse windup and heave the lamp straight into the front window. The plate glass explodes, falls like a frozen waterfall, and the security system starts making that obnoxious noise. My mouth opens in silent, nervous laughter.

While I'm loading the rest of my belongings into my car, the armed-response patrol appears at the curb. Another exciting day in Hancock Park. The guy opens the car door and stands with one foot propped on the threshold. "Hi, Mrs. Franklin. We got an alarm on one of your sensors."

"Yes, I know. It's nothing. I accidentally threw a lamp through the window." I smile at him. He watches me for a few minutes. "Can you give me a hand with this?" He obligingly loads three boxes into the front seat. "Thanks. Those books are heavy."

Every thirty seconds the system pauses, resets, and starts squawking again. His gaze shifts from me to the jagged glass of the window. "We... uh... should probably get that sensor turned off. Cops'll be showing up any minute."

"Good idea. The neighbors are probably going nuts." I get in my car.

He scratches the back of his neck. "Mrs., uh... Franklin, could you maybe unlock the door?"

"I'm really sorry... Ted," I read off his name badge. "I just can't right now." I put the car in reverse and ease out with him walking along-side. Several people have appeared in doorways and driveways to check out the uproar at the Franklin homestead.

I back into the street, and Ted's arms open wide in a gesture of helplessness. "What should I do?"

I turn and smile at him. "I don't give a rat's ass."

Top down, loaded to the gunwales with suitcases, bags, boxes, tele-vision, boom box, the odd shoe, tennis racket, curling iron, and tele-phone, I look straight out of *The Beverly Hillbillies*. I cruise down the street in the balmy fall afternoon, waving at my former neighbors.

There's only one place I can go—to the house in Encino where I grew up and where my mother still lives. Just driving down the winding sub-division street lined with pseudo-Spanish, Hansel and Gretel split-level, and California pagoda-style tract houses makes my stomach clench. It hasn't rained in months, and the surrounding hills look like brushfire fodder, but the lawns are sprinkler green and neatly edged. The little twigs planted forty years ago in the wake of the bulldozers have turned into trees—spruce and sweet gum, birch, kaffir, melaleuca, jacaranda, Chinese rain trees, palm trees, cactus. That's southern California. Whatever you want, stick it in the ground. It'll grow.

I park in the driveway of my mother's fake colonial, and sit with my purse in my lap, keys in hand. Finally I get out and walk up the used brick path with the border of purple pansies, past the reproduction gaslight, and try the brass knob. It isn't locked.

"Mom?"

Footsteps. Johanna Kohlmeyer Morrison appears at the top of the stairs. "Wyn, honey, what is it?"

To say that my mother and I are dissimilar is to wallow in understatement. Fifty-eight years old, petite, with a delicate, refined beauty, she could easily pass for forty-eight. I take after my father's family of tall, rangy farmers. Whenever we go places together, I always feel like one of us should be on a leash.

She's everything I'm not—perfectly groomed, efficient, organized, tactful, reserved to the point of being stoic, and most important, she is that nebulous, hard-to-define entity, a Lady, with a capital *L*. She always knows the proper dress, behavior, etiquette—fill in the blank with the noun of your choice—for any occasion. *And* she's the type of woman who irons underwear.

In spite of our differences, she can usually take one look at my face and know when something's wrong. She shows remarkable restraint now, letting me explain without interrupting to tell me that she told me I shouldn't have gone to Seattle. By the time I finish, I've worked myself into a frenzy. She perches on the edge of her sewing chair, silent, hands in her lap, while I pace in front of the phone table in the hall, listening to David's work extension ring.

"David Franklin's office, this is Andrea Wells." It's his overqualified assistant. I try to keep my voice low and calm.

"Andrea, this is Wyn. Is David there?"

"Hi, Wyn. He's here, but he's in with Hank and Grady. Can I take a message?"

"I need to speak with him. It's an emergency."

She hesitates. "He told me not to disturb them for any—"

"I bet he did. Andrea, please tell him to get his ass out there and pick up the phone."

Her voice becomes anonymous. "One moment, please."

It's actually less than a moment till he says, "David Franklin speaking." Like he has no idea.

"David, what the hell do you think you're doing?"

"Wyn, for heaven's sake, I'm in a meeting with Hank and—"

"I don't give a shit if you're naked in a teacup with Hank. What the hell do you think you're doing locking me out of my own house?"

"In the first place, it's not your house." His voice is icy. "In the second place, you left me, so I had every right to—"

"Left you?" I shriek. "*I* left *you?*"

"You moved out. You never returned my phone call."

"I went to visit my best friend. I was gone exactly ten days."

"I didn't expect you to come back." His voice has the exact tonal modulation of Darth Vader's.

"You knew damn well I was coming back. I told you when I left, and I called last night and left a message on the answering machine."

"I never got the message."

"Bullshit. What you did is illegal."

"I assure you, it is not illegal. You have your things. The house is mine."

"California is a community property state, in case you've forgotten."

"In case you've forgotten, I bought the house before we were married."

Tears of rage are beginning to choke me. "You bought it for us to live in. Or that's what you said."

"Yes. I did." Impatience snaps the ends off his words. "But we never added your name to the title. Therefore the house is legally mine. Listen, I'm in the middle of something very important. We're going to have to talk about this later." *Click.*

The receiver sits heavily in my hand. I stare at the little phone table.

Mahogany, I think, with a white marble top. There's a message pad with watercolor pansies imprinted in the upper-left corner. On the top sheet is a partial shopping list. A crystal bud vase that belonged to my oma holds three pink dianthus from my mother's garden, and their sweet, peppery smell is the only thread connecting me to reality.

When the off-the-hook noise prompts me to hang up, I walk into the den and my mother's eyes lock on mine. I can't stand the way she's biting her lip, but apparently I look stupid, too, because she looks away first.

"Honey," she says. "Oh, Wyn, I'm so sorry."

Five

❧

It's after dinner when I finally catch up with CM's friend Jill Trimble and get the phone number for her attorney, Elizabeth Gooden. When I call her office Wednesday morning, her secretary puts me through to her immediately. "Jill told me to expect your call. Tell me what's happened up to this point." Her voice is low and there's a clipped formality about her speech that suggests schooling in New England.

I give her the broad overview, acutely conscious of how much like soap opera this sounds. She says, "I can check and see if the house is in his name only. If it is, then he's right, you probably can't get back in. We can get an order for him to let you in to get your things, however. And he's going to have to come up with some money for your maintenance."

"I have what I want from the house."

"Do you have any financial records with you—information on bank accounts, investments, real estate?"

"Of course not. I was only going to visit a friend." I hate the way I come off, like a snotty rich girl, but she seems not to notice.

"It sounds like your husband wants to play hardball. If he's the only one who has access to the records regarding the marriage property, he can make it difficult for us to find out exactly what your fair share of the estate should be." *Estate? Sounds like someone's died.* "... should sit down and make a list of everything you can think of that's jointly owned."

"Oh, God. This is insane," I say to myself, almost inaudibly.

"Mrs. Franklin, marriage is about love. Divorce is about money. We don't know if your husband—it's David?—has already begun the paperwork for a divorce, but my advice to you would be to get ready to file as soon as possible. Even if he's already done it, you'll have to reply within thirty days anyway, and the more time we have to prepare, the better off you'll emerge."

"It's just that this is all so weird. I'm numb."

"Of course you are. That's how he planned it, I would guess."

"I can't believe he'd   I suppose you hear this all the time."

"Unfortunately, I do."

I sigh. "Can you tell me your rates?"

"One hundred seventy-five dollars an hour. I can send you a copy of my fee agreement, which spells out my charges. I generally ask for a twelve- to fifteen-hundred-dollar retainer to start, but if you're strapped, we can get started with five hundred. I always try to recover my fees from the other side as much as possible. And, of course, I won't bill you for this call."

I know I'm supposed to be grateful. I gnaw at the inside of my cheek. What if I hire this woman and then David realizes he's being stupid? Maybe he was upset about something at work. Maybe they lost a big account. Or something political—Grady Polhurst, he's always been jealous of David, and Andrea said he was in the meeting. David must be under incredible pressure. Maybe he's having a nervous breakdown. Men don't handle stress well. And then I call up and start screaming at him, no wonder he was angry—

"Mrs. Franklin?"

"Yes. I'm sorry. Listen, Elizabeth, I really appreciate your time. But I just can't— I need to think. I'm sorry."

"I understand. I'll check on the title to the house and get back to you tomorrow. In the meantime, please consider what I've said. Time is of the essence. Oh—and it's best not to have a lot of dialogue with your husband. You need to get used to thinking of him as the enemy."

My mother was born in San Francisco to parents of German descent. These two factors, when combined, have been known to produce a free-floating superiority complex and an innate assurance of correctness in matters of taste. Living in L.A. for thirty-odd years has only reinforced her notion that she is not overdressed; rather, everyone else is underdressed.

After my father died, she took a job as school secretary at Hubble Middle School, fifteen minutes from our house, but she went out the door every day for fifteen years dressed like a financial consultant in classic suits or dress-and-jacket ensembles. Parents, school board members, and sundry strangers who wandered into the office were always mistaking her for the principal, Elsie Howe, who usually came to work in double-knit pantsuits.

So Thursday morning when I come downstairs, it's not a complete surprise to see her wearing her black linen suit with the faux Chanel jacket, a white jewel-neck blouse, and her pearls. She takes a plate out of the warming oven—cheese omelet, two strips of bacon, for God's sake, which I haven't eaten in five years, two pieces of cinnamon toast.

"Mom, this is really very nice, but I don't eat like this. I'll weigh two hundred pounds by next Friday. All I want is some yogurt and fruit. Maybe a little granola. Coffee."

"Wyn, you need to keep your strength up. Stress can be very debilitating. You can't afford to get sick on top of everything else. Now just sit down." She points to the table where my breakfast waits, attended by a rose in a bud vase, a napkin folded like a swan, and the *L.A. Times*. "I have a job interview at ten-thirty, but I want you to have a nice, quiet morning and eat every bite of your breakfast."

"A job interview?" It hasn't even been a year since she retired from Hubble.

"I couldn't stand it. How many times can you clean a house? I don't want to end up like Doreen Whitaker." She rolls her eyes.

"What's the matter with her?"

"Her world ended when her last term as garden club president expired. She's always trying to weasel her way into board meetings so she can feel important. I told her she should get a job, but she'd rather pester the new officers to death."

I pull out my chair and sit down. "So what job are you interviewing for?"

"Office manager."

"Which school?"

She smiles a secret smile. "Not a school. It's a big architectural firm in Santa Monica, very busy, gorgeous offices. There's a lot going on."

"How do you know?"

"I went on a little reconnaissance mission yesterday. They've got a lot of pretty young girls floating around, arranging their hair and inspecting their nails while the phones ring off the hook and people stand around waiting for things. They need someone to take charge."

I take a bite of the perfectly cooked omelet. "They'll never know what hit 'em."

Thirty minutes later, she's out the door looking like organization personified. Why can't I see life the way she does—or the way I think she does—as a challenging puzzle that requires only logic and hard work to be put in order.

I spend the morning wandering aimlessly through the house, sitting down to thumb through the book on divorce she brought home from the library, getting up to wander again. I don't know when she found time to bake mint–chocolate chip cookies, but she did, and every time I wander through the kitchen, I stuff one in my mouth. Soon, very soon, I'm going to be fat. I think about going over to the gym to work out, but I'll see lots of women I know and don't want to talk to.

As an antidote to the thought of fat, I tie on my jogging shoes, start for the front door. The phone rings.

"Wyn, hi. It's Lisa."

"Hi, Lisa. I'm sorry I didn't call you about the publicity com—"

"Oh, that's okay. How are you?"

"Fine. I just—"

"How's your mom?"

"Fine."

The silence is about a half second too long. "I thought— I called you last night to see if you guys were coming to dinner Saturday. I mean, since I hadn't heard from you in a couple of weeks. David said your mom was sick and you were staying over there. I hope it's not serious?"

My mind goes into overdrive. "No, she's...doing a lot better, thanks."

"That's good." Another silence. "Wyn, is everything okay?"

Tom Hathaway, Lisa's husband, is one of David's biggest clients, and of all the women I know in this town, she's probably the closest to an actual friend. But I'm not ready to start confiding in her quite yet. "Of course. Why?"

"I don't mean to be nosy, but when I talked to David about Saturday..." Her voice fades. "He said that you didn't want to leave your mom alone."

"Well, I—"

"But he said he'd like to come. And he asked if he could bring someone from the office. Some account manager he wants Tom to meet."

The Grand Canyon opens up in my stomach.

"Wyn?"

"Lisa, can I call you back? My mother's calling me, and I really need to go see what she wants. Why don't we have lunch one day next week?"

"Okay." She's waiting. Fishing for information. Or maybe I'm just paranoid. "Wyn, call me. If you need anything at all. Or if you want to talk."

After she hangs up, I dial David's number.

"Hi," he says. His voice is warm, almost affectionate. "I'm sorry I couldn't talk when you called the other day. I didn't want to discuss things in front of Andrea and everyone."

He seems oblivious to my confusion.

"David, tell me what's going on. Why did you lock me out?"

"Wyn, I can't talk now. I'm at work and—"

"So close your door. I want some answers."

"Look, I . . . care about you. Very much." Meticulous word choice.

"Then let me come home."

Long sigh. "I don't think it's a good idea."

"A good idea? We're talking about our marriage. If you still— If you care about it, about me, we need to talk—"

"Things have to be different for a while." He cuts in smoothly. "Till I get— Till I figure out what I need to do. I can't be living in the same house with you. You wouldn't move, so I had to do something." His tone suggests that locking me out was a perfectly reasonable something to do.

"I just talked to Lisa."

He waits. "And?"

"Who are you taking to their dinner Saturday night?"

"Kelley Hamlin." It almost sounds matter-of-fact.

"So it's official. We're dating now."

"It's not a date. I want to introduce her to Tom—"

"Can't he find his own blonde?"

"Stop it. You're being ridiculous. She's going to be taking over the account. I'm trying to assign some of my own clients to other account managers. So I'll have more time to manage the marketing side." His tone shifts. "I'm trying to slow down a little. Like we talked about. I thought you'd be glad."

"I've talked to a lawyer." Ungrateful shrew that I am.

"Oh, Wyn." Surprised and hurt. "Are you going to divorce me?"

That word hangs in the air. He says it so easily, and I can't. My throat closes up every time I try.

Another dejected sigh. "I know I can't expect you to be patient forever. It's not fair to you. If you feel you need to make a clean break, I understand."

How did this suddenly become something I'm doing to him?

"David, we need to talk. We need to sit down face-to-face and—"

"We could have a drink one night. If you want to."

"What night?"

"I'll have to see how my schedule's shaping up. I'll call you."

"When?"

"Soon. In the next couple of days. I promise. Okay?"

"I don't think—"

"Oops, I've got a call waiting. I'll talk to you soon."

Before my mother says a word, I know that the job is hers. She looks pleased, confident, but not wildly ecstatic. "Ladies don't give it all away in a rush, Wyn. Keep a little mystery about yourself. Play things down"—her favorite admonition when I was busy letting it all hang out.

"I see congratulations are in order. Who's the lucky company?"

"Prentiss Culver Architectural Design. I start next Wednesday." She takes off her jacket and hangs it in the hall closet instead of draping it over a chair, like I would have. She picks up the mail sitting on the hall table, flips through it, sorting it into piles. Catalogs, bills, trash.

"Let's get takee-outee for dinner. To celebrate your job. Maybe you've even got a bottle of champagne lurking in the pantry."

She looks up from the pile of bills, brows knit together. "Oh, honey, I wish I could. I've got the garden club board dinner tonight. I'm sorry, it's too late to change the meeting; otherwise I—"

"No, it's fine. Tomorrow night, then."

She grimaces slightly. "Tomorrow night I have a date."

"A date?"

"Yes." She perks up. "In fact, you should have a drink with us before we go to dinner. I think you'd really like Ed, and I know he'd like you."

"Mother, I could never go on a date with you. That would be too weird."

"Having a drink before dinner doesn't constitute going with me on a date."

"Who's Ed?"

"He's a detective."

"Like a private eye?"

She laughs merrily. "Don't be silly. He's a police detective. With the Encino PD."

"Where on earth did you meet a cop?"

"He helped us set up our Neighborhood Watch program last year. He was so nice and so...thorough." Obviously that was the deciding factor.

My eyes narrow. "Are you sure he's single?"

"Of course. He's a widower."

"Did he show you the corpse?"

She ignores me and opens the Williams-Sonoma catalog.

She comes home from the garden club board dinner with the names of two therapists and one attorney.

"I guess you got tired of discussing perennials, so you just sat around dissecting my life?"

"Of course not. But all of those women have children and most of them have been through this at least once. By the way, Georgia and Tim Graebel are coming to dinner Monday night. Will you be home?"

"I might go to a movie."

"It would do you good to be with friends. The Graebels know what's happened. They don't expect you to be vivacious and entertaining."

"How do the Graebels know what's happened when I'm not even sure myself?"

"I told Georgia, of course."

The phone rings and I grab it.

"Mrs. Franklin, it's Elizabeth Gooden. Sorry to call you so late. I was in court all day. The title to the house on Woodrow is listed in the name of David Franklin only."

"Oh" is all that comes out.

"Have you had a chance to make a list of community property?"

"Um...no. Not yet."

"Then there's really nothing else to be done at this point. I hope you'll consider what we talked about yesterday. I'll wait to hear from you."

I replace the receiver. My mother's looking at me, waiting for me to tell her something, but I head for the stairs. "I'm going to lie down for a while."

I open the window a crack, stretch out on top of the bedcovers. Without thinking, I reach for the remote, turn on the TV. An old black-and-white movie flickers soundlessly. *Love in the Afternoon.* Audrey Hepburn and Gary Cooper cavorting through Paris. I've seen it so many times I know it by heart. I love the ending, where he's going away and she's walking along beside the train, giving him this line of bullshit about all the lovers she's going to have when he's gone. The train picks up speed and she's talking faster, and then she's running alongside until suddenly Coop realizes that he can't live without her and he reaches out and sweeps her off the platform onto the train, beside him. Kiss and fade to black.

Pretty soon she'll be coming home to their gorgeous apartment in New York to find the locks changed and all her clothes in the hall. I hit the remote control and the screen goes blank with an electrical pop.

My mother is playing the piano when Detective Ed Talley comes to pick her up Friday night—a Bach prelude, something she could play in her sleep—and I'm upstairs in the bathroom with the water running full bore in the tub. As soon as I hear the front door shut, I dart across the hall to peer out around the shade of my bedroom window.

He looks like a character in a detective novel, the one they always describe as "beefy." His navy blazer seems stretched tight across his broad shoulders, and even from up here, I can see he doesn't have any neck. His hair is Grecian Formula black, arranged in kind of a whorl around the little pink circle of barren scalp on the top of his head. He takes my mother's arm possessively and opens the door of his gold Camaro for her. He shuts it, then looks directly up at my window. He can't possibly see me, but I have the creepy feeling he knows I'm here. The gaslight glints off his amber-tinted aviator shades.

God, Mother. How could you?

· · ·

At four o'clock Monday morning, I'm lying awake in the dark. I hear every creak of the still house, every sigh of wind, every barking dog. I sat around all weekend pretending to read, trying to watch TV, waiting for David to call. My mother finally talked me into going to the El Torito Grill last night, and I was a wreck all during dinner. When we got home, I went straight to the answering machine. Nothing.

He didn't call. He's not going to call. I know it in my stomach, which has always been the seat of my emotional responses. Not my heart, the way most people feel things. When I'm happy, it's my stomach that feels all fluttery. When I'm nervous... well, that's not something I talk about in polite company. I'm just as likely to throw up as to cry when I'm upset. And when I'm sad, like now, for instance, my whole abdominal cavity seems to be lined with lead.

I burrow under the covers like a mole, trying to shut everything out, then I'm too warm. I push the blanket away, turn on the lamp, hang over the edge of the bed, stretching for the box of books just beyond my reach. My hand settles on a worn paperback: *The Tassajara Bread Book* by Edward Espe Brown. I roll up my pillow under my neck and tilt the lamp shade so the light falls directly on the pages.

A relic. Published in 1970 by Shambhala Publications, its pages are spattered with hard little specks of dried dough, stained with grease and smudged with fingerprints. One corner of the back cover is charred where I set it down too close to a burner on the gas stove in my first apartment. I scan the contents and the first page of each chapter. I like the way the recipes are laid out—there's a basic procedure, actually no more than a set of suggestions, followed by a list of variations. The whole thing is liberally laced with Brown's Zen philosophy of bread making.

"Bread makes itself, by your kindness, with your help, with imagination running through you, with dough under hand, you are breadmaking itself..."

I read bread recipes until the sky turns quicksilver.

At 6:15 A.M. the Ventura Freeway is already jammed. Must be a SigAlert or a CalTrans closure. I should have listened to the radio. I get off and take Sepulveda south to Ventura Boulevard, zigzag over the Santa Monica Mountains on Laurel Canyon. Not any faster, really, but at least it's green and the air is cool and fresh, crisp with eucalyptus. Then east on Santa Monica to Highland and south into Hancock Park. I stop at the curb, half a block from the big white contemporary where I used to live. The gold Lexus sitting in the driveway isn't really a surprise.

At 7:20 the front door opens and Kelley steps out, stunning in a red miniskirted suit, checking her watch. My husband follows, checking his watch. Like they're synchronizing for some planned battle. While I sit there staring, he kisses her—not some impassioned embrace, but sort of a married-people kiss, casually affectionate, which is even worse. His eyes follow her as she walks to her car and that's when he sees my little red Mazda sitting down the street.

I have to hand it to him. He's cool. He smiles, waves at her as she drives away. When she's out of sight he walks in my direction, calmly, purposefully, no longer smiling. I promise myself that the tears pressing from behind my eyes will never see daylight. He steps off the curb, walks around to my side of the car. He's wearing his charcoal Jhane Barnes suit, a gray-and-gold-patterned tie with little random diamonds of emerald green, and a smudge of red lipstick at the corner of his mouth.

I turn my face as he bends down to the window. "Early morning meeting?"

He looks stern. I have a flash of my father preparing to scold me. "Wyn, this kind of behavior doesn't help anyone."

I swear to God, if I hadn't just seen him kissing his girlfriend, I'd burst out laughing. As it is, I feel like if I don't keep a tight rein on things, any expression of emotion could escalate into full-blown hysteria. I fumble in my purse for a tissue and hand it to him.

"Better get rid of the lipstick. It's not a good color for you."

He sighs audibly, wipes his mouth. "It's not what you think."

The scene through the windshield goes suddenly wavy, like an El

Greco canvas—the gentle curve of the street, the overarching pepper trees, the precise lawns, the exuberant flower beds. The snarl of traffic on Highland is muted to a gentle hum. "Wyn," he says, "why don't we have a cup of—"

I miss the end of the sentence as I pull away, narrowly missing his foot.

The drive back to Encino is a bit of a blur. If I make any illegal turns or run any red lights, no one notices. There's a note from my mother that she's gone to run errands and to shop for dinner and that there's coffee made. I pour a cup and sit down at the oak table in the kitchen where I did homework and carved pumpkins and decorated Christmas cookies. My mother's well-thumbed copy of *Mastering the Art of French Cooking* sits open to page 263: *Coq au Vin*.

I stare at the page. It says that in France, this dish is usually accompanied only by parsleyed potatoes, so that's undoubtedly what we'll be having. In my mother's house, Julia's word is law. I drink my coffee and flip the pages backward, letting my eyes skim the recipes for chicken, fish, shellfish, hors d'oeuvres, soufflés, omelets, stocks, sauces, while my brain slips into neutral and memory engages.

I was half-excited, half terrified when the plane landed in Paris. For a kid who'd never been anyplace more exotic than Rosarito Beach, France could just as well have been Mars. I'd had four years of French in high school and two at UCLA, but the instant the Air France jet's wheels met the tarmac at Orly airport, it all vanished from my brain.

At immigration, the guy stared for a long time at my squeaky clean American passport before he stamped it and handed it back. It was 1976. The Vietnam War was relegated to some nightmare past, but Americans still weren't winning any popularity contests in Europe. Since I was obviously a student, the *douane* (customs) agent decided to take everything out of my suitcase to make sure I didn't have a kilo of dope sewn into the lining. I was close to tears by the time he finished.

When I finally wobbled up the ramp into the light of day, the first thing I saw was a girl holding a sign with my name on it. I introduced myself, and she kissed me on both cheeks. She was Sylvie Guillaume, and she'd come to take me back to Toulouse on the train. The Guillaumes were my host family and I would be working for her brother, Jean-Marc. Overwhelming relief blotted out every other emotion.

Sylvie Guillaume was a college student like me, but she didn't look like any of my school friends back in L.A. Small and finely made, with dark eyes and black hair cut in a sleek, head-hugging cap, she projected effortless chic. Yes, she wore jeans and a T-shirt, but she had a long lavender and green scarf around her throat, one end tossed back over her shoulder. Her face just looked French—something about the way they hold their lips when they talk, as if they're perpetually expecting a kiss. She actually wore purple lipstick.

As soon as we were settled in the train compartment, she produced a slim gold cigarette case from her purse. And she puffed with such aplomb that I didn't even mind inhaling her secondhand smoke. She managed to run through her entire supply between Paris and Toulouse, all the while drinking Perrier and telling me about her family and their bakery. I'd already memorized most of the information from reading my info packet at least once a day for the preceding two months. Her English was excellent, charmingly accented but clear. I worried in silence about how the French would enjoy hearing my heavy American voice steamroll over their musical language, flattening the vowels and clipping off the wrong consonants.

Even though it was late afternoon when we arrived in Toulouse, she insisted on going to the bakery—La Boulangerie du Pont—as soon as I was installed in my bedroom on the third floor of their house. *Du pont* means "of the bridge," and even though the bakery wasn't near any bridge, the whole town was built around the Garonne River, so I guess that's where the name came from. I snapped a picture of it from the corner of the Rue Aquitaine, one of the narrow, curving lanes that radiated out from the circular park called Place President Wilson. It looked positively medieval, all the buildings made of stone and the famous pink brick of Toulouse. When I blurted this out to Sylvie, she laughed.

"Toulouse is much older than that," she said. "There has been a set-tlement here since before Christ. It was the capital of the Visigoths."

"Oh, that's right," I muttered. Like it had just slipped my mind. Then I walked over and looked through the front window and fell in love, first with Jean-Marc and then with the *boulangerie*.

Inside was a man several inches shorter than me, built precisely to the specs of a French baker—barrel-chested, muscular. He looked like he might be able to deflect small automobiles if they veered into his path. In the dim light of late afternoon, his face was an artist's melan-choly sketch, with dark hair and eyes only suggested by thick charcoal strokes. He was deep in conversation with a customer, both of them say-ing at least as much with their hands as their mouths. Sylvie showed me around while we waited for her brother to finish.

My fingers brushed the raised design of the old brass cash register, the fine grain of the walnut cabinets, the cool marble countertop. The tiny white hexagonal floor tiles had been worn smooth over the thresh-old by generations of Toulousain feet. The cases were fronted with etched glass; the price cards hand-lettered in spidery script. A huge wrought-iron rack behind the counter displayed the day's remaining loaves like works of art. A mural of rivers and bridges covered the walls.

When the customer finally left, Jean-Marc embraced Sylvie and shook my hand solemnly. His eyes were so dark I couldn't tell pupil from iris. "*Bienvenue à Toulouse, Mademoiselle Morrison.* You are ready to learn much, work hard, *n'est-ce pas?*"

By the time I met Jean-Marc Guillaume, he was in his thirties, and totally obsessed with bread. He'd been through the arduous *Compagnon Boulanger du Devoir*, the traditional apprenticeship program for French bread bakers. Beginning at age fifteen, he'd worked for seven years in different towns and *départements* of France learning to make the differ-ent regional breads in every type of establishment, from a tiny shop in a remote village of the Camargue where a lone baker tended a wood-burning brick oven, to a huge Parisian *boulangerie* with molders and proofing cabinets and stainless steel ovens watched over by numerous apprentices and *maîtres*. While doing this, he was also required to attend regular school classes one week a month. Sylvie bragged that only a small percentage of those who began the program ever finished. Apparently, to his mother's consternation, he had yet to show any inclination to marry; his only outside interest seemed to be the Toulouse rugby team, the Stade.

When I finally laid my head on my soft, square pillow that first night, my dreams were full of a French film CM and I saw once, called *La Femme du Boulanger—The Baker's Wife*.

My mother staggers in, loaded down with grocery bags, just as I'm dumping bread dough out of the KitchenAid onto the counter, sending up a little cloud of flour. "What on earth are you doing?"

"I thought you might like to have a little *pain ordinaire* for dinner."

"That would be lovely." She beams at me. "Does that mean you'll be here?"

"Yes, I'll be here."

"Where did you go this morning? To work out?"

I sigh. "Actually, I went over to talk to David. Since he hadn't called."

A slight frown drives her perfectly shaped eyebrows together. "And?"

I don't look at her. "He wasn't there. Already left for work, I guess."

I'm making a half-hearted attempt at presentability when the doorbell rings at seven o'clock.

I finish smoothing foundation over my nose, pick up the tube of concealer and start to dab it under my eyes. Ridiculous. What difference does it make whether I look polished and pulled together, or like the business end of a wet mop? I dust on some finishing powder, a bit of blush. I dip the end of my little finger into the pot of clear lip gloss and give my mouth a quick pass. Then I scoop all the bottles and tubes and brushes and boxes into the top drawer and shove it closed.

I step into black rayon slacks and pull on a red knit shirt. The red makes my skin look pale, or maybe it's the bathroom light. David liked me in tailored clothes. Clean lines. Ralph Lauren for casual, Anne Klein for daytime business, Armani for evening. I don't remember what I liked me in.

My mother and the Graebels are sitting in the den and I know they're talking about me because conversation dies when I come bounding in. Georgia gets up to kiss me and Tim hands me a glass of red wine.

"Wyn, the house smells divine," Georgia says. She's about the closest thing my mother has to a hippie-chick friend. She's skinny and still wears her long hair in a braid hanging down her back, even though it's liberally laced with gray. She's never discovered makeup, except for pink lipstick, and she wears full skirts that hit her about the ankles. She's always seemed kind of cheerfully out of it, as if she were perpetually stoned. "Your mom told us you made bread this afternoon. I'm so excited. I love French bread."

Tim says, "You get prettier every time I see you." He was a corporate attorney at Andersen Development where my father was finance VP, and I grew up with his and Georgia's two kids. I remember him as being kind of nerdy, the type who probably carried a briefcase in high school. But then he started dabbling in commercial real estate, retired at forty five, and took up competitive sailing. Now he's silver-haired, tan year-round, and suddenly women seem to find him very attractive. I'd feel sorry for Georgia, but I don't think she's ever noticed. To her, he's probably still the sweet, geeky guy she fell in love with.

"It's great to see both of you."

When my mother goes to check on the *coq au vin*, Georgia turns to me. "We're so sorry to hear about you and David."

I have to remind myself to breathe. "Thanks. I was kind of sorry to hear about it myself."

"I hope he's being reasonable," Tim says.

Georgia frowns at him. "Tim, for heaven's sake . . ." She pushes some magazines aside, sets her wineglass on the coffee table.

"I just mean, if you need an attorney or any financial advice, I know a lot of good people."

"I think I'm set, thanks."

"Do you have any plans?" Georgia asks.

"Nothing concrete." It gets really quiet. I can hear the two cocker spaniels next door going nuts over some imaginary intruder.

"If there's anything we can do . . ." she says.

"I appreciate it. I guess it's just one of those things you have to wade through." Finally, my mother calls us to the dining room.

My mother tells the Graebels all about her new job. Georgia talks about her work at Project Literacy. Tim regales us with stories of breaking in his new crew in time for the Trans Pac Race. I nod and smile a lot. We eat *coq au vin* with parsleyed new potatoes, followed by salad and cheese.

"Jo, I always forget how French you like to do everything," Georgia says with a giggle. "I was thinking you forgot the salad, but we're doing it the continental way." I can hardly look up from my plate, but my mother laughs without a trace of embarrassment.

Back to the den with the rest of the wine. I take charge of the music while they reminisce about old times and gossip about people they know. Inevitably, Tim and Georgia start waxing nostalgic and talking about my father.

"Do you think he would've stayed with Andersen?" Georgia asks my mother.

She smiles wistfully. "I don't know. Probably not."

"I think he would've gone on his own, don't you, Wynter?" Tim looks directly into my eyes, and it's disconcerting.

I shrug and look away. "It's hard to know what someone would do. People change, I guess."

"Glenn couldn't have changed that much. He was a risk taker at heart. He used to say that the most dangerous thing in the world was too much safety." He leans back in the leather chair that was my father's favorite, clasps his hands behind his silvery head. "One thing's for sure, he'd be very proud of you, Wyn."

That's when I go out to the kitchen to take care of dessert and coffee.

I'm standing there watching the coffee drip into the pot when Tim announces cheerfully that he's come to be my assistant. He pushes up the sleeves of his yellow cotton sweater.

While I pour half-and-half in the pitcher, he gets the cups and saucers down from the cupboard. He puts it all on a tray, carries it into the dining room. I cut the *tarte tatin* that my mother labored over and dollop *crème fraîche* on each piece.

"I've always been pretty handy in the kitchen," he says, reappearing. "Do you remember?"

"I remember you as the charcoal king," I tell him.

He laughs with exaggerated heartiness and then he says, "Wynter, I can't believe you're all grown up. I still think of you running around our yard with Jim and Terry like a bunch of little Indians."

"Well, that's what happens when you're not looking. Little Indians grow up."

"But they don't all grow up as lovely as you."

"Thanks." I take a step toward the dining room.

"Wynter." I look at him. "I know this is a difficult time for you. I'm sure you're lonely. I just want you to know that if you ever need anything. A friend. Or advice, or anything at all, I hope you won't hesitate to call me." Not *us*. *Me*. He holds out his card. "I have a little office at Marina del Rey. You can usually reach me there."

I want to tear it into shreds and stuff it down his throat. "Thanks, Tim. But I'm sure my mom has your home phone."

Tuesday morning, my mother's upset because I eat only one piece of French toast. We're sitting in the kitchen with sun streaming in through the double windows over the sink. A chorus of lawn mowers and leaf blowers is getting started outside. There's a dusting of gold pollen on the table from the pink and yellow zinnias in the white porcelain vase.

"You're not going to catch one of those eating disorders, are you?"

"Mother, you don't catch an eating disorder."

"I know, but I mean, it's a psychological thing from being upset. It's a control issue, and I know you must be feeling very out of control right now."

"I'm not feeling out of control, I'm feeling fat. I've got a long way to go before anorexia sets in."

She reaches over to push some hair off my face. "Don't frown, Wynter. It wrinkles your forehead. You're certainly not fat. You look wonderful. Tim was mentioning last night how pretty you are."

I set down my fork. "Tim Graebel is a son of a bitch."

"Wynter, what is the matter with you?"

"He was hitting on me out in the kitchen while his sweet little wife was sitting in there drinking coffee, totally unsuspecting."

My mother laughs.

"He was," I insist. "You should have heard him, telling me he knew how lonely I must be. What a *difficult* time this was for me. How I should call him if I needed a friend."

She laughs again. "Ah, yes. The old I'll-help-you-in-the-kitchen routine. What's so funny is that they all think they've invented it."

I stare at her. "You mean you know? You knew?"

"Wyn, I've been single for fifteen years. Quite an amazing number of friends' husbands have tried that one on me. Including Tim. Make no mistake, Georgia's not so unsuspecting."

"What did you do?"

"I laughed at him. I laugh at all of them."

"What does she do?"

"She ignores it, of course."

I shake my head. "Why do women put up with that bullshit?"

"You know, your language has gotten quite vulgar."

"I can't believe this. You're more upset about me using a four-letter word than you are about your friend's husband making a pass at me. And you." I wad up my napkin, toss it on the table.

She takes a sip of her coffee and sets the cup back in the saucer with a delicate clink. "Men can't help themselves, dear. It's up to women to maintain the standards."

"Standards aren't gender specific."

She picks up my napkin, smoothes out the wrinkles, folds it into a neat triangle. "Wyn, I agree completely. But men really are the weaker sex; they need guidance. And women have either forgotten their moral authority or they've become afraid to use it."

"Mother, please."

"All right, I won't bore you with facts. Your mind is obviously closed."

I get up and carry my plate to the sink, rinse it, and load it into the dishwasher while my mother sips her coffee and smiles into the sunlight.

After my mother has gone off to snatch order from the jaws of chaos at Prentiss Culver Wednesday morning, I call Elizabeth Gooden's office and leave a message with her answering service. Then I sit down at the kitchen table with a cup of coffee, a cream-cheese-smeared bagel, a notebook, and a pen.

Now I begin to grasp the full scope of my ignorance. For starters, I have no idea what David's compensation agreement with JMP is. Hey, I just spend it. I know last year he made over $400,000, but I don't know whether that includes his bonus, stock options, the Mercedes lease, the club membership, or if all that's on top of the $400,000.

I don't know what kind of IRA or pension plan he has, although I'm sure there's something. I know our joint bank account number and how much we usually have in it at any given time. And there's my bank account for household stuff and walking-around money. But for all I know, he could have other accounts. I don't know diddly about investments, although I do know our broker. We have a ski condo in Aspen, but that makes me wonder if he's ever bought other property without my knowledge. I know he has insurance, but I can't remember who wrote the policy.

Elizabeth's office is in a small, Spanish-style building on Ventura Boulevard, in Studio City. The sign on the door says "Gooden, Hedwick, Attorneys-at-Law," and the office behind it is comfortable, not overly luxe. The Shaker-style couch and chairs are upholstered in blue and white, mid-price reproduction, probably Ethan Allen or something. No endangered mahogany, no glass and chrome.

The only other client in the office is a very pretty, very young Asian woman with red, swollen eyes who sits clutching a handkerchief and staring at the closed door across from her chair. I've barely touched down on the couch and opened a magazine when the receptionist calls my name and motions for me to follow her down the hall.

Elizabeth is shorter than I am, but then, most women are. Old-fashioned combs hold the dark hair back, away from clear, gray eyes that telegraph detached friendliness. She wears a navy blue suit with Joan Crawford shoulder pads, and her scarf could pass for a man's tie, navy blue with flecks of red. I amuse myself by imagining it's the spattered blood of an adversary. She shakes my hand firmly, shows me a chair, and sits down at her desk, where a file folder with my name already on it sits on top of a stack.

"So you've been married to David Franklin for seven years." She opens the folder, pulls out a sheet of paper, takes the cap off a Mont Blanc pen. "How would you characterize the marriage?"

The question takes me by surprise. It sounds more like a shrink's question than a divorce lawyer's. "I'm not sure I understand what you're asking."

"Would you say that it's been a happy marriage or an unhappy one, overall?"

"Happy," I blurt out. "I guess. Well, at least until the last year or so. I mean, unless he was unhappy before that and I didn't know it. Which is possible..."

Give it a rest, Wyn.

"Okay." She rubs the tip of her nose with the pen. "Suppose you tell me about it, starting from where you first realized all was not well."

This is worse than making the list of assets. I try to condense everything, to leave in the important facts and leave out the extraneous details. The problem is, I'm no longer certain which are which.

When I get to the lock-out scene, she interrupts me. "Some of the questions I'm going to ask you may seem more personal than professional, Wynter, but these things are relevant to how we want to proceed with the case. This friend you were visiting in Seattle, is it a female friend?"

"Of course."

"And she is simply a close friend. There's no other kind of relationship between you."

"Absolutely not."

"I don't mean to offend you. But you said your husband tried to imply that you had left him. He and his attorney could be planning to say that you left him for this friend—male or female. As your attorney, I can't overemphasize the importance of being completely candid with me."

"CM's been my best friend since the third grade. That's all we've ever been."

She scribbles on the piece of paper. "How would you describe relations between yourself and your estranged husband since the day he changed the locks?"

"Practically nonexistent. I've only talked to him once or twice. Once I went over to the house and that's when I saw him with Kelley. His girlfriend."

She purses her mouth. "So you haven't had sexual relations with him since he locked you out?"

I can't help laughing. "It's been a bit longer than that."

"How long?"

"God, I don't know. Months."

"Do you have any idea how long he's been seeing this woman?"

My stomach knots. "No. But I have a feeling it's been a while."

She cocks her head to one side like a curious little bird. "Why is that?"

"It sounds silly, I guess, but it was the way he kissed her. Kind of casually. Not the way you kiss someone when things are brand new."

"Good observation." She nods. "Do you have any financial records in your possession?"

I look out the window at the parking lot full of Mercedes and Jaguars and BMWs. Several lines are ringing out in the reception area.

"No. I . . . all that was at the house." I pull my skimpy list out of my purse and hand it across the desk. She looks at it silently. Her face doesn't give away anything. "I know it's not very complete." I shrug, helpless. "I guess I haven't been very smart."

"Don't beat yourself up over it. It's a lot more common than you probably think. It makes things a bit more difficult, but certainly not impossible. We would simply have to rely on discovery to ferret out any concealed assets. If he's uncooperative, it might entail using an information specialist and a forensic accountant." At the look on my face, she volunteers, "Yes, it does mean more money up front. But you stand to gain substantially. Do you want to go ahead and prepare to file?"

"Not yet." It's out before I can think. My face burns. She must think I'm either an idiot or a masochist. "How long do I have?"

Elizabeth leans back in her chair, matching the fingertips of one hand to those of the other. "As long as he doesn't file, you aren't required to do anything. If he serves us with papers, we have thirty days to respond. My suggestion would be that we file first, put him on the—"

Tears pool in my eyes. "I'm not ready."

She smiles. "Then my next suggestion would be that we file for some separate maintenance for you. And we get an investigator to start nosing around. Just in case. Generally speaking, if you turn over enough dirt, you're bound to dig up a worm."

I write her a check for twelve hundred dollars, which pretty much cleans out my personal account. I should feel relieved, but I don't. What I feel like is the time CM and I went to New Orleans for Mardi Gras and got caught in the mob watching the Rex Parade. At one point we lost sight of each other and I was trying to cross a side street to a door-way where I thought I'd seen her. But everyone else on the sidewalk was going the other way and I suddenly found I was going with them; my feet weren't even touching the ground. All I could do was keep my elbows up and let myself be carried along.

Six

ornings are the worst. You have to drag yourself out of the comfortable black hole of sleep and face it all over again. Yes, it's true. He's with someone else. Probably at this very moment. Doing all those warm, sweet morning things.

The only remedy is to eliminate morning. So I sleep all day. My mother says it's a symptom of clinical depression. She comes home after work, pulls me out of bed, shoves food at me. I sit at the table in my old pink chenille bathrobe, glassy-eyed, while she tells me about her job, where she goes to lunch, which coworkers she likes, the ones she loathes. Nothing registers. I belong over in Riverside at the Cryogenics Institute—frozen in liquid nitrogen till a cure can be discovered for divorce.

She hammers relentlessly at me about seeing a shrink, says I can get an antidepressant. I promise to think about it, and I do. I turn it over and over in my mind like a grooved stone. At night it sounds like a good idea, but in the morning, taking action seems overwhelming. The one thing I do with a certain amount of energy every day is strip the bed and wash the sheets. I've taken to sleeping in the nude, and I'm addicted to the smell of fresh sheets, their icy smoothness against my skin.

My mother says it's pathological.

Maybe clean sheets are important to me because I'm awake all night, reading until my eyes ache, till they're dry and scratchy when I blink. I have to keep feeding my brain with words, keep it chewing and digesting. The danger comes when I stop. When I close my eyes, the words are replaced by images of David. The way he smiles. How he looks reading in his leather chair, fair hair spilling onto his forehead. The way he chews his food, thoughtfully, as if considering every fine shading of taste. His effortless, almost professional tennis serve. The comical way he lifts his eyebrows in time to music. His elbow resting on the open car window when he drives. The sound of his voice. The scent of his Polo cologne.

So I plow methodically through the two cartons of books that I brought from the house. I don't read them from beginning to end, I skim a few chapters of one, then pick up another. It's an odd assortment, as if he went through the bookshelves and threw in every third book. *The Mosquito Coast* and *The Great Gatsby* and the *Lord of the Rings* boxed set and *The Female Eunuch, Atlas Shrugged, Anna Karenina,* and the complete set of Sherlock Holmes. The copy of *Night Flight* that was my father's. The Tassajara book and *James Beard on Bread,* Julia Child volume two, Carol Field's *Italian Baker.*

And the first edition of Elizabeth David's *English Bread and Yeast Cookery* that CM gave me when I went to France. Talk about asking someone what time it is and they tell you how to make a clock. This book is 250 pages of the history of grains and mills and yeast and bread back to Mesopotamia, plus about 350 pages of recipes. At the back there's a chapter of suggestions for further reading—as if there could be anything further.

One night, my hand brushes something rough textured, large and flat, wedged in the bottom of the second box. I pull out a three-ring binder covered in denim, corners frayed and bent. It's the notebook I started the year before I went to France, a bread journal full of recipes and notes in blue ink, sources for ingredients and equipment in green, quotes on bread, both philosophical and practical, in black. The sections are separated by tab dividers. My God, how anal. I'm my mother's daughter after all.

I close the binder and lay it on my night table, pick up the Elizabeth David book and plunge into the chapter called "Our Bread Grain: Wheat, Rye, Barley, Oats and Pease." This should cure my insomnia.

Two hours later I'm still reading, seduced by the elegant prose, bound by tendrils of wit and romance. This isn't just the history of bread, it's the story of the world, how the growing and milling of grain and the making of bread shaped all of civilization. By the time I've worked my way through thirty centuries of the wheat grain's progress from Kurdistan through Egypt and up into Europe, I'm exhausted. And we haven't even gotten around to milling the stuff yet.

I turn the book upside down on the quilt, reach for my eyedrops. Artificial tears, the doctor called them. Ironic, since I've been able to produce plenty of the real McCoy lately. I recoil at the sting, blink rapidly, then close my eyes for just a second, to let the fake tears lube my lids and fill the gullies in my eyeballs. The next thing I know, my mother's standing there in her teal silk dress and white jacket. Sunlight's flooding the room, and I seem to be waking out of a coma. I feel like Scrooge asking "Boy, what day is this?"

My mother frowns and tells me it's October twentieth. And Elizabeth Gooden's on the phone. Is it possible that the information specialist has unearthed something already? I picture some Danny DeVito–looking guy in a shiny blue suit and fedora sneaking around after David with a miniature camera. It makes me laugh out loud for the first time in weeks. One small corner turned, if you believe in such crystallizing moments.

I step into my flip-flops, pull on a T-shirt, pick up the phone.

"Good morning, Wynter. I hope I didn't wake you." She's probably been up since five, run three miles, and had breakfast with a judge.

"No," I lie, "I was just in the shower."

"You'll be getting the paperwork in a day or two, but I wanted to let you know that your husband's been ordered to pay temporary support of $3,000 a month. He'll be making the first deposit in your account on the thirty-first. Are you going to be okay in the—"

"*Three* . . . ? Three thousand dollars?"

"I asked for five, but Hochnauer convinced the judge that you had deserted the marriage—"

"Who?" My toes are gripping the edges of the flip-flops.

"Ivan Hochnauer, your husband's attorney, a.k.a. Ivan the Terrible," she adds cheerfully.

"Oh. Is there any good news?"

"Yes. We'll go back and get an increase, but I need some time to prepare, and I wanted you to have some money in the meantime."

"Well…" Strange how quickly you forget what confidence feels like.

"Wynter, are you doing anything? I mean, getting out, seeing friends, going to movies, exercising?"

"Well…"

"That's what I thought. You need to be in motion. Even if you don't feel like it, you'll be better off over the long haul if you stay active."

"I will. I'm just—"

"But no dating, okay? And don't get a job. At least not a serious one. If you start making any money, it may be harder to get an increase in your maintenance."

"I don't think there's much danger of that."

"Good. Now remember what I said: Stay active. I'll be in touch."

After my mother disappears in a cloud of Guerlain, I get dressed and drive to the health food store, returning with several different kinds of organic flour, seeds, honey, raisins, and yeast. I flip through my battered notebook to a recipe for basic whole wheat bread.

3 cups lukewarm water
1 tablespoon yeast
¼ cup honey or molasses
1 cup dry milk
6 to 7 cups whole wheat flour
1 tablespoon salt
¼ cup oil or butter
1 to 2 cups flour for kneading

I open the new jar of yeast, stir it around with my little finger. It feels gritty as sand, but nearly weightless. I know that yeast is an organism, a single-celled plant. I know it reproduces by budding, producing a whole new generation about every five hours. I understand the chemistry, how it feeds on sugar and starch, breaking them down into alcohol and carbon dioxide.

Even given what's known, and the fact that you can walk into any grocery store and buy it off the shelf, it's still impossible to dismiss the magic of the process. In the merrye olde England of Geoffrey Chaucer, one of the names for yeast was "goddisgoode," because it was considered a gift from heaven. But until I went to France, I always thought of yeast as something manufactured, something you got in a jar or an envelope at the grocery store.

My very first morning at the *boulangerie*, Sylvie volunteered to walk with me, even though I had to be there at 5 A.M. The river breeze was cool and fresh, and shadows were long in the early light. We turned into the narrow alley behind the bakery. Jean-Marc stood just outside the rear door, leaning against the ancient brick wall, one foot up like a stork, drinking espresso from a tiny white cup and smoking the first Gauloise of the day.

When he saw us, he threw down his cigarette and ground it out under one heavy brown boot. The aroma of baking bread curled out the door like an invitation.

"Vous êtes en retard." He frowned. "The day is nearly finished." I started to apologize, but Sylvie laughed and I noticed the slight twitching of the corners of his mouth, which was the most obvious and sometimes the only sign that he was making a joke. *"Venez,* I show you the *fournil*—the baking room." We stepped through the door and the heat became a tangible presence. "It takes one hour for the oven to be hot."

We passed a small storage area filled with huge sacks of flour, and entered a long, narrow room with a very high ceiling. At the back was the oven—stainless steel, six feet tall, five decks. The cooling racks lining the side walls were already full of crackling-hot, hissing loaves in different shapes and sizes and I thought I would faint with pleasure at their smell. Two men in front of the oven were using a long rack with a canvas stretcher on rollers to load dozens of baguettes into the oven. They worked stripped to the waist, sweating from the fiery blast of air. Within minutes, I had beads of perspiration on my forehead and Sylvie was dabbing her face delicately with a handkerchief.

"You see the high ceiling," she said, pointing up. "Jean-Marc made this." There was a barely discernible line about eight feet up the wall where the bricks changed slightly.

"Some of the *boulangeries* where I work at school, the top is very low." He held his hand just over his head. "Especially in Paris. All the *fournils* are in the basements. It is very hot to work there. This is much better." He looked around the room with a self-satisfied air.

Jean-Marc led us across a narrow hall into a room filled with refrigerators and proofing cabinets and kneading machines with blades the size of airplane propellers, and a huge wooden worktable. One of the men we'd seen loading baguettes into the oven was pushing a wheeled rack full of bread up to the front of the shop. As he passed by the door, Jean-Marc stopped him, took a small, warm, crusty loaf off the rack, handed it to me.

"Pain au levain," he said. "You want to taste it." It was a command, not an invitation. I ripped off a chunk

"Pain de campagne?" I said.

Jean-Marc shook his head. *"Pain au levain.* It is different from *pain de campagne.* Taste it."

The crust was thick and golden brown, the crumb pale gray with an irregular texture. I took a bite. Sweet but with a slightly sour aftertaste. The interior was dense, moist, chewy; the crust crisp and nutty.

I stopped eating it long enough to say, "This is wonderful. What is it? How do you make it?"

His little half smile did something funny to my stomach that had nothing to do with bread. *"Levain* is like your sourdough, the *levure sauvage.* The wild yeast, *oui?* We put the whole-grain flour with the white. To make it more strong. *Plus fort, vous comprenez?* The *levain* that is firm, it make the bread less sour. The *levain* that is . . ." He rubbed his fingertips together, searching for the right word.

"Wet?" I suggested.

"*Oui, bien sûr,* the wet *levain* make a more sour bread. Like your San Francisco bread."

That loaf of *pain au levain* was the best bread I ever tasted.

Bearing in mind the gospel according to Jean-Marc, I cut the yeast in half, eliminate the powdered milk and oil, reduce the honey to an eighth of a cup, and throw in some toasted walnuts.

I mix the ingredients together in the KitchenAid. Any urgency I feel is about getting it out on the counter and into my hands. Kneading is what you miss with a bread machine—the feel of bread. You forget what it is to get lost in the rhythmic fusion, the way you can tell by touch the exact moment when the dough comes alive, when it's ready to rise up and grow. This is what it means, the part about "You are breadmaking itself."

I leave the dough to proof in the cool air of the laundry room and go upstairs to strip the bed.

The loaves have perfumed the whole house by the time they emerge from the oven. I set them on cooling racks, feeling like a sculptor with a new work on display. Awash in goodwill, I can't wait till my mother gets home. I want to tell her the worst is over. That I know I've been a pain in the ass, but I'm going to make it. It will take time, of course, but the healing has begun. I'll thank her for her patience and support, tell her I realize it's time for me to be getting my own place, looking for a job, making a life for myself.

The phone interrupts my enraptured gushing. My stomach balls up. *Wyn, it's me.* He sounds sad, lonely. *Look, I know I've been acting weird.* Try pond scum, David. He sighs. *It's true. I've been acting like pond scum. But I've been thinking about you so much. I can't stand this. I must've been crazy to—Wyn, I love you. Do you think you could—*

"Wyn? Hi, honey." It's my mother. "How are you feeling?"

"Fine. I'm . . . better. I've been up and I—"

"Oh, I'm so glad. Listen, honey, I'm going to go have a drink with some people from the office, and if we get hungry, we might go out to dinner, so don't wait for me, okay? There's some of that lasagne left in the fridge for you and there's salad in the bin."

"Okay."

"What did you do today? Besides wash the sheets." Her voice is bright. She's trying to be funny, to cheer me up. I want to scream at her.

"Nothing exciting. I made some bread."

"Oh, did you? I'll have to try some when I get home."

"You don't *have* to. It's always optional." I hate myself.

She sighs. "Okay, Wynter. I'll see you later."

I hang up the phone, try to ignore the mass of tears that's pushing on my sinuses, inciting a major headache. It wasn't David; it's never going to be David. Get used to it. My mother has a life. She's going out with friends. I should be happy she's not here trying to force-feed me and happy that she's enjoying herself. If I weren't up to my neck in shit, I'd be ecstatic.

I pour a glass of milk and rip a corner off one of the still warm loaves. I stand at the kitchen sink, dunking the bread in the milk and eating it and crying noisily. When the streetlights start to glow, I go upstairs, remake the bed, take all my clothes off, and crawl between the sheets with Holmes and Dr. Watson.

I'm asleep when my mother comes home and she doesn't wake me up when she leaves in the morning. I can't really blame her. I wouldn't want to have much to do with me either. I get up and take the sheets off the bed, throw them in the washer. I pour a cup of coffee out of the thermal carafe she's left for me and take it back upstairs.

When I go into the hall bathroom to get clean sheets from the linen closet, I catch a full-frontal look at myself in the mirror and it's not a pretty sight. In fact, it's so shocking that I stand and stare at my reflection for several minutes. My hair is wild—owing, no doubt, to the fact that it hasn't been combed since Monday. My skin is pasty. Except for the bruised-looking hollows under my eyes. My face looks pinched, the way I look when I have the flu.

I take a sip of coffee and my eyes travel down my body, as if they're following the coffee on its journey. My collarbone protrudes sharply from the neck of my shirt and my jeans are suddenly gapping at the waist. In earlier times, that would have pleased me immensely, but I've learned the hard way that the Twiggy look doesn't flatter a frame like mine. Instead of looking chic, I look like a Dorothea Lange photograph.

This time when the phone rings, I give myself a little shake. It's not David, so don't hold your breath. If it's my mother, she's probably pissed off at me. The most likely scenario is that someone wants to sell us a new roof or some aluminum siding.

CM's familiar voice says, "Hi, Baby. Are you all right?" I want to weep with relief.

"I'm surviving."

"Have you talked to Asshole?"

"Not really. I saw him, though." I sing her my sad song of David and Kelley's early morning meeting, Elizabeth Gooden's cheery philosophy of divorce, my mother's sudden renaissance, Tim Graebel's casual betrayal of his wife of thirty years.

"Your biggest problem right now is that you've got too much time on your hands," she says. "You need to get your own place and get a job. What are you using for money, anyway?"

"I have an allowance. David has to deposit three grand a month in my account or they come and put him in the stocks and let little kids throw rotten eggs at him."

She sighs. "God, sometimes I have trouble working up sympathy for you. Does David have any single friends who'd like to marry me and then dump me so I can have an allowance?"

"I'm not going to dignify that with a reply."

"Well, you still need to get a job. When you have things you have to do, you won't have time to brood."

I kick off my sandals and lie down on the bed. "Maybe you're right. If I don't get something else to think about pretty soon, I'll go nuts."

"In fact, I think you should come up here."

"I can't go anywhere right now."

"Why not? You can stay here. We're starting our master class series a week from Monday, and I'll be gone for three weeks. You'll have the whole place to yourself and you can use my car—"

"I can't, CM. Not till something gets resolved."

She switches to her drill-sergeant voice. "Well, then, what are you doing to resolve it?" My silence tells the story. "You know, I'm really sorry I'm not there to kick your butt," she snaps. "I know you're laying around down there, wallowing in self-pity—"

"*Lying.*"

"Whatever." Her voice changes again. She would have made a great radio actress. "I was at the bakery yesterday. Ellen asked about you. She told me they're still looking for a bread baker."

"I can't leave right now. Period."

"Okay, but the invitation stands, if you should suddenly come to your senses."

I'm curled up on the couch reading *Middlemarch* when my mother walks in with soup and salad from Gelson's. She studies me intently, apparently deciding it would be best not to say what she wants to say. She hangs her coat in the hall closet.

"Why don't you put some of your bread in the oven and we can have it with dinner?"

While we eat, she chats, keeping her tone carefully neutral and upbeat. "This bread is wonderful. I sneaked some when I came in last night."

"I'm glad you like it." I take a big gulp of wine and poke at my salad.

She sets down her fork and looks at me. Here it comes. "Wyn, you can't go on like this. Have you taken a good look at yourself lately?"

"Um, actually, yes. Just this afternoon. Although I'm not sure I'd call it a *good* look."

"Can you stop being a smart-mouth for five minutes? I'm concerned about you."

"I'm sort of concerned about me, too." I try to smile. "I was having a good day yesterday. When I made the bread. I was feeling somewhat functional."

She frowns. "So what happened?"

"You called. I mean, when you called to tell me you weren't coming home for dinner, I just felt . . . I don't know. Deflated. I wanted to show you my bread." I can't believe the way my voice is cracking. "Like a little kid, you know. It's . . . really stupid. And"—I inhale deeply—"and, when the phone rang, I thought it might be—"

"David," she finishes. "I know. I used to think that about your dad. After he died, I would sometimes imagine that I'd pick up the phone and he'd say, 'Hey, Jo. Put that roast back in the freezer. Let's go out for dinner tonight.'"

Now we're both sitting there crying in our salads.

"But he was dead," I blurt out. "He didn't dump you for some fucking bimbo." Suddenly I realize I've just said the F word to my mother. I start to laugh. Then she laughs.

"Oh, Wyn." She gets up and pulls two tissues out of the box on the counter. "I want you to do me a favor."

I dab at my eyes. "What?"

She sits down in her chair. "Come to dinner with Ed and me tomorrow night. Please," she adds, before I can get out my automatic no. "We're going to a new place in Beverly Hills. Le Jardin. It's supposed to be wonderful. Please come."

"I can't."

"What you mean is, you won't. Look, Ed's a really nice, interesting man and I don't think I'll be seeing him much longer."

"Why not?"

"He's getting too serious, and I just don't feel that way about him. I enjoy his company. He tells great stories. But he thinks he's in love with me, and I can't let it go on. In fact, if you'd go with us, he wouldn't be able to get all maudlin and romantic and it would be fun. Please? Come on, say you'll go."

At seven-fifteen Thursday evening, I'm squished into the backseat of Ed's gold Camaro. My mother offered to let me sit up front, but Ed looked so crushed that I couldn't bring myself to do it. The rear speakers are blasting out Van Halen, and he's thwacking his ring on the steering wheel in time with the bass.

So they're up front yakking away and I can't hear a word of it. I just sit with my knees up under my chin and stare at the back of his head. The super-short cop coiffure stands up in stiff little spikes above his collar, like my father's old boar-bristle brush, and there's a tiny bit of shaving cream stuck to the back of his earlobe. Just then he catches my eye in the rearview mirror and I realize he's said something to which he's expecting a reply.

"Sorry, I can't hear you."

He reaches for the volume knob. "I said, have you heard anything about this place, Le Jardin?" Except he calls it "Lay Jardeen."

"No, I haven't. And it's pronounced 'Luh Zhardanh,' by the way."

My mother doesn't have to turn around; I can see her spine stiffen.

Ed laughs good-naturedly. "That's right. Your mom said you spent some time in France. So it's Le Jardin." This time he hits it pretty close.

"That's good," I tell him.

"Anyway, ol' Ruthie liked it."

"Who?"

"Ruth Reichl. *L.A. Times.*" He looks in the mirror again. "And she's pretty persnickety." Like she's a close personal friend of his. "Took me a couple weeks to get a reservation," he continues. "It's the new happening spot."

He weaves through the traffic on Sunset Boulevard, one hand on the wheel, the other draped casually over the other bucket seat, with the aplomb of a man who spends a lot of time behind the wheel and likes it. Every so often his finger brushes my mother's hair.

I look out the window, eyes half closed so that headlights and tail-lights, traffic signals and neon signs run together in a river of multicolored light. Almost as many colors as Ed's plaid jacket. I saw my mother carefully compose her face when she opened the front door to him earlier. His tie is paisley, in a totally different palette. I wonder absently if he's color-blind. A lot of men are, I guess.

By the time we arrive at Le Jardin, I know I'll never be able to uncoil my body. Ed gives me a hand, yanking me unceremoniously out, like a cork from a bottle, and the valet parking guy gets a nice flash up my skirt. Ed gives his name to the maître d', who tries not to stare at the jacket.

He consults his black book and then looks at us down the full length of his long, pointy nose. "There must be some mistake. I have a reservation for two. Now there are three?"

Ed unbuttons his jacket, hooks his thumbs behind his belt buckle, and smiles. "It's not like we're trying to sneak her into the circus without a ticket, is it? Just drag up another chair. You can tell by looking at her she doesn't eat much."

I have to compress my lips to hold in a very undignified guffaw. Our poor maître d' probably doesn't have much experience with guys like Detective Ed Talley. He weighs the matter for only a few seconds before snapping his fingers at one of the busboys. "Chair," he hisses.

The dining room really is a garden. Palm trees and ferns, climbing vines, boldly colored bromeliads and delicate, pale orchids are cunningly arranged to screen most of the tables from each other. White lights twinkle everywhere, like fireflies reflected in the crystal. A harpist plays in one corner, and it's quiet enough that you can actually hear her.

My mother smiles. "Oh, Ed, this is lovely. It's like fairyland."

Ed beams and orders a bottle of Taittinger Brut Rosé, which he pronounces "Tatenjer." I don't bother to correct him.

The plates I can see on other tables look more like works of art than food, but that's L.A. for you. Bread appears, rustic and flecked with herbs. I nibble a piece while I read the menu. Warm rabbit ravioli with tarragon butter. Charred rare ahi. Angel-hair pasta with three caviars. Salmon sashimi with cucumber spaghetti. Baby vegetables. Precious little duck taquitos with mango salsa. It's probably all wonderful, but not what I want right now. Maybe what I want isn't on any menu.

After the waiter brings the wine and announces the specials like they were handed down on stone tablets, Ed holds up his glass and says, "To the two prettiest ladies in the room."

My mother smiles graciously and I take a large gulp of champagne. Then she pushes back her chair and stands up. "Excuse me for just a moment." And disappears in the direction that looks most promising for the ladies' room. I can't believe she's left me alone with him. I drink some more champagne and study the menu and pretend an interest in the few other tables I can see.

"Johanna told me about your husband." This must be his interrogation voice, calm, quiet. In the good cop/bad cop scenario, he'd be the one to lay his hand on the prisoner's shoulder and say, "How 'bout a cup of coffee, son?"

I continue to read the menu, but he won't give up. "I just want to say I'm sorry. I know how hard it is."

I look up sharply. "I thought your wife died."

"My second wife. The first one left me." His expression of neutrality never falters. Jesus Christ, how much did she tell him?

I make my mouth curve up. "I'd really like to talk about something else."

"Sure. I understand." He smears a whole pat of butter on a piece of bread. "It's hard, though, when that's all that's on your mind. So if you want, I'll do the talking. I'm pretty good at it. You can just relax."

"Fine." I lean back in my chair. "Tell me about some of your exciting adventures with the Encino PD."

When he laughs, it sounds like a roar in the jungle. Heads turn. He doesn't notice. "Not too many with the Encino PD. But before that, I was with the Orange County Sheriff's Department. Now there were some interesting times. Like the Sunday morning we got a call to the

Bartholomae place on Balboa. You should've seen this place. Imagine six hundred feet of waterfront property on that peninsula. Moored out front is this ninety-eight-foot ketch called the *Sea Diamond.*" Shake of the head. "What a beauty." In spite of myself, I lean forward.

What happens next is very quick. It's not one big thing, but a series of small actions like a scene in a play. The waiter materializes to take our order. My mother returns from the powder room and Ed stands up to pull out her chair. The maître d' sweeps by with two couples in his wake. One of which is David and Kelley. It's almost comic, the way everybody sees everybody at the same instant and the action stops.

Fortunately, I can't see my own face, but I feel the way I felt one time when I was pitching for a coed softball team and I got hit in the stomach by a line drive. My mother assumes the stance of a momma grizzly whose cub is endangered, glaring at Kelley. The waiter has his bored hauteur look on, probably expecting us to start doing air kisses and chitchat. Kelley's benign smile sharpens into a feral grin. David has the grace to look a teensy bit flustered. Then his glance falls on Ed and the plaid jacket, and he actually looks at me with the suggestion of a smile and raises one eyebrow. It's a look we've shared countless times, laughing at something or someone we considered beyond the pale.

As if on cue, the maître d' turns around to look for his lost ducklings. Their friends look impatient. David and Kelley resume their flight plan. My mother sits down. I start breathing. It took all of ten seconds and no words were exchanged, but everything is suddenly, unmistakably clear.

The waiter says, "Have we made some decisions here?"

Somehow I order. When he's gone, Ed looks at my mother, then at me, and smiles wolfishly. "Should I have his car impounded?"

I excuse myself to the ladies' room, walking as if the floor were carpeted with ball bearings. I lock the door behind me and sink down onto the rose-print slipper chair in one corner. I just sit, as still as you can sit when you're shaking. I pull a tissue out of my purse and blot the sweat off my forehead and upper lip. When I stand up to wash my hands, I feel nauseous, dizzy, so I inhale, exhale, deeply, slowly. I put on lipstick even though I don't need to, and I unlock the door and step out. On my way back to the table, I hand the maître d' a ten-dollar bill and ask him to call me a cab.

It's a very long taxi ride back to Encino. For once, I'm thankful the driver doesn't speak English. I sit wedged into the corner of the seat and think about Kelley. It's funny that David would choose someone who looks the way I always wanted to look—almost as if he'd consulted me on his selection. She's the kind of woman who stops traffic wherever she goes. Tall and lithe, perpetually tan, but not too dark. Just enough to set off her mane of straight, gleaming blonde hair and perfect smile. Kelley Hamlin is what everybody thinks of when you say "California girl." Actually, she's from Wisconsin or Minnesota or one of those other whole-milk states. Watching her blaze through Le Jardin in her body-hugging blue dress and three-inch heels, I could understand how David would be smitten. What man wouldn't be? And I sat there, squirming inside my chalky-white skin, brown hair curling like old Easter basket grass, dark hollows under my eyes. With Ed and his carnival coat, my mother in her Encino-matron silk finery.

Nothing left to do but slink home to my clean sheets and my books. Maybe I'll get wild and crazy and have a glass of wine.

While David and Kelley enjoy a leisurely dinner with friends. Or knowing them, probably clients. And then they go to her house? Our house? How silly of me. I mean, *his* house. Maybe they'll have a fire in the fireplace, a little cognac. Laugh about the clownish trio at the restaurant. While the laughter is winding down, their eyes meet. His hand brushes her bare shoulder. He kisses her neck lightly. He's good at those little teasing moves. I really don't want to think about this, but once I've started imagining . . .

I'm her. Kelley. I feel the tip of his tongue dip into the hollow at my neck and shoulder. He unzips my dress, easing down the top. Am I wearing a bra? Maybe a blue lace demi. It fastens in the front, but he knows all about those. One little click. My breasts tumble out and his mouth chases them, teasing the nipples, making me crazy. We're on the floor now. Well, only if we're at my house. If we're at his house, he won't want to get stuff on the sheepskin rug. My beautiful golden hair billows around my face like backlit clouds in a movie. His hand skates up my thigh to that place he knows will make me scream if he touches it just right and he's so close. Oh god oh god oh god. I bite my lower lip. I lurch forward, banging my shins on the back of the seat.

"Dis de house?" says the driver.

About ten-thirty, my mother comes in and sits on my bed. Wasting no time on pleasantries, she says, "Wynter, don't let that Barbie doll run you off. Fight for what you want."

I drink some water from the glass on my night table. "I don't know what I want anymore."

She takes the glass from my hand and finishes the water. "You're too quick to let go. David's acting like a jerk, but most men do at some point. He's also gorgeous and smart and talented. He's taken good care of you for a long time. I think he'll come around if you don't abandon him."

"Mother, I believe he's made his choice." I pick up my book. She takes it out of my hands and lays it on the bed, just out of my reach.

"I saw him look at you, Wyn."

"Yeah, and don't I look terrific."

"You look wonderful."

"I look like the undertaker's daughter."

"You just look sad. It didn't hurt for him to see that." She sighs, closes her eyes in the expression of frustration I know so well. "I realize you think I don't know anything about anything, but I'm telling you, wait it out. Don't make any sudden moves. The odds are in your favor. And if he persists in being an idiot, you'll still end up a very wealthy young woman."

I put an index finger at each temple and massage in a circle. It's quiet for a minute and then she says, "I told Ed I couldn't see him anymore."

I raise my head and look at her. "I guess it was the humane thing to do. Was he destroyed?"

"Of course not. He took it like a gentleman. Kissed my cheek and wished me well."

"Heartbreaker." I have to smile a little. "Too bad. I was kind of getting to like him. Now I'll never find out what happened at the Bartholomae house in Newport Beach."

"A very rich man got murdered."

"Well, it's something to consider."

She yawns. "And on that note, I'm going to bed." At the door, she turns around. "Think about what I said, Wyn. You've got nothing to lose."

I wake up at ten till seven, and I know from the stillness of the house that my mother's already left for work. I snuggle down, savoring the familiar smells of my room, the dry scent of the wool blanket, the sachet from the linen closet clinging to the sheets, lemon-oil furniture polish, and, still, even after all the years, a trace of Bluegrass cologne. It was my teenage favorite, and the gallons of it that I sprayed into the air, the small explosions of body powder and splattered drops of lotion must have eventually seeped into the walls and rugs and furniture.

Mr. Moon, the night-light my oma gave me when I was five years old and plagued with nightmares about the dark, sits on the dresser, his glow all but invisible in the pale gray light. Next to the dresser is my bulletin board, covered with limp football schedules and brittle newspaper clippings of CM in recitals, photos of us—the best is the one CM's dad took at Burroughs High School graduation. L.A. is in the grip of a killer heat wave. It's 102 degrees at 5 P.M. The senior class is assembled outside the football field, preparing for "Pomp and Circumstance." CM's dad snaps us, gowns flapping open to reveal shorts and halter tops, mortarboards tilted jauntily over huge dark glasses. We're grinning broadly, holding a banner that reads "Too Cool for School."

On top of the bookcase, in a silver frame, is my favorite picture of my father. He's wearing Lacoste tennis whites and holding the new racket I gave him for his birthday. I hated baby-sitting for the brats in the neighborhood, some of whom weren't much younger than I was, but I did it for a whole year at least once a weekend and hoarded my earnings to buy him this new titanium racket that he wanted. I don't even remember what kind it was.

I pull the covers up under my chin and hold them tight. My bed, my desk, my books, my pictures, my room, everything just as it was, and me, safe in the middle. Suspended, like some prehistoric insect in a drop of amber.

Tim, the scumbag, was right about one thing. My father was a risk taker. I wanted to be like him, but I was always torn between wanting to please him and following my own, more cautious instincts.

A summer day at the beach with my parents. I'm seven or eight years old. My father is treading water out beyond the breakers. I want to go out there with him, but I'm afraid of the waves. He calls me, motions me to come, while my mother sits on her towel, pretending to read, chewing her lip. I start wading out.

"Swim!" my father yells. "Dive into the wave!" But I'm too scared and I keep trying to walk through the heaving swells. Suddenly, what appears to be a tower of water looms over me, crashes on me, knocking me off my feet and tumbling me like clothes in a washer. I try to swim, but I'm disoriented and I smack into the sandy bottom. When I scream, brine burns my mouth and nose, up into my sinuses, down into my lungs.

Then I'm in my father's arms, coughing and crying, and I hear his soft chuckle as he carries me up out of the water. My mother runs out to meet us, but she doesn't say anything. They hold me till I stop choking. She's pressing the water out of my hair and he's blotting my face with a towel. He kisses my cheek.

"Now you know how it works, J. W.," he says. "When you're ready to go out to the deep water, you have to dive into the wave. If you wait for it to come to you, it's going to knock you on your keister."

I reach over and pick up the phone. Within an hour, I've talked to Ellen at the Queen Street Bakery, Elizabeth Gooden, CM, Alaska Airlines. Then I lie back in bed and indulge myself in a moment of smugness. I've daringly changed the whole direction of my life before 8:30 A.M. Without even getting out of bed.

There's just one more thing I have to do.

I'm sitting on the porch when David's car pulls into the drive. He digs his briefcase out of the backseat and walks toward the front door. He can't see me because it's dark and he's neglected to leave the porch light on, but I can see him in the yellow glow of the streetlight, and my heart breaks. He walks slowly, for him, head down, shoulders rounded. He looks exhausted.

"David."

At the sound of my voice, his head jerks up. Caught off guard, he can't hide his surprise, and the tiny beginnings of a smile.

"Wyn. What are you doing here?"

"I used to live here," I say softly.

He looks away, fumbles for his key, inserts it into the lock but doesn't open the door.

"Can I come in?"

Reflexively, he looks over his shoulder, like maybe my lawyer put me up to this and it's being captured on film.

"You never called me." I keep my voice low, try not to let it tremble. "We never got to talk."

"I know. I'm sorry. I— This isn't a good time, Wyn. I'm tired—"

"I'm tired, too, and there's never going to be a good time. Is there?"

He turns abruptly, pushes the door open, stands aside while I go in. He flips the switches, flooding the front of the house with light. I look around—the living room, back to the dining room, down the hall toward the kitchen, up the open staircase to the gallery. The rooms seem only vaguely familiar, like a hotel you've seen in a brochure, but never visited before.

I follow him into the living room. Dead ashes from an old fire give off their stale odor.

"Could I have a brandy, please?"

He takes off his coat, folds it carefully, drapes it over the back of the couch. "Of course." His footsteps clack on the slate floor and I hear him rummaging through the liquor cabinet in the kitchen. He's hardly been gone a minute when there's a sharp rap on the door. I can't decide whether he didn't hear it, or he figured he'd never beat me there so he's decided to let the chips fall where they may.

I must be the last person Kelley expected to see here. Certainly the last one she wanted to see.

She recovers quickly. "Hello, Wyn. What a surprise."

"I imagine so." I try to smile, but it's difficult to do when all I can think of is how her skin would feel under my fingernails. I look at my watch. "Nine-forty's a bit late for dropping off files."

"Where's David?" Her voice exudes perfect control. She must be dynamite in those high-stakes, high-stress pitch meetings.

"He's getting me a brandy. We have some things to discuss tonight. Feel free to wait on the porch."

Two spots of color bloom on her smooth, tan face, but before she can say anything, David appears with two crystal snifters of brandy.

"Well..." he says.

The three of us stand looking at each other like an exhibit at Madame Tussaud's until he says stiffly, "Wyn and I have some things we need to talk about, Kelley. I'll see you at the office tomorrow."

She turns without a word and disappears, shutting the door gently behind her. He hands me one of the snifters and we adjourn to the living room.

"Thank you." That's all I trust myself to say until the brandy is burning the back of my throat. I promised myself that I'd be dignified, not lose my cool, and absolutely no tears, but there's a huge knot in my throat that I can't talk around. A few yoga breaths, a few more sips of brandy, and finally it begins to melt away.

"What would you like to talk about?" He sets his drink on the glass-topped table.

What would I like to talk about? I want to scream at him, throw my glass at his perfect face, but I manage not to do either.

"I thought we could talk about us, David." I like the way it comes out. Very low-key.

"Okay." He loosens his tie. The fact that he's wearing one means they must have had a client meeting today. He leans back in the chair, gazing expectantly at me.

"I'm going back to Seattle for a while." Is it my imagination or does he look relieved? "And I was wondering if you've given any more thought to . . . the situation."

Based on what's just happened, that's probably a stupid question, but he shakes his head gravely. "No, I haven't. I've been so busy—"

"If something's important enough, you make time to think about it."

He leans forward, elbows on knees. "Wyn, I'm sorry. I can only do what I can do. Maybe the problem is, you expect too much of me. I'm sorry if you're disappointed."

"Is it expecting too much after everything that's happened, that we might sit down and talk about our marriage? Or do you just not care? Can't you just tell me how you feel?"

He looks straight at me for the first time since he stumbled over me on the porch. His face is drawn and there are dark circles under his eyes. "I can't tell you because I don't know. I don't know how I feel. I don't know what's going to happen. I know you want more than that. You deserve more . . . but I just don't know. Things are crazy at work. We lost Hathaway today and some heads are going to roll. One of them might be mine. I—I'm sorry."

"You lost Hathaway?" It's almost a gasp.

He nods. "They went with Foote Cone."

"But Tom was—"

"It was a business decision, Wyn. Nothing personal." His voice is dull. It's suddenly clear that this was the wrong night to force the issue. I stand up, hugging my jacket to me, and walk over to him.

He looks up at me.

"I love you, David."

He takes my hand and holds it briefly against his cheek, but he doesn't say anything.

"I'm leaving Sunday. If you get a chance before then, call me."

"I will," he says, but we both know better.

"You're doing this because I told you not to." My mother leans in the doorway, watching me French-braid my hair. She's wearing her five-year-old sweatpants that still look brand new, and a long-sleeved T-shirt with a hand-painted bouquet of flowers on the front. She bought it at one of the Christmas bazaars she always goes to in November.

I try to keep it light. "You didn't tell me not to go to Seattle."

"I said you shouldn't make any sudden moves." Her gray eyes meet mine in the mirror. "Wyn, you're cutting off your nose to spite your face."

I drop my carefully subdued hair and it escapes from the braid. "Mother, you may find it hard to believe, but this is not about you."

"You're letting this creature just walk in and take over your husband. You're running away. Giving up without a fight. That's not the Wynter I know."

"What should I do? Invest in a Kelley voodoo doll? Should I start stalking her? Let the air out of her tires? Punch her lights out in the lobby of the JMP building?"

She walks over to stand beside me. "Of course not. Just don't let go. Stay here. Be present. Talk to him. Fight the divorce. Make it difficult. Look nice. Flirt with him. Seduce him."

I throw my comb up in the air and it bounces off the dresser and onto the floor. "Why should I make a fool of myself?"

"Because you love him, that's why. And I think, deep down, he loves you." I roll my eyes, but she ignores me. "Young women of your generation like to pretend that there's no fundamental difference between the male and the female of the species, but there is." Her voice is rising, the Aimee Semple McPherson of marital relations. "It's biological, behavioral, genetic, ingrained over thousands of years..."

"Mother, you were born too late. You would've made a great Victorian."

Now she's pacing back and forth in front of the window. "Wynter, men get what they want by taking it. Women get what they want by persistence, by holding on till everyone else gives up and goes home."

I turn and stare at her. "Great image, Mom. Woman as Gila Monster."

Her eyes close in exasperation. We've been playing this scene for years. "Wyn, please listen to me for once in your life. If you're determined to throw your marriage away, at least get your share of the money. I know too many women who've lost what's rightfully theirs because they didn't have the backbone to stay and fight for it. There are ways of hiding assets, circumventing laws, devaluing the—"

"We live in a community-property state."

"If it were that cut-and-dried, Los Angeles wouldn't be home to thousands of divorce attorneys."

I get up and seize her hands. "Mother, please, please, try to understand this. I can't stay here."

"So get your own place."

"Not *here*, here. I can't stay in L.A. I don't want to be afraid to go places because I might see them. I don't want to have to answer everybody's questions. I don't even want to hear the goddamn questions. I don't want to see the looks on people's faces. Oh, poor Wyn. Her husband left her for this gorgeous blonde. She'll probably be opening a needlepoint shop—"

"That's ridiculous. Your friends aren't going to think less of you because David—"

A laugh explodes out of me. "Friends? I don't have friends; I have contacts. All the women I've been hanging out with for the last five years were hand-picked and cultivated for their economic potential. I haven't had time to make friends."

"So what are you going to do in Seattle? Cry on CM's shoulder every night?"

"As a matter of fact, I've been offered a job. Making bread."

"Oh, Wyn." Her tone drips disappointment. "Honestly, I don't mean to be critical..."

"*But...*" I supply helpfully.

"But how can you make any money working in a bakery?"

"I don't need a lot of money. I've got my monthly allowance from David."

She actually laughs. "Wyn, you can't live on that." Emphasis on *you*.

I feel my fingernails digging into my palms. "Elizabeth said she'd get me an increase."

It's like she hasn't heard me. "And you have a teaching certificate, for heaven's sake. A degree in English and French. Why do you want to do manual labor?"

"Because I like it." We're facing each other now, in the middle of the room, like gladiators. If I look up, I might see Nero giving me the thumbs-down.

"This is utter nonsense." Her eyes cloud with frustration. "If you insist on baking bread, you can do that here. At least you could live with me and not have to—"

"I don't want to do it here. I've already got a job there."

"You're as pigheaded as your father." That's her concession speech. I take it as a compliment.

Seven

❦

Ellen wants me to start yesterday, but I tell her I need a week to get settled. I waste several days looking in the classifieds for a place to live. CM says I can stay with her, but the idea of having my own place has taken root in my brain. I went from living with my parents to sharing an apartment with CM. In France, I lived with the Guillaumes. The only time I was on my own was the six months before I married David, when CM was in New York. And even then, I was over at his place most of the time.

Apparently, Seattle has a surplus of cramped, dirty, one bedroom apartments with sculpted carpeting and peeling fake-wood paneling and moldy bathroom tile. I feel as if I've seen every single one. I drag myself back to CM's in the afternoons, tired and depressed. Finally, someone at the bakery gives me the phone number of a leasing agent named Daisy Wardwell. She's a breezy blonde with perfect makeup and a seemingly vast collection of pastel warm-up suits. She takes me to some places that aren't listed in the paper. They're better than the ones I've seen on my own, but they're also more expensive, to allow for her commission. When I explain what I'm looking for and how much rent I want to pay, she looks at me like I'm crazy, but says she'll see what's "out there."

The very next day she calls, gives me an address on Fourth, tells me to meet her at ten-thirty. Standing in the street, I stare at the faded number on the curb. Daisy must have given me the wrong address, or else I transposed the numbers when writing them down. The house is a huge, creaking Victorian in the process of being restored or demolished, it's hard to say which. With its gray siding and white gingerbread trim faded and cracking, it looks like the "before" photo in a *House Beautiful* renovation story. The "after" shot would involve white wicker furniture and Boston ferns, afternoon tea spread out on a table.

Sidestepping the missing and rotted planks, I pick my way up the steps and around the porch. One of the tall front windows is broken and boarded over; the others are all filthy. I peer inside, hands cupped on either side of my face, but all I can make out is a massive piece of furniture sitting in the middle of the room, covered with drop cloths. The original door has been replaced by a metal lumber-mart special, locked up tight.

Daisy's black Jeep Cherokee screeches to a stop, bumping the curb, and she jumps out, breathless. "Hey, kiddo. Sorry I'm late."

"Tell me this isn't the place."

She laughs. "You're about half right. Come with me." I follow her up the gravel driveway at the left of the house, past a screen of hemlocks to a small, new clapboard cottage at the rear of the property.

"They were building this last spring," she says. "I don't think it's ever been used." The welcoming committee of spiders and piles of mouse droppings on the wood floor tend to bear that out. "Of course, it would be cleaned up and checked for pests, but it's kind of a cute place, don't you think?"

The living room is small, but there's a wood-burning stove, a basic Pullman kitchen. The bedroom has one decent closet, but no shelves or cupboards. Then again, I don't have a lot of stuff to store at the moment. There's a skylight in the bathroom and the square bathtub still has the manufacturer's sticker on it. I wander back out to the covered front porch where I envision myself sitting in the mornings with a cup of espresso. The rent isn't much more than some of the bombed-out studios I've seen.

"What's the catch?"

Daisy smiles. "The catch is it's month to month. I'm not sure how long it's going to be available. The woman who lived in the big house passed away. Her will is in probate; her only son and his wife were restoring it, but she's just filed for divorce ... It's kind of a mess."

"Sounds like my life." There's an empty terra-cotta flowerpot sitting next to the screen door; I picture it full of red geraniums.

"The only problem I can see is that, with no one living in the big house, you're kind of isolated back here. There are neighbors all around but no one can see the house from their porch or anything." She looks at me appraisingly. "This is a pretty quiet neighborhood, and you don't seem the skittish type, but it's something to consider if you..." Her voice trails off.

Standing there in the warm autumn sun, it's hard to picture burglars or homicidal maniacs slinking around. What I see is a hummingbird feeder and flowerpots. Me curled up in a rattan chair with a good book, a Vivaldi violin concerto wafting out the open door. I love the way the house nestles into the trees that surround it, like a woodcutter's cottage in a fairy-tale forest. I picture the porch swathed in vines, and wonder if the front gets enough sun for blood-red trumpet vine. I have to jerk myself up by the collar. Whoa, girl. This a rental. No need to be landscaping the place.

"I think it suits me."

"Okay, then. Let's go back to the office and do the details. I can have it ready for you this weekend."

Linda LaGardia, the Queen Street bread baker, has got an attitude the size of the Yukon Territory. When Ellen introduces us a few days before I'm to start work, she checks me out the way my oma used to inspect a rib roast, and snorts. "We'll see how long this one lasts."

I watch her carry two lidded buckets of flour back to the storeroom, her biceps bulging. From the back, she resembles a bowlegged fireplug, from the front, an English bulldog. She has thin, yellow-gray hair that looks like it was styled with an electric carving knife, small pebble-dark eyes, and one of those big moles on her cheek with a couple of black hairs sprouting from it.

Ellen shakes her head, as if amazed. "She's been here for twenty-five years."

"Are you sure she wants an assistant?"

"Actually, I'm sure she doesn't." She pats my arm. "But don't worry, she's all bark, no bite."

I tell myself that I can quit any time.

On Saturday, UPS delivers my boxes of clothes and books to CM's, and the next afternoon we cart them over to the cottage to join the odd collection of furniture I've managed to acquire in the last two days. She sets down a small but weighty carton and looks around, hands on hips. There's a green paisley wing-back chair and a gold-and-brown, very ugly plaid club chair in front of the woodstove, courtesy of the Salvation Army thrift shop; a small round table sits between them. At a junk shop on Capitol Hill, I snapped up a ladies' writing desk with a broken leg, now mended with Super Glue. The ladder-back chair and tarnished bronze torchère lamp caught my eye yesterday at a neighborhood garage sale.

CM peers into the empty bedroom. "What are you sleeping on?"

"I ordered a mattress and box springs, but they can't deliver it till Wednesday."

"May I make a suggestion? Why don't you get a futon and a frame instead? Then you'll have a couch and a bed."

"Good idea. How come you're so smart?"

"I've had lots of experience making do." The "and you haven't" is understood.

One last trip to the car to fetch the old brass table lamp with a green glass shade that she's donating as my housewarming gift. She sets it on the counter next to the sink. "Wyn, this is so ..."—she gropes for a polite description—"... spartan. Are you sure you're going to be okay? I mean, you're not exactly used to ..." Her voice trails off.

"I'll fix it up," I say firmly. "It'll be fine." Am I paranoid, or does she sound like my mother?

She laughs. "Well, you know you can always come back to my place if it gets to be too much like camping. I still don't see why you won't stay there at least till I get back."

"I just want to be on my own."

"If I'm not there, you can hardly be more on your own." She looks at me. "Oh, never mind. You're wearing your pigheaded look." She hands me the keys to her apartment and car. "Just in case. I've told the manager you might be in and out, so she won't have you arrested. Although you might be more comfortable in a nice cozy cell."

Most of the clothes that I wore in Los Angeles are useless here. They're clothes for lunching and shopping in Beverly Hills, lots of short skirts, party dresses, sexy lingerie, high heels. Hardly anything I can wear to work. Not to mention the fact that I don't have any place to store them. God, my brain has atrophied from disuse. I put aside the jeans, a pair of sweatpants and two or three sweaters, three long-sleeved T-shirts, some workout clothes, jogging shoes. I pack everything else back in the box.

As the light fades, the temperature drops, and I start looking around for the thermostat. I look on every wall, in the closets, the cupboards, even under the sink. From the file that Daisy gave me, I extract the information sheet on the place and skim till I see the word "furnace." On the opposite side of the column is the word "none."

Oh, yes. I vaguely remember some discussion about this, but in my haste to make a nest for myself, I must have glossed over a few details. There's an asterisk next to "none," and then in tiny type: "heated by Jotul woodstove." Which is fine, except I haven't got any damn wood for the damn Jotul woodstove.

I sit down on the braided rug in front of the cold, silent stove. I look around the room at the boxes of expensive, nonfunctional clothing, my few sticks of furniture, which seem lost even in this small space, the basket of dishes and glasses I scavenged from CM.

Okay, what *am* I trying to prove? That I'm not a spoiled twit? That I can be Ms. Thoreau on Walden Pond? I guess I could've sprung for some furniture. But all this is temporary. If David calls and wants me to come home, I don't want to be stuck with a bunch of stuff. *When* he calls. Not *if.*

I bring home a pizza from Dan's Market and eat it sitting at my writing desk in the amber light from the floor lamp. My gaze settles on the glued leg and I wonder distractedly how it got broken. Kids playing touch football in the living room? A family brawl? Dropped by movers?

I forgot to light the gas water heater, so when I rinse my plate, a thin sheen of grease clings stubbornly. I try to read for a while, but I'm too cold. Should I call CM and ask her to come get me? I get as far as picking up the phone, but then I hang up. She doesn't need the aggravation, and I don't want anyone, even her, saying they told me so.

At eight-thirty, I pull on tights, jeans, sweatpants, a turtleneck, a sweatshirt, and a sweater. Seat cushions from the two chairs are my makeshift mattress, and I pull up the three blankets I borrowed from CM. I feel like the casserole my mother sometimes made on Saturday nights—pigs in a blanket. I'm wearing so many layers, I can't even bend my knees. At nine-fifteen I add another pair of socks and my parka.

Loneliness and pain have brought on temporary insanity. There's no other explanation for my behavior. I can get up tomorrow, pack my things, and go home to L.A. I'll lose a few hundred bucks' rent and some face, but I'll be comfortable.

I flip over on my back. I can get my own place, of course, but I'll still have to field my mother's questions, at least appear to consider her suggestions, and listen to her theories about the moral authority of women. I can get a job there. Probably not making bread. I'll probably cave in and renew my teaching certificate and go back to wrangling junior felons.

And then some night when I'm going stir-crazy, I'll accept a blind date with one of my mother's friend's son's cousin's roommates from Antelope Valley Junior College, a nice, quiet guy. He'll turn out to be the Sepulveda Slasher and the next day they'll find my mutilated body in a ravine in Angeles Crest National Forest. I'll be on the front page of the *L.A. Times* and David and Kelley will see the story while they're having breakfast. Kelley's eyes will get very round and she'll say, "Weren't you married to her a long time ago?"

And David will peer over her shoulder at the paper and say, "The face doesn't look familiar, but I recognize that hair."

Monday morning I huddle, shivering, under my blankets and reach for the rental file. Daisy included a sheet with names of some outfits that sell firewood. "The ones that are starred will deliver and stack it for you," she said. "They're a bit more expensive, but unless you have a pickup truck or know someone who does..." I don't think CM would appreciate my hauling wood in her Camry.

I call the one whose name makes me smile—Norwegian Woods. The guy tells me that for a woodstove, I need hardwood, says they have alder, gives me the price for half a cord. When I tell him I want to check some other places, he says, "Gus Doyle and Raven Woods charge the same thing and we all deliver and stack it, so save yourself some trouble. When do you want it delivered?"

"Now," I say. He says Tuesday morning is the soonest he can deliver it. "I need it now. I have absolutely no wood, and I'm freezing."

"Sorry," he says. "It's that time of year. Everybody wants their wood yesterday."

"Forget it then. I'll find somebody who can bring it today."

"Good luck to you," he says politely and hangs up.

I call all the other names on the list. The soonest I can get wood from anyone else is Thursday. I crawl back onto my makeshift mattress, pull up the covers, and cry hot tears of frustration, which are about the warmest thing in the cottage. The place must have zero insulation.

When the tears run out, I push myself into a sitting position, plant my feet squarely on the floor in a big yellow puddle of sunlight. Its warmth rises up my legs as if by osmosis. I pick up the phone, call Norwegian Woods again. The same guy answers.

I talk softly, hoping he won't recognize my voice. "Can I get a half cord of alder delivered tomorrow?"

"Sure," he says, "over on Fourth Street, right? But I've got some other morning deliveries now. It'll probably be around three by the time we get there."

It's pitch-black and freezing when my alarm goes off at eleven-thirty Monday night. I turn on the light immediately so I won't be tempted to go back to sleep. I peel off the sweats, step out of the jeans just long enough to remove the tights. It's the first time I've ever gotten undressed to go to work. I brush my hair, pull on a jacket. I linger for a minute, sleepily wondering what it is I've forgotten. My ring. It wouldn't do to get it encrusted with bread dough.

I told David I didn't want a big-rock engagement ring. This was his idea of a simple wedding ring—five baguette diamonds set across a wide gold band. Well, it is gorgeous. I still catch myself staring at it sometimes, mesmerized by the way light dances over the facets. I pull it off my finger, put it in the little cloisonné box where I keep the few pieces of jewelry I brought with me.

Then I'm crunching down the gravel drive, turning into the silent street.

I move quickly from one streetlight to the next, stepping-stones in a dark river. A siren wails downtown. Ferryboat horns. An occasional car whips by me. People going home. To bed. Sensible people. Then there's me. Getting up in the middle of the night to go to work for eight bucks an hour. With someone who doesn't even want me there.

I pass a small Tudor house with a yellow porch lamp blazing. A man sits in profile to the picture window, leaning forward, elbows on knees. The reflected light of a TV screen flickers across his face and the glowing tip of his cigarette seems suspended in the dark. I imagine that he's waiting for his daughter to come home from a date, the way my father waited up for me a few times. Maybe he doesn't like the boy she's with and they're out past her curfew. His wife has gone to bed, but he sits in the living room, trying to watch some stupid rerun, angry and worried.

I go down the alley behind the bakery and knock on the back door. When Linda opens it, I smile. "Hi."

She doesn't say anything, just steps back with a grunt to let me in. She goes to the storage room, comes back with two buckets of flour, walks out again. I get an apron off the pile of clean ones by the sink, slip it over my head, tie the strings around my waist. She comes back with two more buckets, glares at me, walks out again. This time I follow.

"Can I help?" By the time I get to the narrow passageway, she's roaring back out like a locomotive, with more buckets, and I have to flatten myself against the wall to keep from being run over.

"That's what you're here for," she throws over her shoulder.

The storage room is floor-to-ceiling shelves, housing a mind-boggling array of buckets, sacks, tins, and boxes. She strides in and slaps a wrinkled piece of paper into my hand. "Get those things and bring 'em out."

It takes a few minutes to figure out the storage system, but eventually I find everything on the list and stack it in the center of the floor. When I drag the first bucket out, she's standing there, hands on hips. "Well, that didn't take long."

"Sorry. It was a little confusing to find things." She watches me drag the remaining ingredients out, even though we could do it in half the time if she helped.

"Maybe we should get a dolly," I suggest.

"A what?"

"One of those little platform things with wheels. It would be faster to get everything out of the—" She stares at me like I've just arrived from Venus. I dust my hands. "Now what?"

"Are you gonna be askin' me that every five minutes?"

"I'll have to as long as you're not volunteering any information."

Her eyes narrow, giving her the look of an angry sow. "Don't be smart-alecky with me," she says.

"I'm not being smart-alecky. But you're going to have to give me some kind of clues about what you expect."

"What I expect is for you to watch and learn. And don't get in my way." Her voice ratchets up a few decibels. "And don't be rollin' your eyes, missy."

She must be used to dealing with eighteen-year-olds. "My name's Wyn."

"What kind of a silly name is that?"

She looks and sounds so much like Darlene Grabinski, the fat little playground bully who terrorized me in first grade, that I can't help laughing. After I pull myself together, she takes a black loose-leaf binder down from a shelf over the sink and hands it to me.

"We're doing whole wheat walnut and white sandwich first." She points to a stack of huge stainless-steel bowls. "Weigh out the flours on that scale and put them on the worktable." I ask if I can play some music and she grudgingly agrees. "Just don't play any of that boogie-woogie stuff."

While I'm digging through the drawerful of tapes, I notice on the shelves next to Ellen's desk dozens of books on baking, including quite a few on bread.

"Do you ever use any of the bread books?" I ask.

"Nope."

"I've got some good ones at home, too. Maybe we could find a different kind of bread to try sometime."

I can't tell if she's actually considering my suggestion or if she's distracted. Then she says authoritatively, "Don't do to be messing around with different things all the time. If it ain't broke, don't fix it."

Linda isn't quick to give up her personal history and she's not the slightest bit interested in mine. Every attempt I make at conversation is rebuffed, so I quit trying and just do what she tells me. Based on my hazy recollections of working in France and information I've picked up from baking at home, she seems to be a competent but unimaginative journeyman baker, doing everything by rote. The same breads on the same days of the week, the same way she's done them for twenty-five years. I suppose it could also be called tradition.

I'm wetting the worktable and scraping the dough off with a bench scraper when Ellen arrives at 6 A.M. "Morning, ladies," she sings out, flipping the light switch out front. Linda grunts.

Ellen bustles around, turning on the espresso machine, grinding coffee, wiping the counters, putting money in the cash register. I roll out a cooling rack laden with warmly fragrant loaves and I have the sense that she's trying to read my face. "How'd it go?"

"At least she knows how to clean up," Linda says grudgingly.

I smile sweetly. "Fine. Had a busy night."

Ellen looks at me for another few seconds, then rubs her hands together with forced cheer. "How about an espresso? How's your place shaping up?"

When she finds out where I'm living, she smiles sadly. "Oh, the Keeler place. Stanford and Adele. Now there was a soap opera."

"Do you know everyone on Queen Anne Hill?" I ask.

"Pretty much." She says it with a straight face. "Adele was so beautiful. A former ballet dancer. She was on all kinds of charity boards, the arts. You know."

I nod silently. Yes, it happens that I do know. "She's the one who died? Whose will's in probate?"

Ellen's grinding the coffee beans, lost in her tale. "Stanford was a lawyer. Big shot in county Democratic politics. But such a *mensch*. A real pussy cat."

Her expression changes to one of total disgust. "Adele, on the other hand, was a bitch on wheels, pardon my French. Totally self-absorbed. He was absolutely nuts 'for her. They were sort of Queen Anne Hill Royalty." She pauses for dramatic effect. "There was a big blowup. Right after the last mayoral campaign. Some big politico's wife left him, said he was having an affair with Adele. Not only that, but the guy had apparently been diverting funds from the campaign war chest, and he claimed Adele was in on it. Running the money through one of her worthy causes—although it was never proven."

"So what happened?"

"Poor Stanford was just devastated. They divorced—she fought him tooth and nail for every cent. At that point, I don't think he had much heart left to fight. He died about two years later. Of course Adele was persona non grata in town, and she became practically a recluse. Just sat in that house that she wanted so much, and let it fall apart. Finally died last year. I heard it's in probate because she didn't have a will. Her son was barely speaking to her by then."

She hands me a tiny majolica cup of espresso. "Now the son and his wife are splitting? The place must be jinxed."

Which may or may not be the case, but I'm quickly being disabused of any residual belief in happy endings.

I decide that a hot shower will make me feel more human, and it does, but just as I'm reaching for the towel, I hear someone pounding on the front door.

Dripping wet and shivering, I dive into my robe, twist my hair into the towel, and run for the door. I open it a crack. A man is just stepping off the porch.

"Yes?"

He turns around. "Where do you want the wood?" It's an effort not to shrink back. He looks like he was sent over by central casting to play the psycho-killer handyman. His next shave should have been yesterday. Brown hair hangs down almost to his shoulders in fat, wet snakes under a water-stained baseball cap pulled low on his forehead, so his eyes are barely visible. I have the impression of a wolf peering out of a cave.

"Over there." I point to the garage.

I finish drying, pull on sweats and a raincoat, run out into the gray drizzle, the towel still wrapped around my head. He's laying out four-by-fours next to the garage and he stands up when he hears me.

"They said three o'clock."

"We had a cancellation and you were in such a hurry, I thought you'd be glad if I came early. You have a tarp?"

"You might have at least called."

His teeth flash white against his dirty face. "I might have. But I didn't. You want a tarp?"

"Do I need one?"

"Unless you want to try burning wet wood." He squints into the thick mist, in the direction of the street. "I've got a few in the truck if you want to buy one. Twelve dollars."

"For a piece of plastic?"

"It's not plastic. It's waterproof canvas. It'll last forever."

I want to tell him that nothing lasts that long. "Well, the wood's probably already wet, isn't it? I shouldn't cover it now."

He shakes his head. "Our storage is covered, so it's just a little damp from the ride over."

"Oh, all right, bring me a tarp."

Every few minutes, I set down the hair dryer, pull back the curtain to watch him push wheelbarrows of split wood up the drive, stack it neatly against the garage. I'd forgotten that he wouldn't be able to drive a truck back here. When I hear boots clomping on the front porch, I go to the door, check in hand.

In spite of the cold, sweat runs down his face and he smells like workout clothes that have been sitting at the bottom of a gym bag for a few days. I have to breathe through my mouth. "I put some of it up here." He points to a small stack by the door. "So you don't have to keep running out to the garage."

"How much do I owe you?"

"You're welcome."

I can't believe this guy is giving me etiquette lessons, but there's enough of my mother in me to be embarrassed. "Thanks," I mumble. "Where's the tarp?"

"On the wood." He looks at me as if I'm an idiot. "It's ninety-four, total." I fill out the check and hand it to him. He hands it back. "Sorry, I can't take an out-of-state check."

I forget to breathe through my mouth, and the smell almost makes me fall down. "That's all I have."

"I'll have to get cash, then."

"I don't have ninety-four dollars stuffed in my cookie jar," I say indignantly. "You didn't mention that little detail when I called."

"I assumed your check would be local. We don't get a lot of half-cord deliveries to California." He takes off the cap, pushes the hair back with one hand, replaces the cap. "How much cash have you got?"

"I'll have to look." I'm replaying Daisy's warning about the isolation of this house, the fact that no neighbors can see the front door. I can't even see the street in this fog. As if he can read my thoughts, he steps back, lounges against the porch rail while I raid my wallet. "All I have is forty-five dollars."

He holds out his hand. "I'll make up the difference for Rick and you can pay me tomorrow."

"Is that okay?" I ask.

"It'll have to be." He folds the bills, stuffs them into the pocket of his grungy wool shirt. "I'm sure not going to load it back up and cart it out." He's looking past me at the Jotul stove. "Good stove," he says. "You know how to work it?"

"Yes," I say quickly. "The leasing agent showed me." No way is he getting in my house. Aside from the fact that he looks incredibly seedy, I'd have to have the place fumigated.

"Then I'll see you tomorrow. About ten."

I wait till I hear the truck drive away before I go out to bring in some wood.

. . .

I've been reluctant to open a checking account here. As if it would commit me to something more permanent than an extended vacation. Apparently, the account services rep at Washington Mutual shares my unease. My California driver's license engenders a deep suspicion of my worthiness to store money in her bank. When she finds out I've been gainfully employed for a week, she wants to know why I haven't gotten a Washington license yet.

I smile pleasantly. "Because I don't have a car." She says I need to get a state photo ID card. "I'll do that first thing tomorrow." I think she knows I'm lying, but since I have my passport, she opens the account anyway and sends me off with my temporary checks and one hundred dollars in cash.

In the linen department at the Bon Marché to buy a down comforter, I discover that David has canceled my MasterCard. The clerk says he was asked by the authorization center to pick up the card. I write him one of my new checks, which he doesn't like very much, but accepts because he can't find anything materially wrong.

When I get home, I sit in my ugly plaid chair and dial David's work number. "It's me. Can you talk?"

"Of course. I've been trying to reach you all week."

"You have?" My stomach lurches.

"I've decided to sell the house. I need to know if you want any of the furniture."

My knees are wet cement. "So . . . does this mean you want—"

"No, Wyn, it doesn't mean I want a divorce." It's the talking-to-a-retarded-child voice. "I just think that while we're living apart, it's best not to have the expense of a big house, particularly when I'm n— hardly ever there." Then with exaggerated civility, "I hope that's all right with you."

"Fine." Then I remember the reason I called him. "Why did you cancel my MasterCard?"

"Because you started piling up huge charges."

"What huge charges?"

"Someplace called the Bon Marché for five hundred dollars."

"Five hundred dollars isn't huge. I bought a futon and a frame. And some kitchen stuff."

"What the hell for?"

"Because I have my own place now. I couldn't stay with CM forever."

A brief pause. "You're living up there?"

"Yes. For a while. I got a job."

"Doing what?"

"Baking bread."

"Baking bread?" He says it slowly, incredulously. "Wyn, for Chrissake. What are you trying to prove?"

"Not a damn thing. And I'm paying my own bills, so what difference does it make to you how much I spend?"

"I don't want my credit involved with yours. In case you default. Since you're working, you can get your own cards now."

"At eight bucks an hour, I can hardly get the kind of credit I had."

"Look, Wyn, I don't want to argue with you about—"

"Of course you don't. You just want me to quietly disappear."

"Oh, for Chrissake. I do not." He lowers his voice. "And I can't be having these kinds of discussions at work. Why don't you call me at home?"

"Because I never know who's going to answer the damn phone."

"Look, I've got to go. I'm late for a meeting. We're going to have to talk about this later."

"When, David?" I'm practically shouting, but he's already gone.

I want to rip the phone out of the wall and heave it through the window, but I think that would be counterproductive.

A pounding noise wakes me. I don't even know where I am at first. I stagger to the door and look bleary-eyed at a lanky, crew-cut guy in baggy denim overalls and a filthy sweater. "Yes?"

He says, "Hi. I'm Rick. Norwegian Woods. You got some money

for me?" He fishes around in his pocket for a dirty piece of paper. "Forty-nine dollars?"

"Oh." I turn quickly, take the forty-nine dollars out of my wallet. He counts it before shoving it down into his pocket.

"Brought you some cedar." He smiles, revealing a couple of missing teeth. "Just in case."

I follow his gaze to about half a dozen small logs next to my pile of alder. "What for?"

"Kindling," he says. "Cedar's dry and splintery, and the bark peels off in nice, flat pieces. Perfect for kindling. Smells great, too. Like a campfire."

"Oh. Thanks. Thank you very much."

He hands me a business card that looks as if it's been run over by a truck. "If you need anything else, give us a call."

I watch him limp down the driveway, wondering what happened to the psycho-killer handyman.

On Thursday night, I no sooner get to work than I'm in the bathroom throwing up.

"If you're sick, I don't want you here," Linda says in her most sympathetic voice.

"I feel fine."

Her eyes narrow. "Are you getting any sleep?"

"Well, it hasn't been easy because I've been trying to get settled."

"What time you been goin' to bed?" She leans the big wooden peel against the side of the oven.

"Monday I went to bed at eight-thirty at night. Tuesday about noon. Wednesday at five. Today at two."

"There's your trouble, right there." She folds her arms and gives me a disgusted look. "You gotta get your routine down, sleep at the same time every day or your body never will get used to flip-floppin'."

"What time do you sleep?"

"Soon as I get home. I have some toast and tea and hit the sack. Get up about four."

"What about on your days off?"

"Same thing."

"But how can you have any kind of normal life if you're up all night and sleep all day on your days off?"

"Who said bread making was any kinda normal life? I knew you wouldn't like it."

"It's not that I don't like it . . ." I feel my face heating up.

"You kids are all alike, never done a honest day's work in your life."

"First of all, I'm not a kid, and I don't think you're in any position to know about what I've done in my life."

"Horsefeathers. Look at you." She holds up her hand, lets her wrist go limp. "Little manicured nails. Polo pants." She bats her eyelashes and it's hard not to burst out laughing.

"What?" I look down at myself and the logo on my Ralph Lauren sweatpants looms upside down at me. "They're just sweatpants."

She turns away, as if I'm too painful to contemplate, heads for the storeroom.

"Think whatever you like," I holler after her. "As long as I'm doing my job, you have no complaint."

Eight

⚜

Linda notwithstanding, I love my job. Even the tedium of doing the same breads every week is okay for now. Till I find the rhythm again. Till I can look at a bowl of flour and know how many cups or grams there are. Till I can grab a fistful of dough and say with certainty that it's too wet or not wet enough.

I love getting off work at seven in the morning, walking home as the city's just starting to hum and cats are slinking under porches. I love knowing that most of the people I pass are lock-stepping to their daily obligation and I'm done. The day belongs to me.

Taking Linda's advice, I start going to bed right after breakfast. With a down comforter to keep me warm, my futon opened up in front of the woodstove, and blackout shades on the windows, I'm having my best sleep in years.

If it's not raining when I wake up, I walk the neighborhood. I begin to recognize neighbors at work in their yards, mothers with their baby strollers, kids with their dogs. We smile, say hi or nice day or think we'll get some rain tonight? I discover a tiny park at the top of the hill on Eighth Place and Highland, with a bench that has a 180-degree view of the Sound and the Olympic Mountains.

Sometimes I read; sometimes I just sit there, lost in the way the sun glints off the water like handfuls of diamonds. I watch the Washington state ferries chug to and from Bainbridge Island through swarms of bright spinnakers. When the sun falls into that slot behind the mountains, the wind picks up and the temperature drops, but it's worth the cold walk home to see the Olympics catch fire in the sunset or a huge white bank of fog unroll off the water.

Sometimes I manage to forget the reason I'm here. That I'm waiting for David to figure out what he wants. Whether the package includes me. I sit on my bench and have heartfelt imaginary conversations with him. He tells me he loves me, that it's been a terrible mistake, he can't live without me, he's told Kelley it's over. I smile sadly and murmur that I'm just not sure if it can ever be the same with us.

His voice cracks as he says, "Believe me, Wyn, I understand, but if you let me make it up to you, I swear you'll never be sorry."

Laundry has never been an issue for me in the great cosmic scheme of things. For the last seven years, Hildy, our housekeeper, took care of it along with almost everything else. Sheets, towels, clothes magically appeared in drawers, in closets—washed and ironed, folded or hung up. The closest I got to the process was buying more detergent whenever she said we needed it.

Now it's a logistical thing. I have no washer, no dryer. So when I run out of things to wear, I stuff all my dirty clothes in a pillowcase and drag them down to the Queen Anne Launderland on Queen, across from the A & J Meat Market.

It's a colossal waste of time. You have to sit there while your clothes go through the whole fill, wash, spin, fill, rinse, spin. Then you have to wait while the industrial-strength dryer makes *pommes frites* out of your Calvin Klein briefs. Yes, you can read. But if you get engrossed in a book and you don't jump up and get your clothes the second the machine stops, you run the risk of some grimy-fingered guy waving your black push-up bra overhead and yelling, "Whose 38B?"

Okay, this might sound just a bit too fastidious, but I worry about germs. I have no idea what these people do in their clothes. They could be out rolling around in nonbiodegradable toxic wastes for all I know. And then I have to put my stuff in the same machine?

After two forays into this alien culture, I finally figure out that the best time to go is early in the morning. I take my pillowcase/laundry bag to work with me and hit Launderland on my way home. Seven-thirty is too early for anyone else to be there except for one or two retired couples drinking their early bird half-priced coffee and clipping coupons, and some guy in a baseball cap who never even looks up from the notebook he's scribbling in. Plus, at that hour you have at least the illusion that the place is clean.

The bakery officially closes at two, but Diane and Ellen are usually there with Jen and Misha, the day crew, till five or six, doing special orders, wholesale stuff, and prep work. I drop in one or two afternoons a week to hang out for a couple of hours.

I watch Diane put the finishing touches on cakes to be picked up early in the morning, and I help her wrap freshly baked layers for the freezer. Ellen plows through paperwork, makes entries in the ledger book that she keeps in her desk. Her actual baking time is limited, but she supervises the afternoon crew making cinnamon rolls, muffins, cookies, and Mazurka Bars, arguably the bakery's most famous product.

Ellen invented Mazurka Bars—at least her version of them—when she lived in New Hampshire, and she brought the recipe out west with her, just like the pioneer women. Except she came in the seventies, driving her derelict Volkswagen Beetle instead of a covered wagon.

I never heard of them till I started working here, but I soon discovered how wonderful they are—a bar cookie with a thin, flaky crust on the bottom, then the lemon or chocolate/espresso or apple/raisin or raspberry filling, and over that the crumble layer that other bakers would kill for. It has a habit-forming, sandy crunch. It's not too sweet and it doesn't disintegrate all over your clothes when you take a bite.

While the recipe for Mazurka Bars is as closely held as the formula for Coca-Cola, Ellen's not at all averse to telling me their history.

"I was messing with one of my mother's old recipes," she says. "I wanted some individual desserts I could take to a picnic, but at first they were so crumbly. And the only filling she ever used was lemon. How boring is that?"

Without waiting for an answer, she rambles on, absently stacking bills in alternating vertical and horizontal rows. She tells me about the first months she lived in Seattle, when the only job she could find was waitressing at the Five Spot.

"It was okay, you know. I wasn't making a killing, but they were nice people to work for, and the regulars were fun. Of course, they wouldn't let me cook, and I was dying to. So I just started baking Mazurkas in my apartment and wrapping them in plastic wrap and hauling them downtown on the bus.

"I'd hang around outside movies and down at Seattle Center when there was a Sonics game—"

"Always one step ahead of the health department," Diane pipes up.

Ellen laughs. "They never knew where the Mazurka Bar lady was going to surface next."

My oma used to say it's amazing what you can hear when you're not talking, and I learn all manner of interesting tidbits in those idle afternoons, in addition to the history of Mazurka Bars. Like the secret to a well-risen cake is to cream the butter and sugar forever, so a lot of air is incorporated. Diane usually walks away and does other things while the Hobart beats the bejeezus out of the stuff.

She wraps strips of wet towels around the cake pans to make the cake rise evenly, eliminating that dome in the center. I discover that spritzing hazelnuts with water before you toast them steams the skins and they slip right off without a fight. That all the small products—muffins, scones, even cookies—can be frozen unbaked and then baked without thawing. I watch Jen cut perfect slices of cheesecake with dental floss and Misha use a thin-bladed knife to surgically remove the charred crust from an overdone cake.

But maybe the most important thing I learn is that almost any disaster, no matter how awful it looks, can be salvaged if you keep your head and don't just start dumping things into the garbage.

Payday is every Friday. Since I'm not completely confident of the reliability of David's monthly deposits, I've gotten into the habit of picking up my paycheck on Friday afternoons and taking it over to the Washington Mutual branch on Queen Anne Avenue. When I unlock the back door one misty November afternoon, the work area is dark and empty, but I hear water running. Out front Tyler bends over the sink, shirtless, pouring blue liquid on her head. The fact that she's easily seen through the front windows either hasn't occurred to her or doesn't disturb her.

"Hi, Wyn." She squints at me upside down, then answers my unspoken question. "Ellen lets me do my hair here because my dad won't let me do it at home."

I look around at the puddles of blue liquid everywhere. "Does that stain?"

"Sort of. It comes out eventually."

"Ellen's not worried about contamination?"

She giggles. "It wouldn't hurt if it got in anything. It's just Kool-Aid." She points to a crumpled packet on the counter.

"One little package makes your hair look like that?"

"Well, I had to strip the color out first. Twice, 'cause my hair's, like, really dark." She straightens up, pressing her head with a blue-stained towel. "So what are you doing here?"

"I just came to pick up my check."

"How're you getting along with that paragon of personality, the lovely Linda LaGardia?" She's doing her strung-out disc jockey voice.

"Let's just say we're getting used to each other." I perch on the edge of a tall stool next to the counter and watch her fluffing her hair with the towel.

She pulls on a black T-shirt, picks up the crumpled Kool-Aid packet, aims, and fires a perfect hook shot into the trash. Then, oblivious to my stare, she executes a perfect back jump and falls into the splits.

"You were a cheerleader?"

"In a former life." She grins. "I got tossed from the squad when I dyed my hair blue."

One of the tables is covered with paper. Watercolors. Scenes of Seattle in the rain. A dish of water, a box of paints, and some brushes sit on a half-sheet pan on the counter.

"Are these pictures yours?"

"Midterm projects," she says. "They're all due Monday."

"They're beautiful."

She grimaces. " 'Too derivative.' That's what the teacher said last time. Like I give a shit."

"They remind me of the Impressionist pictures of Paris in the rain." I'm determined to give her a compliment, whether she wants it or not.

Her look is gently reproving. "That's what they're supposed to remind you of. That's why they're too derivative."

I laugh. "I still think they're beautiful. Do you like doing water-colors?"

She shrugs.

"Why are you taking the classes?"

"Gotta do something. I'm too dumb for college."

"You're not dumb. You're just nonlinear."

She laughs, flinging her blue-fringed head forward, then back. " 'Nonlinear.' Cool. I like it."

I look around at all the art on the walls. "Is any of this yours?"

"Nah. Ellen said she'd hang something of mine, but I haven't got anything I like that much. I did the menu board, though."

"It's classy. I love illuminated capitals."

She looks at me with marginal interest. "How come you know about art? Like the Impressionists and illuminated capitals."

"I know a little bit about a lot of things, but not a lot about anything."

She nods sagely, disappears into the bathroom. A few seconds later,

I hear the whine of a hair dryer. I study the watercolors, imagining how one might look in a frame on the wall of my living room.

Tyler emerges from the bathroom sporting a halo of blue fuzz that makes her look like a toy Easter chick.

"Done?" I ask.

"Almost. Gotta do the spikes." She opens the door of the Traulsen. "You need an egg yolk?"

"Not really."

"I use the whites for my spikes, but I don't need the yolks. I think you can do facials with them."

"It's the whites you do facials with," I tell her.

She frowns, grabs one egg from a flat and deftly separates it, stashing the yolk in an espresso cup. She beats the white with a few drops of water and heads for the bathroom again. "I'm going to the U2 concert tonight."

"Have fun."

I tuck my check into the inside pocket of my coat and let myself out. For one minute, I wish I was going to the U2 concert, never mind that I don't even like them. I think of CM and me at Tyler's age, running wild in the Valley with a pack of girlfriends. Going to the Sepulveda Drive-In Movie (a.k.a. the Finger Bowl) in my ancient black Chevy with red baby-moon hubcaps and no backseat. Hamburger Hamlet and Jake's Pizza and Topanga Plaza.

The bank guard locks the glass door behind me. It's four o'clock, and mist halos the streetlights in the early darkness. Queen Anne Avenue is teetering on the edge of Gentrification Gulch without falling over. Yet. Trendier places like Starbucks and Häagen-Dazs, Sonora Southwestern Gourmet, Avant Card, and the new bookstore are popping up seemingly overnight, like mushrooms on the forest floor.

But the old-timers still dominate the street—Arch Plumbing Supply with its windows full of tools and parts predating Liquid-Plumr. Fancy Fabrics, where you can barely squeeze between tables piled with bolts of chintz and dotted swiss and worsted wools. The seedy-looking Greek restaurant that Ellen swears has the best hash browns in Seattle. Another bakery, featuring the kind of Danish my oma loved and cakes with that Crisco/sugar icing that crunches between your teeth. A consignment shop called Rags to Riches, a state liquor store, Thriftway, and a couple of bars.

One of the bars is Bailey's. I've passed by it plenty of times. It looks like a typical neighborhood pub, low-key, nonthreatening. The kind of place where a single woman could go and have a glass of wine and read. Or write a letter. Or just mope if she felt like it, without being pestered. I'm not used to going out alone, particularly not to bars. But the mist has turned to rain now, and walking in it isn't quite as much fun. I hesitate for a minute with my hand on the door.

No. Not yet.

Without noticing exactly how or when it happens, Linda and I settle into an uneasy accommodation. She quits making snide remarks about my name, age, and work history; I quit trying to make our relationship personal and pushing new ideas on her.

I think she's even started to like having me around. Well, maybe not me personally, but someone. She wears wrist braces for her tendonitis. Industrial-strength support hose peek out below her too short slacks. She complains about pain in her right shoulder, probably arthritis. She has to be glad that I'm strong enough to lift the sheet pans, heavy with wet dough, to drag fifty-pound sacks of flour, to do most of the loading and unloading of the oven decks. Of course, she'd eat ground glass before she'd admit it, even to herself.

I tell her about Jean-Marc. How he saw me rubbing my neck one day and told me, "A little pain is good, Wynter. It is how the trade enters your body." She gets a big hoo-ha out of that one.

My antennae start picking up snippets of information about her. There's a husband. Then I discover he's an ex-husband. She calls him

Bubba. Ellen tells me his name is Walter and that he's still lurking in a corner of the picture.

Tyler mentions that he used to be a captain on the ferries. "Pulled down some pretty good bucks, but he got busted down to seaman for drinking on the job. I think that's when she kicked his ass out. They have two kids, you know."

"No, I didn't."

Ellen frowns. "You know how I feel about gossip." Tyler and I look at each other and try not to laugh.

Just before Thanksgiving, the weather goes from bleak to abysmal—gray, wet, bone-chilling—every day for a week. Ellen laughs at my whining. "Honey, you ain't seen nothin' yet. Wait till February when it's been raining nonstop for two months."

One evening, in an attempt to regain my rapidly loosening grip on sanity, I call my mother. The machine answers and her voice tells me that "the Morrisons" are unavailable at the moment, but that "one of us" will be glad to call back as soon as possible. It's nine-fifteen, no, almost nine-thirty. Where is she? I don't leave a message. Just as I settle the receiver back in its cradle, it rings and I jump.

"So you haven't drowned."

"CM! Are you home?"

"Yes, thank you, Jesus."

"How did it go?"

"Great. We got lots of good video, but I'm beat."

"Are you going to L.A. for Thanksgiving?"

"I'm not going anywhere near an airport for a long time. What are you doing?"

"The bakery's closed for the whole weekend."

"Come over here and we can make turkey on Thursday?"

·   ·   ·

I call her on Tuesday to see what she wants me to bring. She still sounds tired, but she says she's taking the rest of the week off and she's positive she'll be fine by Thanksgiving Day. She calls me Wednesday night, and I know as soon as I hear her voice that she's not fine.

"I hate to wimp out on you," she says, "but I've got some kind of bug."

"Oh, damn." I stare at the blackness outside my window, listen to the rain pelting the glass. "What can I do? You need anything from the drugstore? Groceries?"

"I'm set. The doctor sent out some antibiotics. I've got chicken soup in the fridge. Not that I can eat anything. I'm planning to sleep for the next forty-eight hours."

"Don't forget to take your medicine. Call me if you need anything. I'll be here all weekend."

About noon on Thanksgiving Day, I get up and open the blackout shades, climb back into my warm burrow. Fog, so thick you could squeeze it between your fingers, hangs outside the windows. I stare at the textured ceiling. It's not bad, my little house. Plenty of people would consider it the apex of luxury. I've decided the barrenness is oddly restful, like camping in the high desert.

Okay, the place is depressing. Cold, stark, and empty. I'm sick of the color—polar-bear-in-a-snowstorm white. My eyes sweep the blank walls; nothing to stop or direct my glance. Out of nowhere, a bossy voice in my brain says, *So, paint.*

Silly. You can't paint a rental.

Of course you can. You can always paint it white again when you leave.

I sit up, and the comforter falls from my shoulders. My stomach flutters with an unlikely excitement. Everything's closed today, but I could get the paint tomorrow morning. There's just the two rooms. How long can it take? Suddenly I'm pulling on my sweats, my socks and shoes, sweater and jacket. An hour later I've returned from the convenience store with an armload of decorating magazines to peruse while I'm eating my oatmeal.

I flip the pages, barely focusing on the articles, simply letting the pictures bombard me with color. Here's my problem. I've been suffering from acute color deprivation. I gulp it greedily. The food colors— dark chocolate, pale salmon, tart grape, and spicy cinnamon. Flower hues—lavender, fern, jonquil, heliotrope. The earth shades—clay and teal, pewter, mahogany. By my second cup of coffee, I've decided on terra-cotta for the back room and bath, yellow for the main room. A warm, sunny yellow, like my little bedroom on the third floor of the Guillaumes' house in Toulouse.

My French immersion experience was just that—immersion. It was more than being in another city, another country, a different culture. It was like being a freshwater fish suddenly deposited in the Pacific Ocean—wildly disorienting. At first I floundered, exhausted by the sheer effort required for something as simple as asking directions and processing the response.

It wasn't quite the same as French class where the important topics of conversation included the weather—*Il fait beau aujourd'hui, n'est-ce pas?* Or the deviant behavior of various small animals—*Le chat est sur le lit et le chien est sous la table.* Everyone spoke rapidly, especially my peer group, and of course they never teach you slang in class. After my one attempt to just let it rip, when I called someone a *connard* (approximate translation, "shithead") instead of the more harmless *canard* (duck), I decided to stick with textbook French, even if it did sound rather stilted.

Sylvie's friends were all very nice to me, but I felt like Gulliver among the Lilliputians. Not one of them was over five-five, all thin and sylphlike in spite of the fact that they ate like stevedores. Most were pretty, but even those who weren't managed to be attractive simply by being French. They could wear jeans and a T-shirt and then just throw on a scarf or some leather high-heeled boots or a buttery-soft suede jacket or a trendy hat and look like something out of *Vogue*. And they knew how to do things. How to smoke or sit, how to walk across a room or a street, how to order an aperitif, while no one my age back home even knew what an aperitif was.

Dinner chez Guillaume was a thing I anticipated every day with dread. In addition to making polite conversation, and watching Sylvie to see what each spoon or fork was for, I tried desperately to figure out what I was eating before I took an irrevocable amount into my mouth.

Not until I'd been beaten down, like at boot camp, and accepted the fact that everything, including the air that I breathed, was totally alien, did I begin to relax. It happened suddenly, only two weeks into my stay. One night at dinner, I slumped in my chair, too dazed with fatigue to talk, to care if I was using the fish knife correctly, to wonder exactly what I was swallowing, and all at once the realization stole over me. I was getting at least the general drift of the conversation without even thinking about it. Probably because I wasn't thinking about it. Suddenly I sat taller in my chair. My eyes focused on Jean-Marc, over whose head I'd been staring, spaced out, and he gave me what for him was a pretty big grin.

"*Bienvenue,* Wynter," he said.

After that night, I settled in, feeling at long last that I was where I belonged. Class became less nerve-racking. At work I was able to focus on the baking instead of worrying about what people were saying to me and how I should reply. I was more comfortable hanging out at the cafés with Sylvie's group, checking out *les types,* the guys, or reading fashion magazines and listening to Francis Cabrel.

Not that it was effortless, but it was like running, the way you sometimes wear yourself out by pushing too hard. Your muscles burn from lactic acid, your body feels leaden, your lungs ache. And then when you think you can't go ten more yards, suddenly you hit your stride and the miles unwind beneath your feet and you could run all day.

On Saturday, the clouds part, and the sun spills down benevolently. I'll never take it for granted again. I catch the number 13 bus downtown, leaving all the windows open to air out the smell of paint, and conveniently forgetting that this weekend is the kickoff of Christmas shopping madness.

The overheated air inside Westlake Mall reeks of stale popcorn and a dozen different designer fragrances the stores are touting. It's wall-to-wall bodies in Williams-Sonoma and Timberland, Jessica McClintock, Godiva, and there's a steady drone, like a convention of angry bees. I push past an a cappella group dressed in Dickensian costume. Some fragment of melody or flick of a long skirt stirs memories of holiday parties in the big white house on Woodrow.

Every year we had an open house the first weekend in December, invited all our friends and everyone from JML, every client, potential client, and former client in David's files. That made it one big write-off. So we could have the trendiest caterer, a string quartet one year, a zydeco band, or another time, mariachis. Once we had a whole high school choir in the front yard, singing carols as everyone arrived. Okay, that was a bit over the top.

I have to get out of here. Through the glass doors, out into the crisp breeze. Holiday banners float from every light pole and the store windows are outlined in colored lights. A steel-drum band does their pleasantly tinny take on Christmas carols in front of Nordstrom, and the entire population of Seattle seems to be drinking Stewart Brothers coffee and grooving on the rare November sunshine. Bicycle messengers in their Day-Glo orange vests dart and weave through the throngs like bright tropical fish.

I wade into the crowd and out the other side, down to Second Avenue where the music is only a faint twang. Down here the buildings aren't renovated yet, their beaux arts friezes still black with grime. Whiskery old men in drab sweaters huddle in doorways, smoking, eyeing the hookers in satin shorts and high-heeled boots, goose bumps on their thighs.

In a junk shop where the sign advertises "Articles of Interest for the Collector," I buy a 1915 ladies' magazine full of botanical prints, and two ornate frames. Then it's down to Cost Plus for some red-and-yellow plaid bedspreads to tie over my ugly chairs and drape over curtain rods, a fake Tibetan rug to lay in front of the woodstove.

As I wend my way back up to Third Avenue, I notice the clouds have returned, but they're thin and pale and aloof, not the full-bellied, low-slung kind that promise more rain.

My house has the ambient temperature of a meat locker, but the paint smell has mostly dissipated. I dump all my packages on the futon and rush around slamming windows, starting a fire, turning on lamps, filling the teakettle. I remove my purchases from the bags, tear off the price tags, lay out the rug. I tie the makeshift slipcovers over the chairs and drape the faux curtains over the blackout shades. When the kettle boils, I make myself a cup of tea and set out some soup for dinner. While I drink my tea, I leaf through my ladies' magazine, deciding which botanical prints to frame.

I dial CM's number, but it rings and rings. The machine doesn't pick up, so I know she has it unplugged. I stare at the phone for a minute, finger on the hang-up gizmo, contemplate calling David. No. Kelley might answer. Or if David answered, he'd probably just be pissed off at me for bothering him.

I dial my mother.

"You've reached the Morrisons. None of us is available right now . . ."

At the beep. "Hi, Mom, it's me. I just wanted to say hi and see how you—"

"Hi, honey. How are you?" She's slightly breathless.

"I'm okay. How are you?"

"I'm fine." It sounds like a conversation between two telemarketers.

"Where have you been?"

"Nowhere. Why?"

"I've tried to call you a few times and you never seem to be home."

She laughs. "I'm working very hard, you know."

"At night?"

"Well, I go out occasionally. With friends and . . ." Her voice keeps trailing off, as if she's trying to talk to someone else at the same time.

"Are you dating anyone?"

Hesitation. "Yes, I suppose you could call it that." Her tone changes abruptly. "But how are you? Any news from David? Or your... Miss Goody?"

"It's Gooden. No news."

"What did you do for Thanksgiving?" she asks brightly.

"I painted."

"You painted? You mean, like pictures?"

"No, Mom. Like walls. I painted my house."

"Really?" There's a silence, and then she says, "That's interesting," in a way that lets me know she's not paying the slightest attention to anything I'm saying.

"Mother, do you have company?"

Another silence. "Yes, actually, I do. I have some... people over."

"Why didn't you just say so?"

"Because I wanted to talk to you, of course."

"You seem distracted. Why don't you give me a call when you're not busy?"

"I'm not busy, Wyn, it's just—"

She's still talking when I hang up.

After Thanksgiving, the bakery erupts into frenzied activity. Linda and I are making panettone and Ellen's mother's Hanukkah orange bread. Linda's not thrilled about having her routine disrupted, but I'm glad to be doing something new. Diane's taking orders for *bûches de Noël* (yule log cakes).

We all get to make cookies—Diane does gingerbread boys and girls in her inimitable style—one for every occupation and hobby imaginable, ballerina to dogcatcher. Customers fight over the ice skaters and skiers. Ellen has the rest of us working on French and Italian cookies. We make *brutti ma buoni* (ugly but good), bites of almond paste clogged with candied citrus peel; buttery *baci di dama* (lady's kisses); *zaletti*, raisin-cornmeal cookies; hazelnut *biscotti*; and sesame-seed wafers. We make *dentelles Russes* (Russian lace cookies) pungent with dark rum, sandy-golden *sablés, carrés aux marrons* (chestnut squares) glazed with bittersweet chocolate, and, of course, madeleines.

The display case looks like a cover shot for *Bon Appétit,* and I love the richness of different tastes and textures. But one morning as I stand admiring the bounty, a memory of my oma's plain, round cookies decorated with colored sugar dredges up an old happiness that's more like an ache. The second I'm inside my door, I'm on the phone to my mother. Of course, she's already left for work.

"Hi, Mom, it's me," I tell the machine. "I was just calling to say hi. Again. By the way, do you have Oma's sugar cookie recipe? I'm going to bed pretty soon, but I'll be up about three-thirty. Could you call me tonight?"

Her voice is all chirpy when she calls back. Must've been a good day. "I found Oma's recipe," she says. "Shall I fax it to you at the bakery tomorrow?"

"The bakery doesn't have a fax machine."

She's lost her place in the world for a second. "They don't have a fax? How can any business compete in today's—"

"Mom, it's not a business with a capital *B,* okay? It's a small bakery. Very low-tech. I was hoping you could just read it to me."

"Of course. Got a pen?"

Oma's Sugar Cookies

1 cup cold butter, cut into small pieces
1 cup granulated sugar
2 eggs
1 teaspoon vanilla
3 cups flour
1 teaspoon baking soda
1 teaspoon cream of tartar
¼ teaspoon salt
Grated zest of one lemon

Granulated sugar for rolling cookies
1 cup confectioners' sugar
2 tablespoons lemon juice or milk

Cut the butter into the sugar until the mixture resembles oatmeal. Beat in eggs and vanilla. Sift together flour, soda, cream of tartar, and salt. Add to butter mixture along with lemon zest and beat with wooden spoon until blended.

Preheat oven to 350°F and lightly butter cookie sheets. Knead dough for 15 to 20 minutes, adding a little more flour if necessary to prevent sticking. Roll dough into walnut-size balls and roll balls in granulated sugar to coat completely. Place on prepared cookie sheets. Using bottom of a glass dipped in granulated sugar, flatten each ball to about a ¼-inch thickness. Bake for 12 to 15 minutes, until light brown. Using spatula, transfer to cooling rack. Glaze while still hot, if desired, with mixture of confectioners' sugar and lemon juice or milk. Makes about 5 dozen.

"Thanks." I shake the cramp out of my hand. "I'd forgotten the kneading part."

"That's what gives them that great texture." Her voice goes all dreamy with nostalgia.

I hesitate. "Thanks for calling me back. I'm sorry about hanging up last time I—"

"No, it's okay. I was distracted. I'm sorry, too."

"How's the job going?"

"It's a lot more challenging than working at Hubbell."

"David used to say 'challenging' was a euphemism for pain in the ass."

"Actually, I'm enjoying it. I'm learning so much. How's the baker's life?"

"I like it. Except the woman I have to work with is . . . challenging." She laughs and then a silence plops down between us like a fat lady in the middle seat on a plane.

"What are your plans for Christmas?" I ask. "I only have one day off, so I can't go anywhere. I was sort of wondering if you might want to come up here. My place is small, but I think we could—"

"Oh, Wyn, I'd love to, but— I wish you'd asked me sooner. I'm going to Tahoe with some people from the office."

"That's okay. I just thought if you weren't doing anything."

"I'm sort of committed. We've made deposits."

"It's okay." I don't want to be pissed off, but I am. She's only been working there since September, and they're chummy enough to go spend Christmas together? She didn't even bother to find out what I was doing.

"I could see if I can get a refund."

"Mother, stop. It's okay, really."

"I hate for you to spend Christmas alone."

"I'm not going to be alone. I've had two people from work invite me for dinner, and if CM's here, I'll be with her. Listen, I need to go eat something. And I've got stuff to do before work. So, I'll talk to you."

"Wyn, I'm sorry about Christmas."

"I'll come home this spring for a few days."

It isn't a total lie. Tyler and Ellen both invited me for Christmas Day dinner. But I envisioned myself making polite conversation with their families and sitting through endless explanations of family rituals and cute little stories about the year Uncle George set Muffy the cat on fire while lighting the candles, and then I declined as graciously as possible.

December 15—my thirty-second birthday. My mother has sent me a check and a card. She calls at 9 A.M., forgetting that I sleep in the morning, so she's embarrassed and I'm grouchy. CM calls next, from her grant-writing seminar in Phoenix.

Last year—where was I? Oh, yes. My mother's house. David had to be at a client meeting in Cancun or someplace. But two years ago, on my thirtieth, he took me to Paris for a long weekend. It was our first time away together in over a year, and it was like a second honeymoon. We stayed at the Ritz, sleeping late every morning, waking up to make love and eat perfect croissants dunked in steaming *chocolat chaud*. Every afternoon we walked the boulevards in the winter darkness. The naked trees scratched at the steely sky and the city glowed like a giant lantern, lit from within. We rode the *bateau mouche* one night, bundled up against the icy wind, and my birthday dinner was at Taillevent. I felt like a princess. Is it possible that he's forgotten the date?

I get up and take a Tylenol PM, unplug the phone, and float away into a dream.

First day in a new school. Unsure where to go, I wander down long halls with closed doors on both sides. The other students are all taller than I am, and they smile at each other over my head.

Finally, I come to a classroom with the door standing open. People are going in, so I follow them, but there's no place left for me to sit. Everyone's already working on something. Then a girl in the back gets up from her desk and comes over to me, putting her arm around me. It's my mother. I go limp with relief. I know she'll show me what to do.

She takes me back to her desk, sits down, goes back to what she's working on. I just stand there watching her. She looks at me and smiles from time to time, but it's clear I'm not going to get any direction from her.

At Thriftway that afternoon, I buy all purpose flour and granulated sugar and a box of food colorings. In the parking lot, couples are picking out trees; women are buying garlands and waterproof bows while their kids run splashing through puddles. Everyone's bundled up in heavy coats, with bright mufflers and knit caps, and there's an old guy in a patched sport coat, roasting chestnuts on a little brazier. I buy a small bag, and as the first one crumbles into creamy smoke between my teeth, I know I have to have a tree.

Linda has a black eye. Actually, "black eye" is something of a misnomer. It's more a hideous purple-green, and the white of the eye has a slick red patch along one side from a broken blood vessel. Her lower lip is twice its normal size.

It's not the sort of thing you can pretend not to notice, so I say, "What the hell happened to you?"

"My ex-old man, that's what happened to me," she says.

"I hope you gave as good as you got."

"That I did, missy. That I did." She cracks a tiny smile. "Stupid son of a bitch came over drunk. Howlin' like a coyote. I had to let him in before somebody called the cops. 'Course then he tries to get all lovey-dovey, and when I told him to stick it in a knothole, he hauled off and slugged me." She touches her jaw tentatively. "We mixed it up pretty good before a couple of the neighbors came down and threw him out."

"Are you going to press charges?"

Her expression is contemptuous. "Big waste of time. Mine, mostly."

"You could get a restraining order..."

Her laughter is wheezy, and she flinches from the pain. "What am I gonna do? Say, 'Lookey here, Bubba, this paper says you can't come around me'? Restraining order, my ass. I could paper my walls with 'em."

All at once she remembers who she's talking to, and she's especially pissed off because I look sympathetic. "Nothing you'll ever have to worry about, missy."

Christmas morning I wake up at five o'clock. I should have kept to my schedule, as Linda's forever preaching, but I couldn't face being up all Christmas Eve with nothing to do but remember other Christmas Eves. I turn over. It's still dark, maybe I can go back to sleep. Too late, I wish I'd made some plans for today. Just going through the motions is hard, but sometimes not going through the motions is worse.

At seven-thirty, I get up, wrap a blanket around me, curl up in the chair. A red and shrunken remnant of last night's fire glows in the stove. The smell of wood smoke carries memories of Christmases at Lake Tahoe, the cabin we used to rent. My father loved spending Christmas in the mountains. I think it reminded him of his New England childhood, and there was always the tantalizing possibility of snow. I lay in my loft bed every night of the holiday and prayed for a blizzard. I wanted to be stranded in our cabin, with my dad building huge blazes in the fireplace and my mother making hot chocolate with little marshmallows bobbing on top.

Every year, my mother complained about the cold, but she seemed to enjoy it once we were there. She would sit on the couch by the fire and read, absently munching popcorn, while my dad and I went walking in the afternoons. And at night, too, if there was a moon. Each year as I marched behind him, I noted the size of my footprints in his. The air was silent, cold and so crystalline you thought it would shatter and fall to the ground in icy fragments at the slightest noise. We never talked on those hikes. If he wanted to show me something, he would point to it. The only sounds were the puffs of our breath, the crackle of dry pine straw, or the squeak of new powder under our boots, and once, the glorious whoosh of a huge barn owl passing right above our heads.

We always had a little tree that we cut ourselves, and we made decorations from popcorn and cranberries and gingerbread and paper. That was my mother's turf. She had learned origami from a Japanese friend of her father's, and she fashioned birds and stars, cats and dogs, trees and angels. She would make tiny holes in both ends of an eggshell, blow the egg out, and then meticulously paint the shell. She could sit and work on those things for hours, like the sailors who carved scrimshaw by lantern light during long nights at sea.

It's hard to accept that she could traipse off to Tahoe with a bunch of perfect strangers, when it was our place for Christmas with my dad. I wonder if she's sitting around in front of the fire complaining of the cold like she did with us, or if she's all bundled up out in the snow, being a good sport so everyone will say, "That Johanna! She's up for anything, isn't she?"

Christmas always turned David into an Armani-wearing, Mercedes-driving ten-year-old boy. Every night when he got home from work we had to sit down together and read all the cards that had come in the mail that day. And there were dozens, mostly from business acquaintances who were artists, designers, writers, so each one was a miniature work of art. We displayed them all over the house, along with miles of garland and shimmery silver ribbon. It was the only time of the year he could tolerate clutter.

We had to have a big tree—eight-, nine-, once a ten-footer. It had to be flocked, and it had to be decorated in white and silver balls, clear glass icicles, and tiny white lights. We always had a fire in the fireplace and mulled wine to drink. Those years when southern California spent December basking in eighty-degree temperatures we simply turned the A.C. on full blast and proceeded as usual.

He was an extravagant and imaginative Santa. And after the presents were opened, there was always one more, something special, hidden somewhere in the house. One Christmas Eve when we went upstairs to bed, an exquisite gown of pale yellow silk was draped over my pillow. Another year, a diamond tennis bracelet was casually fastened around my Christmas stocking like an anklet; another time, tickets for a cruise were rolled up inside a toy boat floating in the Jacuzzi.

This morning I can't help wondering what he's giving Kelley. What she's giving him.

Hopefully, something that requires penicillin.

By nine-thirty the grayness that passes for winter morning light is spilling into the darkest corners of the room. I stand up, stretch, decide not to spend the day moping. I feed the fire, put on my stovetop espresso pot, and drag my two unopened presents out of the closet.

I open the one from CM first. It looks like two very large blue baked potatoes. On the end of the box, it says "Down Booties, size 10." I smile. My ever practical friend remembers that my feet are perpetually freezing. I pull them on, walk around. They have inch-and-a-half-thick foam soles, and they make my feet look approximately the size of rowboats, but within five minutes my toes are warm.

My mother's present is a hand-knit fisherman's sweater, made from a rag yarn the color of oatmeal. I wonder which of her Christmas bazaars it came from. Underneath it in the box are two cotton turtlenecks, one purple, one teal, and a check for a hundred dollars.

Well. That was fun. I put the butter into the freezer to make it easier to cut into pieces, set the eggs out to come to room temperature.
Collect the flour and the sugar and the food coloring together on the
table. I suppose there are worse ways to spend Christmas Day than
making cookies.

Out on the porch in my new down booties, I sip at my espresso,
hardly feeling the dew that soaks into my sweatpants. Fog obscures the
outline of the big house, and hemlock branches poke out of the mist like
the arms of sleepwalkers. I've consumed about half my coffee when I
notice my little Douglas fir tree sitting on the bottom step. In the mad
whirl of my holiday social activities, I forgot to take Doug inside. He
was probably happier out here, anyway. I pick up the pot and bury my
nose in his soft green needles, sparkling with tiny droplets. The clean,
aromatic scent is simultaneously piercing and calming. I'd thought I was
all cried out, but apparently not.

Walking to work is cold, but so many houses have Christmas trees in the
windows and those tiny white lights draped all over their shrubs that it's
like walking through fairyland. Even if you're lonely, it's nearly impossible to be sad in the face of this fantasy. And I'm beginning to feel the
first rumblings of resentment at David for acting like I don't exist. Kind
of a good feeling.

Linda seems subdued tonight, not so much as a sneer about the
cookies I brought her. That's what Christmas does—brings out the vul-
nerability, even in people who are mostly immune to the ravages of sentiment. Of course, she doesn't thank me either.

"What did you do today?" I ask as we're loading the first batch of
bread into the oven.

She shrugs. "Just another day, far as I'm concerned. Got up at four.
Had some soup. A little company." This last part is so quiet I almost
miss it.

"Company? Your ex?"

"Huh. Not likely. He probably passed out about noon. My kids."

"I didn't know you had children," I lie.

"Why would you?" She glowers. "Sometimes I don't even know I have 'em. They only show up on holidays. And only if they think there's somethin' in it for 'em."

"How many do you have?"

"Two."

"Boys? Girls?"

"Boy and a girl."

I slide the last two loaves off the peel onto the baking tiles of the top deck. "What are their names?"

"What difference does it make to you, missy?"

"I was just curious."

She looks over the tops of her glasses at me. "Didn't you ever hear what bein' curious done to the cat? Kilt him, that's what."

"Okay, forget it." I open the notebook, start setting up ingredients for the cinnamon-raisin and cheddar-cheese breads.

"You been doin' this for three months now. Haven't you got those recipes memorized yet?"

"Nope." I try to keep my voice cheerful.

"Kinda slow on the uptake, aren't you?"

I snip the string on a bag of white flour and pull the threads till I find the one that unravels the closure. "I forget everything as soon as I walk out that door, and that's a good thing. Because if I remembered every day that I had to come to work with you, I'd probably never come back."

She snickers, reveling in her image as the Bad Ass Baker from Hell.

The bakery's quiet since a lot of people aren't going to work today. After Linda leaves, I make myself a decaf espresso and take a table in the front. Ellen comes over to sit with me.

"Post-holiday slump," she mutters, dropping into the chair. She has circles under her dark eyes. "Had twenty people for dinner yesterday. And I'm Jewish, for Pete's sake. Lloyd's family. Those cookies of your

Nine

‫⬥‬

I've never been a big celebrant of New Year's Eve. I prefer going to
sleep in the old year and waking up with the new one firmly in place
and functioning. In grammar school and junior high, CM and I
always took turns staying over at each other's houses. If the adults were
having a party, we skulked around watching everyone get drunker and
sillier as midnight approached. We usually got a thimbleful of champagne at the appropriate time, and then we volunteered to help clean up
so we could polish off the leftover drinks and food.

In high school and college, there were the usual drunken orgies, but
I never enjoyed them, and I don't think CM really did either, although
she talked a good game. For us, the best part of any New Year was
watching the Rose Parade on TV in the morning while we stuffed ourselves with leftover Christmas cookies or cold pizza from the night
before.

This year, she shows up on my porch at five o'clock on New Year's
Eve, carrying bags of food from the Market. A wedge of Stilton, some
Brie and Parmesan, vegetables to be made into soup, and three bottles
of champagne from Pike & Western Wine Shop. And a small gold box
containing six chocolate truffles, for medicinal purposes.

"What smells so good?" She takes off her coat, hangs it on one of the
hooks I pounded into the wall by the door.

grandmother's were great, by the way. I think next year we'll do those here." She rolls her head around, rubs the back of her neck. "This is where I carry all my stress. What did you do? Weren't you going to CM's?"

"I was, but she ended up going to L.A."

"So you were alone? I wish you'd called. I could have used the moral support."

"That's nice of you, but I wasn't up to being with a bunch of people."

She smiles. "Who said anything about being with people? I would have come over to your place and hid from them all." She pushes up the sleeves of her black knit dress, leaving floury prints. "I should never wear black to work. Look at that." Her eyes slide over to me. "Did you hear from Shithead?"

"No." I blot my eyes with a napkin. "Didn't really expect to, though."

She puts her arm around my shoulders for a minute. "We never expect, but we always hope. That's the bitch of it."

I set the bags on my new drop-leaf table. "You're my guinea pig for a new bread. Yeasted orange poppyseed."

"Always glad to oblige. Hey..." She does a 360. "This looks fabulous. I can't believe it's the same place." She wanders into the bedroom, now my office/den, where I put the desk and the wing-back chair. "These colors are terrific. Where'd you get these botanical prints? I love it." Back in the main salon, she admires the watercolor I paid Tyler twenty-five dollars for, the curtains and slipcovers made of plaid bedspreads. "Oh, I love paperwhites. They smell so good." Her shrewd green eyes focus on me. "Quite a little nest you've made yourself. Or maybe I should say a cocoon."

I laugh. "Yeah, it's a cocoon. I'm going in as a butterfly and coming out as a caterpillar."

"A reversal of fortune." She smiles. "By the way, have you talked to Jerkoff?"

I shake my head. "I tried to call him last week and his assistant said he was out of the office for the holidays. He's probably up at Aspen with Barbarella."

"Barbarella? Let's see. Would that be the love child of Barbie and Godzilla?"

I laugh again—twice in five minutes is pretty good. "Something like that. I here." I hand her one of the bottles of champagne, stash the other two in the fridge. "Open that puppy. Let the party begin."

She pours two glasses and we settle in to scrub and chop vegetables for our soup.

For a while we work in one of those silences that's only possible between two people who know each other so well that conversation is superfluous. I'm thinking about times past and I know she is, too, probably the same ones. But when the champagne in our glasses reaches a certain level, she starts telling me about her work in progress, set to Canteloube's *Chants d'Auvergne.*

"What's it about?"

She smiles patiently. "There's not much of a story. Canteloube was from the Auvergne and this work was sort of a hymn to the region. The music is gorgeous; it's for orchestra and one soprano voice." Her face takes on a rapt expression. "The choreography starts with a solo female dancer—namely, me—and then the others join her. All during the piece they're moving together and apart, so the number of dancers visible is constantly shifting." I sit there, nodding, not saying a word, until she looks up from the carrot she's mutilating.

"Neal called me on Christmas Eve."

"And?"

Her posture is a study in nonchalance. "He said he wants to see me. He's in Palo Alto right now, but he's coming up here for a seminar in February. He wants to have dinner. Or something."

I smile and throw a handful of green beans into the pot. "It's those 'or something's' you have to watch. What did you tell him?"

"I said I'd think about it."

"I assume you've thought about it by now." When I stir the onions that are slowly caramelizing in olive oil, their sweet, musky fragrance fills the room.

Heavy sigh. "I actually haven't thought about much else in the last week." She gives me a pleading look. "Help me out here. Tell me what to do."

I hand her the church key. "For starters, open these."

In spite of the fact that she's never been shy about trashing David, I've always been reluctant to criticize Neal. I think it's the old reverse psychology. Whenever my parents criticized some guy I was seeing, I became even more enamored of him. "You probably couldn't find anyone less qualified to offer relationship advice."

The chicken broth gurgles as she pours it on top of the vegetables. "No fair copping out. When you needed advice, I told you to get a job."

"You already have a job. Do you want to see him?"

"I must, or why would I be agonizing over it?" She tosses the cans into my recycle bin.

"Problem solved." I ransack my pantry, pulling out bay leaves and peppercorns, and add them to the pot.

When she shakes her head, her hair flows from side to side, catching the light in its red-gold depths, just like in the shampoo commercials. If she wasn't my best friend, she'd be easy to hate. "You don't think it's a good idea, do you?" she says.

I rest my chin on my hands. "It doesn't really matter what I think, if you want to see him again. Maybe it would be good. Maybe you've both learned something. If not, at least you won't have to waste any more time wondering what might have happened."

"Very sensible indeed." She finishes chopping the last carrot and throws it into the pot. This is obviously what I was supposed to say.

I dump the sautéed onions into the pot and light the burner. She refills our glasses and puts out a bowl of *picholines*, the little green French olives that we both adore. We curl up on the futon in the warmth from the woodstove to listen to *Motown's Greatest Hits* and watch the old year die.

Ever since I moved into my first apartment with CM our junior year in college, my mother and I have had an unspoken agreement. She doesn't call me unless there's a pretty compelling reason. So when my phone rings the afternoon of January first, it doesn't occur to me that it might be her, even though I haven't talked to her since Christmas Eve. In fact, when I hear her voice, my heart stops.

"Mom, what's wrong?"

Her laugh tinkles up the telephone line. "Nothing, honey. I just have some news. I'm getting married."

I slide into the club chair. "Married?" Oh, God. I'm going to have a cop for a stepfather.

"Richard has asked me to marry him."

"Who?"

"Richard. Richard Travers. The architect. My boss."

"What about Ed?"

"What about him? I haven't seen him since you left."

"Mother, who is this guy? I don't even know him." I have the sensation of being in a Fellini movie.

"You will."

"Well. Congratulations."

"You don't sound convinced." She laughs, but there's an edge to it.

"Should I squeal?"

"Wynter." She's trying to be patient. "I know you're going to like him. He's a wonderful man. We've been working together very closely ever since I started there and we've been almost inseparable for the last month."

"Are you sleeping with him?"

A short silence. "That's none of your business."

"Well, don't you think I should get to meet this person before you go running off to get married?"

Now she's laughing so hard I'm afraid she's going to choke.

"What is so goddamn funny?"

Every time I think she's winding down, she gets hysterical again. "Oh, Wyn . . . you . . . if you could . . . oh, God, if you could hear what you sound like . . ." This is followed by gasping for breath and some little groaning noises. Then she blows her nose. "Wyn? Are you there? I'm sorry, honey, but you sound like my mother."

I think if you feel faint, you're supposed to put your head down between your knees. So the blood rushes to the brain. It just makes my head hurt.

"I don't know what to say." I sit back up.

"How about 'Congratulations, Mom, I'm really happy for you'?"

"You haven't even been working there that long. What do you really know about him? Maybe he's a con artist who preys on lonely widows. Maybe schizophrenia runs in his family. He could have a crim-inal record or a wife in Toronto or—"

She's still laughing. "He's divorced. Trust me, I know what I need to know. Besides, the wedding's not till February fourteenth—corny, isn't it? That gives me two extra months to discover Dr. Jekyll."

"Mr. Hyde. Dr. Jekyll was the good guy."

"Wyn, I want you to be my maid of honor." As if she's making me a peer of the realm.

"Well ... okay."

"Okay?" Her voice is rapier sharp.

"What the hell do you expect me to say? I don't even know the guy. You're sneaking around seeing him—"

"Don't be ridiculous. We're two single adults. There's no reason why we shouldn't see each other."

"Well, you work in the same office. I'm sure they don't know anything about it."

"Of course they do."

"Does his family know about it?"

"His son knows, yes."

"But you didn't tell me?"

"Why would I tell you?"

"Because ... just because. Why wouldn't you tell me?"

"Quite frankly, I didn't think you'd be interested. You never seemed to be when you had David and—"

"What's that supposed to mean?"

"Exactly this, Wyn. When you were married and had a wonderful, exciting life, there wasn't a lot going on between you and me. Now, suddenly, because you're lonely and unhappy, you want me to confide in you."

The conversation has become a runaway train, captive of its own momentum. I want to hang up, but I can't. Neither can I make a single word come out of my mouth. I stare at Tyler's watercolor of Pioneer Square with diagonal slashes of rain, umbrella-toting tourists.

"Wyn? Are you there?"

"I'm here."

"I'm sorry. I shouldn't have said that." I notice she doesn't say she didn't mean it. "I was so happy and I wanted you to be, too. I wasn't even thinking what a shock it would be for you. I'm sorry, honey. Please don't be upset."

One long exhale. Then I hear myself say, "I'm not upset. I'm just surprised. Sort of disappointed that you didn't tell me before. That's all."

"Does that mean you'll come?"

"I'll be there if you want me."

"Of course I do. Valentine's Day's a Saturday. Do you think you can take off work and—"

"Not a problem."

"I can send you a ticket if—"

"I can afford a ticket. Maybe I'll even bring CM."

"That would be nice." The silence winds out till it's about to snap. "Well...I guess I should let you go. I'm sure you have things to do. We'll talk again soon."

I open my door and stand in the freshening air, goose bumps racing up and down my arms. Three-thirty in the afternoon and darkness is coming on fast. Gusts of wind thrash the hemlocks. I need to get out of here before I start breaking windows. I pull on my new sweater and my rain parka and head out the door, my hair streaming out behind me. By the time I reach Queen Anne Avenue, the sidewalk is spotted with tiny, dark star bursts, and then the rain arrives in earnest. I flounced out of the house without my umbrella, so in a very few minutes, I manage to absorb quite a lot of water. I run from one closed shop to another, sheltering in doorways. It's New Year's Day. Nothing's going to be open. I dash under Bailey's ragged green awning and lean panting against the rough wooden door. It swings inward. I follow it, shivering and waterlogged, looking around in the dim light. It's a funky joint. One of those places where the floor smells like it's absorbed more beer than the clientele, and right now it's empty.

Then I see the bartender. He has his back to me, drying glasses and putting them away. He turns around, surprised. "Sorry, we're not open till five." Then he laughs. "God, you're soaked."

"You have a gift for stating the obvious." I turn back to the door.

"Hey, come on in. You can stay if you want. I just can't serve you till five. Go sit by the fire and I'll get you some towels." He disappears through the swinging doors at the end of the bar, and I hang my dripping coat on the rack. The place is bigger than it looks from outside. There's a pool table in the back, a fireplace burning cozily on one wall, four tables, half a dozen booths. My shoes squish wetly as I drag a chair up to the fire, sit down, stretch out my legs.

He hands me two white towels and sets a steaming mug on the table. "It's just hot tea." He grins. "But I accidentally spilled some brandy in it when I reached for the towels." He puts a bear-shaped plastic bottle of honey down next to it. "Let me know if you want more."

"Thanks." I blot the water out of my hair, which is already kinking like mad, hand the first towel back to him, sopping wet. He takes it away and resumes drying glasses while I sit watching him. He's tall and his brown hair is cut extremely short, but instead of bristling like a crew cut, it lays down soft and close to his head, like a child's hair.

I squirt a golden rope of honey into the mug and stir it around. My first sip gets me a noseful of brandy and starts the heat radiating out from my core. I settle into the chair. After a few minutes, he must feel my eyes boring into his back, because he turns around. "You okay?"

"I don't mean to stare, but do I know you from someplace?"

He looks sheepish. "Launderland. I think I've seen you there. I'm the one with the notebook."

"Oh, right." I remember him now, head bent, scribbling furiously. He hovers over the notebook the way you did in school so no one could cheat off your test. "So what are you writing?"

"Nothing exciting. A journal." He scoops out a dish of something and brings it over to me. Peanuts. "Just throw the shells on the floor. It's a tradition." He parks his butt on the edge of the table. "You haven't been here before, have you?"

"No." I smile without understanding why. "I didn't plan on coming here tonight, but I thought if I didn't get out of the house I might start smashing things."

"Cabin fever."

"I guess I'm not used to the rain yet."

"It takes a while. Some people never get used to it. Where're you from?"

"Los Angeles."

His eyebrows go up, making his dark eyes look huge. "What brings you up here? Or shouldn't I ask?"

His face is open, direct, pleasantly anonymous. Like a priest. You want to tell him your life story. "Asking's your job, isn't it? Bartender slash therapist?"

"Not much of a therapist. I'm a good listener, though. And very discreet."

"Sometimes that's all a therapist is."

"Good point. By the way, I'm Mac McLeod." He holds out his hand.

"Wyn Fr—Morrison." We shake, and his hand is cool and smooth except for a callus at the bend of his thumb.

"I better finish getting set up. You want some more tea?"

"Well…"

He picks up the mug. "Come sit at the bar and keep me company."

He sets my refill down on a Red Hook coaster. I sip in silence, letting my eyes wander over the rows of bottles behind the bar. On the liqueur shelf, electric-green Midori, golden Galliano, red Campari, Chartreuse, the warm amber of Courvoisier, deep-berry Chambord, red-black port, and startling blue Curaçao. They remind me of this drink my father liked to make when he had an audience.

"Do you know what a pousse café is?" I ask him.

He sets down a stack of napkins and gives it a sharp little twist with his knuckles, so that it fans out into a spiral. "Let's see—grenadine and crème de menthe and Chartreuse…I forget the others. Not many people around here would even know what it is, much less ask for one."

"You forgot my favorite—*crème de violette*." I can see my father pouring each liqueur carefully over the back of a spoon so it would sit on top of the one below, not mixing, looking like a rainbow in a tall skinny glass.

"How do you know about a pousse café?"

"My father. He didn't drink them, but he liked to make them."

"So what does he drink?"

"Not much, these days. Unless they serve Manhattans on the other side."

"The what?"

"He's dead."

"Sorry."

"He liked a dry martini every once in a while, too."

"Sounds like a man's man."

I rest my elbows on the bar. "He was an everybody's man. People loved him."

He slices a lemon with surgical precision, filling an old-fashioned glass with quarter circles of yellow. "Your mother live in L.A.?"

"She's getting married." I drink some more tea. It's odd saying it to him, but not uncomfortable. I guess because he doesn't know me.

"Do you like the guy?"

"Never met the guy." Two tears surprise me by running down my face. I look around, as if someone might be watching, but there's only him, and he doesn't say anything. He just sets a clean bar towel down in front of me and goes back to slicing a lime.

"How long has your dad been gone?"

I give my face a quick pass with the towel. "Almost fifteen years."

"Your mom's been alone all this time?"

"She never even dated much until...recently. I guess. I mean, she doesn't tell me anything." He lets that one percolate while he opens a white canvas bag, starts counting money into the register drawer. "You like this? Being a bartender?"

Over here, under the hanging light, I see that his eyes aren't really brown, but somewhere between gray and green. "There's worse ways to make a living." He laughs. "And I've done most of them."

He cleans his hands and pushes the Play button on a dinosaur of a reel-to-reel tape player. A piano kicks off some kind of jazz lite riff and he looks apologetic. "I know. It's awful. Harte likes elevator music during the week. He buys these god-awful prerecorded tapes from a mail-order catalog. Like *The 101 Strings Play John Lennon.*"

"That sounds pretty scary. Who's Harte?"

"The owner. On weekends I play what I like."

"Which is?"

"Friday night is blues night. Saturday's sort of eclectic—rock plus whatever else talks to me."

"Does Mozart ever talk to you?"

He shakes his head, laughing. "Never. Although I throw in a couple of arias now and then."

"Opera?"

"Sure. It's a distant cousin to the blues. Same worldview, don't you think? Life sucks."

The door rattles open and a white-haired man in a plaid wool jacket comes in, shakes off the rain. He gives Mac a nod, like he sees him every night, and shuffles over to my vacant chair by the fire.

"Hi, Morey. ESB?"

The guy takes off a Seattle SuperSonics baseball cap and slaps it against his knee, sending a shower of spray hissing into the flames. "No hurry. She's prettier 'n me."

"Where do you work?" Mac says.

"Queen Street Bakery." Before he can ask, I say, "I bake bread."

"How'd you get into that?"

"It's a long story. Too long for tonight. I have to get ready for work."

"Next time, then." He draws a Red Hook ESB and takes it to the guy in the plaid jacket.

Outside, the rain hasn't stopped so much as paused, and the air is cold and scoured clean.

Okay. Next time.

There were basically two ways to do anything at the Boulangerie du Pont: Jean-Marc's way and the wrong way. So I learned his way, one step at a time, one day at a time: *le pétrissage,* the mixing and kneading; *le pointage,* the first rising; *donner un tour,* to punch down the dough; *le pesage,* the scaling or weighing to make loaves of the prescribed weight; *le façonnage,* the shaping; *l'apprêt,* the proofing; *le coup de lame,* slashing the loaves; and *la cuisson,* the baking.

The mixing and kneading were all done by machine, but the loaves still had to be shaped by hand. It was hard work physically and it was hard to remember the different techniques for all the different shapes: *la baguette, l'epée, la couronne, le bâtard, le boulot, la boule.*

One morning, Jean-Marc brought me a metal bucket of dough that had somehow failed to meet his standards for bread. He cut it into one-pound chunks and showed me how to form a small round *boule* and a *boulot,* or torpedo. I watched as he dragged the dough along the work-table. The bottom stuck to the table, causing the top skin of dough to tighten, and the mass rounded itself into a perfect dome. Simple enough.

Then I tried it. I pushed too hard and flattened the dough, so I pushed more gently and succeeded only in rolling the ball over so that it looked like an upended turtle. He watched me in silence, and I had the sense that he was biting the inside of his cheek to keep from laughing or shouting at me. After I'd tried three more times without producing that perfect, smooth dome, I looked up apprehensively. His face was impassive.

"You must practice a long time, Wynter," he said. "You do not have the . . ." His hand made a circular motion just above the table.

"The touch." I sighed.

"*Oui.* The touch. *Ne vous inquietez pas.* It will come." He placed his hand on my forearm, and I stared at the fine dusting of flour that covered the olive skin all the way to the elbow. "*Vous êtes trés forte.* Very strong. *C'est bon.*"

Besides learning to make bread and studying French language and culture, I was hoping to put my virginity to rest on French soil. It had become an embarrassment. It was the seventies, after all. Everybody was doing everybody. And here I was still walking around *virgo intacta.*

I found no shortage of candidates in my afternoon classes at the university. There was a dark, doe-eyed Parisian boy, pale and slender like a starving artist. An English guy, all crisp profile and soft, shaggy blond hair. Sylvie had a few cute cousins—rugged Gascon football-playing boys. The problem was, I was in love with Jean-Marc. I compared them all to him, and they came up looking green and silly. And after waiting this long, I wasn't about to jump in the sack with the first *beauzeau* that floated down the river. I was determined to have Jean-Marc, so I set about trying to figure out how and when to seduce him.

As it turned out, the when part was easy. Jean-Marc and Sylvie's *grandmère* lived near Saint-Antonin-Noble-Val, a beautiful little village on the Aveyron River about an hour from Toulouse. Nearly every weekend, the whole family went to stay at her *demeure,* an ancient pile of stone near a fortified mill. She was a stiff old broad and stone-deaf, but that didn't excuse anyone from making polite conversation with her. It was pretty tedious.

The best part of the weekend was Sunday afternoon. After the two-hour, five-course *déjeuner,* everyone would embark on a stroll down one of the paths by the river. Everyone, that is, except Jean-Marc, whose work ethic would have shamed the Puritans. Indolence of any kind made him uncomfortable, so he usually found some work around the house to attend to while the other dozen of us headed off for the after-noon constitutional. It occurred to me soon enough that this would be the perfect time to make my move.

One Sunday when everyone was arranged on rocks by the river, like an Impressionist painting, napping or watching the rowboats drift by, I headed back to the house on the pretext of retrieving my book. Sylvie gave me a strange look, but she didn't say anything. When I think about it—even after all these years—I still feel incredibly stupid. I mean, Jean-Marc was thirty-something years old and French. He'd probably seen it all. But I blithely assumed he was secretly pining for me. Wasn't I from California?

I found him on a ladder, trimming the creeper vines that were threatening to swallow Grandmère's caretaker cottage.

"Wynter, what are you doing?"

I gave him my best smile. "I forgot my book." I went up to the house and rifled through my suitcase, only then remembering that I hadn't brought a book with me. Oh well. I tried to walk at a leisurely pace back down to the cottage.

"Have you found it?"

"No, I must have forgotten it." I leaned against the wall of the house, in the shade, watching him. We chatted a little. He kept looking down, probably trying to figure out what the hell I was doing. Or maybe he knew.

"You should go back to the river," he said gently. "Where it is cooler."

"It's so damp down there." I piled my hair up on my head and leaned back, the better to give him a good view of my neck. I'd seen Raquel Welch do it in a movie.

Finally, he finished the job and got down off the ladder. He came over and picked up a cleaning rag he'd left on a small table. He began to wipe the pruners slowly and deliberately. He must have cleaned them for ten minutes while I stared at the curly black hair on his arms. My heart was fluttering like an injured bird and my head was full of the scents of tobacco and coffee and bread—yes, and sweat—that clung to him.

He set down the pruners and the rag, but he didn't move. I thought if he didn't either kiss me or get away from me, I'd faint. We made eye contact.

"Jean-Marc..."

"*Oui?*"

I took a deep breath. "Would you like to kiss me?"

I've always been grateful to him for not laughing. He sighed. He raised his heavy eyebrows. "*Bien sûr,* Wynter. What man would not like to kiss you? But then what will happen?"

I had my fantasies, of course, but I wasn't exactly clear on the progression of events.

He tilted his head to look at me. "Suppose for a moment that I desire to kiss you and we find ourselves *en amoureux.* There is more to love than kissing, as you know. I cannot compromise a young woman who I have promised to protect. *Ce n'est pas bon.*"

I was twisting my class ring around and around my finger. "I'm an adult, Jean-Marc. I don't need protection."

"*Oui,* but then consider what happens. We have a brief love affair, which is not good for our work together. We part sadly." He ran a hand through his short, wiry hair, causing it to stand up adorably. "Or, I suppose we can marry." He paused. The look on my face must have made great stories for years to come. "You will, *bien sûr,* become *Catholique.* And we must live in the house with my mother."

"Well..." I stammered.

"You will cook and keep the house and have children. At least four, possibly five or six. My mother will take care of them and you will run the shop while I bake the bread... *Que pensez-vous?*"

Mon Dieu. I was thinking Henry Miller and Anaïs Nin; he was talking Ozzie and Harriet. He sighed again, attempted to look sad. "You see, Wynter, *malheureusement,* I do not think this will work."

Merde.

Ten

✥

I love the Queen Anne Thriftway. It's less pretentious than the gourmet markets in L.A. with their artistically arranged strawberries and
Tuscan estate-bottled extra-virgin olive oil and designer goat
cheese and candied rose petals. Thriftway has all that, but they've got
regular food, too, and everything doesn't cost more per pound than a
vintage Stutz Bearcat. The clerks are called "clerks," not "sales associ-
ates." They carry some respectable European-style breads with good
sturdy crusts, which they don't ruin by sealing in plastic bags. Plus, they
have an espresso cart and they play great oldies on their sound system.
I've gotten to where I actually look forward to grocery shopping, a chore
I always hated at home.

The Wednesday after New Year's Day I'm tooling up and down the
aisles with my mostly empty cart, sipping a decaf latte and humming
along with the Carly Simon/James Taylor cover of "Mockingbird."
Okay, I'm dancing in front of the dairy case—the mashed potato—the
way CM's big sister Katie taught us, and trying to decide which flavors
of yogurt I want.

"If yogurt makes you feel that good, they're probably not charging
enough for it." I wheel around, feeling a scarlet flush ride up my neck.
Mac the bartender smiles at me.

"I was just—" Excuse me, why do I feel compelled to explain myself?

He says, "I like that song, too. But the Inez Foxx version's better."

I grab two cartons of yogurt, no longer caring what flavor they are. "I don't think I've heard it."

"Come to Bailey's Saturday night. I'll play it for you." He rips the top off a plastic bag of precut carrot sticks and pops one in his mouth like a cigar. Then he holds out the bag to me.

"No. Thanks." I grip the handle of my cart. "I'm not in the habit of going to bars by myself. Especially not on weekends."

He twirls the plastic bag around and ties the open end in a knot. "Bailey's is a neighborhood joint. We even have a bunch of grandmothers that come in. You won't get hassled. I promise." He uses the carrot to cross his heart.

"Well, maybe. I'll have to see what's going on." *In my extremely busy social life.* My hands are actually sweating on the cart handle.

"I'll save you a place at the bar."

Before I can think of anything else dumb to say, this cute little blonde comes flying around the corner, all dewy smiles. "Mac, hey. I thought I recognized your voice. How long has it been?"

While he's trying to figure out the answer, I slink off to the produce aisle for my bananas. Old wallflowers never die; they just go to seed.

Tassajara yeasted banana bread is good—dense with whole wheat, minimally sweet with honey, the banana really only an aftertaste. But I know it can be improved. On impulse, I cut a piece and take it to work with me. Linda handles it like it might be radioactive.

"What's in here?" she demands.

"You tell me. Taste it."

She chews like a cow, her lower jaw making a complete rotation. "Cinnamon." She swallows. She looks up at the ceiling, side to side.

"What else?"

"I don't know. Somethin' else. Come on, I haven't got all night. What's in it?"

"Banana."

"In yeast bread?" She looks outraged, then disgusted, then she takes another bite. "Yeah, it's banana all right. Can't hardly tell it."

"Isn't it good?"

She shrugs. "Why bother putting banana in it if you don't even know it's there?"

I laugh. "It's called 'subtlety.' "

"I call it silly. Puttin' in something you can't hardly taste."

"I think it could use something else..."

"Yeah, like more banana." She cracks herself up.

"I was thinking nuts. Maybe hazelnuts. What do you—"

She shakes her head vehemently. "No sir. I tell you what it needs. It needs more cinnamon. And sugar."

I stare at her. "Damn, Linda. I think you're right. Make it like a cinnamon swirl bread."

"That's what I said." She looks half embarrassed, half pleased with herself.

"Let's try making some tomorrow night."

"No way," she snaps.

"Why not?"

"We got plenty to do tomorrow night. The bread we're s'posed to be doing. Don't need to be messing with bread that has bananas in it but you can't tell."

"Oh, come on. I'll come in early—"

Her teeth clamp together. "I don't care if you come in at three in the afternoon, we're not doing it here. You want to mess with it, do it at home."

So I do. I add two more bananas to tenderize as well as flavor the dough, pat it into a rectangle, brush it with melted butter, sprinkle it with brown sugar, cinnamon, and raisins, roll it into two fat spirals. It gives off an almost narcotic aroma while it's baking so that it takes all my willpower to wait for it to cool before cutting into it. I let the loaves sit for fifteen minutes, turn them out of the pans, and drizzle a bit of confectioners' sugar glaze over the tops.

Sitting at my table with a warm slice of banana-cinnamon swirl bread and a glass of cold milk, I think it doesn't get much better than this. Maybe sex. But only incredible sex with a French film star at the George V in Paris. This stuff would sell like gangbusters on weekends, but I know Linda's not going to let me try it. I don't understand her. She's got the right instincts. She knew that a little more sweetness and spice would make it come together, but she won't take the next step.

She reminds me of this girl CM and I used to see at the pool every summer. About once a week, she'd climb the ladder of the high dive and walk out to the end of the board. She'd stand there for a few minutes, looking down at the water, sometimes even bouncing a little. Once she backed up and started her approach steps. But she stopped short of a dive every single time. She'd stand there hugging herself till the life-guard blew the whistle and told her to either go or get off the board, then she'd give this little shrug and climb back down, making everybody move off the ladder to let her by. She always seemed embarrassed and I felt sorry for her until CM pointed out that no one was forcing her to publicly humiliate herself every week.

The second week of January, a front blows down from Canada and makes everything so clear and cold that the city seems sculpted in ice. For days, the only clouds are little white puffs floating in an ocean of blue sky. There's a heavy capping of snow on the Olympic Mountains, making the view from the park into a travel poster. Linda and I have to play with the bread's rising times because the ambient temperature in the bakery is much lower than usual and there's virtually no humidity.

"Did you guys hear what happened up on Galer?" Ellen comes in breathless on Tuesday morning, locks the door behind her. "A woman was raped and murdered."

"On Galer?"

Ellen's dark eyes look huge. "In her home, for God's sake. I just heard it on the news. I guess it actually happened yesterday. They haven't released much information yet because there's a suspect, but he's still at large. They're warning all women who live alone to be supercautious."

Linda gives her trademark snort. "Anybody ever grabbed aholt of me, they'd turn loose fast enough once they got a look."

I'm inclined to agree.

When Tyler comes in at six-thirty, she says she heard the killer got in through an unlocked basement door. At seven, when the rush starts, you can feel the electric crackle of fear. It's all anyone's talking about. Linda and I are drying the last of the aluminum bowls when Ellen walks back.

"Wyn, are you all right to go home by yourself?"

"Sure. I just need to get a door chain or something, I guess."

"A door chain? Don't you have a dead-bolt lock? What about window locks?"

"It's just a guest cottage. It wasn't really designed for maximum security."

"You're not staying there alone one more day without some decent locks."

"I'm okay, really. I'll go by Ace Hardware when I wake up this afternoon and get a book and some tools."

"This is no time for do-it-yourself. I'll send Lloyd over when he gets home."

"Ellen, I'm fine, really. I'm sure your husband has better things to do than—"

"I'm not going to argue with you, Wyn. Don't buy anything till Lloyd looks at the place. He'll know exactly what you need."

In the movies, Lloyd Gannaway would play the stoic ex-con, trying against all odds to go straight. Tall and lean, white-blond hair, flinty eyes in a face ravaged by acne and sun and hard living, he doesn't seem a likely match for Ellen. But the longer I'm with him, the more I can see how it works. For one thing, he doesn't do a lot of talking—the perfect foil for Ellen's running commentary on life.

In fact, after he introduces himself, he just walks around my house, looking at the windows and doors, testing the locks, tapping things, shaking his head occasionally. Then he says, "Let's go." And we drive off down the hill in his faded-blue Toyota with the missing front bumper.

The hardware store is doing a brisk business in panic. It's like being in a hardware store in L.A. after an earthquake. The aisles are crowded with single women and their brothers, fathers, boyfriends, sons. By tonight, there probably won't be a lock left in the place. Lloyd selects a dead bolt for the door and insists on getting a peephole and some screw-in locks for the double-hung windows.

Doug, my little fir tree, is still sitting in his pot on the porch, still wearing his red bow.

"You should plant the tree," Lloyd says when we come back.

"I don't know how long I'm going to be here."

He picks up the pot, squeezes it gently. "Well, you might have to leave it behind. But if you don't stick it in the ground soon, it'll get root bound and die. I've got a shovel in the trunk."

While he drills a tunnel in the door for the peephole, I dig a new home for Doug, just in front and to the left of the porch. When I knock the tree out of the pot, I see that the roots have already started to curl under and double back on themselves. I untangle them gently and spread them out over a mound of earth in the hole, scoop dirt around the root ball, tamp it down. I imagine him sighing and wiggling his toes in the dirt.

I lean the shovel against the porch rail and come inside. "Will it bother you if I watch?"

Lloyd shakes his head, absorbed in the mechanics of putting in the locks. The little piles of sawdust under the windows escape his notice. But then, I'm used to David, whose tranquility could be marred by fingerprints on a glass tabletop.

"Would you like some tea or a beer?"

"Tea's good. Thanks."

I put the teakettle on and make a fire in the stove. As the room warms up, he pulls off his sweatshirt and uses the inside of it to wipe his forehead.

"Good fire," he says.

"My father taught me." I hand him a cup of tea and close the air vent on the door of the woodstove.

He looks around. "I think that does it."

"I really appreciate your help."

"No problem." He has the quietest voice for a guy. "You oughta get yourself some tools, though. Learn how to use 'em. Since you're gonna be livin' alone."

Hello. I'm going to be living alone? Not really. At some point, David's going to come to his senses. Or worst case, eventually there will be a replacement. Alone is temporary. A vacation. Hearing it pronounced in Lloyd's flat, steady voice makes it sound alarmingly final. It's like being hit in the back of the knees. "Yes," I manage. "I guess I should do that."

He calmly sips his tea, oblivious to having just turned my life upside down. "What's in the boxes?"

"Mostly books. Clothes."

"You could build some shelves," he says.

I laugh weakly. "I've never built anything in my life."

"Be a good first project."

"I can't afford to run out and buy a bunch of tools and wood and stuff right now. Maybe in the spring."

"I got some tools you can use." It's as if he hasn't heard me. "I'll give 'em to Ellen to bring to you." He gazes at me steadily, daring me to decline.

"That's very nice of you." Okay, I'll take the damn tools. That doesn't mean I have to use them. I can go out and buy some shelves.

"Be a lot better 'n what you can buy in the way of shelving these days," he says. Another sip of tea. "They're all particleboard."

"Ellen said you're a boatbuilder. Where do you work?"

"Whidbey Island."

"You commute to Whidbey Island?"

"Once or twice a week. The other nights I stay on my boat over there."

"Oh. That's great. So how did you meet Ellen?"

"She saved my life once."

"Oh. Really?"

"Really." When I don't ask the next logical question, he answers it anyway. "I was a junkie. One night I was so strung out, hurtin' and full of self-pity, I decided to just kill myself quick instead of slow." His eyes never move from mine and I find that I can't look away. "But before I pulled the trigger, I picked up the phone and called the crisis hot line. Ellen answered the phone.

"She talked to me for two hours. Got me to go to a detox clinic. Whole time I was in rehab I used to call the hot line and hang up till I got her." He smiles minutely for the first time since I've met him. "Finally talked her into meeting me for coffee. Think I was already in love with her before I ever laid eyes on her. Goin' on ten years now."

"That's"—I clear my throat—"some story."

"Yep." He drains his cup, takes it to the kitchen sink and rinses it out. "Thanks for the tea." He pulls his sweatshirt back on, drops the drill in his tool kit. "You have any questions about usin' the tools, I'm home most Saturdays." He disappears out the door.

Well, I really do need some shelves.

Eleven

❧

I love to watch Diane assemble and decorate cakes, especially the wedding cakes, because they're the most elaborate and some of them are pretty different from your average white wedding cake with flowers. Like the one she did for this couple who both work for Greenpeace. They wanted a cake that represented (their words) "the oneness of life and the harmony of sea, earth, and sky." Other than giving her the theme, they said she was (their words) "free to unleash her creativity."

She spent weeks leafing through photo and nature magazines, art books, doing sketches. In the end, the cake was three layers—chocolate, lemon, and hazelnut—stacked asymmetrically. White-chocolate buttercream frosting was colored greenish blue on the bottom to represent the ocean, chocolate in the middle for earth, then sort of a marbleized pale blue on top for the sky, with wispy white clouds. It sounds weird, but it was beautiful. Diane fashioned exotic sea creatures and animals and flowers and birds to populate the three layers. The bride and groom were represented by a little mermaid and merman—I guess that's what you'd call a guy mermaid—porcelain figures that the bride had found somewhere.

Anyway, the couple had a friend who worked for the *Post-Intelligencer,* and a color photo of the cake ended up on the front page of the "Style" section and now the phone never seems to stop ringing.

It's so busy that I don't get to sit and watch anymore. Diane drafts me for making buttercream or doing the crumb coat, which is the first layer of icing that you put on to cover the crumbs and make a smooth base for the finish frosting. She does it so quickly that it looks easy. Just glob some icing on and smooth it like glass with that offset spatula. But I found out immediately that it requires more hand-eye coordination and patience than I possess.

One dark afternoon, when it's just the two of us, she enlists my help with a new recipe for orange frosting to go on a chocolate fiftieth-anniversary cake. Standing in front of the stove watching sugar melt and turn brown is normally about as fascinating as watching paint dry, but the risk of experimenting with a cake that's due to be picked up at ten tomorrow morning intrigues me.

"What if it doesn't work?" I brush sugar crystals off the side of the pan with a wet pastry brush.

"Then I'm here till midnight redoing it. So let's proceed bravely but carefully." She turns on the burner under a pan of milk.

"If you majored in art, how on earth did you get into this?" I ask her. "Was your mother a baker?"

Her laugh is sharp. "My mother is the real estate queen of Baltimore. Or was till she retired. She was never home long enough to bake. Or do much else. Be careful with that. Nothing burns quite like hot caramel."

The sugar is a deep golden brown now, and the mercury in the candy thermometer is nudging 360 degrees, so I turn off the flame. It boils up like a cauldron as the milk goes in.

"To answer your question, my gram was a fabulous baker. She raised my two sisters and me. Till she died—then I inherited the job."

"What did your father do?"

"Drank himself into liver failure." Her voice is flat and free of emotion. She peers over my shoulder into the pot. "This looks ready. Why don't you start on the Italian meringue."

I separate the eggs by letting the whites slide through my fingers the way she showed me weeks ago—a slimy but efficient method.

"I think that might be why I loved art and sewing and cooking," she muses. "All the things my mother didn't seem to care about. To spite her for not being room mother or baking us birthday cakes or taking us to buy Easter dresses or even putting Band-Aids on our goddamned skinned knees."

With the egg whites whipping in the small mixer, I put the sugar and water on a burner to make a simple syrup. "It's funny. My mother drove me nuts because she was there all the time doing all that stuff. Trying to teach me piano and sewing. Maybe there's no way they can win."

Diane stops beating the crème anglaise and stares into the middle distance. "Who knows."

For a second, I think she might cry. Instead, she sniffs a little bit and sets the bowl of crème anglaise into a larger bowl filled with ice.

"Where are your sisters?"

"In Baltimore. Married, with children, the image of domesticity." She laughs ruefully. "They made their peace with my mother a long time ago and just did what they wanted to do. Now they take her casseroles and she baby-sits the grandkids and it's all very huggy/cozy. Me, I had to run off to West Timbuktu to make it on my own. And not just any business would do. It had to involve all the things she either couldn't or wouldn't do." Her laugh is tight. "Guess I showed her, huh?"

I squeeze some oranges and boil their juice down to a concentrate while she beats three pounds of butter to white satin in the Hobart.

"Do you get back there very often?"

"I've never been back. It's almost six years now." She pushes her bangs off her face with her forearm. "Okay, here goes." Her determined smile is almost a grimace. She adds first the crème, then the meringue, then the vanilla and the orange syrup to the butter as the paddle turns steadily in its prescribed arc. At the end, she tosses in a dab of orange-paste food coloring and the grated orange zest.

She has a funny way of tasting things, putting a dab on the center of her tongue and pressing it against the roof of her mouth a few times to spread it around. "Mmmm. Try some."

I spoon out a little. It's one of those flavors that explodes in your mouth. "I love it—the burnt sugar taste with the orange and the silkiness... I want to rub it all over me."

"A waste of good buttercream." She laughs. "Unless you've got someone in mind to lick it off."

On the first Friday morning in February, Tyler calls in sick with the flu.

Ellen looks pained. "Wyn, I hate to even ask you, but is there any way you can stay till about nine-thirty, ten? Just to get us through the morning rush."

"I don't have a problem with staying, but I don't know anything about using that machine."

"Misha can sling the espresso. You can go back and do muffins and scones with Jen. By the way"—she gives me a knowing smile—"I've got some tools for you out in the car."

I take my mocha back to the work area, where Jen's wearing the biggest grin I've ever seen on her face. Short and chubby, with fair skin and dark hair, she looks like the Pillsbury Doughboy's sister.

"What's up?"

"Nothin'. I'm happy because Misha has to work out front and I don't."

"Is it that bad?"

She shrugs. "I guess it all depends on whether you like dealing with customers. Personally, I'd rather shovel shit with a teaspoon." Her blue eyes spark wickedly.

She pulls the bucket of bran-muffin batter out of the Traulsen, hands me an ice cream scoop. "We do three dozen of these. When you're done, the dry ingredients for the cranberry muffins are over there." She points to the other end of the huge worktable. "Mix in the wet and then you can scoop those, too."

In a few minutes, Ellen comes back, dabbing at her forehead with a tissue. She picks up a tray of cooling blueberry muffins. "It's crazy this morning. What muffins have we got for tomorrow?"

"Cranberry, bran, and I'll make some pumpkin when I get through with the cinnamon rolls," Jen says.

"I can do the pumpkin."

"That would be a big help." Ellen jerks her head in the direction of her old brown desk. "The recipe's in that red notebook."

I wash my hands and riffle through the pages till I find it.

Misha's Pumpkin-Millet Muffins

1¼ cups unbleached white flour

½ cup whole wheat flour

¼ teaspoon baking powder

1 teaspoon baking soda

¾ cup sugar

2½ teaspoons pumpkin spice mix (see below)

½ cup millet

2 eggs

½ cup vegetable oil

1 cup pumpkin

⅓ cup water

2 tablespoons maple syrup

½ cup raisins or currants

Mix together dry ingredients and millet. In a separate bowl, beat eggs, oil, pumpkin, water, syrup, and raisins or currants. Add wet ingredients to dry and mix just until combined. Scoop into muffin tins that have been greased or lined with paper liners. Bake at 375°F for 25 to 30 minutes. Makes 1 dozen.

PUMPKIN SPICE MIX

¼ cup ground ginger

¼ cup ground cinnamon

3 tablespoons ground cardamom

3 tablespoons ground cloves

Mix spices thoroughly and store in a jar.

Jen laughs when she notices me frowning. "We make six dozen at a time," she says. "The proportions are on the back. And the spice mix is in the storeroom, first shelf on the left. I think you'll have to open a new can of pumpkin."

She works with her back to the café, but I keep looking up from my muffins to watch the first assault—yuppies in their power suits, parking their BMWs at the curb, pickups full of blue-collar guys who work across the bridge in Ballard, local merchants up and down Queen. Between eight-thirty and nine, the second wave hits—left-over hippies, punkers, and students, and, finally, about ten, the neighborhood moms with their strollers and toddlers, and the blue-hair set.

The hum of voices is punctuated at intervals by the bang of the door, the scalding hiss of the espresso machine, the coffee grinder whirring, the cash register dinging, and the traffic noises. It's sensory overload compared to the stillness and the rhythms of making bread at night.

Jen sticks a pan of cinnamon rolls in the oven about the time I finish the muffins. I wipe my hands on my apron. "Can I watch you make the scones? I love them, but mine never turn out like these."

"There's two schools of thought about scones." She smirks a little. "At least around here. There's fluffy scones—they've got more cream and eggs. Kind of like biscuits. And there's short scones, which I prefer. They've got more sugar and a lot more butter. They're denser, almost like shortcake." She depresses the button on the food processor, cutting the butter into the dry ingredients in about five long pulses. She dumps the crumbly mass onto the worktable and flips it gently twice, patting it into a long rectangle. "What we make here is sort of a compromise."

She holds up two floury fingers. "Two things. The butter's gotta be really cold, even frozen's okay. And don't handle the dough any more than absolutely necessary. That makes them tough. You can use a knife or a biscuit cutter or whatever you want, just make sure it's sharp. The sharper it is, the higher they'll rise." She uses a Chinese cleaver, swinging it back and forth, separating the dough into triangles. We load them onto half-sheet pans and stash them in the freezer to bake off tomorrow.

· · ·

Ellen insists on driving me home at eleven and helping me carry the five-gallon bucketful of tools that Lloyd has selected as my learner's set. The bucket has a blue canvas liner—Ellen says it's called a "tool apron"—with pockets for different hand tools. A drill and a heavy orange extension cord are in the middle. There's also a circular saw that would make a formidable weapon should you happen to be attacked while it's plugged in.

I sigh. "Never in my wildest dreams did I envision myself with power tools."

Her eyes close when she laughs. "Never in my wildest dreams did I picture myself with someone like Lloyd. I hope he wasn't too pushy."

"I'd call him persistent. And he's right, I guess. It's probably a good idea for everyone to know how to use a screwdriver." I drop my backpack on the chair. "He told me how you guys met."

She waves her hand dismissively. "He tells everyone that story. It's his evangelical Lutheran upbringing. Every time he tells it, my shoulders start itching, like I'm going to grow wings. Well, I better get back to work and let you go to bed. Thanks for sticking around this morning."

After she leaves, I stash the tools in my office, curl up in my down comforter without bothering to open the futon frame, and fall into an exhausted, dreamless sleep.

"Missed you last night," Mac greets me as I scoot onto my stool at the bar.

"One of the women at work has the flu, so I worked an extra five hours yesterday. I didn't even roll out of bed till eight."

I've become a barfly. Sort of. I've taken to spending three or four evenings a week perched on this stool, reading and nursing my one glass of wine. Two, if I don't have to work that night. I always felt sorry for people who hung out in bars, and slightly condescending toward them—like, if you had a life, you wouldn't be there—but I've decided there's a lot to recommend it. Of course, you have to choose your saloon carefully.

I'd be willing to bet that everyone who comes to Bailey's lives within a three-mile radius of upper Queen Anne. If you didn't, you'd probably never venture in. It's not the sort of place where enthusiasts congregate to taste the latest boutique pinot noirs from Oregon. I always take a book, but a lot of times I find myself staring at one page while I listen to the guys debate obscure sports trivia or brag about their kids' free-throw averages.

Girlfriends gather at the big tables by the fireplace to gossip and complain about their boyfriends while a group of older women calling themselves the "Thursday Night Grannies" shoot pool and exchange recipes for things like Mississippi Mud Cake and Baked Artichoke Dip.

I don't get involved in a lot of conversation, except sometimes with Mac and the other bartender. Kenny's older, maybe around fifty, short and husky, with thinning dark hair, watery blue eyes, and a nose that looks like it's been broken at least twice. He used to box, but now he just coaches kids at the community center on Capitol Hill.

These two work well together in the small space behind the bar, probably because they work on different planes. Kenny's motions are direct, short and jerky, but efficient, just what you'd expect from a fighter. Mac is tall—over six feet—with an odd, lanky grace. They're both in constant motion, never getting in each other's way, never forgetting what they're about, never reaching for something to find it's not there. I like to watch them.

Okay, I like to watch him. Mac. I like the way he works, as if there were nothing in the world he'd rather be doing at the moment than getting some old codger his Ballard Bitter. I like it that he gives his full attention to anyone who talks to him, even if the person is obnoxious. The way he gets so caught up in the music that he doesn't even know he's mouthing the words.

He told me one afternoon that he's from New York, that he dropped out of NYU his sophomore year to wander around. He came through Seattle on his way to Alaska and he was low on money, so he took a job tending bar at some place down in Pioneer Square and just stayed.

I've heard about his ex-girlfriend Laura, who owns an art gallery in Bellevue. They broke up six months ago after two years of hot-and-cold-running romance. She told him that he was financially challenged and always would be, and she needed someone with a little more ambition.

He's not racehorse gorgeous like David, but then, who is? Mac has more the look of a hawk, with his long nose and high cheekbones, deep-set gray eyes—a certain fierceness that's not unattractive.

But Mrs. Morrison didn't raise any daughters dumb enough to sit around staring at some bartender and wondering how he'd look in those nice faded low-rise jeans if he just took his shirt off.

I've told him a little about David. Okay, I've told him a lot. It wasn't intentional, but he's so easy to talk to, it just slipped out. Anyway, he said he knew I was married the first time he saw me. When I asked him how he could know that, he said, "You looked sad. I see a lot of it going around."

On Saturdays, I can stay till last call if I want, since I don't have to rush home and eat dinner and go to work. The music's every bit as good as Mac promised. I like the way he puts the tapes together.

Sometimes he starts wild, like Billy Idol, and then drops back into the Platters, then punches it up with the Stones, sliding back into mellow with Joni Mitchell. Other times he'll kick off with something sad and slow like "That's How Strong My Love Is" by Otis Redding, and gradually work up to Chuck Berry or Eric Clapton. If he gets on a roll, there might be a solid hour of Motown, or the British Invasion, or surf music, but usually it's an interesting mix.

And every so often he'll come down to my end of the bar and say, "You like this one?" I'll have to stop and listen and figure out that The Drifters are singing "There Goes My Baby." Then I'll say, yes, I do like it, and he'll point out to me that the lyric is actually in blank verse.

Or he'll say, "Wyn. Check out the kick-ass horn section on this Otis Redding. See how they echo the lyrics? The way they pull you right into the next line?"

Usually, Saturday night the place is packed, but tonight's the finals of the high school district basketball tournament, so a lot of people are at the game. He's playing early Dylan from *Blonde on Blonde* and *Highway 61 Revisited*. I'm in the middle of a P. D. James mystery, Superintendent Dalgliesh explaining to Sergeant Martin why the blackmailer had killed the head of the clinic, when Mac raps his knuckles on the bar in front of me.

"Hungry?"

"I'm getting around to it. But don't bring me any more peanuts. I'll just eat them."

"You want to go get Italian with Kenny and me?"

"Where?"

"Lofurno's. Down on Fifteenth. You can either go with us after we close up or we'll stop by your place about one-thirty."

It doesn't occur to me to wonder how he knows where I live until he's at the front door. He's lounging against the porch rail, and when he reaches for the visor of his baseball cap, the picture stops rolling and comes into perfect focus. I stare at him.

"Oh my God."

"What's wrong?"

"You delivered my firewood. That's why you didn't have to ask where I lived."

The corners of his eyes crinkle with amusement. "Took you long enough."

"Your hair. It was really long."

"That was the day before my annual shearing."

"Why didn't you say something before?"

"Well..." He sticks his hands down into his jeans pockets. "I had the distinct impression that you were pretty grossed out that day."

"Grossed out? I thought you were the psycho-killer handyman."

His knees bend when he laughs. Then I'm laughing, too, and shortly we're both bent double, wiping tears away. I recover myself, pull the door shut, turning the key in the dead bolt. "Come on, Kenny probably thinks you got lost."

We step off the porch and crunch about halfway down the gravel drive before he says, "Kenny bailed on us. His wife wanted him home tonight." He brushes a hemlock branch aside for me to pass by.

"I didn't realize he was married."

"Is this okay?"

"As long as they're happy."

A battered, white pickup truck noses up to the curb. It looks held together with barbed wire and chewing gum, and the left-rear fender is gray with primer.

"My God, it's the Millennium Falcon."

"Sorry, the Beamer's in the shop this week."

I climb in. "What *is* this thing?"

"An Elky." When he slams the door, I half expect the window to fall out.

I sit running my index finger over the tuck-and-roll vinyl upholstery while he walks around to the driver's side and gets in. "What's an Elky?"

"El Camino 454 SS. Nineteen seventy-one," he says proudly. The engine hacks and strains and dies. Three times.

"Do you realize what the emissions on this thing must be like?"

"This truck and I have been through a lot together."

"There's probably a hole in the ozone layer with your name on it." On the fourth try, it kicks in. He puts it in drive and we pull away from the curb. "In seventy-one, nobody was thinking about hydrocarbons and nitrous oxides and particulate— And what kind of gas mileage do you get?"

We stop at the corner and he looks over at me. "I think of it as recycling. If I wasn't driving it, it'd be rusting in somebody's front yard."

Lofurno's is another place that you'd never find by accident. Just driving by on Fifteenth, you wouldn't notice the peeling, gray clapboard building huddled at the foot of a bluff. And if you did notice, you'd probably think it was vacant. There's no sign, no visible window lights, only a few cars in the muddy parking lot. In a linoleum-floored hall just inside the front door, a bare lightbulb hangs from a black cord. On the left is a plain wooden door, to the right a flight of stairs.

Mac opens the door into what could be a movie set for a speakeasy. The air is heavy with garlic and cigarette smoke, warmly lit by amber lamps. A black woman in purple chiffon sits at a baby grand piano, sipping a clear liquid that's too viscous to be water. Her hair is silver, but her face is smooth and ageless. She winks at Mac, brings her cigarette to her mouth with a jeweled hand and takes a drag, exhaling a slow stream. Two couples sit at the dark-wood bar that runs the length of the room, and one of the guys looks up when we come in.

"Hey, Mac. How's it goin'?" He slides off his stool and lumbers over, hitching up his pants. He looks like Victor Mature, with those sculpted lips and a large, handsome nose, black eyes, and a wave of steel-gray hair breaking over his forehead. They do this shoulder-clasping thing that I've never seen anywhere except in movies about the Mafia. His name is Tony—what else?—and when Mac introduces me, Tony gives me this kind of macho nod that reminds me of an old joke about Italian foreplay. Then he picks up two menus and leads us to one of the high-back booths opposite the bar. In a few minutes, a waiter in a black vest and a long white apron brings a bottle of Chianti and two glasses.

"Is red okay?" Mac asks me. "Or would you rather have something else?"

"Red's fine."

The waiter pours the wine and says, "We're out of the scallopine, and we've only got one lasagne left."

When he leaves, I lean forward and whisper, "Where's the guy in the dark suit and white tie with a tommy gun in the violin case?"

He laughs. "This place is sort of a throwback. The food's great, though. And so's Arlene. The singer."

"She looks like she's through for tonight."

He shakes his head. "She's just taking a break. She'll sing till everybody's gone. Her voice reminds me of Lauren Bacall. Was it *To Have and Have Not* where she sang?"

" 'Am I Blue.' And Hoagy Carmichael played the piano." I look at the open menu. "What's good?"

"Everything. But I hope you like garlic."

"I love it."

"Good. Then let's get a Caesar."

After we order, Mac gives the waiter a five to put in Arlene's overflowing goldfish bowl. She's lighting another cigarette with the tail end of her last one, but she smiles and pulls the voice mike around. "You got it, babe."

Then she flounces her skirt, flicks ashes off her dress, and plays the intro to "Every Time We Say Goodbye." Suddenly I hear Ella Fitzgerald's throaty purr, see my father in his chair, eyes closed, gently tapping his thumbs on the book that sits in his lap.

Now that we're sitting here across from each other, I suddenly feel the nakedness of my third finger, left hand. Lately I've realized how a wedding ring works like a talisman, granting protection to the wearer. You can talk to a man, laugh, even do a little judicious flirting and no one automatically assumes that you're looking to get laid. Without the ring, you're on your own.

"So do you still work at Norwegian Woods?"

"I just help Rick out during busy times."

The waiter makes the salad at our table in a huge wooden bowl that he's smeared with a smushed garlic clove, the way it's supposed to be done. It's one of the best I've ever had—lemon, anchovy, and garlic in perfect tension with each other, the coddled egg and olive oil smoothing it out, freshly grated Parmesan, just enough Tabasco for a slight afterburn. There's sourdough bread with a quarter-inch-thick crust that I use to mop up the last of the dressing. I could quit right now and be perfectly happy, but then the waiter brings my tagliatelle Bolognese and

I'm glad I didn't quit. I've never tasted meat sauce like this, sweet and creamy. I chew it slowly, practically sucking it, trying to figure out how it's done.

I look up at some point to find Mac smiling at me—almost laughing—and I realize he's been sitting there, keeping my glass filled, and I haven't said a word to him in the last ten minutes.

"I'm sorry I'm being no company at all, but this is so . . . incredibly, unbelievably good."

"Are you always this intense?"

"Only about food. How do they do this?"

He shrugs. "Ask the waiter. I don't think about it, I just eat it."

"This place seems very New York. Or New Jersey maybe. Is that why you like it?"

"I like it because it's a great place. I don't have a lot of nostalgia for the East Coast."

"It occurs to me that you know an awful lot about me and I know very little about you."

He twirls spaghetti around his fork like a pro. "Does that make you uncomfortable?"

"It makes me curious."

"You're free to ask questions."

"Okay. Where have you been? For about the last ten years."

"After I left school"—he looks thoughtful, as if he's sifting out what to tell and what to leave unsaid—"I drove west. Spent three years in Colorado and Utah."

"What did you do there?"

"A lot of skiing and a little waiting tables."

"You can't ski in the summer."

"Then it was rock climbing and construction."

"Rock climbing? You have a death wish, then."

"Not really. It's based on learning a set of skills, just like any other sport."

"Yeah, it's just like other sports. Except your butt's hanging over the abyss."

He laughs, leans his head back against the booth. "It's a matter of engrams."

"Of what?"

"Do you know how to drive stick shift?"

I nod.

"It's like that. Or like a golf swing or a tennis serve. It's just a series of movements that sets up a sequence of nerve impulses in your brain. Every repetition reinforces the pattern. That's an engram. Once it's established, you can perform that series of movements almost automatically, so your brain's free to concentrate on other things."

"Like the fact that your butt's hanging over the abyss. Okay. Then what? After the rock climbing."

"Then I hitchhiked around New Zealand for a year. Then Italy and Switzerland for another year."

"That's five."

"Then I came home. That lasted for about six months, and then I started working my way west again. Then, like I told you before, I came here and stayed."

I rest my elbows on the table. "You do that very well. Cover a lot of ground and a lot of time without revealing anything substantive."

"Good word, 'substantive.' " He grins. "There's just nothing very interesting to tell."

"No brushes with the law? No duels?"

"Nope."

"Ever been married?"

He hesitates for barely a nanosecond. "One close call."

"What was her name?"

"Gillian. She lived on a sheep station in New Zealand."

"Can you tell me?"

"Some other time."

After I've stuffed as much tagliatelle as possible into myself and the rest into a take-home container, I do ask the waiter how they make it. He smiles and pours the last of the wine into our glasses.

"It's the milk," he says. "You cook the meat in milk before you add any tomatoes. And then, of course, you simmer it for a long time—four, five hours. Would you like coffee?"

"In a few minutes," Mac says. Then he looks at me. "I guess this means you like the place."

"It's wonderful. Thanks for bringing me here. I never would have found it."

Now Arlene's playing "Blues in the Night." Mac smiles. "She's angling for another tip. By the way, Jimmy Turner's coming to Bailey's next Friday."

"Who's he?"

"A local blues artist. He usually plays at some pretty down-and-dirty places, but every once in a while, he comes up on the hill. You'll like him."

"I'll have to find out some other time. I'm going to L.A. Friday morning."

"Too bad." He waits a second before asking, "Is this the big day?"

"I'm afraid so." The glow of the evening seems to have taken on a coat of tarnish.

He sets his glass down, twirls the stem around. "Why is this so hard for you?"

"I'm not sure. There's this knot in my stomach every time I think about it."

"You don't seem like the kind of person who'd begrudge her mother a chance to be happy. Not after ten years or whatever it is."

"Fifteen." I shrug. "It doesn't matter, anyway. I'll get through it. My best friend's going with me."

"It matters if it makes knots in your stomach." He drinks the last of his wine, sets the empty glass near the edge of the table. "You think you'll see—"

"David? No. He doesn't even know I'm coming."

The waiter brings thick, inky coffee in white cups and hot milk in a pitcher. I know I should have asked for decaf, but it doesn't seem right after a dinner where every single thing was so uncompromisingly real to drink fake coffee.

Mac dumps in a whole packet of sugar and carefully blends in a few drops of milk. He has a funny cowlick directly above his left eye, at the scalp line where a little tuft of hair grows backward, in opposition to all its brethren. As if to emphasize the difference, the hair in that one spot is shot through with gray.

"Why did you drop out of school?" I ask. He doesn't look up from his coffee. "Don't you want a degree?"

A tolerant smile. "It's just a piece of paper that says you did what's expected."

"It's too easy to trivialize things like education—or marriage—by saying it's just a piece of paper."

"Those things have already been trivialized. The purpose of going to college isn't to learn, it's to get the paper. The purpose of the paper is to get you the job so you can keep on doing what's expected."

"Are you really that cynical?" I blow on my coffee to cool it, take a tentative sip.

"I'm not cynical. I'm realistic. I like my life. I don't need any more than what I have."

"That's fine for now. You're young and strong. What about the future?"

"The future is something dreamed up by insurance companies and high school guidance counselors to keep you from enjoying the present."

"You're going to get old, Peter Pan. What if you get sick? What if—"

He laughs. "I prefer to burn my bridges as I come to them."

The second we finish our coffee, the waiter is there with a refill. When we decline, he presents the check. It's 4 A.M. I reach for my wallet.

"I've got it," Mac says easily.

"No." My voice is too loud in the nearly empty room. "This isn't a date. We'll split it down the middle."

He holds up both hands in surrender. "Okay, give me fifteen bucks."

We don't talk much on the way home, and when he pulls up at the curb, he says dryly, "Since this isn't a date, I won't walk you to your door. Just blink the light when you get inside."

Twelve

❧

onday afternoon. Biology class. We're dissecting frogs. The sweet, sick smell of formaldehyde clings to my hands. Weird, the things that stay with you. One of the secretaries from the office comes in and takes Mr. Ansel out in the hall. Then he sticks his head in and calls for me to come out.

"Wynter," he says, "your mother's down in the office and she needs to speak with you."

It's strange for my mother to show up in the middle of the day and call me out of class, but it never occurs to me that anything could have happened to my father. All the way down to the office, I'm thinking I'm in some kind of trouble, although I have no idea what it could be. The secretary doesn't say a word, but she keeps looking at me out of the corner of her eye.

The second I see my mother's face, her eyes swollen and red, I know. I end up on my knees, doubled over, screaming for CM. Some quick-thinking person shuts the door so the rest of the school won't think I'm being beaten with a rubber hose, and they go to fetch CM from dance production. I hear her coming, bare feet slapping on the linoleum as she runs. She's wearing a red leotard and black tights and she smells like the locker room. She drops to the floor, crying, too, and holding me, rocking me back and forth.

One of the secretaries throws a trench coat over CM, and she shrugs it off. The woman must think it's slipping off by itself, because she keeps pulling

it back up. Finally, CM turns around, snatches the coat out of her hands,
wads it up in a ball, and throws it on the floor, where I promptly vomit all
over it.

The SuperShuttle lurches to a stop, waking me. Still half-asleep, I pay
the driver and take my bag up to the porch. Before I can touch the
doorknob, the door opens and my mother rushes out to hug me. It's a
bit overwhelming.

"Mom, hi. You look great. Your hair and everything."

Her index finger smoothes the curve of her chin-length bob.
"Thanks, honey. I decided the long hair looked kind of old-fashioned."
She doesn't mention it, but the gray is gone, too. "I'm so glad you're
here. Where's CM?"

"She couldn't make it. They went into rehearsals for her big project
yesterday. She sends her love." I'd half-forgotten the reason for that sick
feeling I had when I woke up in the van.

"Oh, that's a shame. Run and take your bag upstairs. Your dress is
on the bed." She adds almost shyly, "I hope you like it."

I run up the stairs, planning to dump my bag and come right back
down, but the dress laid out on my bed stops me in midstep. It doesn't
look like anything my mother would have chosen. It's the color of sun-
rise, a rosy-gold panne velvet that feels like water against my skin.

"Well?" She stands behind me.

"I love it. It's beautiful."

"Try it on," she says. "I've been dying to see it on you."

I pull off my cotton sweater and step out of my jeans. Even in my
stockinged feet and with my hair in a ponytail, I feel as if the dress was
made for me. It's off the shoulders, and cut on the bias, making it cling
and drape like liquid gold to the softly flared hem.

"That color is gorgeous with your hair."

"Where did you find it?"

She smiles. "The same store where I found mine, this little boutique in Santa Monica called The Whole Nine Yards. Richard took

me there." I try not to let my stomach tighten. As I'm wiggling back into my jeans, she says, "Oh, before I forget, there are two boxes of your things in the den and one in your closet. If you want them, you should take them with you. I'm running out of storage space around here."

"I thought you sent me all my stuff."

"The one up here came out of the cedar chest. The two downstairs are ... David brought them by a couple of weeks ago. He said they were more books and some photographs and cards he thought you might want."

I've been fooling myself, how thinking of him wasn't so bad, just a glancing blow. But now, hearing her say his name out loud is like walking into a wall of glass.

"Right." My breath jumps raggedly. "Just some trash he forgot to dump out on the porch."

"You know," she says slowly, "he could have thrown it all away. But he went to the trouble of boxing it up and bringing it over here."

I jerk open the zipper on my bag, pull out my cosmetics kit, set it on the dresser. "What a prince."

"I think he wants to see you."

"Mother, don't." My voice sounds like a knife being sharpened, that metallic scrape that always makes me shiver.

"Has he filed for divorce yet?"

"No. At least I haven't seen any papers. Who knows what'll be waiting for me when I get back."

"I don't think he's happy," she says. She rests one hip on the edge of my bed, not quite sitting, as if she might jump up suddenly.

I turn around too fast, losing my balance. "Is this based on empirical evidence or is it strictly conjecture?"

"He just seemed sad. Or—"

"His shorts were probably twisted from their afternoon quickie."

"Honey, bitterness doesn't serve any purpose."

"Sure it does. It gives the hurt less room to maneuver." From the look on her face, I see that I'm raining on her parade. I take a big breath and paste on a smile. "Let me see your dress."

In her bedroom, she pretends not to notice that I notice Richard's shaving kit, a pair of slacks, some folded underwear. She's already ironing his boxers.

"What do you think?" Her wedding dress is a simple, elegant, long sheath of silk in an old-fashioned color that she calls "ashes of roses." "Richard picked it out. I know he's not supposed to see me in it till the wedding, but, Wyn, he's so artistic and he has such great taste . . . I knew he'd choose something wonderful."

"It's beautiful, Mom. It's your color." I wish I sounded more whole-heartedly engaged.

She looks at the clock. "There's so much I want to tell you, but I was thinking maybe you'd like to lie down for a while. We're going out to dinner about seven-thirty."

"We?"

Her smile dazzles me. "You and me and Richard. We thought it would be good for the three of us to spend a little time together. So you can get to know him before the wedding."

A golf ball–size lump is lodged in the middle of my chest. "How well do you think I can get to know him by tomorrow?"

She acts like she didn't hear me. "He's taking us to Rex," she says. As if the choice of restaurant would somehow make me more receptive to his charms.

I move to the window, hold the curtain aside with one hand. "I'm really pretty tired. I worked last night and I didn't sleep on the plane."

"Wyn, why are you acting like this?"

I turn around. "Like what? Like I'm tired? Probably because I am. I haven't slept in twenty-four hours."

She chews on the inside of her lip, always a bad sign. "Okay, Wynter, do it your way. I was hoping you could forgive me for being happy when you're going through a miserable divorce, but apparently—"

"This has nothing to do with my— with David." I still can't say the word.

"Then would you please tell me what it does have to do with? You're acting like a spoiled... oh, schist! I don't care!" Her idea of profanity. She yanks open the top drawer of her dresser and starts rifling through her underwear, pulling out panty hose, a black lace bra—which I didn't even know she owned—a half-slip. "Richard and I are going to dinner at Rex," she says, looking me full in the face. "If you'd like to go, we'd love your company, but the choice is yours."

The bathroom door closes behind her.

I go down to the kitchen, open a can of chicken broth and a package of dried pasta. While the broth heats, I chop some carrots and zucchini and pour myself a glass of red wine. Tiny bubbles bead the surface of the broth. I turn the flame down low and take my wine out to the den. There are boxes everywhere—stacked by the door, stuck under tables, piled on the desk. I sit down in my mother's sewing chair and put my feet up on her footstool, take a sip of wine.

So what *does* it have to do with?

It's only been five months since I've been here, and it feels like a stranger's house. It's not just the moving cartons full of Richard's things. There are other, more subtle changes—the sofa moved back farther from the fireplace and set at an angle. The wing-back chairs grouped with a new table. A collection of small wooden boxes sits on the mantel next to the old school clock. A lithograph in the hall that looks like a buffalo in a sandstorm.

It's stupid. What difference does it make? My father's gone. Been gone for a long time. He's not coming back. I can't get another father, but she can get another husband. And why shouldn't she? Who wants to be a career widow? She looks great; she's obviously happy. And I'll never live in this house again. So let him make all the changes he wants. He could bulldoze it for all I care.

The sound of a key in the front door makes me jump. Footsteps. Then, "Wynter, great to see you." Richard Travers is standing in front of me, filling the room with his presence, a whiff of expensive after-shave, the dampness of his wool jacket. "Fog's coming in," he says.

Jesus Christ, no wonder my mother grabbed him. He's gorgeous. The prototype for tall, dark, etc. With just a suggestion of silver at the temples. His face is modern sculpture, all planes and angles, Howard Roark, the steely hero of *The Fountainhead*.

He takes off his coat, lays it carefully over the back of the couch, and turns his dark eyes back to me. "How's Seattle? Johanna says you're working in a bakery?"

I gather my composure, hold out my hand, and he grips it. His silver-and-turquoise ring cuts into my hand. "Fine. Yes. I'm... It's nice to finally meet you."

He smiles. "I hope you're planning to join us for dinner."

My eyes go automatically toward the kitchen. "Actually, I'm taking a rain check. I'm a little tired."

"I thought you might be. Did you come straight from work?"

I nod dumbly.

"That's rough."

My mother chooses that moment to appear in the doorway. Howard—I mean Richard—walks over and kisses her. In my adult memory, no man has ever kissed my mother like that. Like a lover. I can't watch. I slink off to the kitchen. I'm standing at the stove giving my soup a stir when she appears beside me straightening her lipstick.

"What do you think?" She's fizzing like a candle rocket.

"He's amazing." I give her the best smile I can muster. "Totally gorgeous. You'll have a better time without me anyway."

"Probably," she says. "But I wanted you to get to know him."

"I will, Mom. I promise. I'm just exhausted."

She kisses my cheek, a little coolly, I think. "Well, get a good night's sleep. We've got to be up by seven in the morning at the latest."

"Why so early?"

"To get the house ready before the caterer and the florist and the wedding coordinator get here."

"I thought we were . . . aren't we going to be at the Biltmore?"

She adjusts her clip-on earrings. "We decided to keep things simple and have it here."

From the hallway, "Jo?" At the sound of his voice, her face looks like she swallowed a lightbulb.

Saturday morning at six forty-five, I'm sipping coffee in the kitchen and watching the rain hammer on the glass of the greenhouse window. My mother is scrambling eggs and humming to herself when the back door swings open in a gust of wind to admit Howard/Richard, dashing in a black trench coat covered with fine droplets. He smiles at me, then turns to the object of his affection.

"I hear rain on your wedding day is good luck." He kisses her neck and she nestles back against him.

"We don't need luck," she stage-whispers. "Ooh, you're all wet."

I guess I'm going to have to get used to this. I can't leave the room every time they're together.

After a quick breakfast, the serious furniture moving starts. All the boxes that have been in the den and the living room end up in my bedroom, leaving only one narrow alley for entrance and another between the dresser and the bed. The wedding coordinator shows up. Her name is Amanda Brewer and she is definitely Beverly Hills. Blue-black hair, enough eyeliner and mascara for a raccoon, red silk dress—presumably in honor of Valentine's Day—matching pumps and huge Coach black leather bag. She's so sorry to be late. Traffic was a bitch. And the rain . . . She closes her eyes briefly, as if giving thanks for having survived the trip.

The three of them huddle, and then the furniture gets completely rearranged. I stand around feeling useless, pushing and pulling when told to and not talking much. My mother asks me if I'm feeling okay.

"I'm fine."

"Well, you could try contributing a little more to the proceedings," she says.

"What would you like me to do? I'm at your service."

She sighs, turns her back so Richard won't hear her. "Could you just try being a little more animated? Or something?"

"Mother——"

"Oh, the caterer's here. Wyn, can you let them in and get them set up in the kitchen, show them where things are?"

"The caterer" consists of a tall guy with slick black hair who seems to be the boss man, two short guys who don't speak much English and probably crossed the Rio Grande this morning, and two nubile blondes. They clump together in the foyer, rain dripping off their black windbreakers.

"I'm Ron," says the boss man. "This is Tony and Raul, Heather and Frankie."

"I guess you need to see the kitchen."

"The bartender's name is Gary. He'll be along later. I want to wait awhile before trying to bring everything in, just to see if the weather breaks."

He talks nonstop while I show them around the kitchen and dining room, and just as I'm getting rid of him, Stuart, my mother's hairdresser from forever, shows up with his partner, Jason, who's doing the flowers.

"Wynter, darling! So good to see you." Air kisses. "Still wearing the big hair, I see."

"Don't start on me, Stuart."

He makes wide eyes. "Uh-oh. A little preceremony tension, for sure." Jason proceeds to get into a fight with Ron about whether or not some of the flowers can go in the fridge. While they're going at it, my mother wanders in.

"Here comes the bride," Stuart sings. "Jo, darling!" More air kisses.

My mother looks at her watch. "Oh, my Lord, Wyn, we've got to get dressed."

"Mom, it's only ten-thirty."

"Lupe's coming at noon to clean, and we have to be through in the bathrooms by then."

I look at Stuart. "You heard her. Nobody pees after twelve o'clock high."

Everyone laughs except my mother.

"I think the ladies should have a glass of champagne to take to their boudoirs," Ron says smoothly.

The popping cork is a cheering sound. Ron hands us each a champagne flute and we clink and sip.

"Honey, you'll probably need to dress in my room, since yours is so crowded with stuff." Suddenly, I'm "honey" again.

As soon as she disappears, Jason pouts. "Can I put these orchids in the fridge or not?"

Ron glares at him. "I told you I have salmon mousse and artichoke dip and chicken..."

I sigh. "Oh, come on, you guys. It's forty degrees outside, why can't something just go on the patio table? It's under cover."

Stuart turns me toward the door. "Wyn, you run along and help Jo. We'll take care of things."

I'm almost to the stairs when the doorbell rings. I open the door and find myself looking into golden-brown eyes under a shock of thick, brown hair. He's holding a suit bag and he says, "Hi. I'm Gary."

"They're all out in the kitchen." I close the door after him and point over my shoulder. "Just go on back." I turn and run up the stairs.

My mother's already brought my dress and cosmetics bag in, and we take turns showering in her bathroom. I spend an inordinate amount of time getting ready, using more makeup in one day than I have in the last four months. My feet rebel at being stuffed into pointy-toed, high-heeled shoes after weeks of nothing but cross-trainers, and the strapless bra constricts my rib cage till I feel like Scarlett O'Hara in her whalebone corset. We help each other with zippers and buttons and jewelry clasps. She's totally focused now, past caring whether I'm animated or comatose. As soon as we're decent, Stuart and Jason are admitted to the inner sanctum.

After gushing over our dresses, Stuart starts on my mother's hair and Jason turns to me.

"And how are we wearing our hair?"

"We're wearing our hair in a French braid." I smile sweetly.

"Let Stuart fix it," he says.

"I can do my own hair."

"I'll fix some flowers for him to weave in. You'll look so goddess, Wyn."

My mother hasn't said a word, but she has this sort of pleading look on her face.

I sigh. "Can't pass up the chance to look so goddess, can I?"

The guys smile conspiratorially at each other. After Stuart finishes with my mother, I take her place in the hot seat. He brushes my hair and lifts it up to the light, rubbing it between his fingers.

"You have such great hair, Wyn. Have you ever tried cornrows?" He doesn't wait for my answer. "You know, next time you're in town, I'd love to style it for you. Crank it up a notch."

He squirts something on my head and starts massaging it in.

"Don't make it all sticky, okay?"

"Relax. It's not going to be sticky, but we do want it to hold up for the afternoon." He manages to subdue my mane into a French braid in record time, entwining it with a garland that Jason makes from stephanotis, rosebuds, and variegated ivy. It makes me nervous that they won't let me look. Stuart fusses, pulling tendrils out around my face and at the nape of my neck till I want to slap his hands. He insists on applying more blush.

He smudges my eye shadow with his pinkie. "Subtlety, Wyn. Hard edges are definitely out." He adds a little mascara to my lashes. I'm going to look more Beverly Hills than Amanda. Then he stands back and squints at me with one eye closed. "As close to perfection as you're going to come in this lifetime, darling."

Perfection? Maybe. What I feel as I stare at myself in the mirror is an overwhelming déjà vu. I can almost picture David standing next to me. In fact, if he saw me now, he'd probably forget all about the blonde. This is the way he liked me—all dressed up with someplace to go.

I sweep out of my mother's room just as the bartender is stepping out of my bedroom. He's wearing a dark suit, not exactly bartender attire. When he sees me, he grins, like we're old buddies.

"Can I help you find something?" I use my best Hancock Park talking-to-the-servants voice.

"Sorry. I couldn't find anyplace else to change." He gives me an appraising look. "Nice dress. You must be Wynter."

"I am."

"It's nice to meet you. I've heard a lot about you."

In my brain, there's a tiny slot machine, with all the pictures lining up—oranges, flowers, dollar signs. No jackpot. Suddenly Howard/Richard comes bounding up the stairs. "There you are," he says to the bartender. "I wanted to introduce—" He sees me. "Have you two already met?"

Oh shit. I think I've been ordering my stepbrother-pending around like hired help.

"We were just about to," says Gary Travers.

"I'm so sorry. I thought you were— I'm really sorry."

He has wonderful, thick eyelashes. When he smiles, they make his eyes look sleepy. "I figured that out when I didn't see anybody I knew in the kitchen."

The doorbell rings again. "That'll be Lupe." I make my escape, thoroughly mortified.

Field Marshal Amanda marches us through a quick dress rehearsal of who stands where and who does what to whom. In the intervening fifteen minutes before guests are supposed to begin arriving, I slip off to the kitchen.

If I close my eyes halfway, the scene resembles an anthill frantic with activity. Nobody pays any attention to me, which is good. I get a glass of water and lean against the counter to watch. Boss Man Ron runs a tight ship. Everyone seems to know exactly where they should be and what they should be doing. I'm envious.

Abruptly the water glass is lifted from my hand and replaced by a flute full of bubbles. Gary pours the water into the sink. "Don't drink that stuff, little girl. Fish fuck in it."

I stick my nose over the rim of the glass to inhale the yeast. "They'd probably fuck in champagne, too, given the chance. I know I would." Did I really say that? I feel my ears glowing.

His laugh rumbles pleasantly. "I don't think I've ever seen a woman make herself blush."

"You obviously haven't been around me enough."

"Something I'm looking forward to."

No telling where this might be going, but Ron chooses this moment to insert himself between us to reach for a fruit platter. Heather and Frankie are arranging trays of shrimp puffs and baked new potatoes stuffed with sour cream and caviar. Gary snags a couple and we devour them. I'm hungrier than I realized.

It begins promptly at two o'clock in the living room that my father always referred to as the non-living room because nobody spent any more time there than necessary. Decorated by my mother in the stiffly formal style that she grew up with, it was only pressed into service on the most ceremonial occasions, like having the boss and his wife over for dinner. The gray-haired presiding judge is an old friend of Richard's. He's big on significant pauses and winks and lots of inflection. As a prelude to the wedding service, he tells how Richard and Johanna met at Prentiss Culver and fell in love and got married to dwell happily ever after. I must be the only one who doesn't know any of the details, because the rest of the fifty-odd guests laugh in the appropriate places, nod, and all but hum along.

In spite of my best efforts, I'm reliving my own wedding. Must be those words. "To have and to hold from this day forward. Till death us do part." Except at my wedding, I insisted on changing it to "As long as we both shall live." David found it amusing that I was superstitious about mentioning death. He looked at me just the way Richard's now gazing at my mother, as if she's first prize in a random drawing and he can't believe his luck. How can she not see what's happened? He's taken over her whole life, rearranging the house, selecting her clothes, changing her hair. She's been redesigned and repackaged, a new and improved product. Why is it that they fall in love with a woman, and then they just can't wait to start tweaking the details?

I'm so absorbed in my own thoughts that I'm startled when my mother turns to hand me her flowers so they can exchange rings. When they've finished the formalities and I give the flowers back to her, I notice Gary watching me, eyes brimming with questions. He gets points for being observant.

Then it's over and everyone's clapping for the performance. A blinding flash indicates the presence of subspecies Wedding Photographer. Champagne corks are popping like antiaircraft fire. I hug my mother and kiss Richard's cheek.

I smile. "Take good care of her. Or I'll break your kneecaps."

"Oh, Wyn." My mother laughs nervously.

Richard looks amused. "I don't doubt that you not only would, but could."

I watch them accept congratulations and listen to the details of the wedding trip to Hawaii and how they're going to be living in this house until they decide where they want to build. They pose for pictures with Gary and me and just about everyone else in the house except the caterer. They read telegrams and cards from friends who couldn't come. I'm introduced to people and five minutes later I've forgotten their names. I keep downing champagne, and whenever I finish a glass, Heather or Frankie is at my elbow with a refill.

"So you're the daughter." A man with a brown ponytail and a prominent Adam's apple looms over me. His voice is so loud I automatically back away. "I'm Chase." As if I should know who that is. "You live around here?"

"No, I live in Seattle."

"Seattle?" He shudders delicately. "Rain capital of the world. What do you do up there in Rain City?" I consider pointing out to him that it's raining here, now. Has been since last night.

"I'm a baker." He's one of those people who scans the room for someone else to talk to while he's talking to you.

"Which bank? I've got a lot of friends in banking."

I debate whether it's worth the effort to correct my image, decide against it. "First Queen Street."

He frowns. "Don't know that one."

"Wyn, hi."

When Georgia Graebel wraps me in her comfortable arms, I come perilously close to dissolving into tears. She tells me how beautiful I look and how beautiful my mother looks and what a wonderful man Richard is. "Don't you just love him?" she says, beaming.

"I only met him yesterday, Georgie."

She looks confused, then brightens. "Well, I know you'll love him when you get to know him. He's so, so nice. Worships the ground your mom walks on." She holds my shoulders. "Have you lost weight?"

"No, I just misplaced it."

She giggles. "How are you getting along up in the wild Northwest all alone?"

"Pretty good. I like my job. I have some friends."

"Hang in there, honey." She gives my arm a gentle squeeze. "It just takes time."

Richard and my mother have this magnetic field between them. They can be on opposite sides of the room and, as if on cue, they both look up and smile.

I try to be happy with them, but they're as remote as if I were seeing them through the wrong end of a telescope. It occurs to me in one of those "Aha!" moments of self-revelation that I'm jealous. Love, marriage—okay, I admit it—financial security. All those things I'm supposed to have, that I had. Now she has them. And I don't. I hate myself for the feeling, but there it is.

In the dining room, Tim Graebel hurries over. "Wyn, you look fabulous." He hugs me enthusiastically. "What a happy day this is." He puts on his sincere, friend-of-the-family expression. "I think Glenn would approve."

Before I can say something I'd be certain to regret, Gary is standing beside me with a plate of food. "Have you eaten anything yet?"

I accept it gratefully, although the way my stomach is acting, I don't know how much I'll be able to get down. "Tim, this is Howard's son, Gary." I realize what I've said when they both look at me blankly.

"Who's Howard?" Tim asks, but I'm laughing so hard that I'm afraid of losing control of my bladder, so I excuse myself and stumble to the powder room. My God, what is with me? I look in the mirror. My hair is starting to escape its confinement; there are black smudges of mascara under my eyes; I have no lipstick left. I can barely stand up without leaning against the wall.

The rain's stopped and the clouds are breaking up, but the wind has turned frigid. I wrap myself in an old gray sweater and sneak out through the kitchen, into the backyard. The laughter is muffled and the air smells of wet brick and eucalyptus.

My father laid this patio when I was seven. He worked on it for several weekends, laying out the herringbone pattern and border while I tried to help by bringing him one brick at a time. I march up and down, like a duck, matching my feet to the angle of the bricks. Eventually my head stops sloshing around. I can't remember what I did with my plate of food. All I want is to go back to Seattle, back to my own little house. I don't want to talk to anyone else about anything. I don't have any more fake smiles left. I want to go to the bakery and make bread and then go home and sleep.

Voices are calling my name. "Wyn, what on earth are you doing out here? You'll catch your death." It's my mother, frowning.

"It was so stuffy, I needed to get some air."

"You're shivering. Get inside this minute." My inner child knows that tone of voice and meekly obeys. Then I notice that she's changed into her travel outfit. "Run up and fix your face," she says, more gently. "We're getting ready to leave."

Sunday I wake up before dawn, deservedly hungover. The illuminated numbers on my watch say 5:35.

It's the middle of the night in Hawaii. I imagine my mother and Richard, lying in each other's arms in some sedately luxurious hotel bed. Maybe they turn, moving together in a sleepy embrace. The thought of him touching her, making love to her—and isn't it odd that I keep thinking of it as something he does to her? I can't picture my mother as an active participant, welcoming his touch, pulling him down, wrapping her legs around him, arching her back. The thought is so disturbing that I sit straight up in bed. My head throbs in protest, and I lie down again, deliberately turning off the Hawaii picture.

At eight, I get up. It's raining again. I open the door, step cautiously into the hall. I vaguely recall going berserk last night. Pushing some of Richard's boxes out of my room and down the stairs. I walk out on the landing. Three boxes lie tumbled in the foyer, flaps jutting out awkwardly like fractured limbs. Papers litter the tile floor. Hopefully, nothing's broken. A black windbreaker that says "An Affair to Remember, Catering for Special Occasions" hangs limply over the railing. There's a gap in my memory between the newlyweds' departure and my rampage. There was pizza, I know that. Gary and I ordered a pizza. I remember getting furious because he just opened the refrigerator and got a beer, as if he lived here. He reminded me that his father does indeed live here. The rest is fuzzy.

Downstairs the air is thick, the palpable silence that follows the departure of a noisy crowd. In the den, a pillow with no pillowcase sits on top of a neatly folded blanket on the couch. Oh, yes. Gary informed me that Richard said he was welcome to spend the night if he didn't want to drive back to his hotel. I think that was the match that set off the powder keg. I'm sure my mother will fill me in on the details.

I get a glass of orange juice and wander restlessly from room to room, in pursuit of my father's ghost. He's always just out of sight, but I can smell him. He never wore cologne or aftershave that I recall, but he had his own scent that was clean, glycerin soap and sandalwood. I've always felt his presence in this house, and it's comforted me. He probably won't hang around after the newlyweds get back. Or maybe he'll terrorize them. Materialize next to Richard in the shower some morning.

In the master bedroom, I notice for the first time that the photo is missing from the dresser, the one of my parents. As I turn away, my glance falls on the cedar chest at the foot of the bed. When I was a little girl, I spent long afternoons taking inventory of its contents.

I lift the heavy lid. I sit down next to it and take things out, piling them on the floor around me. The aroma of cedar permeates everything, makes the past seductively comforting. Sometimes my mother would tell me stories about these things. She and I would laugh at the clothing and hairstyles in the high school yearbooks. She showed me my father's college letter sweater with the gold pins for basketball and track. She told me that she went to all the track meets, even though track wasn't as popular as basketball, because she loved to watch him run. She said he reminded her of the god Mercury, with wings on his feet.

His scrapbook from World War II, full of pictures of friends who never came back. Lots of restaurant matchbook covers, photos of two or three couples in a booth, martini glasses at the ready, cigarettes in graceful, gloved hands or between painted lips. Everyone looked so glamorous. My mother always skipped over the yellowed newspaper clippings with pictures of her from piano recitals. My father was the one who told me how gifted she was. He said she could have been a concert pianist. All I remember is the agony of her attempts to teach me piano.

Dried corsages. A tiny red velvet dress from my first Christmas. I was only ten days old, but my father wanted me to have a Christmas dress instead of just a red sleeper, so my oma made one for me. There's a pink organza dress with a tulle overskirt my mother wore for piano recitals. Once when I was playing dress-up, I decided I wanted a ballerina tutu, so I took scissors to the skirt, hacking it off to about six inches long.

The second box I pull out is smaller and has a lid. Inside are letters and cards. A postcard from the Empire State Building sits on top. I flip it over and my chest contracts at the sight of my father's handwriting.

> *Nov. 20, 1958*
> *Dear Jo,*
> *Fantastic view, but I'd forgotten how cold this place gets. Miss you and J. W.*
> *Love,*
> *Glenn*

A man of few words.

I brew coffee and dunk pieces of stale cinnamon roll in it for breakfast. When I can't avoid the inevitable any longer, I climb the stairs to my room and slit the tape on the boxes that David brought over.

The first one's full of ticket stubs, programs from plays and concerts, photos. In a lot of the pictures, I look less than wonderful. I'm talking, eating, yawning, looking away from the camera so that my eyes look all white, like the alien spawn in *Village of the Damned.* David's amazing. He always looks good. His mouth is never open; his eyes are never shut. He never has a stupid expression on his face.

A manila envelope bulges with wedding cards and gift tags, a few leftover invitations. A letter. I was at a colloquium at San Francisco State the summer before we married. It isn't a lengthy letter, but it's the only one I have from him. I pull out the blue, monogrammed notepaper.

July 7

Dear Wyn,

God, I miss you. I detour by your place every morning on my way to work, just in case you decided to surprise me and come home early. I don't really expect you to be there, but I'm always disappointed that you're not. I miss our weekends. I hate waking up on Saturday and Sunday and not seeing you next to me. I love the way you look asleep, with your hair curling all over your shoulders. Shit. Now I'm horny.

A bunch of us went to Hank and Marie's for the Fourth and everyone was asking about you. By the way, I have a BIG surprise for you. It has to do with the wedding, but I can't tell you anything else. I think you should chuck the seminar and come home early. I promise you won't have to work very much longer anyway. I plan to take very good care of you. Call me about what time your flight gets in. (And make it soon.)

All my love,

David

The "BIG" surprise was our house—the same one he locked me out of. He took me to see it the day I got home from San Francisco. He made me keep my eyes shut till we got there. When the car stopped and he said I could look, I gasped with what I'm sure he assumed was surprise and delight. He told me proudly about the architect, how the house had been featured in *Architectural Digest*, he'd managed to get a tear sheet and have it framed. It was the best area of Hancock Park, he said. East of Highland and north of Third.

In the neighborhood of older Italianate, Spanish, and Tudor houses, the stark-white contemporary stood out like the nouveau-riche cousin from Shaker Heights at a gathering of some Brahmin clan. Eventually I got used to it, but I never loved it the way he did. The stark-white walls and steel railings felt chilly to me. The strange angles kept me off balance. A few times after we first moved in, I actually got lost in it.

The doorbell jerks me upright and I look at my watch. One-thirty. It rings again. Maybe somebody with a present for my mother and Richard. I run down the stairs and open the door.

David.

Just to make the weekend a full-blown, unmitigated disaster. I want to slam the door in his face, but surprise has leached the decisiveness out of me.

"Can I come in?"

I'm a mess. No makeup, hair like a whirlwind. He steps carefully around the tumbled boxes, giving them only a cursory glance.

Finally, I blurt out, "What do you want?"

"Your mother said you were coming for the wedding. I was hoping you'd still be here." I recognize the teal cashmere sweater that I gave him one Christmas; it makes his eyes the color of Lake Tahoe.

"How did you slip your collar?"

"Wyn, please." He takes my arm and I jerk away reflexively. His fingers leave an imprint on my skin. "Can't we just talk?"

He follows me into the den. I sit in my mother's sewing chair, cross my legs, fold my arms. He paces aimlessly for a few minutes, stopping to inspect the little boxes on the mantel.

"How are you?"

"If you actually gave a shit, you could've called to find out."

"Wyn, I do give—I do care how you are. Didn't you know I'm in Denver for a while?"

"Last time I heard, they had phones in Denver."

I look away from him, at the little oval table next to me. It's walnut, with impossibly slender, hand-carved legs and a polished burlwood veneer top. My mother isn't big on flower arranging, but someone, maybe Howard, has placed two dozen yellow tulips in an ugly metal vase—brushed aluminum or steel—very architectural. I vaguely recall them sitting on the sideboard in the dining room.

"We got the Coors account. I'm setting up a satellite office to handle it." He lounges against the fireplace, looking like an ad for men's cologne. "I've been up to Aspen a few times. I stayed at the condo. Everything's fine. Up there." He looks around the room as if he's trying to figure out what's different. "How's Seattle?"

"Fine."

"You're still at the bakery?"

"Yes."

"I guess it's kind of relaxing."

"It's not relaxing. It's damned hard work."

"I mean mentally relaxing."

"Sure. Any idiot can make bread."

He sighs. "You know I didn't mean it that way. I've always thought that you could do anything you—"

"David, why are you here?" After I ask, it occurs to me that I probably know the answer.

He makes his way to the couch and sits down on the edge of the seat cushion, hands clasped loosely, finally making eye contact with me. "I never wanted to hurt you."

"Wow. I feel so much better."

The way he ignores my sarcasm tells me that this is a well-rehearsed speech, brooking no interruptions. "I didn't intend to start . . . with Kelley."

"When was the first time?"

There's some small satisfaction in watching him squirm. "Wyn—"

"Was it the Christmas party? Last summer?"

"How could you think that? I didn't start seeing her till you went to Seattle."

"How can you look me in the face and lie?" There's a stubborn little knot forming in my throat.

"I swear." His eyes close. Those long, dark lashes.

I stare at the beige carpet. Richard'll be ripping it out soon. Replacing it with hardwood, dhurrie rugs. When I try to look at him, my vision blurs. "Could you just tell me why?"

The cobalt eyes shift away from me. "I don't know. I think we both changed. We grew apart—"

"We didn't grow apart. You just saw someone younger and prettier that you wanted and you didn't give a shit—"

"Wyn, don't. It wasn't like that at all. You and I were making each other miserable."

"That's just how you rationalized dumping me."

"I'm not dumping you. You're taking this too personally—"

Even he knows how stupid that sounds.

"Wait. You dump me for the bionic blonde and I shouldn't take it personally?"

"That's not what I meant to—"

"So what did you mean?"

He runs a hand through his hair, takes a deep breath. "What I meant was that our splitting up is not a reflection on you. In any way—"

"*David.* Let's get one thing straight. We did not split up. Splitting up implies that it was mutual."

"Well, it should have been mutual." His face is flushed now, eyes angry. "We weren't happy together—"

"So instead of talking about it, trying to work it out, you just said screw this and went on to the next in line."

"I know I changed, too." Back to the calm voice of reason. It's infuriating. "We just weren't making contact anymore. And then, with Kelley, there was this intense . . . communication. She was right there, in the trenches with me every day. We worked so well together. I mean it got to the point where we didn't even have to talk, I knew what she was thinking and—"

"Shut up!" My hands cover my ears like the little hear-no-evil monkey.

"I'm sorry. I shouldn't have come over." He scoots forward as if he's going to get up.

"Then why did you?" I didn't intend to yell, but I am. "Why the hell did you come here?"

He leans back slightly, as if blown by the force of my anger. "The only reason— I wanted to tell you..." I know what he's going to say. I hear it so clearly that the actual words, when he says them, seem like an echo. "I'm going to marry Kelley."

I surprise both of us by bursting into raucous laughter. "I think bigamy's illegal in California."

He blinks at me like he can't quite place who I am. "For God's sake, Wyn. I just wanted to talk to you. To do the right thing—"

"The *right thing?*" When I leap to my feet, suffused with righteous indignation, I inadvertently kick the leg of the delicate antique table. It goes over and the vase full of tulips resting on it gets launched. Water and flowers and those little glass marbles that they use to hold the flowers go flying everywhere.

All those pretty yellow tulips. Now come the tears from some seemingly bottomless reservoir.

"Wyn..." Before I can get a grip on myself, David's got a grip on me, ignoring the broken flowers and sopping carpet, slipping on the stupid marbles. Holding me.

"Wyn, don't. Please, please, don't do this. I didn't want it to be like this. It's for the best. You weren't happy either. Don't you remember what it was like? Wyn..." He's smoothing my hair, wiping tears off my face with a tenderness I haven't seen in months. Years, maybe. Did he think I didn't care?

What happens next belongs on Sally Jessy Raphael or one of those afternoon shows where people say and do things that are beyond the scope of their own imaginings. When I turn my face up to him, there are real tears in his eyes. It's just him and me. Like it was before. Like none of this other shit ever happened.

He loved me. He still loves me.

Just when you think a thing is dead. Hysterical laughter bubbles up in my throat because all I can think of is General Franco. One day he's on life support, the next he's sitting up eating a steak.

My husband kisses me, and my arms lock around his neck so tightly that for one wild second I wonder if I could snap it, the way they do with chickens. Then sanity regains the upper hand. I feel it rising in a cold wave. He extricates himself. "I'm sorry. I shouldn't have done that." He won't look at me.

Unfortunately, he's the only one in the room exhibiting a shred of common sense. I slide my hands up under his sweater, kiss his mouth, right at the corner, graze it with the tip of my tongue. "Hold me," I whisper. "Just for a minute."

Whoever said love has no pride knew what they were talking about.

"Wyn, stop. I can't." It's almost a groan. My right hand slips down to his belt, then down his thigh, and I hear his breath catch, feel him come to life against me. He grips my arms abruptly, thrusts me away. "You're just making it harder." I laugh at his unintentional double entendre, and then more tears.

"David, you love me, I can tell you still love me." I grab his hands and he pulls them away. It's like trying to hold on to a fish.

Now he's back in control, and totally turned off by this vulgar display of emotion. He holds my wrists at my sides. "I'll always...care about you, Wyn. But it's time to get on with our lives. I'm sorry." This is his executive-decision-making voice. I've just been terminated. It's a business decision. Nothing personal.

He looks around the room. "I'll help you clean this up."

"No."

He's already kneeling, picking up the vase. He drops one of the marbles in and it pings rudely.

I try to tuck some hair behind my ears, stop sniffling, dredge up some dignity. "I want you to leave. Now."

He turns the table back upright, sets the vase on it. Then he's out the door. It shuts decisively, like he's afraid I might sprint after him and tackle him on the lawn. The school clock chimes two, startling me, and I stare at my handiwork—boxes dumped in the foyer, broken flowers, soggy carpet. My God. I've become a one-woman wrecking crew.

There's half a bottle of champagne in the refrigerator, so I pour myself an eight-ounce tumblerful. I drop into a chair at the oak table and take a big swallow, letting the bubbles burn my throat. I'm suddenly limp, no bones, just a blob of rubbery flesh. When I wipe the residue of tears away, I smell Polo on my hands.

It's raining when my flight lands at SeaTac Monday afternoon, that kind of gentle rain that makes the locals say, "This? This isn't rain; it's mist." CM's white Camry is waiting outside baggage claim.

"What have you got in here, barbells?" she complains as she heaves a box into the trunk.

"Old things." I pick up her Day-Timer, an empty Styrofoam cup, and a package of pretzels off the passenger seat and throw them into the back. We pile into the front and take off.

"So. How did it go?"

"Good. It was a nice wedding."

"Liar."

"Okay, it was a nightmare. Something out of Eugene O'Neill."

"You want to tell me?"

I shake my head slowly. "Later maybe. I'm too tired to do it justice tonight."

"Okay."

"And then yesterday David came over."

"What for?" She frowns.

"To tell me he's going to marry Barbarella."

"Shit." She pokes her tongue into the side of her cheek. "Well, you sort of knew it was coming."

"Did I?" She doesn't say anything, so I rephrase the question. "Did you ever think he might be involved with someone else?"

She's the picture of intense concentration on the road. "It crossed my mind once or twice."

"Why didn't you ever say anything?"

We stop at a light and she turns to me. "I thought that you knew and didn't want to deal with it." The guy behind us honks his horn and she flips him off.

"The light's green," I say. She turns onto the freeway and puts the hammer down. "How would I have known?"

"It was a textbook case, Wyn. All the signs were there. In fact, from all the stuff you told me, I thought—"

"You're my best friend," I blurt out. "Why the hell didn't you say something?"

For a second, I think she's going to get us killed as she exits across three lanes of traffic. At the bottom of the ramp, she pulls into a deserted parking lot and stops the car, swivels in her seat to face me.

"I couldn't be the one to tell you. For God's sake, I thought you were telling me. All the things you said. You were just dancing around it."

"Like what? What did I say?"

"You were always talking about how he was never home. How he didn't talk to you. That you hadn't had sex in forever—"

"That doesn't have to mean someone's screwing around." I hit the window button, and the cold air revives me.

"No," she says. "Not always." She reaches over to squeeze my hand. "I'm sorry, Baby."

She starts the car again and gets back on the freeway, driving fast. I close the window. Headlights rushing past us in the opposite direction become long streamers of light. Neither of us says another word till we get to the foot of Queen Anne.

"I think you should stay with me tonight," she says.

"I have to go to work."

"I don't want to leave you alone."

"I'll be fine."

After I've unlocked my door and turned on all the lights, we lug the boxes and my bag up from the car and put them in the office.

"Thanks for coming to get me." I collapse into the club chair and she sits down on the futon.

"Look, I'm sorry. Maybe I should have—"

"CM, it's okay. Really. I'm sorry I blew a gasket on you."

She looks dubious. "Are you sure you're all right?"

"Yeah, I'm just exhausted. I should probably try to grab a nap before I go to work."

We trade hugs. I know if I gave her any opening at all, she'd stay. We'd drink some wine, and I'd end up telling her everything. Maybe I'd feel better. Or maybe I wouldn't. Too much sympathy can be worse than none at all. You start holding on to the hurt. You hoard it, stroke it, polish it like some perverse treasure so you can justify all this sympathy you're getting.

Besides, I'm fresh out of openings tonight.

Thirteen

❧

You look like you could use a boat ride." Mac McLeod stands on my porch Sunday morning, smiling with just his eyes.

"What I could use is about three more hours' sleep," I grumble.

"Sorry. You haven't been to Bailey's all week, so I thought I'd check on you."

"I didn't get back till Monday night. I've been trying to crawl back into my rut."

He laughs at my surliness. "Come on, get dressed. We'll just ride over to Bainbridge and back. Being on the water might improve your attitude. Works for me."

We get coffee at the Market, walk down First Avenue past the adult movie houses and used bookstores, the Oriental rug showrooms with their absolutely rock-bottom, no-joke, going-out-of-business-sale signs, homeless people asleep in doorways under dirty overcoats. He tells me the nicknames of all the skyscrapers. Washington Mutual is the Phillips Head Screwdriver building, Fourth & Blanchard is the Darth Vader building. First Interstate is the vacuum-cleaner tube, Century Square is the Ban Roll-On building.

It's cold by the waterfront. The coffee cup feels good in my hands. At the Colman Dock, we run for the *Spokane* with a few other passengers, stand by the aft rail as she pulls away. The wind's still kicking up whitecaps, but the clouds have broken and long fingers of sun test the water.

We stay outside aft, sheltered from the biting wind in the lee of the passenger decks. The boat shakes with the effort of the engines and the wake trails out before us, a white road back to the pier. I hang over the rail. "Tell me a story."

"About what?" he says.

"I don't care. You must hear some great ones at work."

He gives me his little wry grin. "It would be a flagrant breach of professional ethics."

"Then tell me one about you. Tell me the Gillian story." A gull flies up and hovers alongside, eyeing us impassively.

"I don't think this is—"

"Please. Distract me."

"Okay." He pulls his hat down lower on his forehead. "I was hitch-hiking from Auckland to Wellington. This guy in a beat-up old Land Rover picked me up. He took one look at me and asked if I was inter-ested in making a few bucks. I was practically running on fumes, so I was extremely interested. He owned a sheep station and they were in the middle of the shearing season. Somehow a shearing shed had caught fire and it had spread to some other buildings. Anyway, the family and all their regular help were too busy shearing to rebuild, so they were look-ing for guys to work construction in return for room and board and a few bucks. I was thinking I'd work for a week or two and then move on.

"So that night we're having dinner at this long table—about eight or ten guys—and this young woman comes in to help her mother serve. The daughter of the guy who picked me up."

"What did she look like?"

"Not beautiful. Really not even what you'd call pretty. Brown hair, blue eyes. Tall. Rangy. She had that body ease that people have when they've grown up doing hard physical work..." He smiles. "If you looked at her, she looked right back, like she was checking you out. I didn't pay much attention to her at first. She was just there every day, helping her mother. Then one day she didn't come and I realized I was looking for her at every meal. She was gone for a week. She came back the morning I was leaving. In fact, I was walking down the drive when this car pulled up and she got out. We just looked at each other there in the driveway. She smiled. I turned around and went back into the bunkhouse and unpacked my bag. I ended up staying for six months."

"My God, how romantic." I grip the rail, lean back. "So what happened?"

He turns around, his back against the metal pole that braces one of the lifeboats. Over his shoulder, Mount Rainier pokes its snowy head up through a lei of clouds.

"Nothing. She wanted to get married, have kids, raise sheep. I didn't, so I left."

The wind whips a strand of hair across my face and he hooks it behind my ear, being careful not to touch my face.

We get off at the Winslow terminal, buy ice cream from a cart in the parking lot. We stand, shivering and laughing because we're cold and eating ice cream anyway. He asks me what my favorite flavor is.

"Rocky Road." I say it without hesitation, without thinking.

I have a sudden, crystal-clear memory of my mother and me standing in the shade of a eucalyptus grove beside the little Sebastian general store on Highway 1 in San Simeon. We're eating Rocky Road ice cream cones while my father takes our picture. The golden hills and the towers of Hearst's castle rise in the background. I can see the waves of August heat rippling off the road and smell the piercing scent of eucalyptus oil.

"What?" He's looking at me.

My gaze veers to the terminal. "I think they're boarding."

Coming out through the turnstile at Colman Street, he finally says, "So how was the wedding?" One lurching sob and the waterworks open. This is getting old.

"That good, huh?"

He puts one arm around me and lets me cry all over his fuzzy flannel shirt that smells like pine trees. He rubs my back a little, but gingerly, as if I have something sticky all over me and he doesn't want to get it on him.

He hands me his handkerchief, not one of those white, ironed linen things that David carries, but a blue bandanna. As I'm trying to clean up my face and stop hiccuping, he takes my elbow and steers me over to the escalator. "Let's walk back up to the Market."

On the way, I spill my guts. I tell him every gory detail, every disgusting nuance of the weekend. I tell him about my mother and me sniping at each other, about me getting drunk and being a bitch to Gary and pushing Howard's boxes down the stairs.

I say stuff that I wasn't even conscious of until it pops out of me. Like how I thought it was a slap in the face to my father to have the wedding in the house he and my mother shared. I tell him about David giving me my pink slip, even how I tried to seduce him and he wasn't buying it. I tell him about CM and the way we parted company that night. He just walks along beside me, hands in the pockets of his denim jacket, the heels of his cowboy boots making a hollow tap with every step. He doesn't make any noises like sympathy or disgust or outrage. It occurs to me that's exactly why I can tell all this to him and not to CM, say, who'd be all sympathy and righteous indignation, ready to fly to L.A. and kick David in the crotch. He's just letting me dump it.

By the time I'm through, it's almost five, and I ask him if he wants to get a pizza or some Thai food, my treat.

"I'd really like to," he says, "but I have something I have to do tonight, so I'll take a rain check."

Men. Why the hell can't he just say he has a date? And what do I care? I was only offering because he baby-sat me all afternoon.

As soon as I get home, I sit down and call CM. When a man's voice says, "Hello," I think I dialed the wrong number. Then remembrance and recognition collide in my brain. It's Neal. This is the weekend of his seminar.

"Oh hi, Wyn," he says cheerfully. "She's right here. Hold on a minute. She's drying her hands." She probably cooked dinner and did the dishes while he sat on his skinny ass reading some esoteric treatise on the sociopsychological implications of hangnails.

"I forgot this was the big weekend," I say when she picks up the phone.

"No problem." Her voice is elaborately casual. "How are you?"

"I'm fine. I just called to apologize for being so weird the other night, but—"

"It's not a problem," she insists. "I'll call you later and we'll talk."

This has to be the shortest conversation she and I have ever had.

It's there when I pick up my mail Monday afternoon, the plain white envelope with the return address of a law firm in Beverly Hills. "There you are," I say to it. "I've been expecting you." One of the big advantages of living alone. You can talk to inanimate objects without getting a lot of weird looks.

I rip open the envelope and skim several pages of legal war chant. Looks like the way it works is, if one person says the marriage is broken, it is. Never mind what the other person says. It doesn't seem quite fair. We both had to say "I do" to get married but only he has to say "I don't."

The faceless gray army of legislators and judges and lawyers and clerks who, in their infinite wisdom, created our legal system apparently have decided that you wouldn't want to bind someone to you who didn't wish to be bound. So it's no longer necessary to prove insanity or substance abuse or infidelity or nonsupport or abandonment. All you have to do is say "I don't" and start dividing up the stuff. Sort of takes all the fun out of it. No more corespondents, no more alienation of affection, no more medical records or expert testimony from prominent psychiatrists. Just "I don't."

I fold up the papers and slip them back in the envelope.

Every afternoon when I wake up, I think about calling Elizabeth. But I know that once I do, it's the cannon shot that sets off the avalanche. My whole world becomes a rumbling mass of debris, irreversible in its slide to the bottom. I don't know how long I would have procrastinated, but while I'm still floundering, she calls me.

"Wynter, it's Elizabeth Gooden."

I can't help it. My first thought is my father telling me how sharks pick up the minute vibrations of an injured fish flopping around erratically in the water. Then I'm ashamed of myself. She's trying to help me.

Before I can tell her I've been served with papers, she says, "Our information specialist has come up with registrations from some rather pricey hotels in Cancun, in Scottsdale, and in San Francisco. I'll give you the dates, and you tell me if you accompanied your husband on any of these trips."

"I can tell you right now I haven't been to Mexico in at least three years."

"Interesting. Cancun's the oldest one."

I bite my lip. "When?"

"Let's see, that one was . . . last December. December fifteenth to twentieth."

It's like being smacked in the face with a wet towel. My birthday. The important client meeting he had to attend. "And the registration was for . . . two people?"

"Mr. and Mrs. David Franklin."

The ache inside me transmutes to a molten rage, expanding to fill every crevice in my body. I'm certain it's going to flood out of me, like a pregnant woman's water breaking.

"Wynter? Are you all right?"

"Yes."

It's not just that he lied, repeatedly and across a span of months, it's that I believed him. Long past the point where I should have started questioning. I was willfully ignorant. I was stupid.

I remember reading a few years ago about a woman in Malibu who solved her sticky divorce situation by pumping her husband and his girlfriend full of .38 slugs as they slept. I've always wondered what led her to the moment of decision. What was the last straw, the final humiliation? Or was it just an impulse? *Ya know what, Jack? I'm not going to put up with your bullshit one more minute.* And out the door with her Saturday-night special.

I'm especially curious at this moment because, while my own intent becomes instantly clear, I don't recall having given the matter any previous thought. No internal debate, no dividing a piece of paper into two columns labeled "Pros" and "Cons." It doesn't feel as if there's any other recourse open to me. When you're forced to fight, you use whatever weapons come to hand.

I tell Elizabeth that I've received papers from David's attorney, and she asks if I'm coming back to L.A.

"I hadn't planned to. Is that a problem?"

"It makes things slightly more complicated, but we can work around it. What is it you like so much up there?"

"My best friend lives here. And my mother doesn't."

This is the first time I've heard her laugh outright. "I thought maybe it was the weather."

I must be starting to think like a native Northwesterner, because it irritates me the way people are always ragging on about our weather. When I don't respond, she becomes all business again.

"All right, Wynter, here's what I want you to do. Read over the papers, sign them where it's indicated. It's pretty straightforward, but if you have any questions, call me. If I'm not here, Charlene can help you. Make photocopies of everything and start a file for yourself. Then overnight the originals to me and I'll send you a response form to fill out. And just remember, the sooner you get things back to me, the sooner I can—"

"How long could the whole process take? Worst-case scenario."

"Everything depends on how cooperative your husband and his lawyer want to be. My hope is that we can put it to bed by this time next year, but it could take two or three years. Longer if we have to go to trial."

"Elizabeth, I want to drag this thing out as long as we possibly can."

She barely hesitates. "You know, I think we can have it over fairly quickly, and still mop up the floor with him—financially speaking. But the longer it takes, the less money there will be for you as well as for him."

"It's not about the money. I want him to understand very clearly what it's going to take to marry her. I want him to have a good, long time to decide if she was worth it."

"There's a saying, Wynter: 'She who seeks revenge should dig two graves, one for her victim and one for herself.' "

"I'm willing to accept that possibility."

"This isn't the way I usually work."

"I know. That's why I'm telling you up front. I'd like to work with you, and I'd rather give the money to you than to someone else. But if you don't want to handle it, I'll respect your decision."

An audible sigh. "Very well. But there are limits to what I can do."

I was so preoccupied in rehashing my conversation with Elizabeth when I left for work last night that I forgot to take my pillowcase full of dirty clothes to work with me, so now I have to visit Launderland in the afternoon. Kids running around like it's a big, sudsy theme park, screaming, slopping Cokes on the floor. Mothers deep into paperback romance novels or balancing the checkbook or sketching their next tattoo.

And Mac, bent over his notebook, oblivious to the pandemonium in progress all around him.

I divide my clothes into three piles, carefully measure detergent, and feed in my quarters. Then I flop down in the orange molded plastic chair next to him.

He immediately closes his notebook.

"Nuclear secrets?"

"Just stuff."

My face heats up. Maybe he has no interest whatsoever in conversation with me. What if I'm presuming too much? We had dinner once, spent an afternoon on the water. What does that mean?

I pull out my copy of Mark Twain's *Letters from the Earth*.

"Great book," he says.

"You've read it?" I don't mean to sound astonished.

He laughs. "Yeah. Right after I finished *Vampire Lesbian Cheerleaders*."

"I didn't mean..." My voice sounds stiffer than cardboard. I open the book, shuffle past the introduction to the first page, where God sits on his throne, thinking.

"I've never been to California," he says. "What's it like?"

I look at him, first from the corner of my eye, then straight on. "It's not like anyplace else."

"No place is like anyplace else," he says. "Even the most boring, dusty hole in the middle of the prairie is different from all the other boring, dusty holes."

I close the book. "It's big. A lot of it I've never seen."

"Tell me what you know."

"Mostly L.A. The central coast. The High Sierra."

He turns a little bit in his chair. "Actually, I've been in southern California once, the L.A. airport. It looked pretty brown. What's the central coast like?"

I settle down, letting the chair cup my body. Memory kicks in. "It smells so good, the fog, the eucalyptus. The hills are golden all summer, green in the winter, when it rains. That's where William Randolph Hearst built his castle..." I look at the book in my lap. "You'll probably go there sometime. Everyone goes to California eventually."

"Mostly San Francisco and L.A."

"And that's a good thing. Keeps them away from my spot."

"Where's your spot?"

"Pismo Beach."

"What's there?"

"Dunes. Huge sand dunes. My father used to tell me how Cecil B. DeMille had thousands of workers build an Egyptian city there for the 1923 version of *The Ten Commandments*. Hundred-foot walls, even a boulevard lined with statues of sphinxes and pharoahs. Then, after they finished filming, they just left it there, and now the whole thing's buried somewhere under the sand. I always used to think I'd be walking along the ridge someday and I'd drop down and disappear into another world."

"Like standing on top of the ocean," he says softly.

He gets to his feet and starts yanking laundry out of a washer, blue jeans, flannel shirts, and dark socks in with the towels and white clothes. Typical guy. Throwing it into the nearest dryer without turning around, he says, "No, I don't care if my underwear's gray or if the towels get lint on my socks."

"I didn't say a word."

"You didn't have to."

I open my book again.

When the dryers stop, he hauls his stuff out, jams it into a green army duffel, and watches with obvious amusement while I fold everything and pack it carefully in the pillowcase. I turn to say good-bye, but he says, "You want a ride? I'll try not to emit too many fluorocarbons between here and your place."

"Hydrocarbons."

He throws the duffel into the truck bed, my bag into the front seat. After two false starts, the truck grumbles to life, and we roll heavily down Queen in the afternoon gloom, Crosby, Stills and Nash on the radio.

He turns up the volume. My breath makes a little circle of fog on the window. It reminds me of some movie where they hold a mirror in front of a guy's mouth to see if he's still alive. I guess I pass the test. Mac's talking to me.

"Sorry, I zoned out."

"Coming to Bailey's tonight?"

"I'm kind of tired."

"Is that a no?"

When he turns on Fourth, a string of blinking lights draws my eye. "I can't believe they still have their Christmas lights up."

He follows my gaze. "Some people have a hard time letting go of things."

I fold my arms. "Pure laziness."

"Sometimes it's one and the same."

We pull up in front of the gray Victorian. He puts it in park, but doesn't turn the engine off.

"Been inside that place yet?" he asks.

"It's all locked up. I'm sure they don't want anybody wandering around—"

He laughs. "Somebody did a great job of socializing you."

My left hand tightens around the pillowcase while my right fumbles for the door handle. "Thanks for the ride."

"Wyn..." His eyes change color constantly, like the ocean on a cloudy day. Right now the pale irises are amber-flecked. "Listen, I know things are kind of weird for you..." Fingers drum the gearshift knob. "If you need a friend, I'm around."

Tim Graebel syndrome. "That's very nice of you."

"No, really," he says. "Just a friend. No expectations."

I watch his face. For what, I have no idea. "Okay," I tell him. "Thanks."

Two weeks and one day after the wedding, my phone rings at nine in the morning and I know before I pick it up that it's my mother.

"Hi, honey, I hope you weren't asleep. I can never remember when you sleep in the mornings and when you sleep at night. We got home late last night."

"No, I wasn't in bed. How was Hawaii?" I assume this is proper etiquette for asking your mother about her honeymoon.

"It was so beautiful. We had the most wonderful time." She sounds totally blissed out.

"Um, Mom...about the boxes..."

"I found them. Are you sure you want to throw all those pictures away, and all your wedding cards?"

"I'm sure. But I was talking about the other boxes. The ones with Richard's things—"

"Not to worry. He's getting everything out of your room. By the time you come home for your next visit, it'll be just like you left it."

"I mean the ones...in the foyer."

"In the foyer?" She pauses. "There aren't any boxes in the foyer."

I can almost hear Rod Serling's mellifluous baritone. "Wynter Morrison thinks she's been on a trip to her mother's house. But she's been in...the Twilight Zone."

"Oh. I guess...I meant to put the boxes from David down there, but I must have forgotten."

"You're absolutely certain you want to get rid of all that?"

"He came over the day after the wedding. He told me he's going to marry Kelley. I got the papers."

She sucks in a breath. "Oh, baby, I'm so sorry. That dirtbag! That—"

I laugh. "Mom, don't waste your breath. I've got a good lawyer. I'll do okay."

"It's not just the money, it's the way he's...He'd better hope he never runs into me again. Wait till Barbie finds out she's just the flavor of the month. He'll do the same thing to her, you mark my words."

"You don't look so good," Linda says. "You sick again?"

I glare at her. "I can't be sick again, since I was never sick before. I'm just depressed, that's all."

She snorts. "You got nothin' to be depressed about." I reach up on the top shelf over the sink, pull down a stack of aluminum bowls. "Do ya?" I slide my hands into the heavy oven mitts, take the sheet pans out of the oven where the day crew left them to dry, put them on the cooling racks. "You ain't gonna be bakin' bread for long," she persists. "Your husband'll come sniffin' around again pretty soon. Take it from me, they always do."

I have a vision of David on all fours, sniffing my leg. "It so happens that he's just filed for divorce," I shoot at her.

She grins with all her stubby little teeth. "You can still make his life hell, even if you ain't married. I did." The note of pride in her voice is unmistakable.

"Exactly how did you do that?"

"Oh, there's ways, missy. There's ways. You get a lawyer and they can tell you all the ways. There's child support and there's visitation."

"I don't have children."

"There's maintenance. Every time he got a raise, I hauled his ass into court." Her features are smooth with satisfaction.

"But he got drunk. He hit you. I thought you didn't want anything to do with him."

" 'Course I didn't." She rolls her eyes like I'm an idiot. "But I wanted to make his life hell. And I did. From the time I kicked him out, he never had a moment's peace."

"But neither did you," I point out.

She smiles with grim satisfaction. "It was worth every minute."

Phone calls at the bakery between midnight and 6 A.M. are almost always wrong numbers. For the occasional heavy breather or bored soul who wants to know what kind of underwear we have on, Linda keeps a police whistle next to the phone, the better to shatter their eardrums with, my dear. I always worry that some pervert will sue the bakery for injuries that prevent him from practicing his profession, but that's probably a California sensibility.

When she answers the phone about twelve-thirty that night, I brace myself for the blast, but she adopts her habitual look of disgust and holds the receiver out to me. My stomach sinks. I have three options. My mother is deathly ill. CM's been in a car accident. My house is on fire.

Instead, a man's voice says, "Wyn! I can't believe it. I've called every bakery in Seattle. I was beginning think you'd gone into the witness protection program."

"Who is this?"

"Gary Travers. I'm at the Edgewater for a few days on business. I was wondering if I could take you to dinner tomorrow night."

I hesitate, recalling our last and only encounter. Maybe he wants to take me to dinner so he can slip arsenic into my soup.

"Unless you're still mad at me," he adds.

The room has gone stone-silent. From the corner of my eye, I can see Linda walking on tiptoe. She fairly quivers with attention, like a dog with its ears up, whiskers twitching.

"Of course not. Dinner would be nice."

"Tomorrow night, then? About seven?"

"Sure." I give him directions to my house, hang up, and resume oiling pans for cinnamon-raisin bread. Linda's about to have a fit.

" 'Zat your ex?"

"Nope."

Silence except for the swish of the brush and the rhythmic lunging of the Hobarts. "You're not s'posed to take personal calls at work, you know."

I smile. "Sorry. Normally I wouldn't, but it was my brother."

"Your brother?"

"He lives in San Francisco and he's up here on business. We haven't seen each other since our parents got married . . ."

"Since your parents got married?"

"So we thought we'd have dinner tomorrow. Catch up on family news." I push the tray of oiled pans across the table, pull out the black binder, and pretend to study the recipe for cheese bread.

Canlis is the kind of restaurant my father would have liked. Can-tilevered over Lake Union at the south end of the Aurora Bridge, it simulates being inside a Christmas tree ornament, suspended in the dark, while lights that could as easily be candles or stars as headlights shimmer below. The place seems suspended in time as well, an old-style, expense-account watering hole, featuring hunter-gatherer slabs of red meat and premium cabernets. The servers all wear kimonos, which strikes me as odd, but they move easily in them, seeming to glide rather than walk.

We're early for our reservation, so we sit at the piano bar drinking vodka martinis and observing the salespeople and their clients, who seem to be the occupying majority. I don't really like vodka, but I love the tunneling warmth of it going down. And the olives.

After a few sips, I gather the courage to say, "I have to know. What happened to the boxes of your dad's stuff that I jettisoned down the stairs?"

Gary's had a haircut since the wedding, and he looks older, in a pleasing way, less like a refugee from a *Partridge Family* rerun. "I closed them up and put them in the den."

"You came all the way back to the house for that?"

He shrugs, almost embarrassed. "I thought it would be easier on everyone if they didn't come home and find a mess."

"That was a really nice thing to do. I guess it's lucky I was too drunk to push them all down. I feel like such an idiot."

"Don't. I understand why it happened." That makes him one up on me. He pushes a lock of thick brown hair off his forehead. He smiles. "Now it's my turn. Why did you introduce me to that guy as 'Howard's son'?"

I suck the pimiento out of my olive, nearly choking on it. "I know your father's a great guy, he just reminded me of— Did you ever read *The Fountainhead*?"

His laugh explodes, startling the couple on his left. "Man of granite, buildings of steel. Or vice versa. Except Howard Roark had flaming-red hair."

"I always thought that was a mistake."

"Yeah. Men of granite shouldn't be carrottops." He finishes his drink and declines a refill. "So tell me, Wynter Morrison, what are you doing up here?"

"Making bread." I stir the ice around and around in my glass.

"That's not what I meant." At this juncture, the hostess comes to seat us. After we're settled and he's ordered wine and people have ceased fluttering around us, he says, "Back to my question."

I look over the menu at him. "Gary, knowing my mother as I do, I'm quite sure you've heard more about my life than you ever wanted to know."

He gives me the sleepy-eyed smile. "I've heard a few things, but nowhere close to everything I want to know about you."

"The short version is, I'm separated and my husband's just filed for divorce. What about you? You live in San Francisco, right?"

"Larkspur. Marin. And don't think I didn't notice that extremely smooth transition. I'm divorced. One year tomorrow. But we're good friends."

"How very Marin."

"I guess so. But we have two kids, so it makes things easier."

"How old are they?"

"My son is eight. His name's Andrew. My little girl Katie's ten."

"You're not an architect, are you?"

"I park cars."

"Where?"

He grins. "I have a small company. Contract valet parking for events and businesses."

"So what are you doing up here?"

"Growing the business. I've been chasing some clients up here for about six months now. Seattle's a funny town. They don't much like out of towners."

"Particularly Californians." I smile.

"So I noticed. But it looks like a couple of them are finally coming around. I could be up here making a pest of myself every two or three weeks for a while."

The kimonoed waitress is back to take our order. When she leaves, I arrange the silverware, lining all the handles up abutting the edge of the table.

"Wyn." No choice now but to look at him. "I'm sorry if I'm making you uncomfortable. That's not my intention at all." His golden-brown eyes are looking very puppylike.

"You're not." The chain strap of my purse slips between my fingers and then back the other way. "I'm just...not used to this. I mean, I'm not even divorced yet. It all feels very strange."

He touches my hand lightly with two fingers, then withdraws. "Believe me, I know exactly what you mean. I just went through it myself. At the same time, though—"

"Sir?" The sommelier presents the wine with great ceremony and we have to go through the sniffing-and-tasting ritual. Gary gives each step of the process his full attention, focused, unhurried, but never dropping the thread of his thoughts.

"At the same time, though, I have to tell you that I'm extremely attracted to you." A pause. "I think it was the dominant way you ordered me back to the kitchen that day."

A lot of the tension dissipates when I laugh. "That was my Hancock Park mistress-of-the-castle persona."

"And you wear it well."

"Not too well, I hope."

Dinner is good, conversation pleasant, not overly intense, although there's a purposefulness about him that makes me wary. This isn't a man who does anything casually. By the time we're finished, I'm relaxed enough to agree to a brandy at the piano bar.

He tells me about his kids; he and his ex share custody.

"How does that work?"

"They're with me one week, then with Erica one week."

"That seems like it would be difficult on them, shuttling back and forth. What about school?"

"They're in private school, so that's not a problem." My brain is calculating the cost of private school in Marin for two children. "We've made their rooms as similar as possible in both houses so it's not too jarring. Complete set of clothes at both places. We try to keep it as stress-free as possible for them."

"What about for you and her?"

The laugh lines etched around his eyes and mouth are plainly not all from laughing. "We can deal with it easier than they can. Still, it's hard. There's no denying that. Sometimes when I'm driving all over the Bay Area I think it might be smarter if we shared a big house. Or got condos in the same building or something. But I guess that would have its own set of problems."

We walk slowly up the gravel driveway. "I'm glad you called. I enjoyed seeing you."

"Did you enjoy it enough to do it again Friday?"

"Gary..."

"Too pushy? That's a bad habit of mine."

"No, it's not that. I'm just...everything's so tentative with me right now."

"I understand."

I fish the key out of my purse and insert it in the dead-bolt lock. I'm hyperaware of him standing right behind me, closer than necessary, closer than I want, but the heat radiating off his body tugs at me. I want to lean back against him. I know if I turn around now, he'll kiss me. I do and he does.

"That wasn't so bad, was it?" He's still holding my face in his hands. His eyes are deep, but gentle. If I drown, it will at least be pleasant.

"I'm not sure. Maybe we should try it again." The realization of how long it's been since anyone kissed me like this sharpens my need, breaching my defenses like a traitor from the inside. You forget how that little electric spark dances over your skin, the sweet awkwardness of noses and chins, the softness of eyelashes, the burnished smoothness of a freshly shaved cheek.

It's a wrench when I finally pull away. "I have to get ready for work," I manage. *Take a cold shower.* "What time?"

He looks at his watch. "Ten-thirty."

"I mean Friday. What time should I meet you?"

Fourteen

⬥

It's been over a week and CM hasn't called me back. True, she might be out of town, but that's never kept her from picking up the phone before. She might still be pissed off at me, but I doubt it. She's not the type to let things fester. When she's mad, she blows up, cools off, and that's it. That leaves Neal. Either their reunion was total disaster and she's too depressed to talk about it, or it was total bliss and he's still there.

When she phones me Thursday afternoon, I can tell by her voice it's the latter. "Sorry I haven't called. I was thinking I'd stop by there on my way home. If you're not busy."

"Well . . . let me just look in my Day-Timer. Oops! Today's the day Harrison Ford's giving me flying lessons."

"We can talk while you're packing your parachute."

My latest bread experiment is coming out of the oven, all crusty and golden and filling the house with its sweet toasted-corn smell about the time she walks in.

"You shouldn't leave your door unlocked all the time."

"Then you wouldn't be able to barge in whenever you want."

She drops her purse on the futon. "God, that smells great. What is it?"

"Cornmeal-millet bread. Play your cards right and you might get to taste it."

She hugs me. "Have you recovered from the wedding?"

"Yes. And just in time, too. I got divorce papers. Have you recovered from Neal?"

"Oh, God." She's actually blushing. "I feel bad coming over here like some goosey teenager when you're dealing with divorce papers..."

"I'm young, I'll get over it. So tell me."

"It was incredible."

"Besides the sex."

"No, everything. We talked all weekend and he canceled his flight and stayed till yesterday. I think he did some major soul-searching after he left last fall. He was feeling inadequate about losing that job and he was taking it out on me... but he's sort of come to grips with that now..."

"Sort of?"

"I think he has. Anyway, he asked me if I'd be willing to try it again, and I said yes. He's moving back up here in two weeks."

"Into his own place?"

"Well... no. Why would we do that?"

"Maybe to see how it goes?"

"It's going to go fine," she says firmly. "His dissertation topic's been accepted by the committee, so all he has to do is write it."

"Is he going to work?"

"I'm sure he'll find something. Some tutoring, or maybe he can teach in a private school."

I run my tongue between my teeth and my upper lip to keep from saying anything nasty, but I might as well say it, because she knows what I'm thinking.

"He's never going to be a type-A overachiever," she says.

"I just don't like the idea of him living off you."

"I wouldn't mind supporting him while he writes his dissertation." She's right on the edge of defensive. "If that's how it pans out."

"I know, and I'm sure he wouldn't intentionally take advantage of you, but... sometimes..."

"Sometimes what?"

"Sometimes nothing. You're smart enough to know what to do. And I'm certainly no one to be giving advice."

"So tell me what David said. If you want to."

"The whole thing makes me tired. The gist of it is, we both changed. We weren't communicating. We were making each other miserable. Meanwhile, Kelley was there beside him every day. 'In the trenches,' I believe he said."

She screams with laughter. "The *'trenches'*? The closest David's ever been to a trench is when CalTrans had Highland all dug up."

I laugh till the tears come, which is a good thing, because otherwise it might just be tears. "But I haven't told you the good news. I had my first date."

"Really? With who?"

"*Whom.* My new stepbrother."

"Kinky. I like it."

"It feels a bit strange. His name's Gary."

"Good for you. You need a transitional man. To sort of get you back in the swing of things. What's he like?"

"Kind of cute. Nice."

"What else?"

"I'm not sure what else. I'll let you know after tomorrow."

"Does he live here?"

"Marin. He's just here on business."

She rolls her eyes. "What does he do?"

"Parks cars."

"I'm sorry?"

"He has a little company that does contract valet parking."

"His mother probably watched *77 Sunset Strip* when she was pregnant."

"He took me to Canlis Tuesday night, but I don't know where we're going Friday. Maybe we'll just get room service."

She arches an eyebrow. "You be careful. Remember, this is Transition Man."

"Sounds pre-Paleozoic."

"And don't forget to take a raincoat for his little soldier."

That first batch of cornmeal-millet bread tastes great, but it crumbles like baking-powder corn bread when I slice it. Not enough gluten.

I try again, cutting the cornmeal in half, adding another cup of whole wheat flour, and grinding half of the millet in the bakery's hand-crank grain mill. This is more like what I had in mind—chewier, but still with plenty of crunch from the cornmeal and millet. It makes toast to die for, especially slathered with salted butter and a little honey.

I take some to Linda, and she grudgingly admits it's good. "You have fun playing with all these trickity things at home," she warns me, "but if you think we're going to be changing anything around here, just get that idea out of your head right now."

"I wouldn't dream of changing one teaspoon of anything in the sacred black book." She's a one-woman stone wall.

"Why you want to be foolin' with bread on your days off is beyond me anyways." She stands there, hands on hips, her mouth drawn into a thin line, eyes shifting from side to side, as if making bread at home is a subversive activity that she might report to the work police.

It crosses my mind that I could do an end run here, take some of my samples to Ellen, ask her if she thinks we could give them a try. Maybe on Saturdays only. But Linda's hard enough to work with as it is. Going over her head would only inspire her to even greater heights of antagonism.

Gary and I agreed to meet in the bar at the Edgewater, in case he was running late, but he's sitting at a table near the fireplace, and his face lights up like a birthday cake when he sees me. I'm not accustomed to this kind of overt approval just for showing up.

When he stands up to kiss my cheek, my stomach gives one little flip of protest and then settles down. This is okay. I can do this. He tells me I look beautiful and I come very close to saying, "What?" just to hear it again.

"What would you like?" he asks. He's wearing what I've always called an "English-poet jacket"—a tweed sport coat with leather elbow patches. David wouldn't have been caught dead in one.

"Chardonnay, I think."

It takes him a few minutes to get the waiter's attention. David never had to try. There was an aura about him that caused service providers to hover, waiting for instructions. Why the hell am I doing this? When I'm eighty-seven, am I going to be propped up in bed in a nursing home, thinking about how David handled waiters?

After he orders my wine, Gary tells me that his meetings went better than he expected.

I smile. "That's good."

"I'll say. It means I can come back in three weeks."

I think I'm supposed to be enthusiastic at this point. When I don't say anything, his hand moves to cover mine. But gently. I almost don't feel it.

"I was hoping you'd be pleased."

"I am. Really. I'm just ... nervous, I guess."

"Perfectly natural. But I wish I could say something or do something that would make it okay."

I laugh. "Men always want to *do* something. Sometimes you just have to sit tight till things work themselves out." I extricate my hand and pick up my wineglass.

He says, "I talked to Andrew and Katie right before I came downstairs."

It's a few seconds till my brain kicks into gear and I realize he's talking about his kids. "What are they up to?"

"They're at Erica's, my ex-wife. Katie had cheerleading practice this afternoon and Andrew's science project won first prize in the school competition, so now he takes it to the district."

"You must be very proud of them."

He looks at the table, then back up at me. "I guess it's hard to understand if you don't have kids. I just get such a kick out of every new thing they do. Sometimes I tend to run on about it . . . I don't want to bore you."

"I'm not bored." In my head, I hear CM: *"Liar."*

"Do you ever want children at all?"

"I never have."

"Oh. Any particular reason?"

"No. I just think some women are meant to be mothers and some aren't. Besides, I taught high school. I've seen what becomes of those cute little babies."

"I think you'd be a great mom."

"Why?"

He shrugs. "I don't know. You just seem like such a—"

Now I'm laughing.

"No, you do. You're a warm, caring—"

"I'm selfish and spoiled."

"You're lively and interesting—"

"You're scraping bottom, Gary. Besides, I don't relate well to kids. It runs in the family."

"You would if you had some. Or if you met—"

"Oh no. Don't go there. Not even hypothetically. I've always believed that once you have a child, your own life is pretty much over."

"Not true. It's really just the beginning."

"Men can say that because they don't have to hang around and deal with the little—"

"I do." Suddenly he's serious.

"Sorry. Most men."

The piano player sits down at the baby grand and opens his briefcase. Gary looks at his watch. "We'd better get going. We've got a reservation at the Dahlia Lounge in fifteen minutes."

The Dahlia's a pretty romantic place in spite of the fact that it's small, crowded, and noisy. The walls are dark and the booths are lit by exotic-looking paper fish with lights inside. The service is efficient but relaxed. I unbend, even taking the liberty of looking into my stepbrother's pretty eyes. He picks up the cue, resting his arm on the back of the banquette so his fingers just touch my shoulder. For a minute, I want to giggle. He acts like I'm going to drop my chin and take a bite out of his hand.

"How long were you married to David?"

"Seven years."

"What's he like?"

"Oh...handsome, charming, bright, successful."

"Sounds like the ideal husband."

"My oma used to say, 'If something sounds too good to be true, it probably is.' What about you? How long were you and Erica together?"

"Eleven years." He smiles like a man who's found out more than he ever wanted to know about divorce.

"You miss her, don't you?"

"I miss all of us together. The way it was. After she went back to law school, nothing was ever the same."

"I would imagine law school's pretty demanding." I set down my glass and lean back against him just to feel his breath on my cheek.

"It is, I know it is." He shakes his head. "I guess I never understood why she wanted to go in the first place. She was making good money as a paralegal. Or why she couldn't have waited till the kids were older."

"It must have been really important to her," I tell him gently. "Studying law isn't a commitment you make lightly."

"Neither is marriage," he says.

After dinner, when he asks me if I want to go back to the Edgewater for a drink, I know what he's really asking and I say yes. In the lobby, neither of us glances at the bar; we head straight for the elevators. We're the only ones in the car and he pulls me into his arms. He tastes like the red wine we drank at dinner, the apple dessert. I like his aftershave— not Polo. The first recognizable emotion is relief. Number two is grati- tude. It's all coming back to me now—how it feels when a man wants you, how it borders on reluctance, because he's not sure once he's touched you that he can stop himself. It's like a drug, that touch.

But this one can stop, and he does. With obvious effort, he takes me by the shoulders. "Wyn..." His breathing is ragged. "I don't want to push you."

If he only knew how close he is to being jumped in the elevator.

Before the door to room 324 shuts behind us, I'm tugging his shirt-tail out of his slacks. He pulls my jacket down over my shoulders, kisses my neck, my ear, my hair. My jacket drops on the floor and we both step on it in our race to the bed. Captured on video, we'd be candidates for America's funniest. Between kissing and trying to take off our own and each other's clothes, we keep getting tangled up in sweater arms and pant legs.

He finally figures out the hook on my bra.

"God, I want you," he murmurs in my ear. "I just don't want it to be too fast."

I look into those drowsy eyes, now chocolate-dark with lust. "I do. Then we can do it again."

He pillows his head in my neck and we laugh.

It's too easy, almost familiar. My body seems to remember his from another time; it knows his hands, his mouth. He's intense, methodical, obviously used to being in charge, and I'm happy just to ride the sensations like waves. It does seem oddly like surfing, only instead of carrying me to the shore, each wave takes me farther out into dark water. He's a talker, asking me what feels good, telling me how to touch him. Every time I expect him to slip inside me, though, he backs off and starts over.

My fingers tangle in his soft, thick hair. "If you want me to beg, I will."

He smiles, moving his body over me.

The phone rings, probably once or twice before I hear it.

I whisper, "Don't answer it."

He tries. He really does. I can see the battle raging. "It might be the kids."

He's embarrassed, apologetic, torn. But he rolls away from me and picks up the receiver. "Yes? Erica. What's wrong?" He sighs through his teeth. "Well, I thought since I talked to them earlier—no, it's okay. No, I'm not busy. Of course I want to say good night to them."

He chats patiently—no, it's more than patient. He's into it. First Andrew, with the science project. A smile hovers on his face, but their conversation is serious man talk about grades. Haircuts. Andrew says he doesn't need one; his mother thinks he does. She knew, of course. When he talked to them earlier, he must have mentioned he was having dinner with someone. With the intuition that's actually a higher form of logic, she knew the someone was a woman.

It's Katie's turn. The cheerleader princess. His tone is teasing, cajoling. I look at him curled up on his side. Naked except for fuzzy black socks. The Titan Rocket has become a miniature gherkin, lying meekly on his leg. In one flash of clarity, I see a world I've always known existed, but that I've never brushed up against before. This world comprises 6 A.M. Saturday phone calls from Erica reminding him that it's his turn to drive to early soccer practice. Two sweet, freckled, serious little faces, smiling up at me. *You're not my mother. You can't tell me what to do.* Romantic dinners at Chuck E. Cheese. Chicken pox. Escaped pet boa constrictors. *My mother lets me watch MTV whenever I want.*

He's off the phone now, and looking thoroughly miserable. "I'm sorry."

"It's okay." I lean over to kiss his cheek. "I need to think about getting ready for work." I ease off the bedspread with as much dignity as a naked woman can manage.

I pick up my bra and my sweater and my wool slacks. I toss the jacket on the foot of the bed, take the rest of my clothes into the bathroom with me, and turn on the shower.

The wind knifes through my jacket. I scurry down the alley toward the bakery's back door, pondering my aborted transformation from dumped wife to swinging divorcée. Gary insisted on driving me up the hill, apologizing all the way. He said he was sorry so many times, I wanted to stuff my scarf in his mouth. He said he wants to see me when he comes back at the end of the month. I said yes, but my stomach is not totally okay with this.

I knock on the back door, shift my feet back and forth, try to keep warm. Linda must be in the storeroom or the bathroom. I knock again, louder. Still no answer. *Shit, Linda. Don't mess with me tonight. I'm not in the mood.* I take off my day pack, dig down into the zippered compartment, fumble around till I feel the paper clip and metal tag on the end of the bakery key.

Inside, only a few lights are on. None of the flour buckets are out. For that matter, nothing is out. The worktable is clear.

"Linda?" No answer. I get this weird, prickly feeling at the base of my spine. "Linda?"

I lock the door behind me, take a few steps into the room, and then I hear something—not exactly words, more a cross between a groan and a grunt. "Linda, where are you?" Because I didn't have sense enough to turn on the rest of the lights, I trip over her foot before I see her. She bellows something unintelligible.

She's propped against the wall next to the ovens, blocking the narrow passage that leads to the storeroom. Eyes closed, mouth open, a long string of saliva hanging from one corner. Her breathing is noisy, labored. "Linda, are you sick?" When I bend down, I smell the bitterness of juniper berry. Linda is drunk as a skunk. Right on the verge of passing out. An open bottle lies on its side next to her, but it must have already been empty when she knocked it over, because there's nothing on the floor. Looks like I'm making the bread tonight. But what to do with Linda?

In the storeroom, I find a couple of canvas tarps. I make a little nest on the other side of the oven. Getting her over there won't be easy. She's not that big, but she's deadweight. Finally I hit on the notion of a drag/carry like they taught us in Girl Scouts to move an injured person. I lay one of the tarps out next to her and by shoehorning myself between her and the wall, I manage to roll her onto it. By this time she's out cold and it's like trying to drag a beached whale. Fortunately, she can't feel anything, so I end up moving her by bracing myself against the wall and shoving her with my feet. Between pushing and dragging, I eventually get her out of my way, throw her coat over her, dispose of the bottle, and get into high gear for bread making.

When I've got both Hobarts heaving dough around and I'm sitting on a stool oiling pans, I remember Tyler saying that Linda took a nip now and then and that it made her more talkative, but she obviously crossed that line hours ago.

I haul the white bread and whole wheat out of the mixers, into the troughs for their first rise, dump in the ingredients for the raisin bread and cheese bread without stopping to scrape down the mixers. No time for niceties this evening. While I'm measuring out raisins onto the scale, I hear a noise that sounds like a very big Velcro fastener being ripped apart, and I realize that Linda has risen to a half sit and is throwing up. Jesus, Mary, and Joseph, as my opa used to say. Well, at least she's conscious and not choking to death on it. I grab an empty flour bucket, stick it under her head. The stench is overpowering.

When I think she's finished, I wet a towel and toss it at her. She wipes herself, lies back down with the towel over her face, and drifts back into oblivion. I throw the bucket and the towel into the Dumpster, leaving the back door propped open. This is something we normally never do because of security, but tonight no one would want to come in here unless they had to.

At 6 A.M. I'm removing the cheese bread to the cooling rack when Ellen unlocks the front door. There's a silence. Then, "Holy shit, it's freezing in here." Footsteps. "What is that god-awful smell?" Then she's standing there, looking from Linda to me, to Linda, to the back door, to me. "What the hell happened?"

"Linda's really sick," I say. I pick up the peel, stare into the heat of the top deck, shuffle some loaves from back to front.

Linda starts rolling around on the tarp, moaning.

"We've got to get her out of here and get rid of that smell or we won't be selling anything today." Her eyes narrow as she looks at me. "Has she been drinking?"

I shrug, look her in the eye. "Beats me. She was fine when I got here. Then she just sort of collapsed."

Ellen looks at me hard for a few seconds. "I'll call her daughter."

Paige, the daughter, is here in less than thirty minutes, almost as if she were waiting for a call. She's surprisingly pretty, in a severe way, hair pulled straight back, no makeup, white nurse's uniform. When Ellen introduces us, I notice that her pale-blue eyes are red rimmed, as if she's been crying. She stands over Linda, a mixture of disgust and concern on her smooth features.

"I expect she's been drinking since late afternoon," she says. She looks at Ellen. "My father was killed yesterday."

While Ellen and I scurry around cleaning up the bakery, it occurs to me that Linda's loss, while undeniably sad, presents me with an opportunity. I scrape together a fist-size lump of dough from one of the mixer bowls, break it into pieces, and mix it into a cup of water. Throw in two handfuls of flour, and we have a *chef*, the seed of a sourdough starter, covered with a damp cloth and sitting on a storeroom shelf to ripen in the cool, yeasty air.

Jean-Marc showed me how when I told him I wanted a *chef* to take home with me.

"First you must make the *chef*, okay?" "Okay" was his favorite American word. He grabbed a small bowl from a shelf under the worktable and took it over to the flour bins. "You take the flour." He threw a fistful of white flour into the bowl. "And little whole wheat *pour le faire plus fort, vous comprenez?* Stronger. Then the water." He dumped the flour into a mound on the table, made a well in the center, and filled it with water. Then, using two fingers and working from the well, he began to combine the two, first making a paste, then adding just enough flour to make a firm dough. He handed me the walnut-size lump. "Knead a little...."

He wandered around, searching for something, while I gently massaged the little lump on the table.

When the dough was springy, he produced a small earthenware crock. "Okay. *Ici.*" I dropped the dough in. He took a towel, wet it and wrung it out, and laid it over the top of the crock. *"Maintenant nous attendons."*

"For how long?"

He shrugged. "Until it is ready. Two, three days maybe. We wait for the *levure sauvage, vous comprenez?*

"The wild yeast?"

"*Oui.* And you must keep the towel wet. *N'oubliez pas.*"

Two days later, when I took the towel off to dampen it, I was disappointed to find that my lump of dough had solidified into a dead-looking little rock. I took it to Jean-Marc.

"What's wrong? What did I do?"

He laughed. He took the ball from me and began to peel it like a hard-boiled egg. Under its crust, the interior was full of tiny bubbles and it smelled sweet. "*Bien.* It is ready for the first refreshment." He handed it back to me, now half its original size. "*Allons.* I watch you."

"Two hands of flour this time. That is good. Now in the middle." He made a circular motion and I made a well in the middle. "Now put the *chef.* Yes. Now a little water. Yes. No. Do not mix the flour yet. First you..." He rubbed his fingers together.

"You smush it?"

" 'Smush'? This is a word?"

"Absolutely. *Bien sûr.*" I squished the dough and water between my fingers until the lump dissolved.

"*Bien.* Now the flour. We wait again. Tomorrow, *peut-être.*"

"Don't you know how long it will take?"

He looked at me gravely. "Wynter, you do not tell the bread what to do. It tells you. You know from the way it looks, the way it feels, the smell, the taste. How warm, how cold. How wet, how dry. *Vous comprenez?*"

.   .   .

I don't mind the morning fog. In fact, on this particular morning, it suits me perfectly. I drag myself down the street, replaying last night's fiasco in my mind. It all seemed so promising. I suppose I'm rushing things. I should be more . . . "circumspect," my mother would say. I'm not even divorced yet. I can't just go around falling into bed with people. I'm lonely and vulnerable. I could have kissed Pee-wee Herman and it would have felt good.

My jogging shoes crunch in the gravel and I push through the hemlocks instead of walking around them. A movement draws my eye to the porch. Gary materializes out of the fog, in his jeans and red crewneck sweater and battle-scarred leather jacket. He looks like the guy who'd walk a mile for a Camel. Or like big brother Wally in *Leave It to Beaver*. He looks endearing. I want to be happy to see him, but something almost like dismay nips at me. At the same time, I'm thinking about his mouth on my breasts, about how that leather jacket would feel against bare skin—mine, for instance.

He starts to say something, but before he can, I blurt out, "One more apology and I'll never speak to you again."

He laughs. "Okay. No apologies."

Inside, I hold his jacket for a minute before hanging it up. "I thought you were leaving this morning."

"I changed my flight to this afternoon."

"Why?" Okay, it's a rhetorical question, but I want to hear him say it.

"Unfinished business." He holds me gently, resting his cheek on my hair. "I can't believe how good you smell."

"The bakery." I smile. "Want some coffee?"

He's as tall as I am, so when he pulls back, we're exactly eye to eye. "No," he says.

By Monday night, the *chef* has doubled in volume and the surface is textured with tiny bubbles. When I take the towel off, the unmistakable odor of fermentation rises from the bowl. I add more flour and water and mix it energetically.

The third time I check the *chef,* it's doubled in volume again. It's soupy and roiling with life. I pinch off a piece and put it on my tongue. The bitter acidity flares like a match before giving way to a nutty after-taste. It's ready to make *levain.*

I've conveniently forgotten that Linda's coming back until I let myself in the back door Thursday night just in time to see her standing over the garbage can with my *chef.*

"What the hell are you doing?" I shout. Her head jerks around and I almost laugh at the shock on her face. I'm sure nobody at the bakery has ever taken this tack with her.

She recovers quickly. "Who told you to make this?"

"Nobody told me to make it. I did it for myself, not for the bakery, so just leave it alone."

"I don't want it around here." She pulls the towel off, throws it on the floor.

"Ellen said I could let it ferment here. I'm taking it home tonight."

She looks me in the eye and dumps my *chef* into the garbage. Total disbelief combines with frustration to immobilize me. Then I hear myself say, "You are the sorriest excuse for a human being I've ever met."

She's almost grinning, she's so pleased with herself. "What did you say, missy?"

"I said you're a bitch." I turn and walk out the back door, down the alley.

I hear the back door open and she screams, "You're fired! You know that, don't you? You're fired!"

It's what she wanted all along.

I light the stove, wrap a blanket around me, and sit in my chair, drawing my knees to my chest. Mac says I need to let it burn hot for thirty minutes every day or two to clean the creosote out of the chimney pipe. The fire grows, snapping ferociously at the kindling.

Okay, now what? She's a bitch. She's unreasonable, impossible to work with. She's pathetic and stupid. But I'm unemployed and she's not.

Working alone for these three nights has crystallized the image of my future. Unlocking the door and feeling the oven's heat rush out to meet me. Turning on all the lights to find the whole place clean and quiet, expectant. For the first time, I think I understand what CM must feel when she stands backstage, waiting for the music.

I imagine working in the daytime with Ellen and Tyler, Diane and Misha and Jen. The camaraderie would be fun, but what I remember most is the noise. And I'd have to make muffins and scones, not bread.

Other alternatives are even less appealing. How can I work in a shop or teach English or sit in an office all day? I think of Lauren at the employment agency where I went that morning after David's announcement. *"I don't mean to startle you, Wynter, but sometimes we have to do things we hate."* I bet she laughed about me later, sharing war stories with the other client counselors. *"Let me tell you about the one I had today—the all-time queen dumb-ass rich bitch."* And I was. Last year at this time, my biggest worry was whether to wear black or white to the Black-and-White Symphony Ball.

Linda's beyond comprehension, true enough. But why did I let her get to me? It's just a *chef.* Worst-case scenario is, I make a new one. Why did I have to go berserk? Nothing like cutting your own air hose. I reach for my pillow, on the couch.

When I open my eyes it's light out. I have incredible kinks in my back and neck from sleeping in this weird pretzel position, and someone's banging on the door. When I unfold myself out of the chair, my father's old copy of *Night Flight* tumbles onto the rug. I pick it up and lurch for the door.

"Wyn, I'm so sorry." Ellen rushes in before I have time to say anything, shuts the door behind her. Then she looks at me. "Oh, I woke you up. I'm so upset."

"Sit down." I point to the chair. "I must have fallen asleep." I fill the teakettle and put it on. "What time is it?"

"Seven."

"Ellen, I'm sorry I lost my temper..."

She shakes her head vehemently. "I'm sorry you had to put up with her."

"She told you?"

"She was proud of herself. I've already told her she has to apologize to you." She gives me an ingratiating smile. "And I told her you're going to be making some new kinds of bread. That is, if you want to, of course."

I look at her in surprise. "You mean you still want me to work there?"

"Are you nuts? First of all, you're a great baker. Second, you've lasted with her longer than anyone in the history of the place. I can't tell you how many times we've been through this. She's run off everyone we've put in there."

"Can I ask you a question? Why do you keep her on?"

Her gaze shifts to the teakettle, which is starting to whistle softly. "I just can't bring myself to fire her. She'd never be able to get another job. Too old, too obnoxious... She'd end up on unemployment. She'll be retiring soon, but till then, I guess we're stuck with her." She shoots me a pleading glance. "You'll stay, won't you?"

"What I don't understand is why she threw it out, even after I told her it was mine and I was taking it home."

She runs a hand over her close-cropped dark hair. "She's just a miserable human being, that's why. Her bitterness poisons everything she does. And you committed the unforgivable sin of trying to help her. She'll hate you forever for that."

The kettle's blasting now. "Want some tea?"

"No, thanks. I've got to get back. I just ran over here to make sure you weren't pulling up stakes and heading for L.A. Listen..." She hesitates. "I know it's going to be really awkward going back in there tonight—"

I laugh. "It won't be the first time I've shared space with someone who didn't want me there."

·   ·   ·

I don't knock. I use my own key to unlock the door and go in. She's just bringing two flour buckets out of the storeroom.

"Hi."

She gives me a blank stare and heads back down the hall. O-kay. I pull down the black notebook, put on a Mozart piano concerto, start weighing out flour for white sandwich bread. While I'm oiling bread pans, the concerto ends, shutting off the tape deck with a resounding click.

"Linda, I'm sorry about your husband."

Silence. Is she embarrassed or does she just hate me? When I turn around to look at her, big tears are oozing from her eyes, lumbering down her face. Like she's fighting them every step of the way. I start to slide off my stool, but she spits out, "Asshole." Does she mean him or me? "Ya know how he died?" I shake my head. "Asshole," she says again. "Drinking on the boat. He went over."

"I'm sorry."

We labor in silence except for the motors of the two big mixers.

"Ellen said I had to apologize." Her abrupt pronouncement startles me. She stands next to the ovens, squinting resentfully at me, hands on hips. If she just had a corncob pipe sticking out of her face, she'd look like Popeye. "But I'm not going to. 'Cause I'm not sorry."

I sigh heavily. "It doesn't make any difference to me. All I want is to do my job."

"She can fire me if she wants to."

"Ellen doesn't want to fire you."

"Wouldn't be too sure of that, missy."

"Linda, you're making this much harder than it has to be. Bread making is a good job. We could be having fun here."

Her hard laughter fills the room. "Fun? You little Pollyanna nitwit. Sure it's fun if your daddy has money and you can quit whenever you want and run over to Hawaii for a few weeks. You try doin' it for twenty-five years to bring up two kids when your old man drinks up everything he makes. We'll see how much fun you think it is."

The hair is standing up on the back of my neck and a wave of red heat rises in my face. "My father is dead!" I hear myself shout. I hate it that I've let her get to me again. "And I can't take off to Hawaii for a couple of weeks because I'm separated from my husband and I need the goddamn job. Okay? Does that make you happy? So just get off my case and let me do the work."

Fifteen

❦

I've never had a man friend before. Not one who'll sit with me in a stuffy, low-ceilinged dive in the U district through two and a half hours of *Rocky and Bullwinkle* cartoons. I reciprocate by accompanying him to his favorite used bookstores, where we spend hours sifting through dusty volumes in search of anything "interesting."

I blink as we emerge from yet another bookshop on a narrow, grimy street off Pioneer Square, each of us carrying two recycled grocery bags full of books.

"I feel like a pack mule," I complain. "Those places are all so dusty—"

He laughs. "Oh, quit complaining."

"Maybe we could go to a real bookstore sometime. Like Elliott Bay Book Company. You know, someplace where they have new books. What is this fascination you have with books that have been pawed over by two or three other people?"

Even before I catch the sidelong glance he throws me, I already know I've inserted my silver foot in my mouth.

"I can't afford new books all the time," he says. He doesn't belabor the point, and I say a silent thank-you. Most men would have seized the opportunity to remind me that I'm a spoiled brat who's not accustomed to giving much thought to the price of anything.

Mac, however, isn't most men. In fact, he isn't much like anyone I can recall knowing. His brain reminds me of a meticulously organized file cabinet full of interesting but often arcane or useless information, such as the difference between a glade, a copse, and a grove. Why the second law of thermodynamics is actually more important than the first. Get him going, and he'll ramble on about Cubism or horse racing or celestial navigation. But his favorite subject, hands down, no contest, is music, and he's maddeningly opinionated.

I asked him one night at the bar why he never plays instrumentals. He said because they sound like something's missing.

I said, "You think the lyrics are more important than the music?"

"Not exactly. It's best when the words and the music work together. Like that Otis Redding song I was telling you about. The way the horns follow every phrase, kind of drawing you in."

"I don't remember."

He gave me a disapproving look. "You need to learn how to listen."

"You were probably one of those people who used to sit around playing Beatles songs backward, trying to hear them say, 'Paul is dead.' "

"I never did that," he said.

But I think I hit a nerve.

The one thing we never get around to discussing is his love life. He knows my history, of course, and every once in a while he'll refer to David as the "Evil Prince." Gary is "your brother" or "the parking mogul." But he doesn't expend a lot of breath on either one. I know only the basic plot outline with him and Gillian, even less about Laura. And if he's seeing anyone now, he's not talking. I've tried asking him about it, but he's a master of evasion and diversion. It's probably just as well.

Wind gusts up from the waterfront to meet us, blowing my unrestrained hair into a wild cloud. I grab it, wrestle it down, and plop my Dodgers hat over it.

It takes the rest of the afternoon to get back up to the Market because we keep detouring out on the piers or stopping to look in shop windows. The cold sting in the air promises yet another storm, but for the moment, people jam the sidewalks, jostling each other happily, enjoying the break in the rain. Smells of clam chowder and waffle cones remind me that I haven't eaten since breakfast.

"I'm hungry."

He looks at his watch. "I've got to be at work by six. If you'd let me bring the truck, we would've had time to stop somewhere."

"No we wouldn't have, because we would have spent all day looking for parking places."

We compromise by running into Phoebe's Café on Third while we wait for the bus. The eighteen-year-old with two-inch fingernails who waits on us keeps looking at Mac under her mascara-gooped eyelashes. She hands me the white Styrofoam box that contains his croissant and my scone while he empties change out of his pockets onto the counter. I pop the lid for a peek and my blood freezes.

"This is not a croissant." They both look up and I hold open the box as Exhibit A.

"Sure it is," she says between gum pops.

"It's a roll and it's crescent shaped. That does not make it a croissant."

"That's what we call them." Her tone is defensive.

"You should call them crescent rolls."

Mac looks at the ceiling. "Wyn, we're going to miss the bus."

"Crescent, croissant." She shrugs. "What's the difference?"

"Allow me to show you." I set the box on the register and rip the croissant in half crosswise. "What do you see here?" I brandish half under her nose.

"Half a croissant."

"Wrong. You see half of a crescent-shaped roll. This is bread, and not even very good bread. Look at the mushy crumb. A croissant is pastry. Flaky layers, each one separated by butter so that it puffs up crisp and golden. Instead of being dry and bready inside, you should be able to separate the layers into almost transparent sheets."

The girl looks a little scared.

"There's the thirteen." Mac stares glumly at the bus grinding to a halt across the street.

"You want the croissant or not?"

"No," I say.

"Yes, I do." Mac jams the lid back down, grabs my arm, and pushes me out the door. "Goddamnit, we missed the bus."

"There'll be a two along in a minute. I can't believe they try to pass this shit off as a croissant."

We park ourselves on the bus bench. "Eat your scone and leave my crescent roll alone."

The scone feels suspiciously warm and spongy. I stick my pinky into the interior. Just as I suspected.

"What's the matter with it?"

"It's hot."

"You should be happy. It just came out of the oven."

"It's squishy. And hotter inside than outside. That means it just came out of the microwave."

He sighs. "Fräulein Wynter, the bread Nazi." But he's laughing when the number 2 bus pulls up.

At Steve's Broiler early one Sunday morning, we sit in a Naugahyde booth that would easily hold eight people, eating feta-cheese omelets and watching the old guys at the counter suck on unfiltered cigarettes and drink coffee.

A young woman wearing a baseball cap, flannel shirt, and jeans comes in with two little boys and they climb into the booth next to us. The rugrats are cute—about seven and five years old—and they could've been made by the same cookie cutter, except the older one has brown hair and his little brother has blond curls. The kids have coloring books and their mother gives them a box of crayons and tells them to share. She sips her coffee and gets engrossed in a magazine. Mac watches them with more than casual interest.

"So tell me about it. You never talk about your childhood. What you did or what it was like. Was it happy? Unhappy?"

He folds his napkin and lays it next to his plate. "There were actually a lot of factors involved."

"A lot of 'factors'? That sounds like an algebra problem, not a kid. You had a brother. Kevin, right? What about your mother? Your father? Friends?"

"I had buddies." He smiles briefly. "That's the jock equivalent of friends. Except you don't actually have to talk to buddies. You just punch each other in the arm and laugh a lot. I went out for every sport there was. And plotted my escape from New York."

"Lots of kids play sports and punch their buddies and think about escaping from their hometown."

"True." He lets out a long breath. "Okay, here's the *Reader's Digest* condensed version: My mother was an art student. She met my dad— the original happy wanderer—in a museum. In a few hours, they were madly in love. They went to his place and screwed their brains out—"

"Mac..."

"I've kind of distanced myself from the whole thing. Anyway, she got pregnant. I guess in those days there weren't many options in that situation. They got married. Kevin was born. Things were fine for a while, then he got restless. He took off for South America, working for an oil company, I think. After a year or so, he came home. She took him back. Bingo. I'm in the oven."

"Didn't they ever hear of birth control?"

He shrugs. "If they had, I wouldn't be here. So life went on. He'd be home for a while, then he'd get the blues in the night. When I was twelve, he went to Canada to hunt moose or something and he never came home. His plane went down in the Canadian Rockies and they never found it."

"Did you ever wonder if he was really dead?"

"For years, I was convinced that he was alive. I used to make up stories about him being taken care of by some hermit or having amnesia and not knowing who he was. I even wondered if he'd wanted to disappear. Not that he would have planned it all, but maybe it seemed like a convenient out."

"Is that what your book's about?"

His eyes lock on mine. "What makes you think I'm writing a book?"

I start to laugh. "Oh, come on, Mac. I may not listen to all the words, but there's nothing wrong with my eyesight."

"Meaning what?"

"The way you're always scribbling in those notebooks."

"I told you, it's a journal."

"My bullshit indicator is blinking double reds. I suppose it could be a journal, but I'm picking up an intensity. A certain unity of purpose."

He seems somewhat abashed. "Well..."

"I'm not asking you to show it to me. Just to admit to what you're doing. Why are you so embarrassed?"

His eyes are suddenly dark. "I don't want to be an asshole about it. I'm not a writer. I'm a bartender who writes stuff."

"As long as you think of yourself that way, that's what you'll be." I take my last bite of cinnamon-raisin toast.

Sounds of a scuffle draw our attention to the next booth, where the kids are locked in a tug of war over a blue crayon.

"Knock it off or nobody gets to color," the woman says, not looking up from the magazine. The kids act as if they don't hear her. The older boy manages to get the crayon away from the younger one and starts writing on his napkin. The little one chooses an orange crayon and imitates his older brother's artwork on his own napkin. The calm lasts about fifteen seconds, and then the older kid decides he wants the orange crayon, too. He grabs it away from the little guy, who promptly begins to cry.

The mother looks up. "I told you guys to share."

"Christopher took mine," the little one wails.

"So get another one and stop being such a baby." She resumes her reading.

The waitress sets down our check. Mac hands her a twenty and continues to watch the kids while I watch him. The younger boy pulls out a green crayon and resumes his napkin art. The waitress counts out our change and we scoot out of the booth. There's a sharp slapping sound and a yelp. The older boy now holds the blue, orange, and green crayons and the little one's crying again. The mother's looking around like she'd rather be somewhere else.

"Brian, I told you to shut up. If you're gonna sit there and cry like a baby, you can't color anymore."

Suddenly Mac leans over and pulls two crayons out of the older boy's hand. The mother and both boys stare openmouthed as he looms over them. He smiles sweetly and says to the kid, "It's always a good idea to share. Someday he'll have something that you want." He hands the two crayons to the little brother and we walk out.

Spring and winter are having a tug-of-war. Some afternoons when I walk up to Parsons Garden in the mild caress of a Chinook wind, I think spring is winning. Crocuses push up through the dank black earth, yellow and purple and white. Pale green flowers of hellebore, which my oma called Lenten rose, gleam like tiny lamps in the deep shade. I daydream about fiddleheads and fresh asparagus.

By the time I leave for work at night, the wind has changed again, driving cold, stinging needles of water against my face and sending the temperature south. Winter digs in its heels, refusing to budge.

Ellen comes in early one of those wintry mornings, her eyes hollow and red-rimmed, her mouth a soft downturn. She's one of those people who's normally so up in the morning you sometimes want to kick her in the knees, so I start worrying about her and Lloyd. When you're obsessed with your own marital woes, you tend to assume that's the only thing that can go wrong in anyone's life.

But after Linda goes out, slamming the door behind her, Ellen says, "Diane's mother had a stroke last night."

"Oh shit." My very first thought is how she'll be drowning in guilt. I would be. "I mean, that's terrible. I'm so sorry. Is she going home?"

"She's on her way to the airport as we speak."

"Let me help you set up." I turn on the espresso machine, and wring out a cloth in the enamel pail of Clorox solution to wipe the counters.

After she finishes counting change into the register drawer, she rinses the espresso baskets with a jet of steam and fills them with two quick snaps of the grinder.

"I feel awful for her," she says, handing me a double shot of decaf. "And I'm a terrible person for worrying about the bakery at a time like this . . . but we're in a real bind here. We've got all these cake orders. I don't know how long she'll be gone. Two that are supposed to be ready this morning. They're frosted, but not decorated. She was going to finish them when she came in." She looks at me. "I don't suppose you could—"

"Oh, Ellen, I wish I could. Believe me, they'd come out looking like ground zero of a nuclear chain reaction."

A tapping on the glass draws our attention to the door. Tyler's waving at somebody in a green Plymouth Valiant of indeterminate vintage. Ellen and I look back at each other and smile. She jumps up to open the door.

"Hey, I'm really sorry. Marie's car wouldn't start and I had to—"

"Hi," she practically sings. "How are you this morning?"

Tyler shoots her a guarded look. "Okay. Why?"

"I need a big favor. Can I make you a mocha?"

"Ellen, you're creeping me out. What's up?"

"Diane's mom had a stroke last night."

"Bummer." Tyler takes off her jacket, looking from Ellen to me and back to Ellen.

"We have two cakes that are supposed to be ready this morning and—"

"Oh, no. Not me. I don't do that hearts-and-flowers shit. No way."

Ellen impales her with a pleading gaze. "Tyler, it's too late to call them and say we don't have cakes for them. We have to give them something. Please. Only one's a wedding cake, and the flowers are all in the fridge. All you have to do is arrange them. Please?"

"What about the other one?"

"It's a birthday cake. Generic adult. All she specified was the colors—pale peach, lavender, pale green. Like spring. You can do something with that, I've seen your pictures."

Tyler sticks her finger down her throat.

"Come on, please? I'll up your hourly for the time you spend on the cakes."

"Oh, all right." She closes her eyes and puts out her hands like a blind person. "Lead me to them."

I don't get to see the cakes, but everyone laughs about them for the next few days. Everyone except Ellen. She's busy calling people who have orders for the following week, advising them that Diane is away on a family emergency.

"So what happened?" I ask Tyler one morning when Ellen's out in the alley helping the people from Meals on Wheels load up the day-olds. "How did they turn out?"

She glares at me, scuffing her Doc Martens on the rubber matting. "The wedding-cake woman looked at the thing like it came out from under a rock, but she didn't say much."

"What about the birthday cake?"

"She freaked. Totally wigged on me. Started screaming, 'I said peach and lavender. This is orange and purple and neon lime.' " She pushes up the sleeves of her T-shirt. "I told her it was cutting edge. She said it looked like the shirt Sammy Davis Jr. wore when he sang 'The Candy Man.' Whatever that is."

"I think that was before your time. So what happened?"

"Ellen ended up giving it to her for free." She rolls her eyes. "Personally, I thought it looked pretty radical."

"So who's going to do cakes till Diane gets back?"

She gives a little sigh of resignation. "Me. I promised Ellen I'd keep the colors down."

A lot of the advance orders get canceled anyway.

The first time I see Diane, I almost don't recognize her. It's Friday afternoon and I'm making my weekly financial pilgrimage. When I step
around the cooling racks, Tyler's talking to a woman who's arranging
pansies on a small pink-frosted wedding cake. My brain skips to the
idea that Ellen's hired a part-timer till Diane comes back. Then they
both look up and I see that Diane *is* back.

"Hey, Wyn." She smiles at me, an automatic response, but her face
is bleak. She looks smaller somehow, and when I hug her, she feels tiny
and brittle.

"How's your mom doing?"

"Not bad, considering what she's been through."

"What's the prognosis?"

She pushes her bangs back with her forearm. "It's too early to know
for sure. The hemorrhage was on the left side of the brain, so that means
it affects the right side of the body. She hasn't got much mobility on
that side right now. She's either in bed or in a wheelchair most of the
time." She sighs, a sound of utter exhaustion. "She's in physical therapy.
They started that right away. And occupational therapy—"

"Occupational therapy?"

"Yeah, I thought the same thing. What it means is, she has to learn
how to feed herself and take herself to the bathroom and stuff. It's hard
because she has to do it all left-handed now. And of course she can't talk
very well."

She blinks and tears glint in her eyes. "Hell, what am I saying? She
can't talk at all. She makes weird noises and everyone's supposed to
know what she wants."

"I'm so sorry." I feel the total inadequacy of the words.

"Well..." Tyler clears her throat. "It's my turn to cook dinner, so
I'm outta here. Later, you guys." She disappears and I lock the front
door after her, pull down the shades.

"Should I make us a mocha?"

Diane manages a laugh. "And blow us all to Hawaii?"

"Hey, Jen's been giving me private instruction. I can *barista* with the best of them. Well, maybe the vast mediocre majority of them." I turn on the machine.

"Okay, then. I could use a jolt to keep me going."

"You need some help tonight?"

She shakes her head. Her hair is dirty and more the color of dishwater than her usual sunny blonde. "Tyler made all the buttercream, thank God. All I have to do is slap it on." She pulls more flowers out of a white plastic bucket. "How's Linda?"

I laugh. "Some things never change."

When the espresso light comes on, I turn the frother dial to bleed off a little pressure, and tamp ground espresso into two brew baskets. In the time it takes me to finish our drinks, she's crumb-coated the bottom layer of another wedding cake. I hand her a mocha and she takes a sip.

"Good job."

She takes another sip, sets the cup down, and I watch helplessly as her face crumples and she begins to cry. It's not weeping, which I usually think of as a silent function. This is sobbing, an anguished moaning that shoots like a geyser out of some great subterranean pool of grief.

All I can do is put my arms around her and wait.

I lose track of the time till she steps back from me, hiding her red, puffy face in her hands. "I'm sorry."

"I won't even dignify that with a response. Come here and sit."

She collapses into a chair and lays her head on the table. "I am so fucking tired."

I get a clean towel, wring it out in cold water, and hand it to her.

"I've been up and down all night, every night since I left. God, Wyn, she's just impossible. And I would be, too." She holds the towel to her face, muffling her words. "I mean, suddenly your world is gone. You can't do anything for yourself. You can't even talk and make people understand what you say. This is a woman who ran the most successful real estate office in Baltimore. She had three secretaries. She said jump and everyone asked how high on the way up. Now she can't wipe her own ass."

Diane sits up, drapes the wet towel over her head like a scarf. "And she's determined to make everyone in the family as abso-fucking-lutely miserable as she is."

Sixteen

❧

A pril, everyone agrees, is too late for snow. But the weather gods aren't paying attention to the calendar. Or maybe it's just their idea of an April Fool's joke.

In L.A., winter weather means long, dark days, sluicing rain the color of iron, flooded streets and SigAlerts. Snow isn't even vaguely related to all that. Snow is a minor miracle. One year, Encino got a few flurries and CM and I were outside running around, tongues outstretched like pink landing strips, hoping to catch a stray flake.

As a child, I believed that snow existed only at Tahoe because that was the only place I ever saw it. I've never been in a city where it snowed. I suppose in New York and Chicago and places where it happens every winter, it's just an inconvenience. Traffic snarls, people have to shovel their driveways, salt their porches, drag out the snow tires. The majority of Seattleites aren't that jaded.

I love how it slows everything down. Everyone turns, as if they were startled by a sudden noise, except it's the sudden hush that's startling. On Queen Anne Avenue, people clump together on the corners, sipping lattes and hot chocolates and scrunching their boots just for the sound of it. Snow smooths all the rough edges, the cracks, potholes, and splinters, like a glorious white fondant over a none too attractive cake.

Of course, the functioning world breaks down completely. You

can't drive without chains, buses don't run, the airport closes. Gary calls
to say his flight's been canceled and he has commitments for next week,
so he won't be able to come up till the end of the month. "I miss you,"
he says. "I can't wait to see you."

"Me, too." But what I'm actually feeling is something akin to relief.

Saturday night at Bailey's it's like a party. Kenny's made hot buttered
rum in a Crock-Pot. There's microwave popcorn, and somebody
brings in a huge tray of chocolate chip cookies that disappear in about
five minutes. Mac's playing sixties tapes and people are doing the twist
and the jerk. One obvious case of arrested development can't resist
running outside and making little snow balls to slip down his date's
collar.

I'm caught up in the festivity in spite of the little pincerlike pain
that started last night at work and has now turned into a pretty decent
stomachache. I feel vaguely nauseous. Could I have food poisoning? I
wonder if the Alka-Seltzer this morning was such a great idea. If it's a
viral thing, aren't you supposed to let it run its course and get out of
your system? Maybe it's just cramps. Except I don't think I'm due for at
least another week.

I should probably go home and go to bed, but I really don't want to
leave, and the thought of walking home alone in the cold is somehow
daunting. If I just sit here a little longer, nursing the now warm beer that
I ordered because wine didn't sound good, maybe I'll feel better.

When Inez and Charlie Foxx start singing "Mockingbird," Mac
comes out from behind the bar and grabs my hand. "There's your song."
He pulls me off the stool and we manage a few steps before he tries to
twirl me under his arm and I double over. "Hey, what's wrong?"

I straighten up. "Nothing. I've just got a stomachache. Maybe I'm
getting that flu that's going around."

He helps me up on the stool and I lick my lips, only then realize
that I'm sweating. He frowns. "You don't look so good."

"People usually don't when they're getting the flu," I snap at him.

"You want me to take you home?"

I shake my head. "I'll just sit here awhile and then I'll go home. Don't worry, I won't breathe on anyone."

"Let me know if you start to feel worse. The truck's out back."

"I don't need to ride in the smogmobile. I'm not that sick."

He laughs and goes back behind the bar.

By one-fifteen, most of the crowd has departed for the comfort of their warm beds. I must have the flu. I squirm on the stool. My eyes are hot and my stomach is churning. I keep blotting my forehead with my napkin. A ride in the smogmobile's sounding not half bad.

"Hey, Mac."

His grin fades as he focuses on me. "Jesus, Wyn. Are you okay?" Without waiting for an answer he says, "Come on, we're going to the walk-in clinic."

"No, we are not. Just take me home. Please."

"You look like hell. You need to see a doctor." He shrugs into his jacket and helps me with my parka, wrapping my scarf around my head.

I yank it off. "Will you stop?"

"Back in a minute," he hollers at Kenny. The cold air in the alley feels good, but even the snow can't cover the smell of rotting garbage and that's all it takes. I'm on my knees puking my guts out, and since there's not much in there, I start dry heaving.

Mac lifts me from behind and pain rips through my lower abdomen. Pinpoints of light explode in front of me and fade like tiny fireworks. "Try to breathe shallow. Nice and slow. That's it. Keep swallowing."

I must have yelled, because the back door opens and Kenny's head sticks out. "What's wrong?"

Mac says, "Call 911."

I shake my head as vigorously as I can manage. "No!"

Kenny ignores me.

"Come on back inside." Mac grips my arms.

"Too hot in there," I mumble.

"You want to sit?"

I shake my head.

"Where does it hurt?"

I rest my hand on the tight, warm place under my jacket. Mac looks at his watch.

Finally, Kenny opens the door. "I got through, but they said it'll be at least fifteen to twenty minutes. They're swamped tonight. The snow—"

"By that time..." Mac's voice trails off, which is fine with me. I don't think I want to hear this. "Help me get her in the truck." He opens the door and the two of them fumble me into the truck, sliding in the vomit.

"You think you can make it?" Kenny looks dubious, but Mac grins and pats the blue tarp stretched over the bed of the Elky.

"A half cord of oak should give us pretty good traction."

He slides behind the wheel and turns the key. The truck makes a kind of groaning noise, and he strokes the dashboard as if it's a big old dog. Next we get a groan with a grind. I'd laugh, but it would hurt. He ignores me and turns the key again. This time a hiccup follows the groan and grind; the truck starts to chug, slowly.

Snow is falling again in big, starry flakes, and the streetlights are all wearing sun dogs. It would be enchanting, except that I feel like I've swallowed a live ferret. The headlights carve out a tunnel of light in the alley and he turns left, then right on Queen Anne Avenue.

"Where the hell are you going?" He doesn't answer. "Goddamnit, Mac, I need to go home."

He stops at a light. "We're going to Virginia Mason."

His face blurs. My breath pumps out in short, white smoke signals of panic. "Just take me to urgent care, then. I don't need to go to the hospital. Really. I'll be fine. I just need to sleep. They'll give me some pain pills. Antibiotics or something." I brush at my sweaty face and smell vomit on my sleeve. My stomach roils again.

"Breathe and swallow." His voice is calm, but he's gripping the wheel so hard that his knuckles look like a white dotted line. "I need to figure out how to get there with the least number of hills."

The cold glass of the window feels good against my face. Instinctively, I draw up my legs, shivering.

"Fasten your seat belt," Mac says. He flicks the defroster on High and the truck noses into the intersection.

"I can't. It hurts." Every nerve ending in my body is on full battle alert. I can feel every pebble, every change in pavement, every pothole under the truck wheels. I'm never sick. Never sick. I'm not sick. I never get sick.

"How's your boyfriend?" Mac's voice interrupts my litany.

I peer at him through slitted eyes. "My what?"

"Should I call him your brother?" I don't say anything. "You Californians sure do lead interesting lives."

"We had dinner twice. That doesn't make him my boyfriend."

"Did you make him split the check?"

"Are you trying to distract me or piss me off?"

"Your choice." He smiles infuriatingly.

I wince as we take a bump. "What is it? What's wrong with me?"

"Appendix, I think."

"No. Shit, no. It can't be. I can't have surgery. I can't be laid up for a month."

"I don't think you get to decide. Anyway, you'll like it. You get lots of sympathy. Cards and flowers and TLC." He frowns. "The only problem is . . ."

I cut my eyes toward him although even that slight motion hurts. "What?"

"String bikinis are probably out for a while."

My head falls back against the seat. "Fuck you, McLeod."

"Remember, you have to eat with that mouth."

"Will you quit laughing at me? I'm scared."

"It'll be okay. Trust me. I've been there."

"Show me your scar." He laughs, and I feel the tires spin. "Oh, God."

"Just a little slick patch," he says. But I can tell by the way the stuff is splatting against the windshield that it's turning to sleet. The truck crunches forward, gaining traction with its sheer weight. "Recite a poem for me."

"I can't remember—ahh." I pant, grip the armrest, rock back and forth.

"Okay, I'll do one. 'I think that I shall never see a poem lovely as your knee—' "

"You've never seen my knee."

"Sad but true." He turns left, then right. Downtown is eerily beautiful in the falling snow, bathed in the coppery glow of streetlights and spiked with red and green traffic signals. We haven't seen another car since we left Queen Anne. "Okay, how about 'The road was a ribbon of moonlight over the purple moor—' "

"Butcher," I wheeze. "You skipped two lines. 'The wind was a torrent—of darkness among the gusty trees, The moon was a ghostly galleon tossed upon cloudy seas, The road was'—oh, shit—"

"I don't remember any shit in the road. Although there was a horse. 'The road was a ribbon of moonlight over the purple moor, And the highwayman came riding, Riding, riding, The highwayman came riding up to the old inn door.' "

Suddenly the truck founders, slides backward, and swerves to a stop against the curb.

"Shit." He says it under his breath. "This hill . . ." He looks over at me. "How are you doing?"

"I've never been in a hospital. Except to visit people."

Turning the wheel first one way, then the other, inching forward, slipping back, little by little he turns us around, not down the hill, but across it, and then we start to zigzag our way up like a sailboat tacking into the wind.

"Hang on. We're almost there."

"I've never had anesthesia. I don't want it."

He laughs uproariously. "Wyn, it's not natural childbirth. I guarantee you don't want to be awake." I squeeze my eyes against the pain, then dash the tear away quickly so he won't see what a wimp I am.

As we get closer to the crest of the hill, the wind picks up, driving the snow against the windshield. Granted, I'm not at my most alert, but I can't imagine how he can see much. The wheels are slipping again, but I can't make myself care. I pull the scarf around my neck and huddle miserably against the door.

He turns on the radio and the cab fills with a breathless tenor.

> *"Are the stars out tonight?*
> *I don't know if it's cloudy or bright."*

"Oh, good one." He smiles. "The Flamingos."
"Mac . . ."
"Close your eyes. Listen to the words."

> *"I don't know if we're in a garden,*
> *Or on a crowded avenue."*

A high school prom in the fifties. Girls in ballerina-length tulle, shiny page boys, wrist corsages. Crew-cut boys in dark suits with skinny lapels. I let myself drift.

> *"You are here, so am I.*
> *Maybe millions of people go by.*
> *But they all disappear from view . . ."*

Abruptly I feel the unmistakable dip of a driveway entrance. A lighted red cross appears out of the dark and a sign that says "Emergency." Mac leans on the horn as we skid to a halt.

"Stop that. I feel like an idiot."

He's out the door, slamming it behind him, leaving a cold gust, a few swirling flakes to melt into the upholstery, and me curled up around the hot pain.

There's movement outside and noise, lots of people in green scrubs and white uniforms. I'm on my back on a wheeled contraption and Mac's going through my wallet.

"Call CM," I plead, and he nods.

"When was your last meal?" a nurse demands. I look at her stupidly, then say, "Breakfast." She rolls me over on one hip, and I feel the bite of a needle, followed by a wave of warmth. Miraculously, the pain begins to break up and wash away.

I'm signing a paper that I can't read and the walls are moving past me, fluorescent lights speeding down the tunnel over my head. My face flops to the left and Mac is still there. I think he's holding my hand, which is very cold. I can tell he's moving and the white-and-green people are moving all around me, but I seem to be floating. On an air mattress, bobbing easily on gentle swells.

It's like a silent movie with that fuzzy black border. The border is getting wider as the picture gets smaller and smaller, till I can't see any of it anymore.

I'm throwing up. Or wanting to. But the world's perkiest blonde nurse is smiling at me, saying, "Don't vomit, honey. You'll feel really bad."

I shake my head. It would not be possible to feel any worse than I do. My stomach heaves again. I swallow obediently. I want to sleep and she keeps rubbing my hand, sponging my face, telling me to wake up. I just know she'll be in here later trying to give me a sleeping pill.

Later, I wake up in a different room. As the fog recedes, the first thing in focus is CM's worried face. I smile weakly with relief. She scrapes a metal chair up close to the bed and takes my hand in both of hers.

"How are you feeling?"

"Never better. Did anyone get the license number of the truck?"

She gives a little nervous giggle and presses my hand against her cheek. "God, I was so worried about you. How did Mac know how to reach me?"

"Your phone number's in my wallet."

"He seems like a pretty nice guy."

"We're just friends."

"He asked me to call your mom, but I thought I'd better wait till you were conscious..."

"Thank you for that." I sigh. "All I need is her fluttering around here like Florence Nightingale. I'll call her when I'm safely ensconced at home. What day is it?" Sunlight's poking around the window blinds, illuminating various metal contraptions with plastic bags full of liquid connected by tubing to several of my orifices. There's a needle taped in my arm.

"Sunday afternoon. The snow's already melting."

When I try to shift my weight, a quick turn of the screw makes me gasp. "Shit. I think they left a scalpel inside."

"It's your incision, dum-dum. You'll be fine as long as you don't cough, sneeze, laugh, or breathe."

The sound of knuckles on metal draws our attention to the doorway, where a very young guy with hair as curly as mine, and a stethoscope hanging around his blue surgical scrubs, stands grinning. "How's it going?" Naturally, he's talking to me, but he's looking at CM.

"Are you the one who did this to me?"

"Guilty as charged, Your Honor. And it's a pretty bang-up job, all modesty aside. You don't have to leave," he says as CM gets up.

"I'm just going to run down to the gift shop and see if they have any more of these in spring fashion colors." She tweaks my plastic hospital bracelet. His head about swivels off his shoulders as he watches her go. He drags his eyes back to me.

"How do you feel today?"

"Like the magician's assistant who's been sawed in half. When can I go home?"

"Whoa, easy there. You are one very fortunate lady. You were about that close"—he holds his thumb and index finger together—"to a ruptured appendix. In fact, I lifted that puppy out and as soon as I set it in the bowl, it went. Your friend got you here just in time."

"I assure you, I'm grateful to all concerned, but I'd like to go home."

He gives me a bemused smile. "Tuesday. Maybe even tomorrow. As soon as you can pee by yourself. And when you can promise me you won't drive a car for at least three weeks—"

"I can promise you that now. I don't have a car."

"And that you won't do a lot of walking around for at least two weeks—"

"How am I supposed to go to work?"

"You're not. And I don't want you lifting anything heavier than a sandwich for about six weeks."

"You must be joking. I'm a baker. Lifting's half the job."

"Not for the next six weeks it isn't." He shakes his head. "You need to understand that you've just had major abdominal surgery. It's going to be an absolute minimum of six weeks before you can resume a normal routine. Particularly if your normal routine is very physical in nature."

I fold my arms and stare at him. "Well, fine. You want to come home and wait on me?"

"It's not the worst offer I've had, but I can't spare the time right now." He gives me a charming smile, but at the moment I'm way beyond crabby. "Ms. Morrison, all kidding aside, your body needs a certain amount of time to heal properly. That's just a fact of life."

"Here's my fact of life. I live alone. Things have to be done and I don't have a guy named Cato hanging around waiting for instructions."

"Do you know what adhesions are?"

"Should I?"

He sighs. "No. But if you don't let your body heal properly, you will. And it won't be a pleasant experience." By the time he finishes describing adhesions, bowel obstruction, abscess, chronic pain, and future surgeries in lurid detail, I've reluctantly accepted my new status as invalid.

When Mac calls Monday afternoon to see if I want company, I announce that I can pee by myself. I haven't been this proud of going to the john since I was potty-trained.

He laughs. "Does that mean you need a ride home?"

"If you could, I'd appreciate getting out of here ASAP. This place is depressing. It's full of sick people."

"Unfortunately, that means another ride in the smogmobile."

"I apologize for any snide comments I might have inadvertently let slip about the Elky."

"Inadvertently, my ass."

I have to clamp my teeth firmly onto my tongue. "Mac, I most humbly beg forgiveness."

"Okay, you're forgiven. What time can you leave?"

"As soon as you can get the bucket of bolts over here."

He was right about one thing. It's been a long time since I had this much attention. Of course, for the first few days, I'm too drugged out on Vicodin to enjoy it. CM fills my freezer with soup and casseroles; she helps me bathe and French-braids my hair. Ellen and Diane bring me bread and scones and muffins.

Tyler brings me cookies and a wood-block print of a loaf of bread in warm shades of brown and rust.

"Tyler, this is wonderful. This should be hanging in the bakery. Can you make another print of it?"

"Yeah." She shrugs, looks embarrassed by the fuss.

"In fact, I think we need T-shirts."

"What for?"

"To sell, my little nonlinear friend."

"You mean T-shirts with my design on them?" Her eyes flicker with interest.

"Exactly. And maybe coffee mugs, too. Why don't you ask Ellen to call me?"

"Totally inflammatory. By the way, Linda says hi."

"Right."

"No, really. She totally misses you."

"Tyler, stop. It hurts when I laugh."

Mac brings me cassettes for my boom box, and books, which he reads aloud when I'm too groggy to focus. As you get older, you forget how nice it can be to hear a story instead of reading it. It calls up all these primal race memories of storytellers squatting around a campfire in the jungle darkness.

After a week, I stop taking painkillers, so I'm perfectly capable of reading to myself, but he keeps doing it because we both enjoy it. On the three-week anniversary of my grand opening, he shows up at nine-thirty in the morning with a white bag and a copy of *The Great Gatsby*. I crawl back under the covers while he makes coffee.

"If it wasn't for the pain, I could get used to this. Sleeping late, having people bring me food and music, read to me."

"Enjoy it while you can. As soon as you're up and about, I'm planning to get sick so you can read to me."

"Does that mean I have to drive you to the hospital in the smog-mobile?"

"No, I'll get sick at home. Elky would never run for you." He sets a plastic tape case down on the kitchen table. "Here's another tape."

"Who is it?"

He's pawing through my cupboard. "Don't you have any clean cups?"

"Yes, CM washed everything. There's no telling where she put them. Who's on the tape?"

"Bo Diddley, Chuck Berry, Jackie Wilson, Sam Cooke." He hands me a cup of coffee and tosses the white sack on the bed. Inside is one perfect golden croissant, still warm.

"Oh, Mac, thanks." I inhale the buttery scent. "Is this from Le Panier?"

"Of course. You don't think I'd dare to bring you a crescent roll from Phoebe's, do you?"

I clutch my stomach, panting. "Oh, don't make me laugh." I take a bite of the croissant and the hundred butter-crisp papery layers shatter into toasty shards. "Oh, God, this is so perfect. Thank you so much. You want a bite?"

"No, I had one on premises." He sits down in the club chair, props his right boot on his left knee.

"You're out early for a Saturday."

He flips the pages of the book. "Actually, I haven't been home yet. Kenny and I went out last night and ended up at a party on Capitol Hill."

I feel a weird little jab in my stomach nowhere near my incision. "Was it fun?" I ease out of bed and creep carefully to the stove for a refill. "You want any more?"

"You finish it." Just a breath, then, "Laura was there."

"Did you talk?"

"No. She was with somebody."

"How did that make you feel?" I curl back down on the futon, balancing my cup.

He leans his head back against the chair and laughs. "You can take the girl out of California, but you can't—"

"Okay, okay. I just thought you wanted to talk about it. If you don't, fine. Why don't you put the tape on?"

"Because I'm reading and I don't want you to be distracted. You can listen to it later."

I close my eyes and listen as Mac becomes Nick Carraway, lost in the glittering world of the Buchanans, and I recall happily that after reading *Gatsby* for the first time when I was sixteen, I wanted to change my name to Jordan. Now he's at the part where Daisy tells Nick about the birth of her daughter. " 'And I hope she'll be a fool—that's the best thing a girl can be in this world, a beautiful little fool.' "

He snaps the book shut. "Sorry. I'm really tired."

"That's what happens when you stay out all night. Go home and get some sleep. Leave me the book."

He tilts his head from side to side, rubbing the back of his neck. "God, I'm stiff."

"Come here. My dad always said I gave good neck rubs."

"Don't go ripping anything."

"Sit down and shut up."

He lowers himself to the floor, stretching his long legs out in front of him, and I sit cross-legged on the bed, massaging the stiff cords at the base of his skull. Everything's fine until I start thinking about it. Mac and I don't touch each other. It's an unwritten rule with us. A little nudge with an elbow is about as far as we've ever gone. Now I remember why.

Because I'm imagining my fingertips on the smooth curve of his back. I'm staring at the hollow where his neck joins the shoulder, wondering how it would feel under my mouth. God, no, this is all wrong. I need a friend, not more complications.

"Okay," I say, too cheerfully. Slap his shoulder. "That's it. I'm a little sore. I guess everything really is connected to your stomach muscles."

"Thanks." He doesn't get up or turn around.

When my mother was trying to teach me piano, she explained about the *una corda* pedal, the one on the left. When you depress that pedal, the entire action and keyboard shift just slightly, nearly invisibly, to the right, so that the treble hammers strike only two of the three strings. The pianist continues playing just as before, but the music is different, softer. That's how the world has just shifted.

A knock on the door makes me jump, sending a twinge through my incision. Mac scrambles up.

From my angle, I can't see the porch. I can only see Mac's face, the neutral expression that drops like a curtain after the play. He steps back and Gary walks in, both arms hidden by giant bundles of pale yellow roses.

I find my voice. "Gary! What are you doing here? I'm sorry. This is my friend Mac McLeod. Gary Travers." They exchange some kind of genetically encoded male information at a glance and then Gary shifts the flowers so he can shake hands.

Just so nobody misunderstands, he bends down to kiss me. I try to make it a short one.

"I better get going." Mac picks up his denim jacket.

I look around Gary and the roses. "Mac? I'll talk to you soon."

After the door shuts behind him, Gary off-loads the roses onto the kitchen table. He hangs up his leather jacket and sits down next to me, taking both my hands.

"Why didn't you call me?"

"Because there was no need to. I figured I'd be seeing you next week. How did you know?"

"I talked to your mom yesterday. If I'd known, I could have been up here taking care of you." He lifts my hands to his mouth.

I give him a smile that's meant to be reassuring. "All my friends have been taking care of me."

"Like Mac?"

"Yes, like Mac. He's the one who took me to the hospital when I got sick."

He runs a hand through his hair. "I'm sorry, Wyn. Maybe I shouldn't have barged in like this, but when your mother told me you'd had emergency surgery, I panicked."

"You and my mother." I smile. "It was all I could do to keep her from getting on the next plane up here. But I'm fine. I've had my stitches out, and it's just a matter of resting until everything finishes getting stuck back together."

"Then that's exactly what we're going to do."

The way he holds my face in his hands, as if I were some treasured work of art, is guaranteed to neutralize any leftover pockets of insurgency. His kiss is gentle but insistent, and it makes me want to do things I know I can't do yet.

He painstakingly cuts the stems of all the roses and arranges them in my only container, a galvanized bucket. There are so many that they look embarrassingly spectacular.

"Thank you for the flowers. They're beautiful."

"I'm glad you like them." He dries his hands on my dish towel. "I'll just go out to the car and get my bag."

My eyes open wide. "Your what?"

"My bag. My suitcase."

"You mean you're staying here?"

"Well, yes. Unless you don't want me to. I arranged things so I could be up here all week."

"My place is so small..." I feel like my protest is not only feeble, but petty and ungrateful. "You won't have room to—"

"I'm here to take care of you. I won't get in the way, I promise. I have a few phone calls I have to make tomorrow, but for the most part I'll just be your devoted slave." He bends down to kiss me. "By the way, I hope you don't mind, I gave Erica and the kids your phone number. And a few people at work. I told them they could reach me here."

He disappears out the door.

I can stand it for a week. I mean, he rearranges his whole schedule, comes up here with all these flowers. How can I throw him out?

For dinner, he heats up some of CM's soup. He brought a loaf of Paisan extra-sour sourdough with him and two bottles of a Napa Valley caber-net. It's like he doesn't remember that I make bread for a living or doesn't believe that the Northwest produces perfectly good wines. Or maybe I'm just too grouchy.

I do enjoy watching his butt while he's standing at the sink washing dishes, a pillowcase tucked into his belt because I don't own any aprons. At some point, he turns around with his sleepy-eyed smile.

"What are you laughing at?"

"You. In your makeshift apron with your buns of steel kind of rolling back and forth. And I'm not laughing, I'm smiling. Enjoying the after-dinner show."

"You better not talk like that if you can't follow through. Remem-ber the theory of rising expectations."

When he's finished with the dishes, he takes off his Top-Siders and stretches out next to me. One of Mac's tapes is playing, one of the less raucous ones.

"Don't you have anything more romantic than Otis Redding?"

"I think the Big O is pretty romantic. You have to listen to the words. The way they work with the music. If you insist, I think there's a Frank Sinatra up there. I know there's an Ella Fitzgerald."

Pretty soon Ella's singing "Every Time We Say Goodbye" and I'm trying not to think about the first night Mac took me to Lofurno's. Gary pushes up the sleeve of my sweatshirt and tickles the bend of my elbow.

"God, that feels good."

"When are you going to be seaworthy again?" he asks, nibbling my earlobe.

"I don't know. The post-op instructions were kind of vague. All it said was something about gradually returning to your previous level of sexual activity. And they don't even know what my previous level was. I could be Truck Stop Annie."

" 'Gradually'?" His breathing kicks into second gear. "If we have to work up to it, maybe we should start slowly. Now."

"I don't think so."

"How about if I just touch you?"

I smile. "How about if *I* just touch *you*? You're the one with a gun in his pocket."

His breath catches when I run my hand down the ridge in his pants. He unbuckles his belt. I ease the zipper down, and slip my hand inside, freeing up Junior. From the way he jackknifes when I scoot down and take him in my mouth, I surmise that Erica wasn't into oral sex. After the initial shock, he settles down and lets me make him happy. His Class-5 excitement is a turn-on, but his gratitude leaves me feeling vaguely uneasy. Like most men, he has no idea what to do if he can't direct.

"That was incredible," he breathes when he's holding me later. "I wish I could make you feel good."

"Gary, you *are* making me feel good. I like the way you hold me. It doesn't have to always be about orgasm, you know."

Apparently, this is a novel concept to him.

· · ·

The phone rings at seven in the morning and he grabs it before I can even roll over. He spends fifteen minutes going over interview questions for new employees.

"Be sure to give everyone the sheet on drug testing. And let me know how many good candidates we've got. If we don't get at least six, we'll have to run the ad again."

By this time, I'm wide awake. I dread having to get my body clock synched up again when I go back to work. When he crawls back under the covers and tries to get chummy, I give him the evil eye.

"You know, since this is my house, I think I should answer the phone."

"I'm sorry. I didn't want it to wake you up."

"How could I sleep with you reciting your entire employee handbook?"

"I'm sorry."

"It's okay. It's just—it could have been my mother or something." She probably would've been ecstatic to call and find him here, but I don't say that.

"You're right. I won't answer it unless you ask me to."

Around noon, he showers and gets dressed. "I have to go to a very short meeting." He looks worried. "Are you going to be all right here by yourself?"

"Of course. I've been mostly by myself since I came home. People wander in and out and leave me food. I eat, sleep, get fat and lazy."

"Do you feel up to going out tonight?"

"Possibly. Go to your meeting; we'll talk when you get home."

"You want me to heat up something for your lunch before I go?" He shifts that soft leather jacket from one hand to the other.

"No, I can do that. I'm supposed to be up and around more. Go on, scram."

· · ·

When he's gone, I'm exhausted. Like I've been onstage or at least on display for the last twenty-four hours. In the bathroom, the only traces of him are a few stray whiskers in the sink. Everything is wiped up, screwed on, nailed down tight. I run hot water in the tub, until it's about half full, and sit on the edge to sponge myself. I clean my puckery incision and pat it dry per the instructions they gave me. It doesn't hurt that much anymore, but looking at it when I touch it makes my salivary glands twang like too tight guitar strings.

I putter in the kitchen, wash out the coffeepot, make myself a peanut butter sandwich on whole wheat–walnut bread. I take Ella off the boom box and put on the new tape Mac brought me. "Bo Diddley's a Gunslinger," Chuck Berry's "Sweet Little Sixteen." My mind reaches for something. A phantom idea it can grasp, but not hold. Like a wet bar of soap in the shower.

Then Jackie Wilson starts winding out "Doggin' Around." The way he hits that high "Yeah" and slides down into good-man, feelin'-bad blues gives me goose bumps.

"You must be feeling way better. Sounds like party time." CM flings open the door.

"I feel pretty—" The word dies in my mouth when she flashes a diamond solitaire under my nose. "Oh my God."

There's a cavernous silence. "Is that all you can say?" She laughs.

I put up my arms for a hug. "Congrats." I want to smile, but my face is numb. Come on, Wyn. This is your best friend and she's ecstatic. Lie. "I'm really happy for you."

"Yeah, I can see you are."

"I'm just . . . stunned. So when did this happen?"

She holds her hand out and turns it from side to side so the sun shaft coming in the window makes rainbows on the wall. "Pretty righteous rock, don't you think? Last night." She flops into the club chair. "He just came walking in the door with a bottle of Dom Perignon and some roses and I said what are we celebrating and he said—"

I'm wondering, since he's not working at the current running moment, but living off CM, where the hell he got the money for a diamond and Dom Perignon.

"Gee, I hope I'm not boring you."

I look at her. "CM, please don't be mad at me."

She smiles, but I can see her heart's not in it. "I'm not mad. I guess I just expected you to be thrilled or something." She shrugs. "Maybe that's asking too much."

"This worries me," I say lamely.

She stands up, hands on her hips. "Can't you be happy for me simply because I'm happy?"

I swallow carefully. "Can I be totally honest?"

"I have a feeling you're going to be, no matter what I say."

"I'm sorry. I just can't help wondering— Is this what you want?"

"Not really. But I didn't have any classes scheduled for spring, so I thought I might as well get married."

"Sit." I ease down and pat the space next to me on the futon. She walks over to the window and pretends to be looking at something. "I was thinking the other day. About David and me, but it could apply to you and Neal, too . . ."

She turns around, leans against the windowsill. "Yes?"

"This probably sounds silly, but remember that theory you had about who you marry?"

"No."

"You told me one time that you thought people tend to marry whoever they happen to find themselves with when their internal clock tells them it's time to get married. Whether or not—"

"Oh, come on, Morrison. I must've been nineteen years old when I thought that one up. It has nothing to do with present reality."

"Well . . . it wasn't that long ago that you didn't even know if you wanted to see him again. And you don't even like diamonds," I blurt out.

Her eyes narrow. "What's with you? Does it really matter what kind of ring it is?" She starts walking back and forth in front of me.

"CM, I want you to sit down and listen—"

"My ears work fine standing up."

"No, please sit down." I lower my voice. "Please."

She perches on the chair. Right on the edge so she can jump up and throttle me.

"I want you to be happy. You know that." I pause, hoping she'll agree, but she doesn't. "Why did he give you a diamond?"

"They must have removed part of your brain when they got the appendix. Why do you think he gave me a diamond? Because he loves me. He wants to marry me. Is that so hard to fathom? You think you're the only one in the room who can get married?"

I should just shut up. We can patch this up now. Except I can't stop myself. "No, but—he knows you. He knows you don't like diamonds—"

"What the hell are you trying to say?"

"Neal got you a diamond because it's what *he* wanted to give you, not what you wanted—"

"You!" She points her finger at my nose. "You are way jealous."

"Yeah, I am, but it has nothing to do with this." She's already pissed; I might as well go for broke. "Don't you see what's happening? You're in panic mode—"

"Don't you dare. Don't say another—"

"Neal Brightman is not your last chance to get married."

She's on her feet, heading for the door.

"Listen to me." I jump up, too, and the sharp pull of my abdomen makes me gasp. "The man can only love you when everything's hunky-dory for him, don't you remember?"

She turns quickly and shoots me a look that's an Arctic blast in the face. "Every relationship has problems, as you, of all people, should know. At least Neal's not out fucking his secretary." She has the grace to look embarrassed.

"Don't you remember how we always said if one of us was getting ready to make a bad mistake, the other one should tell her, no matter what? I'm trying to help—" The words tumble out, blocks tipped over by a clumsy child.

"The hell you are!" she snaps. "You're jealous. You didn't want your mom to get married and you don't want me to get married. Nobody's allowed to be happy if you're not happy. When did you get to be such a selfish, spoiled..."

She doesn't finish, but I can fill in the blank. She slams the door so hard it bounces open again and I hobble after her.

"CM! Wait a second. Talk to me." I get past the hemlocks just in time to see her car pull away from the curb. I grab one of the branches to steady myself and the needles lie cool and smooth in my palm.

"She's not his secretary," I say to no one but me.

Seventeen

⬦

I want to vomit, but I know how that would feel, so I pop a warm Coke and take little swallows till the nausea passes.

Can't she see how defensive she is? Doesn't she realize this will never work? As soon as his dissertation hits the skids—and it will—he'll be hanging over her shoulder again. Mr. Moody Blues. Accusing her of neglecting him, of being self-centered. He'll bitch and moan and make her feel guilty. Then she'll come running to me.

Just like I always go running to her.

Of course, this whole thing will pass, and we'll take up where we left off. Either she'll marry him or she won't. She'll be happy or she won't. It never makes any difference between us. In a couple of days, we'll be talking on the phone and we'll laugh about it.

Except, how could she think I'm jealous? I mean, I am, but only in general. I accepted that a long time ago. How could you not be jealous of someone who sometimes renders you invisible by her very presence? But jealous about her getting married? Not likely. And that crack about David fucking his secretary. I suppose she thinks she can dip him in horse shit whenever she feels like it. But I say one thing—actually, one pretty tame, wishy-washy thing—about Neal and she's all over me like head lice.

I need to make bread. I need to and I can't.

· · ·

When Gary comes back, I'm on the phone with Jen, taking down her personal recipe for "short" scones.

3 cups flour
½ cup sugar
5 teaspoons baking powder
1 teaspoon salt
1 cup unsalted butter, chilled, cut in small cubes
½ cup dried cranberries, soaked in orange juice for 10 minutes
½ cup chopped, toasted pecans
½ cup milk
1 egg
Zest of one orange

Combine flour, sugar, baking powder, and salt in large bowl. Cut in butter until dough is in pea-size crumbs. Drain cranberries and add to dough along with pecans. Whisk milk, egg, and orange zest in small bowl. Add to dry ingredients and mix just until incorporated and dough clumps together in a ball.

Roll out on floured surface ½ to ¾ inch thick. Cut into desired shape, and freeze or bake at 375°F until golden brown, about 25 minutes (longer if frozen).

He paces until I hang up, then I have to give a report of my activities. I skip the whole CM scene. When I start dragging out flour and sugar and butter, he says, "What are you doing?"

"Making scones."

He looks at me as if I'm delirious. "Why?"

"Because I need to."

"Can't we just buy some—"

"Gary, please. It's not the scones I need, it's making them. I'm going nuts. Why don't you get us a glass of wine and park yourself in that chair and tell me all about your meeting?"

He uncorks the Napa cab and pours two glasses. I confess I'm not listening too closely about the meeting. Something about setting up interviews in Portland. I'm rubbing the butter into the dry ingredients with my fingertips and thinking about CM.

"...so we run ads in the college papers, but then you have to make them understand that people who use valet parking are generally older and they don't feel good about sending their Lincoln or Mercedes off with somebody who looks to them like a wild-eyed radical junkie, so they have to keep their hair short and have clean fingernails and absolutely no beards..."

I enjoy a malicious thought of Neal being told to shave his beard so he can park cars for Gary's company.

I scoop the dough onto the countertop and roll it out with my grocery-store rolling pin. I think of my oma's big maple rolling pin lying unused in the bottom of a drawer in my mother's kitchen. That sucker weighs about two and a half pounds and moves like a skater on a frozen lake. The wood's sleek and golden from years of pie crust and cookies and biscuits. She always cleaned it by rubbing flour into it and wiping it off with a flour-sack towel.

"You never, ever wash a rolling pin," she told me.

"Have you thought about tonight?" Gary says.

The way my head snaps up, he probably realizes I wasn't listening, but he sits there in his blue oxford-cloth, button-down shirt and khaki pants, hair falling clean and soft on his forehead, smiling like a choirboy. Why can't I just accept my good fortune and run with it?

I get out my chef's knife and cut the dough into triangles.

He tries again. "So, what do you feel like doing?"

I pull out a cookie sheet and arrange the scones on it in orderly rows, lay it in the freezer. I turn around. "Can I ask you a question?"

He smiles. "Sure."

"Did you ever cheat on Erica?"

The smile evaporates like water on a hot griddle. "No. Why?"

"Did you ever want to?"

"Not really."

"What does that mean, 'not really'?"

He looks directly at me. "It means I met someone once that I was attracted to, but I never pursued it. Later I realized it was probably just a revenge fantasy."

"Revenge for what?"

"Erica had an affair with a friend of ours," he says quietly.

Batting a thousand today, Wyn. "I'm sorry. That was a stupid conversational gambit."

"You obviously had a reason for asking."

The reason being that I'm in training to be a bitch.

"Is that what happened with David?"

I manage a laugh. "You mean my mother didn't spill all the dirt?"

He shakes his head. "Why would she?"

"Sometimes I don't know why she does things. We don't understand each other very well, I guess." I take out my plastic bench scraper and clean off the counter, wipe my hands.

"Is that what happened?" he asks again.

"Sort of. It was a woman in his office. I guess now they're getting married."

"I'm sorry."

"Doesn't it seem weird, us sitting here talking about our exes? Comparing their liabilities. Like they were former employees or something. Instead of someone you thought you'd be waking up next to for— You know what I want to do?"

"What?"

"I want to go on a tour of that house out front."

"Isn't it locked?"

I shrug. "Maybe we can find a way in."

He rubs the back of his neck. "I think that's called 'trespassing.' "

"We won't break anything. If nothing's open, we won't go in. Come on. Before it's too dark."

· · ·

"This would be the tradesmen's entrance," Gary says. "All these big old houses had one. By the kitchen." The rusted knob is so loose that the door swings open at a gentle push.

We step inside, inhale the damp, stale air. My eyes gradually adjust to the dimness. There's something about a house that's been shut up for a while. Sadness builds up like a static charge just waiting for a conductor.

"The mudroom," he says. There are pegs in the wood paneling, a bench, and a built-in corner cupboard with doors sagging on broken hinges. The bead-board walls are streaked with black, probably mildew.

"What's a mudroom?"

He smiles. "A place to leave mud. Boots, raincoats, umbrellas. So you don't mess up the rest of the house." He takes my hand, pulls me into the kitchen. They got as far as gutting it. The bleached shadows of cupboards and appliances are all that's left on the dirty walls, except for stubbed water and gas pipes.

The dining room's obvious by the chandelier hanging over the spot where the table would be. "Watch your head." He picks up an unopened can of paint, turns it around. " 'Goldenrod,' " he reads off the label.

"I read somewhere that a lot of people split up when they're in the middle of some big project," I say.

He nods, looking around us at the piles of new lumber and boxes of nails languishing under a thick layer of dust. "Planning holds you together because it's fun—mostly imagination and anticipation. Then when you actually have to start working, reality sets in."

The thing in the living room covered with drop cloths turns out to be an ebony grand piano. With one finger, I pick out the melody line of "Moon River," the only song I remember from my abortive piano lessons. Out of tune, but not hopeless. We cover the piano again.

The stairs groan and our footsteps echo off the bare wood. Dust motes dance in the last light of afternoon spilling through a tall, narrow window. We stop on the wide landing, halfway up.

"This is where you make speeches from." He leans on the railing and jumps back smartly as it bows out.

I laugh. "And that's what happens when the speeches go on for too long."

"No one builds landings like this anymore," he says.

"Why is that?"

"Wasted space."

"It's not wasted. Where else are you supposed to stand and let everyone admire your gown?"

The doors leading off the upper hall are closed, except for one. I wander in and he follows. No furniture, just moving cartons sealed with tape and labeled optimistically "Master Suite."

"Look." He points to a box under the bay window. Sitting on top is a pair of fuzzy bunny-rabbit slippers. More endearing than flowers or jewelry, intimate beyond lingerie. Not something you'd buy for yourself. Maybe a birthday present. To say I'm sorry. Or I love you.

I can't breathe in here. I turn abruptly, go back down the stairs, through the living room, dining room, kitchen, mudroom, and out the side door, as fast as I can without my incision protesting. Gary's right behind me, securing the door.

How could you leave someone who gave you bunny slippers?

"You want some more wine?"

"No, thanks." He sits down in the club chair while I rinse the glasses out in the sink. "You still haven't told me what you want to do tonight."

"Well..." I reach for the blackout shade on the kitchen window. Then I walk over to the other window and pull the shade. I lock the door.

"I promise I won't run away." From his silly little grin, I'd say he's picking up the signals okay.

He reaches for my hand. "Are you going to be all right with this?"

"We'll just do what we can."

"I like the sound of that."

When I straddle him, I can feel his erection under me. "Are you ready already?"

"It's getting embarrassing," he says against my throat. "All I have to do is look at you and I'm ready."

I'm dissolving against him, sediment falling through still water. Tears stream out of my eyes, and when he feels them on his face, he looks up at me. "Do you hurt?"

"Not physically. It's just been kind of a shitty day."

"Do you want to tell me?"

"No."

His thumbs gently push the tears off my face. "What can I do?"

I lean over to kiss his mouth. "This will be just fine." I stand up and pull the sweatshirt over my head. The rest of the clothes are laid aside and we settle in carefully. I wonder if this chair has a history. Crazy, but it beats thinking about CM. Or Mac. Or the shadow I was trying to name. It was nearly in my grasp when CM showed up. I push it all away. The only thing I need to be grasping right now is directly under me, seeking an entrance. I'm surprised to discover that I'm as ready as he is. His hands cradle my hips and I lower myself, letting him fill me.

"Are you okay?" he whispers.

I smile. "Better than that."

He begins to move inside me and I fall thankfully into darkness.

Sunday night. My attempts to function on impulse, without a lot of review or analysis, have always met with limited success. Gary is snoring—but softly and considerately—sleeping the sleep of the righteous, while I lie on my back, eyes glued open, brain turning over like an old car suffering from post-ignition run-on.

The whole week has been about him taking care of me, pleasing me, helping me, making me feel good—whether I wanted to or not. It reminds me of being in a mink-padded cell. And just when I get annoyed, just when I feel like I have to get away, at the very instant I think I'll explode if he doesn't go get a hotel room, his breath on the back of my neck turns my knees to water and we end up sprawled on the futon.

He always says my name when he comes. It's comforting to know that the person with whom you are having sex is focused on you alone. I myself have visions of calling out the wrong name, not the sort of thing that's easily explained. If words have the power to wound, the wrong name uttered at the wrong time could be lethal.

When I open my eyes Monday morning, he's lying there propped up on one elbow, smiling at me. Awareness of his imminent departure produces a twinge of something almost like regret. It wasn't so bad. In fact, it was nice. He pulls me closer and I snuggle up against his warm, clean T-shirt smell.

The kids only called three times and Erica not at all. He gave me back rubs and foot massages and touched me in all the best places, fixed dinner and did the dishes. He even tried to brush my hair one night, although it turned into a contest of wills ending in a draw. When you get old, half blind, mostly deaf, and you can no longer tell which stuff in your fridge is edible and which is riddled with botulism, then you want someone like Gary around. He may not be in any better shape than you are, but he'll damn sure be trying to take care of you.

"Wyn."

"Hmm?" I rub my cheek drowsily against his chest.

"I want you to come down to San Francisco for a weekend."

I raise myself too quickly, grimacing at the pain. I sit cross-legged, holding my head between my hands, combing the hair back with my fingers, waiting for the brain to clear. "Why?" I finally manage.

He smiles, unperturbed. "I want you to meet Andrew and Katie."

"I'm going to pretend I didn't hear that long enough for you to come to your senses."

"I think it's time for the three people I care most about to meet each other." He clasps his hands behind his head.

"I cannot possibly be one of those people. You don't even know me."

"I know what I need to, Wyn. And I know myself. I want you in my life."

"Gary, for Chrissake, it's just sex."

"That's not what it is to me." The way he says it, slow and steady and very sincere, makes me ashamed of myself. "I don't think that's all it means to you either, but you're scared. I can understand that. You think if you can diminish it by calling it 'just sex,' you can avoid getting hurt again."

There's just enough truth in what he says to make me hesitate. "My divorce isn't even final. It's probably not going to be for a long time. I can't think about . . . stuff like this."

He sits up, too, facing me. "I'm not asking you to think about anything. I'm asking you to come to my house, meet my kids, have a fun weekend. If we lived in the same town, it probably would have already happened."

"But we don't live in the same town." How do I say I'm glad we don't? That I don't feel up to making this decision right now?

He looks at me with those sleepy eyes while he traces the outer curve of my ear with one finger. Even that's enough to race my motor, and he knows it.

"As Mick Jagger said, 'Time is on my side.' " He leans over to kiss my neck, right at the jawline.

"Irma Tho—mas said it first," I say weakly.

"God, I love that little catch in your voice." He leaves a trail of feathery kisses on his way down my neck.

"Gary, I'm not comfortable with—this."

"Why not?" Around the front, to my collarbone. "You know how I feel. I know how you feel. Everything's"—he touches my throat with just the tip of his tongue and my body responds without consulting my brain—"up front and out in the open." When his thumbs graze my nipples through my T-shirt, they stand up and salute.

He knows he's won this skirmish.

It seems like a good time to divest myself of some of the accoutrements of my former life. Like my clothes. It's only partly a symbolic gesture. The truth is, I need some money to pay my last bill from Elizabeth. Apparently, stalling is pretty expensive.

Mac comes by Saturday afternoon, loads the two boxes into the back of the truck, and drives me down to Rags to Riches. When I climb out and reach for one of the boxes, he slaps my hand away.

"You're not supposed to be lifting anything yet. Go open the door."

The bell over the entrance jingles when we walk in, and the petite blonde behind the counter smiles at us.

"Hi. I'm Wyn Morrison. I called about the clothes."

"Great, just put them over here and let's have a look." Mac goes out and returns with the other box. He sets it down and leans over the counter, watching us. She's pulling things out, exclaiming over them, dividing them into piles. Donna Karan, Ellen Tracy, Diane Freis, Anne Klein, Ralph Lauren, Giorgio Armani. Sand-washed silk, linen, rayon, chenille.

She says, "These are gorgeous. Are you sure you want to get rid of them all?"

"Positive."

"Well, our split is sixty-forty and...oh my God, a Judith Leiber bag? We shouldn't have any problem selling them for you. They're like new." She and I inventory the tights, skirts, slacks, tops, dresses, lingerie, shoes, purses. "These dresses are exquisite. I have one or two people in mind to call about them."

Mac's uncharacteristically quiet on the way home. He's been sort of preoccupied lately, and I tend to blame his close encounter with Laura at the party on Capitol Hill. Or else he's suffering from writer's block, which, like most writers, he takes out on everyone around him.

When he pulls up in front of the Victorian, I ask him if he wants to come in.

"I've got some things to do before work," he says.

I look over. "Are you okay?"

"Yeah. I've just been kind of tired lately."

"How's the book going?"

"Fine." But he's looking out the window.

"Mac, is it Laura?"

"What?" He tries laughing, but he sounds pissed off that I mentioned it.

"Maybe it's none of my business. I just thought you seemed a little depressed ever since you ran into her at—"

He looks at me sharply. "Do me a favor. Don't try to analyze me with your California pop psychology."

"I was only trying to help—"

"Well, don't, okay?"

"Fine. I won't." I open the door and get out, but before I make it to the curb, he calls after me.

"Wyn, wait a second." I stare into the truck. "I'm sorry. I'm just in a shitty mood. I'm going home and get some sleep. I'll see you tonight?"

I shrug. "Probably."

My shoes roll as I start up the drive; I realize there's easily two inches of new pea gravel on top of the old.

Sunday night is clear. Clear like I've never seen in L.A. The debris of the day must be halfway to Japan, and the stars look like this jacket my mother used to have, rhinestones set in black velvet. There is no moon. Mac wants to be on the water tonight.

Dark silhouettes of gulls float against the jeweled towers of the city, and metal clanks against metal on the car deck below us. In the lee of the passenger decks, the fierce wind drops to a ripple.

We hang over the rail, side by side. I'm aware of him so acutely that my fingers ache. The smell of pine bark that clings to his jacket, smoke from the fireplace at Bailey's. Something grassy, maybe shampoo.

He's staring up into the black dome of night sky.

"What is it?" he says.

"I was just— Is that the Big Dipper?"

"Yes."

"That's the only constellation I know."

"If you know that one, you actually know two. The Dipper's the tail of Ursa Major, the big bear." I try to follow his finger, tracing the outline of a long-tailed bear.

"So where's the Little Dipper?"

He looks behind us. "You can't see it from here because of the boat, but if you followed a straight line from those two stars on the cup of the dipper, you'd see Polaris, the North Star, which is the end of the Little Dipper's handle."

"What's the really bright star, just down that line from the Big Dipper?"

"That's Arcturus. It's sort of at the knee of Boötes, the herdsman. And then if you keep looking down that same curve of stars, you can see part of Virgo."

I look past him. "Who knew that the psycho-killer handyman would know so much about stars."

"You can't see that many here," he says. "Too much light. This would be a great night to be up in the San Juans."

Something about the way he says it. I feel hot and cold at the same time, and I know it's too early for menopause.

"I'm probably going up there."

"Probably?" My voice is faint.

He studies something down on the car deck. "No. Not probably. I'm going. Next week." Fortunately, he keeps talking, because I know I can't make any sounds. "That's why I've been sort of distracted lately. I've been in Seattle longer than I've been anywhere else since I left New York. It was a hard decision. Sorry if I've been moody or—"

"What will you do there?" That voice isn't mine. It belongs to one hell of a ventriloquist.

"Write." He turns his face toward me, but it's shadowed. "I got a letter from this agent named Alan Lear. In L.A. I sent him the first three chapters and he wants to see the rest." He laughs. "I didn't want to tell him there is no rest, so I told him I was revising and I'd have it in his hands by September."

"Congratulations."

"I'm not breaking out the champagne yet. He just wants to see it. There's no promises."

"There never are."

He exhales noisily. "Anyway, Rick—the guy from Norwegian

Woods—his family has a cottage up on Orcas and he said I could use it for the summer if I'd do some maintenance on the place. Patch the roof, clear some land, paint. Stuff like that. And the rest of the time I can write."

"Sounds like an offer you can't refuse."

He gives me a little nudge with his elbow. "I'll probably be back in the fall."

"Probably?"

"Yeah. Probably."

The morning air is so thick with spring that it's hard to believe there was a foot of snow on the ground six weeks ago. The Red Riding Hood tulips that Diane planted in the barrel outside the bakery door have opened in a blaze of scarlet. Everyone on Queen Anne is nuts for window boxes, and by now they're spilling over with cascading blue lobelia, red and purple salvia, white dwarf snapdragons, yellow mimulus. Plain green hedges that I've walked past every day have become drifts of white, soft pink, deep-purple rhododendron.

I can practically hear Julie Andrews singing "The Lusty Month of May."

When I get home from work, Mac's leaning against the Elky's passenger door drinking coffee out of a big white cup.

"You shouldn't drink anything acidic out of a Styrofoam cup," I tell him. "The acid dissolves that stuff right into your drink."

"So that means if I drink it slow enough, I don't have to worry about recycling the cup."

"I'm sorry I missed your going-away party. I promised CM months ago I'd go to this dance thing. She had the tickets..."

Has my skill as a liar improved dramatically, or maybe he simply doesn't notice? The truth is, I sat alone through some French film at the University of Washington, letting the images flicker on my eyes, the syncopated rhythm of the dialogue dance past me without registering. It seemed preferable to standing around Bailey's listening to everyone wish him good luck.

I wonder if Laura was there, but I can't ask.

"That's okay. It was fairly sedate, as parties go. I was just on my way out of town. Thought I'd stop by."

"So . . . good luck with the book."

"Thanks. I hope your . . . situation turns out okay."

I smile fixedly. "Jean-Marc used to say the bread might not always turn out the way you want it, but it always turns out."

"Take care of yourself." His mouth brushes my cheek awkwardly. I follow him around to the driver's side. He climbs in the Elky, and the door rattles as he slams it. He rolls the window down as if he just thought of something else.

"Here. I made this for you." He hands me a cassette.

I turn it over. "What is it?"

"All the songs and artists are on the card."

My stomach is making little warning noises. "Mac, thanks. For everything. You've been a great friend."

He turns the key. Of course it doesn't start. We both laugh and then he looks at me. He's wearing a green T-shirt that says "Eat Water: Raft the Colorado." I wonder if he ever did that. Anyway, it looks good on him. Makes his eyes as deep green as river water.

He tries the ignition again and this time it catches. I wave and start walking back to the house. Quickly, so I don't have to see him drive away.

I don't exactly decide to call CM; it's habit. One of Mac's engrams. The machine picks up on the first ring. She's either out of town or screening her calls.

"This is the right number, but you called at the wrong time. Leave a message and I'll get back to you."

"CM?" Could I sound any more pitiful? "CM? Please pick up if you're there." I take a breath. "It's me. Your old ex-best friend. I miss you so much. I'm sorry for what happened. All the stupid stuff I said. I'm glad you're happy. Honestly. Please call me. I need to talk to you. Please don't—"

The machine clicks off. The empty air reminds me of that sound you hear when you put a seashell up to your ear.

Eighteen

❧

It's pouring Thursday afternoon when I wake up. Probably a good
day to delve into my time-capsule box that I brought home from
the wedding. Getting rid of nonessentials always makes me feel
good, sort of clean and strong. Still, I sit at the table after I've eaten my
cheese omelet, stirring cream around and around in my coffee till it's
too cold to drink and wondering if it's raining in the San Juans.

Mac said one time that they actually got less rain than Seattle
because they were in the rain shadow of the Olympics. He explained
what that means, but I can't remember now. Sometimes I think I'm
always paying attention, but not to the right things. There was something with Mac—some tension, a dark shape in my peripheral vision.
How else do I explain it? The vague restlessness when I wake up in the
afternoons. The nagging sense of missed opportunities.

Okay, maybe I was distracted, but it wasn't just that. I mean, he's a
bartender, for God's sake. A college dropout with a low threshold of
boredom. I hardly know anything personal about him, except that he
likes music and rock climbing. Then there's Laura, the phantom ex-
girlfriend hovering in the wings. Another doomed relationship, I don't
need. I'm already involved with Gary. And I'm not even divorced yet.
It's all happened too fast. What was it John Lennon said? Something

about life being what happens to you while you're busy trying to make plans.

I get up and pour the coffee down the drain, leave my dishes soaking in soapy water. I make space on the floor for myself and a giant plastic trash bag. I slit the tape on the box and dump the contents on the floor.

Engagement calendars. I open one, flip a few pages. Most of the names and places scribbled in the squares don't sound even vaguely familiar. I check the first pages to be sure they're mine and not CM's before tossing them all in the bag.

I save my high school graduation tassel, throw out all the cards. I pitch my acceptance letter from UCLA, my class schedules and my grade reports. I save my high school and college diplomas in their folders with the graduation announcements. I throw out all the pamphlets CM and I worked on for the National Organization for Women, and a button that says "Uppity Woman." On second thought, I retrieve the button. A rolled up T-shirt unfurls like a banner, making me laugh. CM gave it to me when my steady boyfriend dumped me just before the senior prom. It says "A Woman Needs a Man Like a Fish Needs a Bicycle."

There are photographs. Halloween party at Zelma Wallis's house. CM and I are standouts. Not just because we're taller than everyone else by three inches, but because our costumes are so weird. All the other girls have gone the glamour route—a queen, a movie star, a ballerina, Amelia Earhart. There's even a Statue of Liberty. CM and I are dressed as Amazons (our interpretation) in frizzy black wigs and fake leopard skin "Alley-Oop" outfits her mother made for us. The nickname "the Amazons" would stick with us for the rest of our school days.

A Polaroid snapshot taken by my mother. CM and I stand by my old black Chevy, leaving for freshman orientation at UCLA. She looks confident, gorgeous. Her long hair is ironed straight, parted in the middle. She wears a dark paisley shirt, crocheted vest, bell-bottom pants. Her woven bag from South America is bulging, probably with cookies, apples, gum. I'm smiling, but still manage to look grimly determined. My hair is barely contained in some weird contraption on top of my head. I'm wearing a tie-dyed T-shirt, hip-hugger jeans, and a belt with a huge brass buckle in the shape of my name. Three hours later, I'll be crouched in a stall in the women's rest room of the administration building, throwing up.

My heart aches and so does my stomach. This is worse than breaking up with a man, sitting around mooning over old pictures and remembering the good times. CM and I have been together almost twenty-five years, longer than a lot of married couples. She knows more about me than my mother. I used to think we were closer than sisters, but now I'm not sure. Sisters at least know they love each other, so they don't always have to like each other.

Sibling rivalry—we had it in spades. I got better grades; she was prettier. There were nights that I cried myself to sleep because some boy I was madly in love with had called to talk to me about fixing him up with CM. She never went out with any of them.

What I loved even more than her loyalty, though, was her absolute fearlessness. She seemed to thrive on getting in trouble, while I was loath to upset my father. He never laid a hand on me, rarely even scolded me. But he could say my name a certain way, not with disapproval so much as disappointment. That's all it took. CM, in one of her brutally honest moods, once told me I would have made a good golden retriever— quick, smart, eager to please him. The strange thing is, it didn't particularly offend me.

On the bottom of the pile is a professional photo taken at the country club the Sunday my father and I won the mixed-doubles tennis tournament. I was fifteen. I think it was the happiest day of my life. In the picture, we're each holding a handle of the silver trophy. His arm is around me and my smile takes up my entire face.

I stack all my high school yearbooks back in the box. They're always good for a laugh. Or when I can't remember somebody's name. Papers I wrote in college. "Woman's Work, Man's World" and "Sociology of Knowledge." "Shakespeare and the Passive-Aggressive Personality." Unutterably boring and pretentious. But they were mostly A papers. Maybe Mac was on to something with his cynical view of higher education. Underneath them is a pile of loose sheets. Every overblown, sophomoric poem I had in the literary magazine. My mother saved every single one.

I'm grabbing handfuls of stuff and jamming it into the bag when a piece of ivory stationery floats out of the pile like a leaf on the wind and settles on my foot. The old-fashioned penmanship is the kind they stopped making kids try to imitate when I was in fourth grade. My oma's handwriting. It's a letter to my mother, or part of one, probably mixed in with the papers from her cedar chest. As I start to crumple it up, my name leaps off the page at me.

> *If he really means to leave you, there is nothing you can do to prevent him. You could make things very difficult and unpleasant for him; but I don't believe you have the strength of will to pursue that course. So it behooves you to consider other alternatives. Of course, you and Justine are more than welcome to stay with us until you decide what to do. However long it takes.*
>
> *Remember, Johanna, that your father and I are standing by, should you need us. God bless you, my dear child, and comfort you. Justine is behaving reasonably well and seems to be enjoying herself.*
>
> *Lovingly,*
> *Mother*

I read it three times. Then once more, just to be sure there's not some other possible explanation of who "he" is. Of course there's not. "He" is my father, and now the wheel of my memory turns easily, gracefully, despite its unwieldy mass. Pictures click silently into place like slides, enlarged, illuminated, and projected onto a screen.

They were an unlikely couple. He was handsome, maybe a little bit wild when he was young—daring, adventurous, self-assured. She was pretty, but sweet, quiet, serious. I found their wedding picture interesting when I was old enough to appreciate the subtleties of people's eyes, their expressions. For that photograph, they seemed to have exchanged personalities. Pleased, proud, exuding stability, he had the air of a man confident of doing the correct thing. While my mother looked as if she might bubble over with laughter at some unexpected adventure that had just presented itself. How long before he realized she wasn't enough for him? How long before she knew?

I reach for the phone book that sits under the little side table and leaf through the A's till I get to Alaska Airlines.

Saturday morning at eleven-fifteen, I'm standing in front of my mother's house. The door is locked, undoubtedly Richard's influence. She's never locked anything. I ring the bell. When she opens the door and says, "Wyn! What a wonderful surprise!" the revulsion I feel at the sound of her voice nearly unhinges me. "How are you? How long can you stay?"

"I have to go back tonight. Where's Richard?"

"Playing golf. Why?"

"I need to talk to you about something. Privately."

Her tone changes instantly. "What's the matter?"

By this time, we're in the den. I set down my purse, but before I can say anything, she says, "Do you want some tea? Or juice, or water? Coffee?"

"Nothing, thanks." I sit down on the couch; she lowers herself gracefully into her sewing chair.

"Honey, what's wrong? You seem upset."

"I found this." I take the letter out of my jacket pocket, unfold it, and hand it to her. "In that box I took home after the wedding."

She opens the reading glasses that she wears on a silk cord around her neck, puts them on. Before she even begins to read it, I see that she knows what it is. Her face is first flushed, then very pale.

"Oh, baby." She must have been holding her breath and she lets it all out at once, like the air going out of a balloon. "I'm so sorry you saw this."

"Please tell me what happened."

"Wyn, it was so long ago, and it wasn't really—"

"Please."

She scans the page and then lays it on the coffee table. She sits back in the chair, hands in her lap. "When you were four years old, your father decided he was in love with someone else." Her voice is calm, matter-of-fact.

"Who?" My voice, by contrast, is more like a squeak.

"No one you'd know. She worked in Andersen's Chicago office. He came home from a trip and told me he was in love with her and he asked me to divorce him."

I've never been anywhere near a tornado, but this is how I think it must be. The black wind howling around you and the dead-calm center. For a second, I'm actually dizzy.

"What did you say?"

"I didn't actually say much. I just cried and got quietly drunk and passed out." The idea of my mother drinking enough to pass out is hard to grasp. It probably took all of two drinks. She brushes an imaginary piece of lint off her slacks. "He moved into a hotel that night."

"Where was I?"

"Thank God you were at Oma and Opa's. The next day I called them and asked them to keep you a while longer. That week..." She pauses. "It was like a dream. No, more a nightmare. Your father was coming over to the house every night to talk about divorce and division of property and who would live where and how we would settle you."

"And you really had no idea he was—?"

"None. But then I was rather naive in those days." She looks away from me, out the sliding-glass door to the patio. "He had an attorney. And a list of attorneys he thought I might want to call. He'd apparently given it quite a bit of thought."

I see David, sitting on the couch in our den, telling me about the great condo he'd found for me. "So...?"

"I begged him not to leave, not to break up the family, but he was absolutely determined."

One of those scenes that burns itself into your brain, but you can't remember why. Waking up one night. Getting up for a drink of water or a potty trip. Walking down the hall, bare feet padding silently on the carpet, past my parents' room. It's dark except for my mother in her chair. She sits in a pool of light, holding a book, and she doesn't look up when I tiptoe past.

"That was the week that Oma wrote me that letter. I was desperate. I was ready to try anything that might put my world back together." The ticking of the school clock on the mantel sounds like a drum in the silence.

I must look thoroughly confused, because she leans closer, peering into my face. "It wasn't such an everyday occurrence then, you know. Things had to be pretty bad before you resorted to divorce." She attempts a laugh. "Divorcées were women who wore too much makeup and used cigarette holders and frequented cocktail lounges."

"So what did you say to him?"

"You have to understand, Wyn . . ." She keeps talking about her desperation, her fear, the pain. She hasn't said anything yet about loving him. In my head, I'm screaming, *Cut to the chase,* but I sit listening. "The next time he came over, I was ready. I started with the house and the car. His salary, future raises, investments, insurance, a college fund for you. He was very accommodating." When her eyes sweep up to mine, I imagine her looking at him in just this way. "And then I said, 'Oh, and one last thing. You will never contact Justine again once the divorce is final.' "

My mouth opens slightly, half in surprise, half in protest. "You can't really do that."

"Not now." She smiles faintly. "Twenty-five years ago, men didn't have many rights as far as child custody. Particularly under those circumstances. Anyway . . ." She shrugs. "I don't know that I would have done it even if I could have. But that's not the point. The point is, I made him believe that I could. That I would." The smile becomes a full-blown triumph. "Two days later, he moved back home."

For an instant, I see her the way he must have. Beautiful, yes. Always. But no longer sweet, accommodating, pliant. He's underestimated her. She's willing to push it to the limit. It's exactly the kind of thing he would have responded to. I can see him falling in love with her all over again.

I should say something now; I just don't know what. She stands up.

"And that, my dear, is pretty much the story. I'm going to have a glass of sherry. Would you like something?"

"No. Thanks."

"It's very good. Quite dry. Richard's favorite."

She goes to the walnut cabinet that came from my grandparents' town house. Amber liquid splashes into a small crystal glass. Standing there in her black linen slacks and expensive white cotton sweater and a chunky gold necklace I've never seen before, she's gathered all the pieces together. She's Richard's wife, not someone's washed-out widow, fending off her friends' husbands in the kitchen.

She comes back and sits down next to me, sipping her drink. "We had twelve wonderful years before he died."

" 'Wonderful'?" I still feel like the cartoon character who's been hit in the face with a frying pan.

"I'm not going to sit here and tell you it was like a fairy tale. But we had a more honest relationship, a deeper one."

She sets down the glass and puts her hands on mine. A tale without words can be read by looking at our hands together. Hers are small, graceful, limber. Her nails are always French-manicured, cuticles neatly pushed back to reveal the creamy white moons at the base. My hands are large, blunt-fingered. No matter how often I have them manicured, there are always a few pesky hangnails. And I could push my cuticles back to my elbows and I'd never have those pretty little moons.

She's looking at me, eyebrows just slightly arched. And the last question is . . .

"Why didn't you ever tell me?"

She appears genuinely surprised. "Why would I do that?"

"So I'd know the truth. About what kind of man he was."

"Wyn, you've always known the truth. Your father was a good man who made mistakes. Like everyone else. But don't ever forget this. He loved you more than anything in the world. When I made him choose, he chose you."

I get up and push open the sliding door to the backyard, set my feet on my father's bricks. The old redwood patio furniture with its ugly green cushions would fetch a bundle in one of the retro-chic shops off Melrose. I sit down on the chaise lounge and lie back, put my feet up. The black walnut tree that's thrived for twenty years under Shoji's judicious pruning shades the whole yard at this time of year. In spite of the dark stains their shells left on the patio, I always thought "black" walnuts was a misnomer. They taste like the color green. The shells were so tough I used to put them on the driveway before my father came home from work so they'd be crushed open by the weight of the car. He used to say that they only tasted good because you had to work so hard for them.

My mother is standing next to me, although I didn't see her come out. I move my feet so she can sit down.

"Did we hurt your feelings a lot?"

She gnaws delicately on the inside of her cheek. "Sometimes I just wanted to be in on the joke. I wanted you to look at me the way you looked at him. Sometimes I even wanted him to look at me the way he looked at you." Her face is flushed. From the sherry, I suppose.

It occurs to me that I have no idea who this lovely stranger is. Haven't had for years. What she thought about, wished for, laughed at, loved. All this time, I've been seeing her in the wedding picture. Mamie Eisenhower bangs. Big smile. Waiting for the adventure to start.

"After he died, people would always say to me, 'At least you have Wyn'" She touches my arm. "But I didn't. There wasn't much left of you. And what there was, you weren't willing to share with me."

"Momma..." The word cracks my voice.

I'm so much bigger than she is, it's hard for her to hold me while I cry, but somehow she does. This hasn't happened in a very long time.

When I get my mail Tuesday, there's a fat envelope bearing the postmark of Larkspur, California. I rip the end off, and an airline ticket drops into my hands. I'd conveniently forgotten that a week from Saturday is the date we finally agreed on for me to stand inspection.

There's a handwritten note stapled to the ticket jacket.

Dear Wyn,

Here's your ticket. Erica's agreed to swap weekends with me, so we'll only have the kids Saturday afternoon. I thought we'd pick you up and go to the aquarium or Fisherman's Wharf. Or if there's anything else you'd prefer, we can do that. Andrew and Katie are excited to meet you.

After we drop them off, we have early dinner reservations at a great little roadhouse in Larkspur and then we'll go to a party at a client's house. We don't have to stay long, but I can't wait to show you off. Sunday we can do brunch in Tiburon and I have tickets for a matinee that afternoon. Or maybe we'll forget all that. I'll take your clothes off using only my teeth and . . . well, you get the idea. Hope you're feeling like new. Take care. I miss you.

G.

I should be happier about this. More excited . . . something. Maybe it's just that I'm upset about CM. I jam everything back in the envelope and toss it on the kitchen table.

My first priority is weaseling my way back into CM's good graces. Bread. Not just any bread, but something special. Sylvie used to do these fabulous window displays at the *boulangerie* with special loaves shaped by Phillipe, one of the bakers who was more artist than artisan. There were sheaves of wheat, ears of corn, little alligators, turtles, fish, cats and dogs, baskets and wreathes, all sculpted from bread dough. I don't have the artistic inclination for something so elaborate, but any fool can make a circle.

A *couronne.* In fact, a double *couronne,* like interlocking wedding rings, will be my peace offering. Jean-Marc told me that the *couronne,* the crown-shaped loaf, originated in rural areas of France where the people were thrifty with their time as well as their money. The four-to-six-pound loaves of bread would last a whole family for a week, but they didn't have enough crust in proportion to crumb until somebody came up with the bright idea of putting a hole in the middle.

I don't have time to wait for a starter to ripen, so I use a *poolish,* or sponge. Actually my oma used to use this method of bread making, but she never let the sponge ferment more than a couple of hours. I can leave it in the fridge when I go to work and give it a nice, cool, slow development.

POOLISH FOR PAIN DE CAMPAGNE
(SPONGE FOR COUNTRY FRENCH BREAD)

½ teaspoon yeast
½ cup water
¾ cup whole wheat flour

Dissolve yeast in water, then stir in flour till mixture forms a thick batter. Beat about a hundred strokes to develop the long strands of gluten. Cover with a damp cloth and let sit at least 2 hours at room temperature. Longer is better, up to about 8 hours. Or let *poolish* ripen in refrigerator for 12 to 15 hours. Keep in mind that it must come to room temperature before you can make bread, so allow an extra 2 hours.

Pain de Campagne

All of poolish
2½ cups water
½ teaspoon yeast
5½ to 6½ cups unbleached white bread flour
1 tablespoon kosher salt or sea salt

When the *poolish* is ready, it will be bubbly and loose, with a definite smell of fermentation. Scrape it into a large bowl, add water and yeast, and stir until the *poolish* is broken up and the mixture is frothy. Add flour one cup at a time until the dough becomes too difficult to stir, then turn out onto a well-floured board and knead for 10 to 12 minutes, adding flour as necessary. Sprinkle salt over the dough and knead an additional 5 to 7 minutes. At first the dough will be quite sticky, but don't add any more flour than absolutely necessary to keep it from sticking to the work surface. A moist dough yields a wonderful, chewy texture.

When you press your finger into the dough and it springs right back, it's ready. Shape it into a ball and cover with a damp towel while you clean and oil the bowl. Place the dough in the bowl, turning to coat the whole surface with oil. This keeps it from forming a dry crust, which will inhibit rising. Cover with the damp towel and let rise at room temperature till doubled in volume, about 2 to 3 hours. When you press your finger about half an inch into the dough and the indentation remains, it's risen enough.

At this point, deflate the dough gently and let it "rest," covered, for about 30 minutes to relax the gluten. Then, cut in two pieces, shape as for *baguettes,* and place on a heavily floured linen dish towel with folds between each loaf for support. Dust tops with flour, cover with damp towels, and proof (let them rise) for 1½ to 2 hours, or until they increase in size about 1½ times.

Preheat the oven to 450°F and put the teakettle on low about 45 minutes to 1 hour before baking. When the bread has risen, place the *baguettes* on a baking sheet lined with parchment paper or covered with a thin layer of cornmeal. Make several diagonal slashes with a single-edged razor or serrated knife and shape dough into two circles, overlapping the ends and pinching them together. Remember, this is a rustic bread; the shape isn't supposed to be perfect.

Adjust the oven rack so it is in the center, fill a heavy pan with boiling water from the teakettle, and set it on the lowest shelf or on the oven floor. Bake the bread for ten minutes at 450°F, then lower the temperature to 400°F and bake another 25 to 30 minutes, or until bread sounds hollow when bottom crust is thumped. Turn off the oven, prop the door open slightly, and let bread sit for another 5 minutes. Then remove and cool on racks. Do not cut or break bread until it has completely cooled.

The night is positively balmy, and I find my pace slowing, my thoughts focused on Gary. It wouldn't kill me to go down there. It obviously means a lot to him. The thought of his note sends a pleasant little frisson of anticipation down my back, and my steps get faster. Yes, that part of it will be fine. Better than fine.

Everything's always fine when he's with me. When I'm looking at him, touching him. But when he leaves, that's fine, too. I don't miss him. It's like he's a convenience, like junk food. Satisfies the craving for something sweet, but without any lasting nutritional value. Jesus, what's wrong with me? He's a person, not a Snickers bar.

My oma never told me, "Wyn, good sex can make you stupid."

It can get you into places where you wouldn't normally go and probably shouldn't be. Unfortunately, that's one of those lessons you have to learn for yourself. Some people are so dense they have to learn it more than once.

Look at David and me. Yes, okay. He liked shopping and classical music. He could balance a checkbook with his eyes closed and he knew the perfect wine to complement mushroom risotto. He had a killer crosscourt backhand.

Of course all that helped. But mostly it was his cobalt-blue contact lenses. The contrast of his sun-bleached hair with his dark eyelashes. It was because he could tie a soda straw in a knot with his tongue, and when he kissed that little fuzzy place in the small of my back, I forgot my own name.

I don't pretend to know what it was for him. He should have married someone like Kelley to begin with. Someone who not only understood what he was about, but shared the same passion. I blush to recall that night in L.A. when they'd just lost the Hathaway account and I showed up, determined to talk relationships. As much as I'd prefer to think otherwise, Kelley was the one he needed that night. She was the one who knew what had happened, what it meant, how he'd feel about it.

And now here's Gary. Sweet Gary. Who thinks he wants to take care of me. Make me feel good. He wants me to meet his kids. He wants to take up where David left off. A different route to the same destination. Marin instead of Hancock Park. Same story, different setting. Same shit, different day. *Why did Erica have to go to law school? She was making decent money as a paralegal.* She had it all, didn't she? You can always find another job. You can always make bread at home. He wants me in his life. But it's *his* life, not mine.

I picture CM, leaning across the table. *Does your life make you happy? Is this what you want to do?*

The double wedding ring *couronne* is, in all modesty, a thing of beauty—two interlocking circles of crusty, golden bread. And it smells like heaven. If this doesn't make CM call me, nothing will. The presentation is another matter. I don't have a box big enough, so I wrap it carefully in a clean dish towel and carry it over to the bakery.

Ellen and Misha are up to their eyebrows in Mazurka Bars, but they stop to admire my handiwork.

"It's sort of an engagement present for CM," I say. "I need something to put it in."

"You can use one of those display baskets if you promise to bring it back," Ellen says.

I arrange the towel in the basket and nestle the bread in the center, covering the whole thing with plastic wrap, loosely, so the crust doesn't soften. Then I pull out the plain white gift card that I bought and stare at it.

"Are you waiting for inspiration to strike?" Misha laughs.

"I just can't decide what to say."

"How about 'Best wishes' or something?"

Ellen shakes her head. "That sounds like something you'd write to someone you barely know. This is Wyn's best friend."

I feel a quick jab of guilt.

"Okay, how about 'Happiness always' or 'To a terrific couple,' or—"

I write "To CM, Love, Wyn" in the middle of the card, then as an afterthought, I scrawl "and Neal" next to her name. We can talk about the happiness and the terrific-couple stuff when she calls me.

Neither of them is home anyway when I take the bread over there.

Maybe it's best. I leave it with the building manager after making her promise to watch for them and deliver it the second they come home and not set it near any open windows or air vents in the interim. I walk home feeling vaguely depressed and anxious. Like I've just delivered my firstborn child into some dubious day care center.

Of course, Gary's first question is, "Is there someone else?"

"No, there's nobody else."

"Wyn, I don't understand. I thought we had something pretty special going on. Even if you want to call it just sex, where's the harm in seeing if it turns into something more?" The man is a born negotiator.

"It wasn't just sex. You were right. I was saying that to protect myself. The harm is that it's not going to work and the longer we drag it out, the harder it gets to break up."

"Why are you so sure it isn't going to work—"

"Because I don't want it to work."

"But why?"

"Because we have different priorities. I'm not willing to give mine up again."

"I'm not asking you to give up anything—"

"You don't have to ask. It just happens. Like quicksand. I sink into your life and disappear without a trace."

"Is it such a terrible life?"

"Not at all. It's just not the life I want."

"I swear, I don't understand. If there's nobody else, why can't you just be with me until—"

"Until you can change my mind? That's what would happen, I know. Because I'm weak and because I really like you. You're very sweet—"

"Geez, the kiss of death."

"No, it's not, believe me. Sweet men are a rare and precious commodity. It would be easy to fall right in step with you. And it's just not where I'm headed."

He sighs again. "I don't understand."

"I know you don't. And it's next to impossible to explain. You're going to have to trust me."

"I'm sorry."

"Stop apologizing!" I bite my lip. "It's not your fault. It's not my fault. We just want different things."

"Wyn, you sound so confused. Why don't we talk next week?"

It's my turn to sigh. "What part of this is giving you trouble?"

I'm not feeling so resolutely, unwaveringly positive that he couldn't change my mind. Maybe if he said, "I love you and we can work around whatever you want to do." Or even if he said, "You know, I don't like being jerked around." But what he says is, "Katie and Andrew are going to be really disappointed."

"Gary, I'm going to hang up now. Take care of yourself."

I send the ticket back. He calls every night for a week, but I don't answer the phone. Every time the machine picks up, he says, "Wyn, I just want to talk to you. Please pick up if you're there." He sounds so miserable that a couple of times I almost do. But the elation of making it this far always gives me the strength to pick up a book instead of the phone.

The calls get farther apart and later at night. The messages on the machine start to include things like he just wants to say hi, see how I'm doing, but I don't call him back. When he calls the bakery, Linda's only too happy to tell him that I'm not available.

Voices wake me. Raucous male laughter. I roll over. One-thirty, Saturday afternoon. I sit up and pull on my sweatpants. I can't see anything through the peephole, so I open the door. A tall, skinny guy wearing a backward baseball cap is standing at the corner of the big house, yelling to a guy on the roof.

I step outside. "Do you mind? I'm trying to sleep." That old Hancock Park voice still comes in handy once in a while.

He wheels around, stares at me. "Who are you?"

"I'm the tenant, and I'm trying to sleep. Who are you?"

He walks toward me offering what I'm sure he hopes is a charming smile. "Sorry. I didn't know there was a tenant." He holds out a card. "Marty Crowley, Arvis Brothers Construction."

"What are you doing here?"

"Putting together an estimate for a Mr. Keeler. I believe he owns the property."

"Yes. Well...I'd appreciate it if you put your estimate together without shouting. I work nights and I'm trying to sleep."

"We'll be as quiet as we can. Like I said, we didn't know anyone lived here."

I go back to bed, but I know I'm not getting any more sleep today. When they've left, I get up and pull on some shorts and a rugby shirt, take a glass of apple juice out on the porch. The air is soft and heavy with sunlight. I've been meaning to buy a couple of those white plastic chairs that you see everywhere, but not having chairs hasn't stopped me from spending time out here. In fact, there's something kind of down-home about sitting on the front steps.

All that's about to change.

I suppose I need to think about getting some white paint. A lot of white paint, probably. It's going to take at least two coats to cover up the color on the walls. Maybe some evening when Mr. Keeler's guests are sitting in front of the woodstove enjoying a glass of wine, my yellow paint will surface through the white overcoat like Lillian Hellman's pentimento.

I'll be leaving Doug behind, too. My little Douglas fir. He's grown nearly a foot since I planted him there. I hope Keeler doesn't rip him out. They do that here. Trees are so ubiquitous and in your face that people don't appreciate them. God forbid one should be situated in a slightly inconvenient position, maybe casting some shade on your porch. They bring in Paul Bunyan and clear-cut the place.

I reach over and absently pinch a spent bloom off the ivy geranium. My herbs are showing modest growth, but I know they're just revving their engines till they get a few good days of full sun before they pop the clutch and take off. I pull a leaf off the lemon balm and crumple it under my nose. It smells like the lemon-drop candies my oma loved.

Doug's not the only one who's rooted here. I feel more at home in this funky little place after eight months than I did in the house where David and I lived for seven years. Maybe because the rest of my life has undergone a seismic shift equivalent to an 8.9 on the Richter scale. So far, I've lost David. CM. Gary. Mac. My house is next. What else could possibly happen?

My oma used to say it was tempting fate to ask questions like that.

The new bartender's name is Shawn. He looks like a very young Kenny—short and squared off, hair the color of wet sand, pretty blue eyes. He has an engaging crooked grin and the kind of swaggering macho that young guys usually affect when they're scared shitless. He calls all the women "babe" or "sweetheart" no matter how old they are, and his musical knowledge could be held comfortably in a teaspoon with room left over for sugar.

That's one reason why I don't go to Bailey's much anymore.

Kenny's eyebrows lift when he sees me; a huge grin splits his face. "Hey, lady, where've you been keeping yourself?"

I return the smile. "How's everything?"

He looks down the bar, moving only his eyes, to where Shawn is trying his damnedest to dazzle two very young-looking women. "Well, it ain't what it used to be, that's all I'll say about that. What are you drinking? It's on the house."

I laugh. "In that case, I'll have a glass of your finest red bordeaux."

He sets a glass down on a napkin. "Château Bathtub for mademoiselle." He scoops out a dish of peanuts for me. I crack one open and pitch the shell at him. He bats it away.

"Have you talked to Mac?" I keep my voice casual and pay closer attention to the peanut I'm working on.

"Couple of days ago. Thursday, I think. He said to say hi. Told him I would if you ever showed your face again." He takes wineglasses out of a washer tray and hangs them by their stems in a rack behind the bar.

I take a sip of wine, turn partway around on my chair. "Pretty quiet for a Saturday, isn't it?"

Kenny shrugs. "We get the regulars during the week, but folks came on the weekend to hear what Mac was going to come up with next. Mr. Cool"—he nods slightly toward Shawn—"don't know his arse from deep center field, music-wise. His idea of oldies is Twisted Sister. And God knows, I'm not much with the tunes. We played Mac's last two tapes till people got sick of them. I guess I'm going to have to see about ordering some tapes from somewhere."

"How is he?"

"Mac? Fine."

"What's he doing?"

"He didn't say much. I guess he's working on Bensinger's place, mostly."

I eat another peanut and drink some more wine before I ask, "Did he say anything about coming back this fall?"

Kenny shakes his head. "He won't be back." He starts loading dirty glasses into the tray he just emptied.

"You don't think he will?"

"He's talking about driving up to Alaska in September. He always wanted to go up there, you know."

I rip off a damp corner of the napkin, roll it into a little crumb. "Does he have a phone or anything?"

Kenny gives me a smile that skates on the edge of pity. "Nope. There's an emergency number, but it's just a rental agency. You want it? Or you want me to tell him anything next time he calls?"

I think for a minute. "No. Just tell him hi for me."

Even though it's the end of June, it's still cool enough at night to use the woodstove. I light a little pile of kindling. When it's burning fast, I open the door and lay a chunk of alder inside. For a minute, the fire dies, as if smothered, then the log catches.

So Mac's finally going to Alaska. I rummage through my tape box in search of the last tape he gave me. I've never played it. I turn it over to read the card and I have to smile. Title, artist, record label, and running time painstakingly printed for each song. I lay it back in the box and pull out Mozart's Symphony no. 40 in G Minor. I always liked that one.

I lie down on the futon, pull a blanket over me, tired but not sleepy. Through the glass doors of the woodstove, the flames lap at the wood the way you lick an ice cream cone. It doesn't even appear to be burning till you look up and it's down to papery white ash.

July. Toulouse was in the middle of the worst heat wave in recent memory. The bakery, of course, was an inferno. Phillipe and Yvon wore shorts and went shirtless, but I didn't have that option. I wore white cotton overalls with a sleeveless T-shirt. My hair was twisted up and covered with a scarf soaked in cold water. The scarf usually stayed wet for less than thirty minutes before the water evaporated, to be replaced by sweat. We drank gallons of water all day long. I thought I'd never feel cool again.

One morning I arrived at the *boulangerie* early to find Jean-Marc loading the oven. I stood in the doorway to the *fournil* watching him. He wore his usual white pants, white shirt, white apron, and he seemed oblivious to the sweat pouring off him as he worked in the oven's fiery blast. When the last of the dough was in, he closed the heavy door and turned away.

"*Bon matin*, Wynter." As if he knew I'd been standing there.

"*Bon matin*, Jean-Marc." Not even 6 A.M., and I was already wilted and cranky. He motioned me out the back door. Even in the alley, it was oppressive. No breeze. I leaned my head back against the wall, closed my eyes.

"It's hotter than hell," I said in my best colloquial French.

He smiled and mopped his face with a white towel.

"*Oui, c'est vrai.* But it is the fire that make the bread, Wynter," he said.

Nineteen

❧

In composition class, they tell you that a cliché is a disaster. The literary equivalent of farting at the dinner table or walking out of the bathroom with the hem of your dress tucked neatly into your panty hose. What they don't tell you is that clichés have become clichéd because they're true. Because they're exactly how most people act.

Like in every romance novel worth its satin bodice, there comes a time when the heroine's lover takes a hike. Crazed with longing, she—get ready, here's the cliché—searches for his face in every crowd.

So even though Mac's been gone for five weeks and he's never called, and I have no reason to believe he'd be in Seattle, and he was never even my lover, I find myself looking for him. Scanning faces on the street, at the park, in restaurants, waiting for the bus, in line at the grocery store, every time I pass Bailey's. Every time I see a tall man in faded jeans and a blue windbreaker or a black baseball cap, every time I see a white El Camino, I have to look, even though it defies logic.

On July first, I call my mother. Just to say hi. I've been doing that every couple of weeks since I came home, and it makes her so absurdly happy, I have to wonder why I never did it before.

After the usual pleasantries, I ask, "What are you guys doing for the Fourth?"

"We're going down to Long Beach."

"Long Beach?"

"We're spending the night on the *Queen Mary*. They shoot fireworks off from the bridge and they have parties in all the different restaurants."

"Sounds like fun."

"I think it will be. Gary and Erica and the kids are coming down."

I nearly choke. "I'm sorry. Did you say Gary and Erica?"

"Yes, we were rather surprised when he told us they wanted to come." She pauses.

As you should be, Mother. Since two scant months ago he was crawling around naked on my futon and begging me to come to San Francisco.

"I'm not sure what's going on. For a while I thought he was rather enamored of you." She waits again. "What ever happened with that?"

"I'll tell you all about it sometime."

"He seems like a very sweet boy."

"He is. Please tell him hi for me. And try to say it in front of Erica."

She gives it her merry laugh. "Will do."

Seattle is having a heat wave, something I didn't know was possible. It has to do with a huge high-pressure area stalled between two low-pressure areas, and it's hanging smack over the city. It's been miserable for almost a week, high nineties during the day, eighties at night. Not a breath from the Sound to bring relief. Even the water itself looks oddly flat and still. It's eerie. Everyone says it's not that unusual, it happens every year or two, but it feels unnatural to me, and I realize that I've gotten used to the cool weather. I'm even maybe starting to like it.

Friday is the Fourth of July and the bakery's closed. I was thinking about going down to the waterfront to watch the fireworks, but Tyler convinces me that I should go with her and Barton the hairdresser—except she calls him a stylist—to Gasworks Park to watch the display over Lake Union. When they come by for me at six-thirty, it's so hot that my own sweat hangs in a cloud around me like a personal steam bath.

Barton the stylist is a tall, thin guy with an infectious grin and bleached-blond hair with black roots. He bats his big, dark eyes at me. "I'm Barton. How do you like my shirt?" The shirt in question is a blue Hawaiian number with ugly red flowers all over it.

I laugh. "It's a great example of the genre."

"Very tactfully put." His eyes lock on my hair. "Ooh, what a lot of hair. How I'd love to play with it sometime. Strictly on a professional basis, you understand. Can I touch?" He rubs a piece between his fingers and holds it against his cheek. " 'Like a virgin,' " he sings. "No perms, no colors. But we can fix that. Let Barton pop your cherry, honey. Strictly on a professional basis, of course."

"Should we take snacks with us?" I ask on the way to Barton's green Plymouth Valiant.

"Barton packed us a gourmet picnic," Tyler says. "With a thermos of his secret-recipe strip-and-go-nakeds."

"Fat, sugar, alcohol, chocolate, hallucinogenics," he intones. "All the major food groups."

Parking is scarce around Lake Union, even under the best of circumstances, so we end up having to schlepp our blankets, basket, and cooler for blocks before we find a patch of grass not occupied by other humans. I'm dripping and miserable and wishing I hadn't come. Barton's first official act as host is to pour drinks out of the giant thermos. He's even brought sprigs of mint for our cups. The concoction is refreshing and lemony; I gulp it down.

"Careful, Wyn, baby," he warns. "It tastes good, but it's got the alcohol content of jet fuel."

I lie down on the blanket, balance the sweating glass on my stomach. "What's in it? Or is that a trade secret?"

"Basically lemonade, vodka, and beer. 'It'll cure whatever ails you,' as my granny used to say."

"That one has to be in the granny training manual," I smile. "Mine used to say it, too."

"I think mine did, too," Tyler says, "but she always talked Polack, so I'm not totally sure."

Barton spreads out the gourmet picnic—two pressurized cans of "cheese product," a box of Triscuits, and a box of lavosh. A huge bag of popcorn, a small can of almonds. A tin of onion dip with the top peeled back, potato chips, Oreos. A box of peppermints like the ones restaurants give away, giant economy-size bag of M&M's. A pie plate of homemade brownies, which I'm certain are loaded.

"Ta-da." He bows with a flourish. "Regional cooking of provincial New Jersey."

I watch the stars appear in the slowly dimming sky, listen to Tyler and Barton chatter about people they know, reach for the salty almonds once in a while.

"Wyn, darling, you're so quiet over there in your little corner," Barton says presently. "Have some food. It's going to be a while before the show starts."

"She's in pain," Tyler says. "A busted marriage, two boyfriends gone missing." She squirts some cheese-flavored chemical onto a cracker and hands it to me.

"They weren't boyfriends. One was my stepbrother. The other was just a friend."

Barton raises one eyebrow, like Vivien Leigh in *Gone With the Wind.* "My, my, my. I have to say, I admire your style."

"I just don't seem to be very smart about men." I swallow the cracker almost whole to avoid tasting it, take another good swig of my drink.

"Now, there's NO pity like SELF-pity!" He does a great Ethel Merman. "Barton knows what will make you feel better." He gets up, comes around behind me. "Sit up, sit up." When I do, I feel the effects of my one strip-and-go-naked. Before I know what's happening, he's taking my hair down, combing it out. "You don't mind if I play with your hair? A new do always makes us feel better."

So we sit, listening to jazz from somebody's boom box, getting high on strip-and-go-nakeds, eating junk food, waiting for the darkness while

Barton braids my hair into lots of skinny braids. I probably look like Medusa, but it does feel good.

Finally, at nine-fifteen, the first salvo goes off from a platform in the middle of the lake. We ooh and aah along with everyone else, but Barton continues to work on my hair. I never tire of watching fireworks. They're utterly useless, just beauty for its own sake, a life span measured in seconds. I even love the smell of gunpowder and the little black puffs that hang in the sky after the glitter disappears. But tonight they seem to underscore the heat. After the inevitable gut-busting finale, Tyler and Barton start packing up our stuff and talking about going to some club on First Avenue. Portable generators hum as lights go on.

"You guys go ahead," I say. "I don't need anything else to drink tonight. I'll catch a bus home."

"We can take you home first," Tyler says.

"I want to sit here awhile. It's too hot to be inside."

Barton gives me a hug and adjusts my braids. "This is a whole new you. Totally tribal. Come see me."

Tyler grins. "You look like Bo freakin' Derek. Miss Perfect Ten. Watch yourself, babes. Don't get in trouble with it."

I laugh, twist my head, whipping the braids from side to side. "I feel like a helicopter."

They disappear into the crowd and I wander over to the kite meadow, a big hill next to the old gasworks. I sit on the grass and watch heads bobbing up and down as people gather their paraphernalia together and disperse lethargically. Kids run away from their parents and slink back, frazzled by the effort. Dogs bark unenthusiastically at each other, moving slowly in the heat. I watch for tall men in black baseball caps. I even see a few, but of course they aren't him. I know I should get up and leave. Most of the people are gone now except for a few bunches of kids. It's probably not a good idea to be the last one here, but a few more minutes won't hurt. I pull my knees up, hug them to my chest, rest my forehead on them, braids falling around me like a curtain.

"Are you all right, miss?"

I look up quickly at a middle-aged couple carrying folding chairs.

He has a crew cut and nice eyes. Her eyes are cautious, like she thinks I'm on a bad drug trip or having a spontaneous abortion.

"I'm fine, thanks."

"You shouldn't stay here by yourself," she says.

I stand up, smile at them. "I was trying to muster the energy to go to work."

"Where do you work at this time of night?" he asks.

"The Queen Street Bakery. On Queen Anne."

She says, "You're kidding. That's where I get my bread. Look." She sticks out her chest to show me her Queen Street Bakery T-shirt.

"That's what I do. The bread."

Her face lights up with interest. "Well, your bread's wonderful. Especially the new kinds. That banana-cinnamon stuff and the cornmeal-millet bread. You really make all that?"

"Yeah, it's great," her husband says.

I think I'm blushing. "Thanks. I'm glad you like it."

"I'm excited to meet you," she says. "Maybe we'll see you there sometime."

I laugh. "You have to get there before seven in the morning."

They wave and move toward the street, but I stand still. Waiting for him to appear out of nowhere, like in the movies. Take off his baseball cap, push his hair back. Smile his great smile and say, "I figured I'd find you here."

Finally, I turn to follow them, and as I do, a current of air rushes past my face. It becomes a full-fledged breeze, deep and fresh, smelling of the ocean. I picture it coming in off the water, pushing little white-caps ahead of it. It cools my face. My head falls back in relief; I look at the stars. The heat wave's broken.

The bus driver has his directional signal blinking, ready to pull out into Eastlake Avenue. As I run for it, I catch a reflection in the glass doors of a building—someone else trying to catch the bus—a famous bread baker, running down the sidewalk, braids bouncing in the wind, yelling at the driver to wait. I slide into a seat, catch my breath, and brush at the dampness on my face.

If I were writing a story about myself, it would begin: "In her thirty-second year, she discovered her Right Livelihood..." Or as CM would say, I've discovered what I am. I've peeled off the outer layers one by one—my father's daughter, David's wife, a divorcée—and I find, at the core, a baker of bread. A woman who likes working while the rest of the world sleeps. Who enjoys living alone, who doesn't own a car or a house. Who's happiest in jeans and a flannel shirt. Who chooses friends for the pleasure of their company, not their usefulness. Who's open to love. Or would be, if she could learn to recognize it.

It's only about eleven when I get to the bakery. Linda's already there. I can see her through the front window. Beyond the darkness of the café, our work area glows like the stage of a little theater. I watch her move between the Traulsen, the ovens, and the worktable, her stubby torso seeming to dance for some unseen audience. She's actually smiling. It occurs to me that she probably enjoys making bread as much as, if not more than, anything else in her life. It's not the same for her as it is for me. She draws comfort from the routine; I need to experiment. But it doesn't make her pleasure less valid.

Sometimes my own arrogance amazes me—I come waltzing in with my Ralph Lauren sweatpants, full of how things were done in France, prodding her to change the way she's been working for twenty-five years. No wonder she didn't want me around.

Saturday morning, I'm getting ready to sack out when there's a knock at the door. I open it and there's Daisy Wardwell, in yellow warm-ups and a white T-shirt, smiling through her perfect makeup. She says she was in the neighborhood and wanted to stop by and say hi.

"Oh my God, look what you've done to this place." I can't tell if she's horrified or impressed. "This is wonderful. It's so...warm and inviting."

"Listen, Daisy, I have a pretty good idea why you're here."

She gives me a mock pout. "Yeah, kiddo, it looks like Mr. Keeler's about ready to take over the property again."

"When do I have to be out?"

"There's no rush. From his perspective. He can't move back in until the house is ready. The problem is, starting in about a month, there's going to be a whole lotta shakin' goin' on."

"Workmen?"

She nods. "Now, if that doesn't bother you, you're welcome to stay till the fat lady sings."

"The problem is, I sleep during the day, so I guess I better start looking around. You know of anything right offhand?"

"Nope. It's not a real great market right now, kiddo. But we've got a couple of weeks. I'll get on it and see what I can find. Meanwhile, you might want to start getting ready, just in case we have to make a fast jump."

"Yeah, probably a good idea."

"Sorry, kiddo." She fluffs her blonde curls.

"No problem. I knew the deal going in."

I've accumulated an amazing amount of stuff in an amazingly short time. Clothes, books, *batterie de cuisine,* tapes, furniture, linens, and, of course, my tools. I appropriate boxes from the bakery's weekly deliveries, fill them with various nonessentials, and stack them against the wall where my long-planned bookcases were supposed to go. After one week, it starts to look like the seeds of a conceptual art exhibit, and I haven't heard any good news from Daisy.

Tuesday night I'm packing the contents of my desk—admittedly, there's not a lot, only about one box worth. It's a warm evening and I've got the windows and door open, entertaining the neighborhood with Van Morrison. One of Mac's all-time favorites. He introduced me to the song "Cleaning Windows." He loved it because it tells a whole life story in four minutes or whatever the time is—what the guy does for a living, who his friends are, what music he listens to, what books he reads, what he eats. It is rather wonderful.

There's nothing specific—I don't hear a noise or see anything, but I have a sense of someone on the porch. I get up and wander into the living room, push open the screen door. CM's sitting on the rail. I think she's been crying, but it's too dark to see for sure.

I fling myself on her, nearly knocking both of us over the rail and onto the ground. In a second, she's hugging me back and we're both crying and then we're both laughing.

"At least you didn't give me a bloody nose this time," she says.

"I love you." I wipe tears away with the heel of my hand. "I missed you. Oh, God, CM, I'm so sorry. I was such a bitch. I promise I'll dance at your wedding."

She wipes her eyes on the sleeve of her sweater. "Thanks for the offer. Unfortunately, there's not going to be one. A wedding."

"What? Why not? What happened?"

She gives me a crooked smile. "You were right."

"No I wasn't. I was petty and bitter. And jealous."

"Maybe." She laughs. "But you were still right."

I slip my arm through hers, pulling her inside. "Let's have a glass of wine and debrief you."

She looks at my box pile. "Where are you going?"

"I'm not sure yet. I have to get out of here. But, later with that. Get us some glasses while I open this."

We sit Indian style on the couch, and she says, "Thanks for the bread. It was great."

"Why didn't you call me when you got it? I thought you hated me."

She shrugs. "I'm sorry. By that time I was too embarrassed. Not too embarrassed to eat it, however."

"So what happened?"

"Exactly what you said would happen. He started having trouble with some of the resources he listed for his dissertation. His adviser claimed they didn't exist. So he was exchanging nasty notes with his adviser and then the whole committee got involved and he went into his Olympic door-slamming routine. From there it was a very short drive to me being selfish and not understanding what he was going through. We were fighting every other night and humping like bunnies in between. I got to the point where I was so wound up I couldn't eat—imagine that, if you will. I couldn't sleep. I started breaking out in this hideous rash under the ring—a sign from God, no doubt."

She waggles her reddened, puffy ring finger at me. "Anyway, I threw it at him last night and told him to get his ass out of my apartment. He stormed out and I haven't seen him since. He probably spent the evening exposing himself to coeds in the stacks."

"So he hasn't officially moved out?"

"He has to come back and get his stuff. If he hasn't gotten it by Sunday morning, I'm putting it on the front lawn for some homeless person." She stops for a long swallow of wine and a sigh. "How did you know?"

I shake my head. "I didn't. I was just being petty. And jealous."

"You were not."

"Yes I was."

"You're not that kind of person," she says firmly.

Which just proves that a true friend is somebody who insists on believing the best of you, even when faced with irrefutable evidence to the contrary.

"Tell me what's going on with you," she says.

"Oh . . ." I lean my head on the back of the futon. The Shirelles are wailing on "Baby, It's You," and I have to wait and hear my favorite part, where it sounds like a calliope. When the song ends, I say, "Remember that oldies record Katie had? The one she taught us to dance to?"

CM laughs. "You mean the one with 'Please Mr. Postman'?"

I nod. "What was the name of that one we played over and over? We kept picking up the needle and setting it down till it was full of skips."

" 'Party Lights.' " She smiles. "God, I hadn't thought about that in a while. Those were the good old days."

I swirl the wine in my glass. "I'll say. All we cared about was getting the steps down so we could look cool. It didn't matter that no one would dance with us because we were too tall."

"We weren't too tall. They were too short."

"Whatever. You know, Mac played that song at Bailey's one night, and I almost didn't recognize it without all those little hiccups."

She pulls her knees up, looping her arms over them. "Justine Wynter, where are you going with this?"

"I don't know. I was just thinking how you get used to things. Even if they're totally wrong. At some point, you start believing that's how it's supposed to be."

She gives me a look of perfect understanding, as only a longtime best friend can. "Gotcha."

"David was absolutely right, you know. He said, 'Don't you even know when you're unhappy?' Obviously, I didn't. If he hadn't kicked me out, I never would have had the nerve to walk away."

"Well, I wouldn't go writing him any thank-you notes just yet. Not till the money's divvied up, anyway. What about the handsome stepbrother?"

"He went back to his ex."

"Really? That's strange."

"Actually, it makes perfect sense. He was more enamored of the nuclear-family lifestyle than of me specifically. And I was starting to have déjà vu. You know—a second term as executive wife in Marin instead of Hancock Park."

"He was a good Transition Man."

I treat her to a Linda-style snort. "The shortest transition in history."

"How's Mac?"

"Fine, I guess. He's up in the San Juan Islands writing the great American novel."

Her X-ray vision burns into my brain. "Too bad. I liked him. For you, I mean."

"I sort of liked him, too. But we never got beyond the platonic."

"Maybe he'll come back to Seattle."

I start chipping orange flakes of Caribbean Sunset polish off my big toenail.

"And what about all this?" She nods at my pile of boxes.

"The owner's ready to start working on the house again. I knew it would happen eventually, but it's not good timing. Daisy says the market's pretty stagnant."

"Wyn, just move into my place. As soon as I can get Butt-head out."

"Don't you think you need some peace and quiet? Some time to yourself?"

"What I need is to have my Amazon blood sister around." She grins. "Just like old times."

CM goes home and I skip off to work in a rosy glow, which lasts until about 5:55 in the morning. At that point, Ellen comes in looking like Death's blue-plate special.

"Diane had to go to Baltimore again," she says in reply to my questioning look. "Her mother hasn't been doing well, and they think she may have suffered another small stroke."

"That's the way the cookie crumbles," Linda mutters. She heads for the door, leaving me to wheel out the cooling rack and arrange the bread on the shelves.

Ellen's floundering this morning. After filling the register, she sinks into a chair and lays her head on her arms. At a loss for anything inspirational to say, I crank up the espresso machine. Now that I've mastered the espresso machine, I confess that being *barista* every once in a while makes me feel undeniably cool. Like some gorgeous, skinny, but well-endowed *signorina* with black hair and pale, flawless skin. Who works at a coffee bar in Milano or Firenze and is secretly—or openly—coveted by every artist in the district. They flock to the coffee bar each morning to watch her hips sway with maddening grace as she pulls their espresso. They kiss their fingertips at her and leave thousands of lire on the bar.

"Are you going to make us a mocha or stand there and watch the steam blow?" Ellen says.

"Sorry." I close the frother nozzle and tamp the finely ground coffee into the brew basket. "Did Diane say when she'd be back?"

Ellen stares at me. "As I just said five seconds ago, she's hoping to come back Friday, but she wasn't sure."

"Sorry, I was thinking about some stuff."

"I guess I have to draft Tyler again." She rambles on, talking more to herself than to me. "And call all the cake orders for this week and tell them Diane's gone again." She turns abruptly. "Word's going to get around, you know. We're going to get a reputation for not being able to deliver."

I hand her a steaming mug. "It's not that we can't deliver. It's just that we can't deliver what they've ordered."

She frowns. "Duh."

"I'm just saying maybe there are people out there who are looking for Tyler's style of cakes, too."

Ellen's expression relaxes. "You think?"

"I don't know. Punkers and artists and students get married, too. They probably don't all want a white wedding cake with alstroemeria and violets. Lots of bakeries are copying Diane's cakes now, although I've never seen any as beautiful as hers. I'm just saying maybe we should try something different. A little edgier. We might tap into a whole other market."

She mulls it over, shifting the mocha from one cheek to the other, before she swallows. "You may be on to something," she says. "I'll have to talk to Tyler about it." She looks at her watch and sighs. "If she ever decides to grace us with her presence."

At twenty to seven, Tyler strolls up to the front door, holding hands with—I hate to be judgmental, but this guy resembles the Incredible Hulk. He's got a shaved head and he's dressed all in black, just like Tyler. The two of them look like some noir version of the Bobbsey Twins. He's wearing one of those dog-collar things with spikes on it, and we watch, fascinated, as they engage in a few minutes of passionate farewell kissing. Finally, he disappears and Tyler makes an entrance.

"Hi, guys." Her purple lipstick is smeared on her left cheek.

I'm dying to know how you can kiss somebody who's wearing one of those things without getting your throat slashed, but this may not be the time to ask.

"You're late," Ellen says.

"Oh. Sorry. Teddy wanted to walk me to work, and we sort of got—"

"You've been late every day this week." Ellen chews the words as if they were rubber. "Next time it happens, I'm docking you. And furthermore, I don't appreciate your standing out there swapping spit with Rin Tin Tin in front of the door at the beginning of our busiest time. If you have to indulge, go in the alley." She gets up abruptly and heads for the bathroom.

Tyler stares after her. "Geez. Who put the Ben-Gay in her Preparation H?"

I try to suppress a laugh. "Cut her some slack. She's totally stressed."

By Saturday, CM's apartment has been cleansed of all traces of Neal Brightman. I move in on Sunday. Most of my furniture ends up in storage, but Neal had set up a tiny office in one corner of the living room and CM assigns it to me for all my books, papers, and tapes. Since her idea of fixing dinner is to nuke a Lean Cuisine, there's plenty of room in the kitchen for all my tools.

"I've always wanted a live-in baker." She stows my whisks and rolling pin and bread pans in a cupboard next to the sink.

We exchange her couch for my futon, but because I'm getting ready for bed about the time she's getting ready to leave for work, we sleep in shifts in her queen-size bed. It all seems designed to work as smoothly as a set of well-lubed gears, but I'm too used to the luxury of solitude. For the moment, living with CM is like playtime, but eventually I'll want my own space. I call Daisy and tell her I now have the leisure to be particular, but not to stop looking.

Only the angle of the sun says it's late August. In L.A., all but the most well-watered yards would be a bit shopworn by now. But here, hollyhocks still nod in the warm breezes and zinnias still shout out their colors up and down the streets. The sky is still an endless blue in the afternoons and Diane's still in Baltimore. Her rationale is that it's better to stay there while things are so precarious than to keep flying back and forth.

Ellen says yes, she agrees, but everyone at the bakery can see the effects of the stress. Her normally cheerful demeanor is submerged in fatigue and worry. She's lost weight and lugs a perpetual set of bags under her eyes. Tyler's unhappy, feeling overworked and underpaid, jerked back and forth from *barista* to cake designer, as the occasion demands. This necessitates pulling Jen or Misha out front to cover for her, and they aren't crazy about the setup either. Only Linda carries on unperturbed.

One morning as I'm putting the bread out, I notice a well-dressed woman pacing back and forth in front of the door. Obviously someone who needs her morning coffee. She keeps looking at her watch and switching her Louis Vuitton briefcase from hand to hand. At 5:45, Ellen appears, shakes the woman's hand, and then a guy in a navy suit comes up and they all shake hands. My stomach gives me a couple of well-placed nudges. When Ellen unlocks the door, they follow her in.

"Hi, Wyn," she says. She sounds almost like her old self, but she avoids looking at me. She doesn't make any move to introduce me to the yuppies, so I just go about my business. The three of them wander back to the work area and I hear Linda complaining loudly about being crowded. Ellen's response is inaudible, but she brings them back up front and they settle at a table.

I know what this is, but it's not until Ellen goes to her desk and comes back with her old green ledger book that I give up trying to formulate other explanations. I stand around staring at them for long enough that she gets embarrassed.

"Wyn, come here a second. I want you to meet Terry Sullivan. With Great Northwest Bread Company. And this is Donna Baird." We shake hands and I manage to get quite a bit of flour on his navy blue suit.

"This is Wyn Morrison, one of our bread bakers. Wyn studied at a *boulangerie* in Toulouse."

"That's marvelous," Donna Baird gushes. "Being trained in the basics is so important. Of course, Great Northwest requires that all bakers go through the Great Northwest program in addition to whatever other training they may have had. Just to ensure uniform quality, of course."

Franchise? Uniform quality? Ellen's having a nervous breakdown, there's no other explanation. Why else would she want to turn the Queen Street Bakery into a bread machine?

They're through with me, resuming some previous conversation, and I hear Terry Sullivan say, "This is a great space. Of course, it would pretty much have to be gutted to make room for the machinery. Those ovens are . . . amazing. I can't believe they're still working. They should be in a museum."

I head for the back door, ripping my apron off over my head.

"Hey, where d'ya think you're goin', missy?"

"Your turn to clean up." I throw the apron in the basket and make myself scarce, leaving Linda to stare after me.

I can't go back to the apartment. My mind is spinning like one of those gyroscope toys. Sleep is out of the question, so I just start walking.

By summer's end, I didn't want to go home from Toulouse. I suppose it was partly just the dread of real life that you always feel when you come back from a trip someplace wonderful. But there was something else—an awareness. I'd discovered the existence of a world that was at once foreign and familiar. I wanted to stay in it. I wanted to walk every morning to the boulangerie *in the heavy, sweet air that lingered under the plane trees. To enter through the back door, an initiate. To feel the blasting heat of the ovens, smell the toasty-caramel smell of a hundred perfectly cooked loaves, to hear the steam sing as it escaped the crackling crust. I wanted to watch the hypnotic motion of the giant kneader blades, feel the cool, rounded dough under my hands.*

I could quit UCLA and go to cooking school. I could work as a baker if that's what I wanted. There was no reason not to. Except that I knew I wouldn't. I would go home and run headlong into all the forces of my old, comfortable life

pushing against me. I wasn't strong enough to make it happen. The knowledge
was utterly depressing.

A horn blares, startling me.

"Hey, excuse me. Could you get out of the driveway?"

I'm standing in front of the Victorian house on Fourth Street.
Workers are already crawling all over the thing and the air is full of
their voices, the whine of power tools, the sharp reports of hammers.

"Sorry." I wave at the driver of a flatbed truck loaded with a dozen
different styles of doors. Pretty soon this place won't even be recognizable.

Turning abruptly, I start back the way I came, my speed gradually
increasing to keep pace with the racing thoughts in my head. When I go
past the bakery, practically at a trot, Terry Sullivan is measuring the
front windows and barking numbers at Donna Baird, who's writing them
down on a clipboard. They look up as I go by and she calls out cheerfully, "See you soon."

I smile. *Don't bet the ranch on it, lady.*

It's been a while since I've been jogging, and CM's is uphill from
Queen Street. By the time I burst through the door, I'm gasping for air
and I've got a major stitch in my side. I drink a glass of water while I
ransack the little desk for my address book, and, finally, I sit down with
it and Dorian Duck.

The air in the apartment seems oppressively close. Beads of sweat
are popping out on my face, running down in little rivulets to drip off
my chin. My heart's pounding so hard that my hands are shaking as I
punch in Elizabeth Gooden's number. I need to start working out again
somehow. Even if it's only—

"Law office."

"Elizabeth Gooden, please."

"Speaking."

"Oh, Elizabeth," I pant, "I didn't recognize your voice. Why are you
answering the phone?"

"Who is this?"

"Wyn Morrison."

"Wynter, hi. I'm the first one here. You sound as if you just ran a race."

I laugh, breathless. "You're close. Listen, we need to talk."

"I'm listening."

"About the divorce," I gasp. "I want it now. I mean, as soon as possible. Forget the foot-dragging."

A few seconds of silence. Then, "Are you certain?"

"Yes, I'm certain. I'm even willing to make concessions—I mean, as long as it's not too much—"

She laughs, a cool, dry sound. "No need to go overboard, Wynter."

"Okay, but I'm serious. I want to proceed with all— What do they call it?"

"All deliberate speed."

"Right. 'All deliberate speed.' " My breath is starting to slow.

"And you're absolutely sure this is what you want?"

"Yes. I'm sure."

"You don't have to tell me, but I have to ask. Why?"

I look around the apartment at the cozy tangle of my things with CM's, out the window to the sapphire-blue water, the buildings of Seattle, golden in the morning sun, and the day is suddenly full of promise.

"I just have better things to do, I guess."

"Okay. I'm going to overnight your husband's financial declaration to you. Go over it with a fine-tooth comb and let me know if anything's missing. We'll proceed from there. Okay?"

"Okay. Thanks, Elizabeth."

"You're welcome, Wynter. And congratulations."

By three that afternoon I'm back at the bakery, still not having been to bed. Ellen clearly doesn't want to talk to me, but I corner her in the storeroom.

"Don't do this. You know you'll regret it forever. Think of what this place will be like as a franchise of the Great Northwest Bread Company."

She spins around to face me. "You think I want this? I'm too old to be selling Mazurka Bars on the street corner." Tears pool in her eyes. "I have no choice."

"Why?"

"Wyn, believe me, I've tried for months to find an independent baker to buy it, but nobody wants to work this hard anymore. At least the franchise will contract with me for Mazurka Bars."

"Months? How long have you known about this?"

She runs a hand through her hair, leaving a floury trail. "Well, I suspected a long time ago that this was where things were heading. Right after Diane went home the first time. I started putting out feelers around the end of June."

"But why do you have to sell?"

"Because I don't know what else to do." She pulls out a tissue and blots her eyes. "Diane's not coming back. She's decided it's her obligation to stay in Baltimore and take care of her mother."

"But she's got all kinds of family back there. Why does Diane have to uproot her whole life and—"

Ellen rolls her eyes. "Guilt is an incredible motivator. It makes otherwise sane women crazy. Anyway"—she lowers her voice—"our partnership agreement states that if one person leaves, the other has to buy her out. Ordinarily that wouldn't have been a problem, but we used up our reserves when we expanded into the candy store's old space. We're maxed out on loans. And I just don't have the money to buy her out."

"Well, I do."

Her expression reminds me of those forties detective movies. Some guy's always getting hit in the head with a blackjack, and he gets this really goofy look on his face just before he drops to the floor.

"What?"

"I've been making some phone calls. I talked to my lawyer and I talked to my mother. My divorce won't be settled for a while, but my mother's loaning me thirty thousand dollars against the settlement."

She laughs ruefully. "Oh, bless your heart, Wyn, it's a lot more than thirty thousand dollars."

"Of course. But there's nothing in the agreement that says you have to pay her the lump sum all at once, is there?"

"No . . ."

"So we negotiate. I think Diane will be amenable, don't you?"

She nods slowly, but I can tell she's afraid to put her full weight down on this solution for fear it might collapse under her. "Why do you want to do this? You do understand that Diane and I never made a lot of money."

I smile. "It's sort of about missed chances."

I hold out my hand to shake on it, but she grabs me in a bear hug. "Wyn, thank you. Thank you so much."

"That, and I'm looking forward to being Linda's boss."

Her sudden laughter bounces off the cement walls of the storeroom.

Twenty

❧

CM and I are having a celebration dinner. Halibut with a white-wine reduction sauce with capers. Puréed acorn squash. Salad of baby lettuces. Champagne. And for dessert, Tyler's Jackson Pollock cake—hazelnut pound cake glazed with white-chocolate ganache and decorated like one of Pollock's paintings in spatterings of chocolate, caramel, and espresso icing.

CM raises her glass. "To my best friend and Amazon sister—now an official bread maven."

"Yesterday I couldn't spell entrepreneur; today I are one. You know, I don't think one bottle of this is going to be enough. Can we put another one in the fridge?"

She crosses her eyes. "We could, except we're out."

"How could we be out of champagne?"

"I don't know, but we are. This is the last bottle."

"I'm going to have to go get some more. Put the top on this one and give me your keys while I can still drive."

She throws me her purse. "I'll make a fire and wash the lettuce. Get some goat cheese, too."

I should never go near Thriftway when I'm hungry. I come back with three bottles of champagne, five kinds of olives, two kinds of goat cheese and a small wedge of lemon Stilton, and a quarter pound of raw cashews, which CM loves.

She peers into the bag. "Are we feeding a gypsy camp?"

A fire's burning cheerfully in her little fireplace, and I'm unloading my purchases when I recognize the music coming from her tape deck. It's the tail end of "Cleaning Windows" by Van Morrison. I get the open bottle of champagne out of the fridge.

The last notes fade out and then a breathy tenor spills into the void.

"My love must be a kind of blind love.
I can't see anyone but you . . .

Are the stars out tonight?
I don't know if it's cloudy or bright."

"What tape is that?"

She shrugs. "I found it in your box. It's got some great stuff on it."

She hands me the card. Twelve songs. Title, artist, record label, running time.

"It's the tape Mac gave me when he left." On the back he scrawled, "Remember to listen."

"Let me see it." She pulls it out of my hand and studies it while I fill our glasses.

"I'm starving. Let's get dinner started." I turn on the fire under the sauté pan and pat the excess water off the fish, but CM reaches around me and turns off the burner.

"What are you doing?"

"You need to listen to this. The person who made this tape has something to say." She takes my hand and pulls me over to the futon. "Don't you see what this is? It's about you."

"Give me a break."

"Look at these songs." She waves the card under my nose, but when I reach for it, she pulls it back and reads, " 'Brown Eyed Girl.' That's you—"

"Right. After all, I *am* the only woman in the world with brown eyes."

She ignores me. " 'Sally Go 'Round the Roses'—that's about finding your significant other with someone else. 'Changing Horses'—about breaking up. 'Tangled Up in Blue' ..." She pushes her hair behind her ears and flops down next to me.

"It's just a coincidence. He likes Dylan."

"Even you don't believe that. Look at this one." She laughs. " 'Cold-water Canyon'—obviously Gary. 'Cleaning Windows'—that's Mac."

"You have a vivid imagination."

" 'I Only Have Eyes for You.' That's so romantic— "

"It's not romantic, it's just—"

"Just what?"

I stare at the lights of the city framed in her window. "It's what was on the radio the night he drove me to the hospital in the snow."

"Wyn, call him."

"He doesn't have a phone. Besides, even if you're right, which I don't think you are, he made that months ago—"

"No excuses. Can't you get him a message? No, you need to go up there. Take the Camry."

"And leave you with no car?"

"Taking the bus won't kill me. Go tomorrow."

"I can't go tomorrow."

"Why not? It's Saturday. You don't have to work."

"I don't know how to get there."

"Piece of cake. I've got maps. Basically, you just drive up to Ana-cortes—it's about an hour and a half—and get on the ferry."

"I don't know where he is."

She smiles. "But you know how to find out. Don't you?"

The last song is playing now. "The Dimming of the Day" by Richard Thompson. He has one of those pure Celtic male voices that's like a knife in your heart.

"CM, don't do this to me. I was just getting used to his being gone."

She puts the tape case down on the coffee table, folds her arms, and gives me her green-eyed stare. "If I'm wrong, you'll have plenty of time to get used to his being gone. If I'm right..."

Later, when all that's left of our celebration dinner is a few pleasant aromas and a chunk of cake covered in plastic wrap, and we've had enough champagne that we sing "The Night They Invented Champagne," and CM remembers how to make the cork-popping noise by flipping her little finger out of her mouth, and after we have one more hug, and she's gone to bed... then I curl up on my side on the futon to watch the last embers of the fire die in the dark.

Maybe I'll be like CM—devote my life to my art. The idea has a certain appeal. But even before I finish the thought, I know it's not the same. CM has something—a steel cable that runs through the center of her life. Around it, all the other threads of her existence are gathered.

Bread is my job, my craft. A *boulangere* is what I am. But I'm not CM. Instead of a steel cable, I have a hollow core. I need someone. But is it Mac? He's truly a man outside my realm of experience. Even if what I feel is... what I think it is, I mean, could it possibly be the L-word? Even if I feel that way, maybe he doesn't. Maybe he's just on the rebound and he needs a Transitional Woman. Or maybe he just wanted someone to fill a space in time till he got ready to move on, and he's no longer interested. And even if he's interested, and I'm interested, there's no guarantee that it would work. I mean, we're so different.

I sit up, punch the pillow, flop back down, roll over on my back.

From the darkness of her bedroom, CM's voice floats out to me. "The car has a full tank of gas..."

The *M. V. Anacortes* glides through a dreamscape of islands that emerge from the fog and then disappear back into it. I've been hearing about the San Juans ever since I moved to Seattle, but this isn't what I imagined—no sandy beaches, no palm trees. Just rocky, conifer-covered mountains thrusting up from the cold, blue Pacific. Air so clean it sears your throat with a sweet ocean smell. CM said that September wasn't too late to spot killer whales, but everything that looks like a black dorsal fin turns out to be a floating log or a duck or a curious sea lion.

The boat's metal ramp clangs down on the Orcas landing, and the Camry bounces cautiously onto the road. I ask the guy who's directing traffic how I get to Eastsound.

He smiles at me as though he doesn't get asked that question five hundred times a day, and says, "This here's Horseshoe Highway. Just stay on it."

The road drops down into a tunnel of trees that opens out on to rolling green hills. Mist pools in the low spots, but the fog is quickly burning away under the persistent gaze of the sun.

I'm scared. Like riding my two-wheeler for the first time after my father removed the training wheels. He'd tried to talk me into it for weeks. He said they hadn't touched pavement in the last dozen outings. But I wanted their presence. I needed to know that if I failed to maintain perfect balance, if that theory about forward momentum was all a lie, that I wouldn't go somersaulting to my doom. In the end, he just took them off. If I wanted to ride, he said, I'd have to just get on and pedal like crazy.

I have no plan, no idea what to say to Mac when I see him. I'm just pedaling. God, why did I let CM bulldoze me into this fool's errand? It's been almost five months since he gave me that tape. What if he doesn't feel that way anymore? What if he never did? I bang my palm on the steering wheel. Goddamn him. This whole mess could have been avoided if he'd had the *cojones* to just say something to me.

Of course, I could have said something to him, I suppose. Like that night on the ferry. But what would I have said? *Don't go?* What if he'd just looked at me and said, "Why not?" I would have jumped overboard.

The highway bends ninety degrees right and I cruise into the village of Eastsound. There are only three or four streets, so I turn on North Beach Road, the first one, and park at the curb. The wooden sidewalk is lined with cafés, a bookstore, two art galleries, a sporting goods store, a small insurance office. I follow my nose to a tiny bakery tucked away in a courtyard, hoping a pumpkin muffin will fix the hollow feeling in my interior. The muffin is moist, dense with nuts and dried fruits, but I put it back in the bag after one bite.

At the end of the block, on the left-hand side, is Jaimie Johnson Real Estate. The door's locked although it's nearly ten thirty. Rick said there'd be someone here at nine. Maybe I've blundered into some obscure island holiday custom of closing offices on the third Saturday of the ninth month. I'm about to walk away when I hear a cheery, "Hi. Can I help you?"

A tall, dark-haired woman is walking toward me, clutching a pink mug. "Dorrie Alesworth." She holds out her hand. "Sorry, I had to have some caffeine and there's no one else here this morning."

"I'm Wyn Morrison. Rick Bensinger talked to someone about my getting a map to his cabin."

"Oh, yes. You know it's occupied right now?"

My gaze slips across the street to the small parking lot, unconsciously scanning for white El Caminos. "It's— I actually need to see the person who's staying there, not the cottage."

"Come on in. I'll mark it on the map for you. It's real easy."

How nice that something is.

I lay the photocopied map on the passenger seat, turning it to orient myself to the yellow highlighter tracings. Back on Horseshoe Highway. The road skirts Crescent Beach and a sign warns potential oyster rustlers to keep off the oyster beds. Left onto Terrill's Beach Road, nowhere near a beach as far as I can tell, then right on Buckhorn Road. In a few minutes, I start to see tantalizing glimpses of water on the left. Exactly half a mile later by the odometer, a sign announces "Madrone Cottage."

I slam on the brakes even though I'm not going that fast, and sit there sliding my sweaty palms around the steering wheel. When I look in the rearview mirror, there's a silver Honda Civic waiting patiently behind me. If this were L.A., or even Seattle, the driver would be laying on the horn by now. I wave an apology and turn in, bumping up the rutted drive.

A white clapboard bungalow appears suddenly, poised on the edge of a meadow as if preparing to dive in. The Elky sits on a patch of gravel to the left of the covered porch. He finally got the fender painted.

I park near a clump of trees about twenty yards from the house and get out, closing the door gently. I can smell the sea, but the only visible ocean is the swaying green and gold meadow grass. A squirrel's piercing chatter makes me jump like a guilty trespasser.

Bob Dylan's nasal twang blasts out the open window. "Subterranean Homesick Blues." I'm almost to the porch when the music stops abruptly.

"I'm going for a run. You coming?"

Obviously, he's not alone. My heart thuds in my ears, less a noise than a vibration, as if it's underwater. If I circle around into the trees, I can wait and see who he's with. If it's a guy, fine. If it's a woman, I need to decide whether to humiliate myself or just slink back to the ferry landing.

Two steps into the tall grass, my left foot hydroplanes and sinks up to the ankle in thick black mud. Shit! My brand-new cross-trainers. I nearly fall down trying to pull my foot out. Wouldn't that be a great scene. He walks out with—God knows who, it could be Laura in there— and here I am floundering around like a rhinoceros on a wet clay bank.

Before I can decide whether or not to bolt, the door opens partway and a face looks out. A face with button eyes and a black nose. A scruffy yellow dog of uncertain parentage wanders out. As soon as he catches my scent, he bristles and starts making that low growling noise in the back of his throat.

"You protecting me from a vicious squirrel?" A stranger steps out, dressed in running shorts and a sweatshirt with the sleeves cut off to reveal tan, muscled arms. His sun-streaked hair is pulled back in a low ponytail and he has a full beard. But his eyes are Mac's.

He stares at me. "Wyn." His gaze ends up on my feet. It looks like I'm wearing one black shoe and one white. "You're all muddy."

"As I previously pointed out, you have a gift for stating the obvious."

Yellow Dog decides I'm okay. He bounds down the steps and starts licking my leg with his warm, sandpapery tongue.

"I don't know quite what to say," Mac says.

At least he looks pleased.

"Must be a first for you." I bend down to scratch the dog's ears. "Who's this?"

"Minnie."

"You named your dog after a mouse?"

"Not likely. 'Minnie the Moocher.' Cab Calloway. She's not really mine. She just keeps me company sometimes. How did you get here?"

I look over my shoulder at CM's Camry. "Drove to Anacortes and took the ferry over." I pause awkwardly, then press on. "This place is so...magical. It's not what I expected."

"It's great, isn't it?" When he smiles, my stomach turns upside down.

Minnie tires of waiting for the promised run and takes off into the woods. Mac says, "I'll get something to clean your shoe."

I ease down on the top step and extract my foot from the gooey cross-trainer, peel off the filthy sock. He comes back with a putty knife and a rag. He sits down next to me, but not too close, takes the shoe.

Scattered high clouds stitch a tapestry of light and shadow on the meadow, sparked by summer's last pink wild foxgloves and fluffy white seed heads of thistle. Blackbirds float in lazy spirals. The breeze is gentle and still warm, but it carries a warning of shorter days.

I rummage around for a clean, unwrinkled smile to wear. "What have you been working on?"

"Painting. Inside and out. Fixed the roof. Cleared some land and built a storage shed." While he talks, he cleans the muck off my shoe, scraping the putty knife on the edge of the porch. "I think you're going to have to scrub this one down."

His expression I remember from the first time I met him. Open, direct. But no longer anonymous. I know certain telling details now. Like he can't stand his brother and he gets one haircut a year. He likes Raymond Chandler and John Irving, Wallace Stegner and Joan Didion.

That he loves the blues and songs that tell stories. Riding the ferries just to be on the water. His favorite flavor is caramel.

"Or you could just hang out here till the mud dries. Then it'll brush right off."

I want to run my index finger down the muscle in his arm that contracts when he grips my shoe. "I don't want to keep you from your run."

He stands up. "I can always run. Come here. I want to show you something."

He pushes the door open, and I step past him into the pleasantly musty interior.

Knotty-pine paneling makes a cheerful backdrop for the thoroughly broken-in furniture: a maroon couch, two green chairs, an old trunk with a piece of glass on top for a coffee table. Bookshelves overflow with books and board games. Rag rug. Brick fireplace.

"It's cozy. Like a grandma's house."

For a minute, I almost think he might take my hand, but he turns and walks into the next room. "In here."

The kitchen floor slants crazily away from the rest of the house. The old linoleum is cool and wrinkly under my one bare foot. There's a vintage Wedgewood gas stove, a refrigerator, a battered wooden table and three chairs.

In the center of the table, like art on display, is a corrugated cardboard manuscript box. He's looking at the box, not at me, so I set down my purse, reach over and lift the lid.

Accident of Birth
A novel
by
Matthew Spencer McLeod

He's trying to look modest and self-effacing, but without success.

I smile, momentarily forgetting that I'm pissed off at him. "Oh my God, Mac. You must have worked your butt off."

He sits on the corner of the table. "I kept thinking about what you said."

"About what?"

"That if I thought of myself as a bartender who wrote stuff, that's what I'd be. So I decided to try thinking of myself as a writer who needed a day job." He gives me his little wry grin. "You want some coffee?"

"No thanks."

I walk over to the chipped porcelain sink, glance out the window into the woods. I can hear Minnie's squirrel-spotting aria.

"So." He folds his arms across his chest. "Are you going to tell me why you came all the way up here? Or am I supposed to guess?"

"Why not? You made me guess." My voice breaks embarrassingly, like a kid entering puberty. "In fact, I forgot. I'm really pissed off at you." I turn and glare at him. "How dare you?"

He looks puzzled. "How dare I what?"

"How dare you give me that tape and then skip town like some fugitive?"

"What was I supposed to do?"

"You could have said something."

"I could have, but I didn't. You weren't listening anyway." His left hand fidgets with the pocket flap on his running shorts. "You were too busy plotting revenge against your ex, and fooling around with your brother."

"He's my stepbrother. Quit trying to make it sound like incest."

"You could have said something, too, you know."

"What was I going to say? Stop mooning around about Laura and try—"

"Laura?" He stares at me.

"Yes, Laura. You were wrecked after you saw her at that party with somebody else."

"I wasn't wrecked. I was half asleep from staying up all night, and then just when things started to get interesting, your brother—excuse me—your stepbrother showed up with the whole flower mart in his arms."

"But you were all depressed and grouchy for days after that—"

He shakes his head slowly. "God, I could never tell what you were thinking. I was depressed and grouchy because I was getting so involved with you, and you obviously had other fish to fry, and I just figured it would be better if I got out of town for a while." He eyes me accusingly. "You didn't have to wait all summer to get in touch with me."

"I just heard the tape yest—a few days ago."

"Why did you wait so long?"

"Why the hell do you think?" I say crossly. "I couldn't listen to it because I missed you."

I love the amber flecks in his eyes that you can only see in a certain light. The way his lashes are dark at the roots but pale as moonlight at the tips. There's a newly sunburned place across the bridge of his nose.

"I missed you," he says, and the feeling I've been holding under house arrest all summer suddenly escapes, flaring up in my chest.

"Kenny said you were going up to pollute Alaska."

"That's the plan." While I'm looking out the window again, he makes the three feet between us disappear. His hand is on my arm. "Why don't you come with me?"

"McLeod, you make me cry and you're roadkill."

He laughs right before he kisses me. His mouth is warm, and the tip of his nose is cold against my cheek. His tongue barely brushes my mouth, like when you knock on a door, then step back politely and wait to be invited in. He smells of freshly cut pine and wood smoke and meadow grass.

I put a hand up to touch the beard.

"Too scratchy?" he says.

I try rubbing it in different directions. "I can see how it might work."

"Come to Alaska with me. It would be so—"

"Can't." This is where I nearly lose it.

"Why not?"

I press my lips together. "You're looking at the proud half owner of the Queen Street Bakery."

"So the divorce is...?"

"Practically a fait accompli."

He smiles. "Is that anything like a done deal?"

The second kiss is longer, more interesting. It takes me places—like flying down the sidewalk on my first ride without training wheels. Like diving into a wave off Zuma Beach. Like spotting France from 35,000 feet and knowing that somewhere down there in a maze of pink brick, the Boulangerie du Pont was waiting for me. It sets me down gently but firmly on this speck of land off the coast of Washington where mud is drying on my shoe and Mac is holding me against him in a way that leaves very little doubt as to his intentions.

When we break for air, he says, "On the other hand, fall's probably not the best time to go to Alaska."

"Maybe you should play it by ear," I suggest helpfully. "At least until spring."

There's a pause, no more than a space between heartbeats. I feel him draw a deep breath, as if he's about to make some monumental pronouncement, but he just winds a strand of my hair around his finger and says,

"At least."

ACKNOWLEDGMENTS

One of the best things about having a book published is getting to mention in print all the people who deserve more, but will have to settle for my undying gratitude. To my parents, Ruth and Doug Huggins, for their unwavering love and wild applause, beginning with those lost-dog and buried-treasure stories.

To my husband, Geoff, for literally supporting me while I labored. For rubbing my back and holding my hand and cheerfully consuming countless pizzas and take-out Thai noodles. To Marilyn Carter for thirty-five years of bestfriendship.

Thanks to all my writing teachers—and they have been legion—but especially to Andrew Tonkovich, in whose fiction class the seed of *Bread Alone* first germinated. To my wise and generous teacher and dear friend, Jo-Ann Mapson, whose books are both inspiration and aspiration for me, and who did me the honor of recommending me to her wonderful agent. To Deborah Schneider, who is now also my wonderful agent, and with whom all things are possible. To my editor, Claire Wachtel, for her warm heart and cool eye, and for helping me tell my story to the best of my ability.

To all my writing-group friends and my book-club friends, who slogged through numerous drafts and revisions with me, particularly my writing part-ner Amy Wallen, for knowing how to be both brutally honest and encouraging in the same breath. To Janet Fitch for dialogue lessons. To Rebecca Hill and Judith Guest for showing me that less is more.

To Kathryn Brown for sharing her clear-eyed perspective on California divorce law. To David Bresard, who welcomed me into his bakery and shared his experiences as a *Compagnon Boulanger du Devoir.*

To all those singers and songwriters whose music still plays in my house and my car and my heart—Bob Dylan, Van Morrison, Jackie Wilson, The Big O, Crosby, Stills, Nash and Young, Richard and Linda Thompson, The Flamingos, and more.

To my bread heroes, Edward Espe Brown, Elizabeth David, Daniel Leader, Nancy Silverton, Brother Peter Rinehart. To Gunilla Norris for so eloquently articulating the connections between bread and love.

And last, but far from least, to Nancy Mattheiss and Jessica Reissman, and the women of the old McGraw Street Bakery for making my time there a feast of food and friendship.